KU-742-619

SWAT SECRET
ADMIRER

BY
ELIZABETH HEITER

MILLS &
BOON

Published in Great Britain 2015
by Mills & Boon, an imprint of Harlequin (UK) Limited,
Eton House, 18-24 Paradise Road, Richmond, Surrey, TW9 1SR

© 2015 Elizabeth Heiter

ISBN: 978-0-263-25303-0

46-0415

Harlequin (UK) Limited's policy is to use papers that are natural, renewable and recyclable products and made from wood grown in sustainable forests. The logging and manufacturing processes conform to the legal environmental regulations of the country of origin.

Printed and bound in Spain
by CPI, Barcelona

Elizabeth Heiter likes her suspense to feature strong heroines, chilling villains, psychological twists and a little romance. Her research has taken her into the minds of serial killers, through murder investigations and onto the FBI Academy's shooting range. Elizabeth graduated from the University of Michigan with a degree in English literature. She's a member of International Thriller Writers and Romance Writers of America. Visit Elizabeth at www.elizabethheiter.com.

For my critique partner, Robbie Terman.
Thank you for convincing me that I could write
romantic suspense, and lending your expertise.

ACKNOWLEDGEMENTS

Thank you, as always, to my friends and family for
your support. A special thanks to Chris Heiter,
Robbie Terman, Ann Forsaith, Nora Smith,
Charles Shipps and Sasha Orr, for your feedback,
and Mark Nalbach, for keeping my website going.

Thank you to my agent, Kevan Lyon, and my editor,
Paula Eykelhof, for always pushing me, and to
Denise Zaza and everyone on the Intrigue team,
for all your help behind the scenes. A big thank-you
as well to the Intrigue authors, for the friendly
welcome—I love being in your company.

Chapter One

"Invisibility in three...two...one...now!"

The words echoed in Maggie Delacorte's earbud as her SWAT teammate stepped back from the neat hole he'd cut in the window. Behind her, everything was quiet in the predawn darkness. But that wouldn't last for long.

The FBI had gotten the word that a wanted fugitive was hiding out in this gang-infested part of DC, armed with an AK-47 and surrounded by a pack of die-hard supporters. Maggie and her teammates were here to make sure his time on the run was finished.

She moved quickly forward, tossing a flash-bang grenade through the window. The world in front of her exploded in white light, a massive *boom* echoing as the flash bang landed. Smoke billowed, providing cover.

"Go, go, go!" Grant Larkin yelled in that deep voice that always sent goose bumps running up her arms, as he used a ram and his massive upper-body strength to break down the door.

Maggie raced around the corner to follow, just as the door flew open into the one-story hideout. Grant went in first, moving right as planned, then the two teammates behind him dodged the splintered door and went left.

Her MP-5 raised and ready, Maggie barely felt the weight of the extra fifty pounds of gear she carried as she darted through the door, clearing it fast the way she'd been trained.

A bullet whizzed by her ear, coming from her left, but she didn't turn her head. That was in a teammate's sector. He'd handle the threat. Maggie's sector was straight ahead, and she stayed focused as she forged through the swirling gray smoke.

Reports came in over her radio as she entered the hallway to the bedrooms. The fugitive's allies were dwindling fast, either from bullets, or because they threw their hands up and their weapons down at the sight of the six FBI SWAT agents converging on them. But there were at least two left, including the fugitive himself, a three-time offender, who was surely looking at a life sentence this time around.

A gangbanger popped out of a doorway ahead of her, his modified AK-47 coming up fast, and Maggie moved her weapon right, firing at center mass.

The threat down, she kept going until she was beside Grant. He outweighed her by a solid eighty pounds and in the narrow hallway, with all their gear, they barely fit side by side.

He nodded his head to acknowledge her presence, glancing briefly her way. She registered it through her peripheral vision, but kept her focus where it needed to be: on the rooms to the right side. One more for her to clear, one for Grant.

Grant went through the doorway to the left and Maggie through the one on the right, her weapon instantly sighting on the threat in the corner. The fugitive himself, all three hundred pounds of him.

His finger quivered on the trigger, and Maggie barked, "Drop it! FBI!"

She'd been on the Washington Field Office's SWAT

team for the past four years, but perps sometimes made the mistake of thinking she wouldn't fire just because she was a woman. So Maggie leveled her meanest stare at him, hoping he could see it through her goggles. She wanted this guy alive, wanted him to rot in a cell and help them bring down the rest of his crew.

He scowled back at her with a nasty grimace even as his eyes watered from the smoke. But the modified AK-47 he'd been clutching fell to the floor beside him.

From the room across the hall, she could hear Grant yelling at another suspect to get down on the ground, and Maggie demanded the same of the fugitive.

She didn't get close until he'd followed her order to lie flat on his stomach on the filthy carpet, his hands clasped behind his head. Then she switched her MP-5 to safe mode, slung it over her back and unhooked the handcuffs from her belt. She approached him and planted a heavy knee in the center of his huge back. Yanking his left hand down fast, she slapped on the cuff then grabbed his right hand.

As she shifted her balance right, he ripped his cuffed hand away, using his bulk to toss her sideways.

She landed hard on her MP-5, and pain tore through her back. That was going to bruise. Cursing loud and creatively, she was up before he could get to his feet. Wrenching his cuffed arm backward, she rammed a foot in his armpit.

He squealed as she muttered under her breath about men who thought bigger meant they had the upper hand. A decade ago, she might have agreed with that assessment. But six years in the FBI, four of them on the super-competitive SWAT team, had taught her it just wasn't true.

She didn't have to be bigger. She just had to know how to leverage her strength, and her skill set.

The fugitive was still screeching as she slapped the cuff on his other wrist and then Grant was in the room, dragging a gangbanger behind him as if the guy weighed nothing. He took a handful of the fugitive's shirt, and the two of them pulled him to his feet.

"Nice job, Delacorte," Grant said.

Her heart rate—which had stayed relatively even during the entire arrest—picked up at the sound of his voice.

Grant Larkin had moved from the New York Field Office to the Washington Field Office, WFO, and her SWAT team, nine months ago. He was just shy of six feet, but even on a team filled with muscle-bound men, he stood out. The guy was *built*, which was why he was usually the door-kicker.

He also had deep brown eyes, light brown skin and an infectious grin, even in the middle of a grueling SWAT workout. In short, exactly her type. If only he wasn't a teammate, making him off-limits. And if only she didn't have baggage from her past that weighed more than he did.

Maggie nodded at him and called in their status over her radio. She got the "all clear" from all sectors and told Grant, "We're set. Let's get out of here."

"Sounds like a plan to me," he replied, letting her go ahead of him with the fugitive as he brought up the rear with the cuffed gangbanger.

The rest of the team was waiting outside the dilapidated one-story, loading a few other prisoners into their vehicle for transport. A couple of her teammates hooted when they saw her pushing the enormous, scowling fugitive in front of her.

She grinned back, because she knew they were laughing at the furious threats the fugitive was making, and not at the fact that she, at five foot eight and a hundred and forty pounds, was bringing him out. She'd worked with most of them for four years, and they'd learned fast not to coddle or underestimate her because she was a woman.

That was why being on SWAT had been good for her. It had shown her exactly how much she was capable of, and she wouldn't trade it for anything.

After they'd loaded the last two prisoners, Grant came over to her, yanking his goggles up over his helmet, and leaving behind indents around his eyes that didn't diminish his attractiveness at all. "I think this calls for celebration."

"O'Reilley's?" Clive Dekker, the team leader, asked. It was the pub the team usually hit after a particularly good or bad day.

It didn't matter that it was almost three in the morning. O'Reilley's catered to cops. They stopped serving liquor at two, but they were open twenty-four hours. And after the adrenaline rush of a high-risk arrest, most of the team couldn't just go home and go to sleep.

"Let's do it," Grant agreed. He turned to her, looking hopeful. "Delacorte?"

She hadn't gone with them in six months. Not since she'd started getting the letters, because the stress of it made it impossible to go out and joke around, to pretend everything was okay.

A lump filled her throat, and she tried to push back the memory that always surged forward when September 1 came around. In exactly thirty days, it would be ten years since the day that had changed her life. The day that had led her to the FBI. To SWAT.

And whatever happened on that tenth anniversary, would she regret not having spent as much time with Grant Larkin as she could?

She nodded at him. "Sure. I'm going to run home first. I'll meet you all there."

He looked surprised, but then grinned in a way that made her positive she'd made the right choice.

She stared back at him, momentarily rooted in place. Maybe it was time to forget her past. Maybe it was time to forget the rules.

Maybe it was time to see what could happen between her and Grant Larkin.

MAGGIE FELT HERSELF smiling with anticipation as she unlocked the bolts on her DC row house and entered, flipping on the lights. She stepped over the mail scattered in the entryway, realizing she hadn't been home in close to twenty-four hours.

As she locked the door behind her and kicked off her boots, it occurred to her that she should be exhausted. She'd worked a full day on her regular FBI civil rights squad, then been out with her brother and best friend when she'd gotten the call to come back for the SWAT arrest. But she was full of energy. When was the last time she'd been this happy?

Six months ago, she realized. Before the first letter had arrived. Grant had been on her team for three months at the time. They'd hit it off from his first day. Besides being a solid addition to the team, he was funny and just so dang happy all the time. Being around him made *her* happy.

SWAT was an ancillary position—agents did it on top of their regular squad duties. Still, dating a teammate, even in a secondary team like SWAT, was forbidden. So she'd tried to keep her feelings hidden. But just knowing that she was capable of feeling this way, after everything…

Stop dwelling on the past, Maggie scolded herself. She knew Grant had been able to tell these past few months that something was wrong. But unlike a lot of agents at the WFO, who'd heard the rumors over the years, she was pretty sure Grant didn't know her history. And she wanted to keep it that way.

She liked the way he looked at her, no trace of pity or worry. He'd never shown any sign that he'd heard about her past. The case agents had been good about keeping her connection under wraps over the years; though inevitably agents who'd been in DC for a long time found out. But Grant had only been here nine months. In that time, the only thing she'd ever seen in his eyes was friendship and camaraderie. And lately, something else, something that went beyond the bonds of the team.

Maggie carried her gear up the narrow stairs to her bedroom, flipping lights on along the way, then stared into her closet. She didn't own date clothes. Not that this was a date.

Everything in her closet belonged to a woman who, somewhere deep inside, was still afraid. Not of being a victim, not anymore. But when was the last time she'd actually wanted a man to look at her with appreciation?

Frowning, Maggie grabbed what she'd always worn to O'Reilley's—jeans, combat-style boots way too similar to the ones she wore for SWAT and a loose-fitting T-shirt. They'd only stay an hour or so anyway, chat and play darts and let the adrenaline fade. Then, one by one, the exhaustion would inevitably hit, and they'd head home and conk out.

She needed to get over there, or she'd miss everyone. Changing quickly, she looked into the bathroom mirror, taking a minute to lift her shirt up and look at the damage to her back. A bruise was blooming fast, huge and purple, snaking its way along her spine in the general shape of a sub-machine gun.

She poked at it and flinched, then pulled her shirt back down, combing a finger through her bob. It was just long enough to cover the back of her neck, and Maggie's fingers twitched as they skimmed the puckered skin there.

The tattoo she'd gotten years ago hid the image of a hook, but nothing could fix the damaged skin underneath. The brand that had been left on her.

She threw some water on her face, then dug through the drawer under her sink until she came up with some lipstick and mascara. The guys were probably going to stare at her as though she'd grown an extra head. Or maybe they wouldn't even notice. Most of them were like brothers.

Only Grant might spot—and appreciate—her pathetic attempt to look a little more feminine, since most of the time she tried to hide it.

She stared at herself in the mirror, resisting the urge to wipe off the makeup, then laughed aloud. She was being ridiculous. Just because she didn't wear makeup to work didn't mean everyone at the bar would know why she'd put it on tonight.

Maggie took the stairs down two at a time, still grinning. It wasn't that she didn't date, but most of the time, even when she truly had feelings for a guy, it felt obligatory. An attempt to feel normal that never quite worked.

But nothing about Grant Larkin felt obligatory.

And she was ready to take a chance. She had no idea how they'd handle the FBI rules—assuming he was interested. But the heated glances he hadn't quite been able to hide over the past few weeks told her he was.

At the bottom of the stairs, Maggie picked up the pile of mail and dumped it on the table and reached for her keys. But before she'd finished turning away, dread rushed over her. The plain business envelope. The corner of a neatly printed return label sticking out from the huge pile of mail like a flashing beacon.

She looked back at the mail slowly, dreading what she was going to find. But she hadn't been dreaming. She didn't have to open it to know. Another letter.

All the excitement drained out of her, buried under a decade-old fear.

Her movements robotic, she walked into her kitchen and slipped on a pair of latex gloves before returning to the front hall, even though she knew there'd be no prints. There never were.

She shouldn't even open it. It was evidence in an ongoing case. She should call the agents from the Violent Crimes Major Offenders, VCMO, squad assigned to the case. They'd have to be called anyway, because this letter would have to go in the case file along with the others. She should just let the case agents open it.

But even knowing what would be inside, she couldn't stop herself from carefully slicing open the top of the envelope. She slid out the plain white paper and unfolded it carefully, only touching the edges. She knew it was useless, but she still tried to numb herself as she started reading.

Anger and resentment—along with the guilt and shame she couldn't suppress—crept forward, even as she tried to remain clinical and approach it the way she would one of her own cases. It read just like the previous letters, three of them over the past six months. To someone who didn't know the sender, it would sound like a love letter, fondly recalling their time together.

But it wasn't. It was a letter from the Fishhook Rapist, the predator who'd evaded capture for almost a decade.

The predator who had started by abducting her on her way home to her dorm room at George Washington University all those years ago. He'd let her go the next morning, drugged and disoriented, carrying a permanent reminder on the back of her neck.

Maggie felt herself sway and clutched the table as she read the last line. It was different from any of the previous letters.

The Fishhook Rapist was coming back to DC. And he was coming back for her.

Chapter Two

"You got another one?" Maggie's older brother, Scott, was scowling furiously, clenching his fists so tightly, the knuckles looked ready to break through skin. He was standing in the entryway to her row house a mere thirty minutes after she'd called him, which meant he'd broken a lot of traffic laws to get there.

Normally, Scott was all charm, all the time, with an easy grin and a swagger. But today, even with his eyes red from being ripped from sleep before dawn, he looked angrier than she'd seen him in a long, long time.

Their best friend, Ella Cortez, had arrived ten minutes earlier; she lived within DC and closer to Maggie's house. Maggie had called them instead of heading to the bar, and Ella had gotten in her car practically before Maggie had finished telling her what had happened.

Now Ella put a hand on Scott's arm and gave him a look Maggie could read as well as Scott could. *Go easy.*

The three of them had grown up together, back in Buckley, Indiana, and Ella might as well have been her and Scott's other sister. After Maggie's assault her senior year of college, they'd made a pact together. Throw out all their plans for the future and join the FBI. Stop this kind of thing from happening to anyone else.

But she couldn't even stop the man who'd hurt her.

Maggie tightened her jaw, tried not to let them see her fear. "Yes. But the letter was different this time. He said he's coming back to DC. He said he's coming back for me."

"What?" Scott shouted.

He ran a hand through his close-cut blond hair, and she could see him trying to rein in his fury.

Scott was a year older than she was. They'd always been close, but since her attack, he'd become even more protective. She'd expected him to worry less once she'd joined SWAT, but it was only recently that his new girlfriend had taught him to loosen up at all. That would change back now.

"Have the case agents taken the letter?" Scott asked. As a sniper with the FBI's Hostage Rescue Team, Scott was used to being able to take action. Not knowing who the threat was drove him crazy.

"Were those his exact words? That he was coming back to DC, coming back for you?" Ella asked. She was calmer, but Maggie still heard her worry.

"They just picked it up," she told Scott, then looked at Ella. "His exact words were, 'I'm coming home for our anniversary.'" She choked the words out. Even saying them made bile rise up in her throat.

Scott swore, and Ella paled, but she still nodded thoughtfully. "Home," Ella mused.

Her brother took a loud, calming breath, but rage still filled his eyes. "What do you think it means?"

Just like her, Scott had gravitated toward a specialty that would let him physically, personally, take down threats. On the outside, they didn't resemble each other at all, though they were only a year apart in age. Scott was a head taller than her at six feet, with blond hair and chocolate-brown eyes. She looked more like their younger sister, Nikki, with her dark brown hair and light blue eyes.

But inside, they were so similar, both of them attacking every challenge head-on.

Ella was different. She'd been the glue that had held them together, kept them from butting heads over the years. And while Scott and Maggie had gone into physical specialties with the FBI, Ella had wanted to understand. So she'd become a profiler with the Behavioral Analysis Unit. If there was anyone who had a chance of deciphering the Fishhook Rapist's motivations—and hopefully his next move—it would be her.

"What does it mean?" Ella repeated. "Well, it could be the obvious."

"That he was born here," Scott replied, nodding. "Okay. What else?"

"Well, we know he doesn't live here now."

Part of the reason the Fishhook Rapist had managed to evade capture for so long was because he moved around a lot. He claimed one victim a year, and never in the same place. His last victim had been in Florida, and the second letter Maggie had gotten had been postmarked from there.

The first one had come from Georgia, and the most recent one had originated in North Carolina.

"Then, what?" Scott demanded.

Ella frowned, her deep brown eyes pensive. "This guy is a narcissist. He brags about what he does. It's why he lets his victims go. He wants the attention, and he gets off on knowing the women he abducts can't identify him. His attacks have become the main source of pride in his life. So the location of his first attack—"

"You think he might see DC as home because it's where he assaulted me," Maggie broke in.

She'd gone to school here—and she'd even finished out her senior year after her attack, putting all her focus into her new goal of making it to the FBI—but then she'd moved back to her parents' house in Indiana for a while, wanting to put physical distance between her and the memories. When she'd made it through the FBI Academy, and they'd assigned her to the DC office, she'd almost backed out.

But she'd stuck with it, then worked her way onto the SWAT team. DC had truly become her home now. It made her sick that he thought of it as his, too.

Ella looked uncomfortable, but she didn't fidget or honey-coat anything. "Yes. It's the start of where he got his name."

The media had dubbed him the Fishhook Rapist after they'd gotten wind of what he did to his victims, branding them on the backs of their necks with the image of a hook. Maggie's hand tensed with the need to touch the puckered skin on her neck that would never be smooth, but she clutched her hands together.

Ella looked apologetic as she finished, "To him, this is home."

Nausea welled up, and Maggie sank onto her couch. Scott sat next to her, wrapping an arm around her shoulder. A few seconds later, Ella was on her other side, hooking their arms together.

"He can write as many letters as he wants, but he's not getting anywhere near you," Scott vowed, in the dark, determined tone he probably used on the job. It sounded convincing.

So did Ella when she added, "We're going to get him, Maggie. He's making a mistake trying to come back here."

She wanted to believe it. Wanted to believe that the

case agents, and her brother and Ella and all of her FBI and SWAT training were enough to keep her safe.

But that fear she'd pushed down for ten years rose up, strong and painful, like the feel of fiery metal on the back of her neck.

Maggie squeezed her eyes closed, grasping her brother and Ella by the arms. "I'm not supposed to be anywhere near the case."

"Doesn't matter," Ella said. She was a stickler for doing everything by the book—except when it came to a possible lead on this particular case.

"We're not waiting for that SOB to come after you," Scott agreed. "And we're not leaving this to the case agents, no matter how good they are."

Maggie nodded, tears welling up in her eyes at their loyalty. "It's time to go on the offensive."

WHERE WAS SHE?

Grant Larkin tried not to stare through the near-empty pub at the entrance to O'Reilley's, but he couldn't stop himself, the same way he couldn't stop himself from taking a peek at his watch. The team had been at the pub for a solid two hours, letting the adrenaline from the arrest fade.

Now daylight was rapidly approaching. Even though it was Saturday, and they got a break, a couple of them were heading out the door, along with the last of the cops who'd been in the pub when they'd arrived.

Maggie wasn't coming.

"What happened to Delacorte?" Clive Dekker asked, looking at Grant as if he would know.

Grant shrugged, but he'd been resisting the urge to call her for the past hour and find out. He'd been shocked when she'd agreed to join them, after six months of skipping out on anything social. Even more shocked by the way she'd looked at him while agreeing. As if she was as interested in him as he was in her.

He'd been drawn to her from the moment they'd met, nine months ago. For most of that time, he'd tried to keep his attraction hidden. They were teammates, a definite Bureau no-no. Lately, though, he hadn't been able to suppress it, and he knew she'd noticed. But she'd never looked at him quite the way she had tonight, as if maybe she wanted more from him. If only...

"Well, I'm calling it, before my wife sends out a search party," Clive said, then squinted, leaning closer to him in the noisy pub. "Is that your phone ringing?"

Grant grinned at him. "I think you're still hearing the aftereffects of that flash bang, old man," he joked. The team leader was thirty-nine, only four years older than Grant. But Clive was the oldest guy on the Washington Field Office SWAT team.

"Ha ha," Clive replied. "It's *your* hearing that's going." He slapped Grant on the shoulder as he maneuvered out of the booth. "That was definitely your phone."

Grant frowned and took out his FBI-issued Black-Berry. Clive was right. One missed call. Hoping it was Maggie saying she was on her way, he held in a yawn and dialed his voice mail.

The message was from the supervisor of his Violent Crimes Major Offenders, VCMO, squad. SWAT was his calling, but VCMO was his regular position at the FBI, the job that filled most of his days.

"We've got a situation," the supervisory special agent said in his typical no-nonsense way. "I need you back at the field office, ASAP."

That was the extent of the message. Grant swore as he slapped some money on the table to cover his drink, then told his remaining teammates, "Gotta go. I'll catch you guys on Monday."

"Hot date?" one of them asked.

"I wish," Grant said. And boy, did he. If only Maggie had shown tonight. "But that was my SSA. Duty calls."

It was a short drive back to the office, which was oddly busy for 5:00 a.m. on a Saturday morning. Not that this was a nine-to-five sort of job, but from the amount of agents gathered in one of the interagency conference rooms, something big had broken. Or they wanted it to.

It wasn't *his* VCMO squad in the conference room, so Grant strode past with only a curious glance inside. His own SSA was waiting in the drab gray bullpen, a scowl on his face as he marked up a stack of paperwork.

"Thanks for coming in," James said, not glancing up as he wrote frantic notes on whatever case file he was reviewing.

Judging from the way his rapidly receding gray hair was sticking out, and the heavier-than-usual shadows under his eyes, the SSA had never left yesterday. But that was pretty standard for James.

"What's happening?" Grant asked, wishing he'd stopped for a coffee instead of settling for the bitter junk they brewed in the office. He'd been up nearly twenty-four hours straight now, and he was heading for a crash that even caffeine could only hold off for so long.

"Hang on." James finished whatever he was writing, then pushed it aside and looked up at Grant, a deep frown on his face.

Discomfort wormed through Grant. In his gut, he knew that whatever was happening, he *really* wasn't going to like it. "What is it?"

James sighed and rubbed a hand over his craggy face. With three divorces under his belt, he was now just married to the job. He was a tough supervisor, and he rarely looked stressed. But right now he looked very, very stressed. "Take a seat. Let's chat."

Grant tugged a chair over and sat down. "Spit it out."

James smiled, probably because Grant was one of the few agents in his VCMO squad who would push him. But the smile faded fast. "You know the situation with the Fishhook Rapist case, right?"

Grant cursed. Everyone who worked violent crime knew the background on that case. A sadistic rapist who grabbed one woman a year off the street, drugged, raped and branded her, then let her go, too disoriented to provide a description of her attacker. There was never any useful forensic evidence.

The guy was way too smart. He surfaced only on September 1, when a new victim would show up at a police station or hospital somewhere in the country, branded with his signature. Then he disappeared again, until the following year, when he'd hit some other state and leave a new victim.

And he'd started with Maggie Delacorte.

That part wasn't general knowledge—they didn't advertise the names of the victims, and they tried to keep the press from getting too much information. They inevitably did, but somehow, the FBI had managed to keep Maggie's last name out of the media for a decade, along with the fact that she'd moved on to become a standout SWAT agent.

Inside the Bureau, however, a few rumors had gotten out over the years, and when he'd moved to WFO and landed on her SWAT team, he'd heard the whispers.

She worked harder than just about anyone he knew, and he was positive she didn't want one terrible incident in her past to color the way her colleagues looked at her, so he'd never said anything. To him, it didn't change a thing. Not about what he thought of her work, and definitely not about how he felt about her as a woman.

"Grant!" his boss snapped, and he realized he hadn't been paying attention.

"Sorry." He ran a hand over his shaved head, dreading whatever he was about to hear. They had a month to go before the guy was supposed to surface, so any news about him now could in theory be a lead to catch him. But judging by his boss's face, Grant didn't think that was it.

"I said, is this going to be a problem for you?"

"What?"

James let out a heavy sigh. "You know about the letters, right?"

"Letters?" Grant frowned and shook his head.

"The perp's been sending them to Maggie over the last six months."

Anger boiled inside. No wonder Maggie hadn't been herself lately.

Did anyone on the team know? He felt his frown deepening, certain she wouldn't have told any of them, no matter how close the team was.

"The case agents checked with the other victims," James continued. "None of the others have received anything. But Maggie got a new one last night." He looked at his watch. "This morning, actually."

Grant looked toward the bustling conference room. So that was why the other VCMO squad had gathered. Maggie must have found the letter when she'd gone home. Which explained why she'd never shown at the bar.

Now he really wished he'd called her, even though chances were, she wouldn't have asked for his help.

"This letter was different from the others. The others were psychological-sick, but meant to hurt from a distance. This one was a threat. And given *your* back-ground…" James stared expectantly at him, not needing to finish his sentence.

Grant had worked in the New York field office for eight years before moving to WFO, and while he'd been there, he'd closed a serial murder case with unusual elements. Specific dates of attacks over a number of years, letters to one particular victim. In that case, it was a woman who had escaped.

"You think my experience on the Manhattan Strangler case—"

"Could help close this one," James finished. "Yes. Kammy Ming has requested you be moved to her squad for the duration of the case. Full-time. We're going to catch him before the next anniversary. There's no other option."

"He said he was coming back for Maggie, didn't he?" Grant asked, shades of the homicide case he'd closed coming back to him. The warm blood spurting on him as he'd driven the perp's knife into him. Carrying the victim out to the ambulance, then being shoved in with her to have his own wounds stitched up.

Grant had caught the guy four years after he'd started killing, but it had almost been too late for the woman he'd come back for. The thought of Maggie being loaded into an ambulance made him queasy.

"Look, Kammy wants your help," James said. "But if you being on SWAT with Maggie is going to be a conflict…"

Suddenly glad he was sitting down, Grant shook his head and hoped for once, James's intuition would fail him.

"Are you sure?" James persisted. "Because once she hears you're on the case, if she asks you about it, you still have to keep it all confidential. Can you do that?"

Could he? He wasn't sure. Worse yet, Grant was pretty sure Maggie had no idea he knew about her past. How would she react to him being on the case now?

Did he even want to be on this case? He didn't have to ask Maggie to know she wouldn't want him involved.

It was one thing to walk into dangerous situations with her—he trained with her and knew she could handle herself. But to go through all the details of what had happened to her a decade ago, back when she'd been a scared college kid? Being her friend now, feeling the way he did about her, did he have any right to dig into the worst day of her life, without her permission?

"Well?" James demanded, staring expectantly.

Then again, how could he sit by and not do anything when he had a chance to stop the man who'd hurt her?

Rage and determination filled him in equal measure, drowning out the nausea. "Yes, I want in on the investigation."

"Good," James said, standing up. "Then, get in the conference room. You start right now."

Chapter Three

"Why now?" Maggie asked as she walked into her living room. "And how long have you been up?" she added, noticing the pillows and blankets she'd put on the couch for Scott looked untouched. The guest room bed she'd made up for Ella was probably still made, too.

She glanced at her watch—10:00 a.m. Which meant she'd been in bed for about four hours. Not that she'd slept much. She'd spent most of the time trying every combat nap technique she'd learned from Scott, who'd trained with military special operations teams for his HRT sniper position. Still, every time she'd drifted off to sleep, she'd startled awake almost immediately.

Despite having gotten out of bed at five in the morning when she'd called them over, Ella and Scott looked wide-awake.

Ella handed her a cup of coffee. "We stayed up."

"What did I miss?" Maggie asked, looking back and forth between them. But neither of them needed to answer. She could tell from their faces. "You talked about how you were going to protect me, didn't you?"

"Don't be ridiculous," Scott said. "We both know you can take care of yourself."

"Thank—"

"But that doesn't mean we're leaving you alone," he

cut her off, putting a hand on her arm. "Get ready for some houseguests. Or pack a bag. And don't even think about arguing."

Maggie was both annoyed and relieved. If it was one of them in trouble, she'd be doing the same thing. They were a team; they always had been.

"Okay. But I want to stay here." They could take turns staying with her—she knew there was no stopping them—but she didn't want to bring trouble to their doorsteps.

Especially since neither one lived alone. Ella's fiancé, Logan, was a cop, and Scott's girlfriend, Chelsie—who'd moved in with him a week ago—was FBI. But neither of them had signed up for this, and although Maggie knew they'd help if she asked, she didn't want to drag them into it, too.

Scott looked surprised at her easy agreement, but he changed the subject, probably worried she'd change her mind. "Maggie, you haven't told Mom and Dad about the letters, have you? Or Nikki?"

"No." She took a sip of coffee, and the hot liquid burned the back of her throat, clearing her head. "And I don't plan to now, either. What are they going to do from Indiana, besides worry?"

She got ready to fight Scott on it—her parents had worried enough about her, ten years ago. She didn't want them repeating it now. And Nikki had only been twelve then, so they'd tried to keep the details from her. Nikki knew now—since the Fishhook Rapist had never been caught, she'd read about him in the news over the years. But Maggie didn't want her little sister to worry, especially not while Nikki was just moving into her first apartment, starting her first job.

"I agree," Scott said, surprising her.

"You do?"

"Yes. We both know Mom and Dad will just call you constantly, insisting you come home. And you don't need the distraction. We need to focus on stopping him. I want this September 1 to be just another day."

So did she. Getting together with Ella and Scott once a year, praying a new victim wouldn't turn up, was a tradition she'd love to forsake. But September 1 was never going to be just another day for her.

"Good," she said. "Then let's get started."

"You don't have access to the case file, do you?" Ella asked.

Maggie snorted. "No." She knew more details than the average victim, because the task force had asked her questions over the years. But they'd never let her officially investigate. She suppressed a shudder at just the idea. Even if it could help, the thought of looking through all the other victim files—and her own—made the coffee churn in her stomach.

"It probably wouldn't tell us a lot more than we already know, anyway."

She didn't have to say why. The news gave them enough details about where the Fishhook Rapist had been, and it was no secret he'd stuck to a pattern. Victimology and the crime itself hadn't changed.

He always struck once a year, on the same date. And he always chose the same type of woman: someone in her late teens or early twenties, with a slender build and long, dark hair.

Maggie touched the hair she'd cut into a bob years ago, after the second Fishhook Rapist victim had surfaced, looking too much like her. She'd worked hard on her physique, too. No longer was she thin and willowy, but lean and muscular.

She turned her back on Scott and Ella, in the pretense of heading for the chair in the corner, but really to give herself a second without being scrutinized to get her game face on. The face she used when she went into a SWAT call and needed a perp who weighed more than twice as much as she did to recognize her as a viable threat. She could do this. She could talk about what had happened to her, with the two people closest to her in the world.

Her bruised back protested as she sat. When she raised her eyes to theirs, she could tell Ella and Scott weren't fooled. In some ways, this would be easier with total strangers.

Clutching the arms of her chair too hard, she asked Ella, "Why now? Why isn't this year the same as every other one? Do you think he plans to target a new victim, too? Or just come back for me? And what—" She choked on the rest of the sentence, but she could tell Ella knew what she was going to ask.

What did he plan to do to her this time?

Ella settled onto the couch across from her, her face scrunched up, and Maggie knew what was coming. A detailed profiler's analysis.

Ella looked pensive as she started, "It was a sophisticated crime. He didn't leave us any forensic evidence, not even the first time. He was probably in his late twenties a decade ago. Young enough to fit in around a college town, but old enough to be self-sufficient, with his own vehicle and the ability to leave town permanently afterward without attracting attention."

Scott was nodding from his perch next to the couch as Ella continued, "He's closing in on forty now, and he's still grabbing women in college or just out of it. It's not as easy for him to blend in anymore. He's starting to realize he needs to think about changing his approach. He's starting to realize his pattern for the past decade has to change, at least in some ways. It's made him reminisce. And ten years is a significant number, in terms of standard anniversaries."

Intense lines appeared on Ella's smooth olive skin, and even her tone changed as she got into what Maggie recognized as her profiler groove. "To this perp, September 1 is more important than any standard anniversary. He's not married, never has been, and for him, this crime dominates his life."

She looked apologetic as she continued, "You're important to him because that day was the start for him. It probably wasn't his first offense, but it was the first time he used the brand." Her voice caught as she said, "And that's his signature. As he's been planning his next attack, he can't stop thinking about how it all started. He's looking for that same thrill, the way it was the first time he decided to act—the fear and excitement and—"

Ella closed her eyes again, and Maggie realized this was as hard for Ella to profile as it was for Maggie to hear. Ella had been there that day, when Maggie had stumbled back to their dorm room, drugged and only able to remember fragments of what had happened. Fragments were all she had today, and in some ways, she was grateful for that.

Scott was standing beside the couch, his jaw locked, his nostrils practically flaring, as he listened silently.

Maggie got up and walked woodenly to the couch, sitting beside Ella, who'd befriended her and Scott when she'd moved down the street from them when she and Maggie were in kindergarten. "It's okay. Keep going."

Maggie could hear determination, sorrow and anger in Ella's voice as she said, "It's hard for me to profile him objectively, Maggie. But I don't think he's planning to go after a new victim this year. I think he means what he says in that letter. I think he's coming back here just for you, to re-create what's in his mind from a decade ago."

"THE DATE OF the attacks has to mean something," Grant announced Monday morning.

He'd been saying it for two days now, and he was certain he was right. The problem was, he didn't know what it meant.

"Maybe." Kammy Ming, the SSA of the VCMO squad where Grant was on loan, still looked skeptical.

They were the only ones in the room now, but in an hour, it would fill up with the rest of the case agents. Kammy was already here because, as far as he could tell, she didn't sleep. He was here extra early because he needed to figure this out, for Maggie.

"Or maybe it's just the day he went after what he wanted," Kammy said. "Maybe it's important *because* it's the date of the attacks. Because it's when he abducted Maggie, so then it became his day for every future attack."

"Yeah, I know that's the prevailing theory," Grant said, rolling his shoulders, which were tight from spending the weekend sitting in an uncomfortable chair in a WFO conference room. "But you wanted me here because of my experience with the Manhattan Strangler case, right?"

Kammy nodded, but she was frowning, looking exhausted after a weekend without much progress. "There are some compelling similarities we can't ignore. But this isn't the same guy..."

"No," Grant agreed. "But in that case, the killer specifically waited for the anniversary of his mother's death to make a kill. Four years, and he was in control enough to wait a whole year in between attacks. With someone who has this sort of compulsion, a year is a long wait."

"Keep talking," Kammy said, tying her graying hair up in a bun as she stared expectantly at him.

She was as much of a workaholic as James. Was that going to be him in ten years? No balance, just the job all the time?

An image of Maggie immediately filled his brain. There was a heck of a lot more than work that he wanted to fill his days. And there was a heck of a lot more than just work involved when it came to solving this case.

"It's the same with this guy," Grant pressed. "He's systematic with the abductions, the branding, every single year. But he can control the urge until September 1 comes along. There must be a reason."

Kammy raised her eyebrows, sinking back into the chair next to him. "You have any ideas *why* the Fishhook Rapist would choose that specific day every year?" Before he could answer, she added, "Why did the Manhattan Strangler wait for the anniversary of his mother's death every year?"

"He was textbook. Overbearing mother he hated. He'd threatened to kill her for years, but could never bring himself to do it. After she died in a car accident, he treated the new victims as surrogates. So he waited for her anniversary for each kill."

Kammy nodded thoughtfully. "Trying to kill his mother over and over again, in the form of women who resembled her."

"Exactly. And the Fishhook Rapist chooses victims with a definite look, so it's possible he's modeling them after someone, too, but it could just be that he has a type. And given the rape, I think his motivation is different."

"Such as?"

It was 6:00 a.m. Monday morning, and they'd been going over the evidence practically nonstop since he'd been called in early Saturday. He was exhausted. But he didn't think he'd be able to sleep even if he wanted to. Every time he closed his eyes, he thought of the case. He thought of Maggie's case file.

He thought of Maggie, the way he knew her now. Light blue eyes bright with intelligence and determination, dark brown hair framing her heart-shaped face, lean body outlined with muscle, primed to rush into a SWAT call. And he thought of her the way he'd seen her in the photographs from her case file, taken at the hospital shortly after her attack. Smaller and much younger, hunched into herself, battered and broken. He never wanted to see her like that again.

Straightening, he shook his head. "I don't know. Maybe we should talk to a profiler—"

Kammy cut him off. "This case has been to the BAU. One of their senior people profiled him for us a few years ago."

"Okay, so what'd they say about the date of the attacks?"

"He said there wasn't enough evidence to be sure either way."

"But if we could figure out what it was, maybe it would help us track him."

Kammy nodded. "Well, you have any ideas, then go for it. In the meantime, let's work with what we know. Why's he coming back for Maggie?"

"Because he couldn't claim her," Grant replied immediately. To him, that one was obvious.

It had been the same with the Manhattan Strangler. He'd come back for the one woman who'd escaped him, the one woman he'd tried to kill who had managed to survive, against all the doctors' predictions.

Kammy's eyebrows drew together. "He *did* claim her. He raped and branded her like the rest—"

"Yeah, but look at her now." Grant cut Kammy off, not wanting or needing the reminder of what Maggie had endured. "She's SWAT. She didn't let him break her. And she was the first one he went after, the one with the most meaning to him."

"You think he knew her personally?"

"Probably not, but I think he watched her from afar for a while. I think there's a good chance he had a legitimate reason to be at the college back then."

"You mean a student?" Kammy shook her head. "The profiler was pretty solid on the guy being older than his victims."

"Maybe he worked there."

"Okay," Kammy said, "We can double-check. But they definitely looked closely at college employees back then. And I'm pretty sure we checked into anyone who moved after that attack, because we know he must have left between then and the following year, when he showed up in Mississippi. But let's go back to what you said about Maggie being different from the others."

Grant spun his chair back toward the conference table and took out eight of the nine victim files, handing them to Kammy. "The other victims. Look at their updates, the follow-ups. Look at where they are now. Every single one of them was derailed by the attack in some way. Either they dropped out of school, so they didn't end up in their planned profession, or they developed other problems like drinking or substance abuse."

Kammy started opening the files. "Okay, you're right about some of them. Two dropped out of school and never went back, which—you're right—seriously impacted their futures. One has a drinking problem and another one has had substance abuse issues, but she's clean now. Still, what about Marjorie? She—"

"Was on suicide watch on and off for two years after her attack."

"Danielle—"

"Dropped out of school, too."

"She's a doctor now," Kammy argued.

"She eventually went back to school. But it set her back about four years. And she's been vocal about her experience since then, including her struggle with panic attacks to this day."

Kammy stared at him. "This isn't all in the files."

"I did some digging. I know Maggie was his first victim, and ten years is an anniversary. But I think it's more than that. Maggie didn't just survive. She went into one of the most physical jobs in the FBI. Looking at her now, you'd never think she endured that. I think he's developed a sick obsession with her, with the idea of her and how he tried to leave a mark on her—psychologically, that is—and ultimately failed. I think he's coming back for her because he wants to break her."

Kammy snorted. "I know Maggie Delacorte, too, Grant. She's one of the toughest agents here. If he couldn't break her when she was twenty-two, how's he going to do it now, when she's SWAT?"

Grant shook his head, frowning. "I don't know." Which worried him a lot. Because the Fishhook Rapist was extremely intelligent. He had to be, to evade them for this many years, with this much Bureau heat on him. So he would have a plan in place.

Yet, he'd advertised that he was going to return for Maggie. He'd never returned for any of his victims. So they would never have expected it if he hadn't told them. Why would he do that? Unless it was part of his effort to break Maggie down.

"Well, whatever his plan is, we need to get to him before he gets near her. I don't care if she can take him down with her bare hands, I don't like this," Kammy said. "I don't like anything about this."

"Neither do I."

"We've got twenty-seven days," Kammy said. "And so far, zero leads."

"Then we'd better get cracking," Grant said, standing. "I'll get the number for the DC cops who handled the original case."

"Just remember," Kammy called after him, "You run into Maggie, and you say nothing."

"Not a problem," Grant said. He hoped she wouldn't discover that he was working the case until it was over. Until they'd put the Fishhook Rapist behind bars for good.

PEOPLE WERE STARING.

Maggie felt uncomfortable as she walked down the drab gray hallway toward the bustling bullpen where she worked at the WFO. Other agents avoided her eyes as she approached, but she could see them watching from her peripheral vision. As if they all knew.

The case agents for the Fishhook Rapist investigation worked out of the WFO, and it had been that way for a long time, so inevitably some rumors had gotten out. But never like this.

She jumped as someone clapped a hand on her shoulder, then spun around to face the office newbie, a tall, reed-thin guy a few months out of the Academy. Still all nervous excitement and no experience. Still too green to know when to keep his mouth shut.

He gave her an uncomfortable smile and said, "I can't believe the jerk is writing you letters. But they'll catch him. Don't worry."

Mind your own business formed on her lips, but she held it in and nodded stiffly back. Until now, only the longtime agents had seemed to know anything about what had led her into the FBI, and by the time they found out, they knew her well enough not to judge her for it. Six years at the WFO, and she'd never felt as though there was an invisible cloud of pity around her no one wanted to enter. It was why she'd almost backed out when the FBI had assigned her here in the first place.

Frustration and dismay filled her, and she gritted her teeth and tried to bury those emotions under anger. After ten years, the Fishhook Rapist shouldn't have this kind of power over her life anymore.

She wasn't going to *let* him have this kind of power over her life anymore.

She straightened her shoulders, and the newbie must have seen something in her eyes, because he stammered nervously about getting to work and hurried off.

"Maggie."

She turned at the sound of the familiar voice, and found Clive standing behind her, a grim expression on his normally friendly face.

"You know," she said, and her voice sounded weak and emotional. She cleared her throat and added, "Does everyone know?"

Did Grant know?

Clive's lips twisted with sympathy. "No, not everyone. But those of us who came in early today heard the case agents working. They had the conference room open, and they were going over the new evidence." He lowered his voice. "This is the first I've heard about the letters. I wish you'd said something, Maggie."

She shrugged, trying not to feel she'd somehow let him down. She knew he was aware of her history, because it had come up when she'd joined his team. But he'd made it clear then that her past didn't matter to him so long as it didn't affect her ability to do the job. And she'd proven, for four years now, that it didn't. "It wasn't relevant. It didn't affect my position in SWAT."

He gave her a small smile. "No, it didn't." The smile faded. "But with everything going on—"

Maggie put her hands on her hips. "You're pulling me from the team?"

"No. But I want you to think about whether it's the best place for you right now. If you want time—"

"I don't." She tried to force confidence into her tone and her expression. "The letters just mean there's more evidence to investigate. They won't affect my performance on the team."

Clive frowned, as if he could see through her. "We've been friends a long time, Maggie. I'm here if you want to talk. And if you need a break, we'll hold your spot. Don't worry about that."

"Okay." She nodded, a lump filling her throat. There were three SWAT teams at the Washington Field Office, and agents tended to stay on the teams for years—positions very rarely opened up, and waiting lists for tryouts were long. Clive offering to hold her spot was a huge commitment.

She needed to remember she had good friends here, and focus on that, instead of the unwanted attention she was getting right now from agents who barely knew her. "Thanks."

"Of course." He gave her a smile that looked a little

forced then headed for his own desk across the room, in the Organized Crime squad.

As he walked away, Maggie surveyed the other agents in the room. It hadn't been her imagination. There was definitely staring.

She dropped her bag at her desk, slid her gun and cuffs into her drawer and headed back down the hall toward the coffeepot.

Hopefully, Clive was right and only the agents who'd come in early today had learned about the letters. And hopefully, those agents would get over it, stop staring and not gossip.

But the thing she hoped for most was that Grant hadn't heard.

She had to believe the Bureau would catch the Fishhook Rapist this time. Before September 1. She refused to think anything else, no matter how dread filled her every time she thought about that date. No matter how the voice in the back of her mind sounded too much like a whisper from a decade ago, telling her, "This is going to hurt."

She had to believe it would all be over soon, and once it was, she wasn't going to let a few bureaucratic rules keep her from taking a chance with Grant Larkin. Assuming he wanted to take a chance with her. Assuming he hadn't learned all of her horrible secrets.

Please, please, don't let him know.

She chanted the words in her head as she reached the coffeepot. As she grabbed the carafe, Kammy Ming strode over, managing to project power despite her tiny five-foot frame.

"Maggie." Kammy greeted her in the subdued tone she seemed to save just for Maggie.

"Hi, Kammy," Maggie replied. "How's the case going?" She clutched the carafe too tightly, certain

Kammy wouldn't tell her anything. Kammy never told her anything.

But this time, Kammy carefully tugged the carafe from her hand, poured her a cup and said, "We worked all weekend. We're going to catch him."

A smile trembled on Maggie's lips as Kammy poured herself a cup, then faded as Kammy turned to leave, calling after her, "Your friend Grant has some good insights."

Grant was *on the case*? Dizziness washed over her, and she would have dropped her mug of hot coffee except a pair of large hands grabbed it and steadied her.

She looked up, and there was Grant, staring down at her with concern and guilt in his deep brown eyes.

He knew. He knew all the horrible details of what had happened to her. It may have been years ago, but that didn't change how men reacted when they found out. Especially men she was dating. Or wanted to date.

She stepped out of his grasp and braced herself.

"I'm sorry, Maggie," Grant whispered.

And right then and there, she knew anything that could have happened between them was over.

Chapter Four

"Get out of here."

"What?" Grant stopped rubbing his eyes and looked up at Kammy.

She was so tiny, she barely had height on him when she was standing, and he was sitting, but she glared like a pro. "You're no good to me if you're so exhausted you can't focus. Go home. Get some sleep. You've been here too long. Come back fresh tomorrow."

Grant started to argue, but Kammy reached for the file in front of him and closed it. Knowing she'd fight him if he tried to stay, he held up his hands in surrender and got to his feet.

As he trudged through the practically empty bullpen and into the equally deserted parking garage, he admitted she was right. He did need to recharge. Pure determination wasn't going to solve a case that had eluded dozens of other case agents and local police over the past decade. He needed to be at the top of his game, and to do that, a solid eight hours of sleep was in his immediate future.

He was already pressing the button to open his doors when he realized someone was sitting on the hood of his car.

Maggie stood as he approached, a familiar "don't mess

with me" glint in those pretty blue eyes, though she usually saved it for the dirtbags they arrested.

He hadn't asked her before agreeing to work on the case. That made him uncomfortable, but the fact was, even if she'd said she didn't want him on it, he couldn't have turned it down. Couldn't have sat by knowing he might have made a difference when the Fishhook Rapist was after Maggie again.

Grant rubbed the back of his neck and prepared for a fight. "You could have called me if you wanted to talk, Maggie. I would have come out."

She shook her head. "I wanted to do this without causing more gossip."

He cut her off before she could get going. "I should have told you. But I wanted to help."

"And you didn't think I'd prefer someone else work this case?" she said, straightforward as always. "We work some heavy calls together. Every time we clear a room now, are you going to think I can't handle it?"

"Of course no—" he started.

"Do you know how hard it is to be in this field office?" Strain filled her voice. "Knowing there's a squad full of agents who've read all about the worst day of my life?"

"I'm sorry." He'd thought about the strength it took to get through that, and the character it took to ignore the rumors. But he'd never thought about how she felt as a federal agent who investigated crimes all day long, to be part of a case file as a victim.

Probably because, even with what she'd gone through, he'd never thought of her as one. He'd always thought of her as a survivor.

"And do you know how much worse it is, knowing you've seen the evidence from my assault?" she whispered.

The information from her rape kit. It'd been one of the

hardest things he'd ever done, reading through it. And he'd read plenty of them over the years.

"They wanted my help," he said, trying to be honest with her. "It doesn't change a thing between us."

"You're wrong about that."

He stepped closer, reached out and lifted her hand, threading his fingers through hers. "I hope not." He stared into her eyes, trying to tell her with just his gaze how he felt.

Considering how surprised she seemed, it might even have worked.

But then she looked down at their locked hands and frowned. "I'm sure you'd love to think it doesn't make a difference, that it doesn't change how you view me. But believe me, it always does."

He tugged on her hand, bringing her closer, and forcing her to look up at him. "How many people have seen the case file?"

She shook her head. "*Knowing* what happened to me always changes how people look at me."

"I don't believe that." And he didn't. Everyone working the case had the highest respect for her.

He could tell she was about to argue, so he cut her off. "Maggie, I've known since I moved to the WFO."

Her jaw went slack, and her eyes widened. "What?"

"I work the violent crimes squads, and those squads share theories. Just because I wasn't on the case…" He shrugged. "I already knew."

"Why didn't you say anything?"

"Why would I say anything? You heard about me getting stabbed in the Manhattan Strangler case a few years back, right?"

She nodded, studying him as though she was trying to figure out whether or not to believe him.

"You never said anything about that."

"It's a little different."

"It's a lot different, I know. But just because something really bad happened to you a decade ago, that doesn't have anything to do with how I feel about you now."

He tugged her even closer, so there was barely any space between them. She was tall, so even though he outweighed her by almost a hundred pounds, he only had a couple of inches on her. She stared up at him, surprise and uncertainty in her eyes.

Then her gaze traveled down to his mouth and back up again, and there was something new in her expression, something that made him completely forget he'd ever been tired.

She was so different than anyone he'd ever known, and he'd had feelings for her practically since the day he'd started with SWAT. But he'd never made a move, even tried to keep his feelings for her hidden, because she was a teammate. He'd been wary of risking their friendship, wary of risking his place on the team where he'd just been accepted, wary of going in too soon and ruining his shot.

Then they'd become fast friends, and he absolutely knew there was no way he could ever have anything simple or temporary with this woman. And yeah, that was a little scary, too.

But right now, with her staring at him as if her feelings were just as strong, there was no way he could resist her.

She pressed her free hand against his chest, and it felt as if the world was moving in slow motion as she rose up on her tiptoes, and he leaned forward.

He brought his hand to the curve of her waist, marveling at how slender she was beneath all that lean muscle. His fingers slid up to the middle of her back, and he brought her even closer. His lips brushed lightly against hers, and he felt her sigh.

He could practically feel his whole world shifting beneath his feet as he made another pass over her lips with his, and then another, until her grip on his hand tightened, and she kissed him back, harder.

If he'd ever managed to keep his feelings for her hidden, the secret was definitely out now.

Then the door into the parking garage opened with a loud *bang* as it hit the wall, and Maggie jumped backward, fast.

The agent who'd come into the garage didn't even seem to notice them as he headed for his vehicle, but when Grant looked back at Maggie, she had taken another step back and was cursing under her breath.

Before he could say anything, she blurted, "That was a bad idea."

"I think it was one of the best ideas I've ever had."

He grinned at her, and she scowled back, her cheeks flushed. "Grant…" She shook her head. "We need to work together. Let's not make this messy."

"I'm okay with messy," he argued, moving toward her.

She held up a hand, and he stopped. "You're on my case. That changes things, whether you want it to or not. I need this guy caught before September."

Grant nodded, getting serious fast. "Okay." But come September 2, when they had the Fishhook Rapist in jail, he was going straight for messy, regardless of what it meant for his position on the SWAT team.

He'd been shocked when a spot had opened up as soon as he'd moved to DC—as though it was meant to be. The idea of leaving the team was like a punch to the gut. The guys—and Maggie—had become like family. A family he didn't want to lose. And the chance of getting onto one of the other SWAT teams without waiting *years* was minuscule at best. But the thought of not taking a chance with Maggie was worse.

"Do you have any solid leads on the case?"

He gaped at her. "Come on, Maggie. You know I can't tell you."

"Really?" Her hands went from being crossed over her chest to her hips. "Because you had no trouble breaking the rules a second ago."

"*You* kissed *me*," he argued.

"You sure about that?"

Was he? Jeez, he had no idea. "Look, Maggie, I promise you, we're doing everything we can—"

"I've been hearing that for a decade, Grant," she broke in. "And if this guy really is coming back for me, I want to be prepared."

Furious at the idea of the Fishhook Rapist getting anywhere near her again, he vowed, "We won't let that happen."

"Neither will I," she said, her battle face on. "So tell me something I can use."

He stared at her, at the stubborn set of her chin, and he knew. She was already investigating on her own.

He swore. "Maggie, this isn't your specialty. You should leave the case to Violent Crimes."

"Well, that's not happening. So help me or don't, but I'm still looking into it."

Worry gnawed at him. But he couldn't deny this was what he liked about her—her insistence on going full force at a problem.

As the only woman on their SWAT team, she could have gotten out of some of the particularly physically grueling jobs on an assignment, but she never did. Half the time, she volunteered for them. And they could always count on her to get it done, no question.

He took her hand, folding it into his before she could pull it back, and said, "Promise me if you come up with anything, you'll take me with you."

"Scott and Ella are helping me."

He should have realized. "Okay, fine. If you find anything, bring me or Scott. Agreed?"

She raised her eyebrows. "Take a guy with me? What about Ella?"

"She's a profiler, not an operator. Your brother is HRT. Promise me."

"Okay, I promise. I'm not stupid. I wouldn't chase after this guy on my own, not when he's after me specifically."

"Good." He looked down at their linked hands, then back into her gorgeous blue eyes. "We don't have anything solid yet, but if we find something, I'll share."

"Thank you." She eased her hand free. "I need to go."

As she walked away, Grant sighed heavily. When he'd been brought into this case, he'd promised he'd be able to uphold the confidentiality. Now, only a few days later, he was already promising Maggie that he'd break it.

The reality was, there was no way he could say no to her if she pressed him. And there was no way he could step away from the investigation, not when it was this important.

He had a bad feeling that before this case was over, his career was going to take a direct hit.

"WHERE WERE YOU?" Scott greeted her as she walked into her house.

Maggie jumped, even though she knew he'd be there, since his SUV was parked in her driveway. She'd given both Scott and Ella keys to her house, and they insisted on knowing her whereabouts every part of the day.

"I told you I was going to be late coming back from work." As soon as she'd gotten over the shock of discovering Grant was on the case, she'd decided to talk to him. That meant waiting around until he left, which hadn't been until nearly 7:00 p.m.

Then the whole drive home, she'd alternately berated and congratulated herself for kissing him. Yes, she'd wanted to do that for months. And she *had* been honest about how his being on the case changed things. Sure, if they'd somehow gotten around the problem of being teammates and started something serious, she would have told him about what had happened to her, eventually. But she would have given him the basics; she wouldn't have handed over pictures from her rape kit and every horrible detail from her interview with the cops a decade ago.

Even thinking about the fact that Grant knew such personal, painful things made a knot squeeze tighter in her chest.

Scott frowned at her. "You okay?"

"Yeah, I'm fine." She squinted at her brother, taking in the stress lines on his forehead that hadn't been there a few days ago, the dark circles under his eyes, then glanced at her watch. "You're early."

He turned away, saying, "Ella will be over in a bit. She was swinging home first to see Logan before he leaves for his shift."

Maggie's stomach growled, loudly, from being unable to eat much all day, and not wanting to go out for dinner and miss Grant leaving work.

"Ella's bringing dinner," Scott added.

Turning all the bolts behind her, Maggie hurried after him. "What aren't you telling me?"

"Nothing."

Maggie grabbed his arm, making him spin around. "Scott, what is it?"

He shuffled his feet, then sighed. "Nothing to do with your case. Don't worry about it."

He tried to pull his arm free, but she held on tighter. "I appreciate you and Ella trying to protect me, but I'd rather hear it straight. *What*?"

He smiled. "How is it that you always know when there's something I'm not saying, but I could tell Nikki I met an alien in the backyard and she'd believe me?"

Maggie rolled her eyes. Their younger sister had been coddled most of her life. A decade younger than Maggie, she'd already been the baby, but after Maggie's attack, the whole family had become even more protective of little Nikki. But for all her blind trust when it came to family, she wasn't a fool. Maggie and Scott had drilled safety techniques into her until she'd finally told them enough was enough, or she'd be paranoid about everyone she met. "She's not trained by the FBI. I am. And she's not *that* bad. So, spit it out."

"It has nothing to do with this case. I just bailed on some advanced defensive driving training I'd signed up for a long time ago. My supervisor isn't thrilled with me right now." Scott shrugged. "He'll get over it."

Maggie frowned, because this *was* about her. Six months ago, Ella had taken personal time and accepted a case on her own because she thought it was related to Maggie's abductor. Ella's supervisor had been surprisingly understanding, but Maggie knew it had cost Ella a lot of trust she'd worked hard to gain in the elite Behavioral Analysis Unit.

Now Scott was putting himself in a similar position. Again for her.

"Don't do that," Scott said. "I can read you just as well as you read me, sis. I make my own choices. And this really isn't a big deal."

She could tell he was lying, but she also knew it didn't matter what she said. There was no way her big brother—and one of her very best friends, to boot—was stepping one inch away from the case.

"Thanks" seemed so inadequate, but she didn't know what else to say.

He patted her arm as the growl of a convertible came closer. "I hear Ella. Let's eat and then figure out how to stop this guy for good."

"I'm on board with *that*," Maggie said, following him to the door to let in Ella, carrying bags of Chinese food.

An hour later, she, Ella and Scott sat cross-legged on the floor of her living room, surrounded by legal pads, laptops and discarded balls of paper.

"Okay, let's think about this," Ella suggested. "He picks a different state every year. These attacks are definitely specific, and he spends real time stalking the women first, which means he's not just flying out to a new state once a year. He's moving from year to year. So he's either got a job that allows him to travel without attracting notice, or he's got a lot of holes in his résumé."

"We've been through that," Scott said. "Salesman, pilot, trucker—"

"Trucker," Ella said, cutting him off. "What about a long-haul trucker? Maybe someone who's independent, who can pick his own routes. Because he definitely stalks his victims first. But a truck would give him a private location for the attacks and the branding. He could soundproof the back."

"I don't know," Maggie started, but Ella kept going. "There's a reason the FBI put together that database on Highway Serial Killers. The interstate travel means multiple jurisdictions that are harder to track, and the nature of the job means they're often around people who are high-risk victims."

"Sure," Scott said, "but aren't most of the victims who were in that database prostitutes? This guy goes for women who are at pretty low risk for being victims of a crime and at a high risk to himself."

Ella looked impressed. "You do listen when I babble about profiling, don't you?"

"Of course, kiddo," he said, using the nickname he'd had for her since childhood.

"I don't remember a truck," Maggie said quietly, and both of them got serious, looking over at her.

"Do you remember that part at all?" Scott asked.

Maggie had always told them both she couldn't remember much about her attack. And it was true. She just had fragments—nothing she'd ever thought would help in an investigation.

She recalled feeling dizzy as she walked out of the college party alone, as though she'd had way more to drink than just one beer. Then, later, being lifted off the ground after she'd tripped and fallen. A low voice, whispering in her ear right before the brand burned her neck. The vague sense of stumbling out of a vehicle before she dragged herself back to her dorm room.

She'd never remembered a face. Never remembered the assault itself. Nothing that would lead police to whoever had hurt her.

Even though she'd always felt some relief about that, she'd tried. She'd even let herself be hypnotized once, attempting to get back the details. But hospital staff and police experts had warned her that date-rape drugs like the one she'd consumed could eliminate huge chunks of time from her memory. They hadn't been surprised when she couldn't provide any details.

Still, for some reason she felt strongly about this part. "I only remember bits and pieces. I couldn't say for sure. But I just don't think I was in a truck."

"Well, a motel room is another possibility," Ella said. "Something off the beaten path a little, somewhere that charges by the hour and expects the sort of customer who'd prefer not to be remembered."

"Or he puts down roots, rents something for eight months then moves on to the next location and starts scouting," Maggie suggested.

"Which would mean he probably works odd jobs and has a résumé full of holes," Ella said. "And this perp is extremely intelligent. So in these odd jobs, he's either hiding that so he doesn't stand out, or he's noticed for it."

"I know the original profiler said he was antisocial," Maggie said. "So maybe he just keeps quiet."

"Yeah, maybe." Ella was frowning. "But we know he arrives sometime after September 1 in each new location, and he leaves before September 1 of the following year, probably at least a few months before, so he can pick out a new victim. So he's either choosing all short-term contract work, or he's suddenly going absent from these jobs and creating a trend."

"A trend we can track?" Scott asked skeptically.

"Probably not. But I'm not sure—"

"Or he's wealthy," Maggie cut in. "Wealthy enough that the money doesn't matter."

"Maybe," Ella said. "But the hook suggests something to do with water, so he could also have some sort of seasonal job in the fishing industry, something that ends before the fall."

"That makes a lot of sense," Scott agreed. "That hook has to mean something."

"Does it?" Maggie glanced between them, knowing her frustration was showing. "Or is he smart enough to do it to throw us totally off track?"

Her eyes were wet, and she blinked fast, hoping neither of them had noticed, but knowing they had. "What chance do we have of finding him? We don't even have the case files. Even the case agents—who worked nonstop all weekend—don't have any new leads."

"We're going to get him," Scott promised.

She nodded, hoping she looked as though she believed it. At work, she tackled every case assuming that if she just worked hard enough, she'd solve it. She tried to treat her own life the same way.

But year after year, the memories added up. Going through the same motions of gathering together and closing ranks with Ella and Scott. Watching the news even as they tried to stay away from it. Hoping that year would be different even when they knew it wouldn't.

And every year, it was exactly the same. Every year, she watched some new woman live out the same horrible thing she had, knowing that just like her, they'd only have partial memories. Knowing that just like her, they probably wouldn't be able to identify the Fishhook Rapist even if he walked right up to them.

In twenty-seven days, would the Fishhook Rapist walk right up to her? And if he did, would she know it before it was too late?

Chapter Five

Twenty days.

There were twenty days left until Maggie's attacker came back for her, and despite the best efforts of some of the most dedicated VCMO agents Grant knew, there were no new breaks in the case.

Despite his nonstop hours at work, poring over the evidence, he wasn't making a difference.

Grant slammed his fist against the wall of the van he was riding in, and the teammate seated next to him gave him a perplexed look.

"Grant!" Clive barked. "Get your head in the game."

"Sorry," he muttered, refocusing.

They were en route to a warehouse in a particularly bad area of DC, where case agents had determined a human trafficking ring was conducting business. Two of their supposed victims had already shown up in the morgue, burn marks on their bodies as apparent punishment before their throats were slit, and case agents expected more would surface unless they acted fast.

Maggie's squad had brought the warrants and the evidence, and requested SWAT for the potentially high-risk arrests. It was well after normal business hours, but surveillance indicated the personal vehicles of the three men listed on the arrest warrants were parked outside. The only three vehicles in the lot.

If SWAT was lucky, they'd be the only people inside the building tonight.

"They've got surveillance cameras everywhere, so we're hacking them and blocking the feed," Clive continued briefing them. "But if anyone's watching the cameras, they're going to know we're coming. So get your A-game ready, people."

Grant pushed Maggie's case to the back of his mind, but he couldn't help glancing at Maggie. She was squashed into the corner of the truck, and even in all her gear, she looked tiny next to the teammate they jokingly referred to as "Tank." Her dark hair curled around her chin underneath her helmet, and even with goggles dangling around her neck and buried underneath Kevlar and weaponry, she made his pulse pick up.

As the van bounced over potholes, she held her MP-5 and stared straight ahead, totally focused. And totally ignoring him, even though she probably felt his stare.

It had been that way for a week. It wasn't as if they weren't on speaking terms, but things were definitely strained between them, and had been since they'd kissed.

Still, he couldn't bring himself to regret it. Given the chance, he'd do it again.

He felt himself smile at the idea, and Maggie finally glanced his way as if she could sense the direction of his thoughts. But then she went back to staring straight ahead, which was typical for her right before a high-risk arrest.

Some of the guys worked off tension by joking around just before they went into a call—usually, he was one of them. Others on the team sat in silence. Maggie always seemed to be envisioning exactly how the raid was going to go.

It wouldn't surprise him if whatever she imagined was usually right—she tended to have a sixth sense on this kind of call. More than once, he'd watched her react to a threat before anyone else knew it was there, before there was any reason for her to know it existed. Some of the guys on the team called it "Maggie's Magic."

As they drove past the warehouse, giving them eyes on the target, he hoped for a little of that magic tonight. The quick look he had before the truck parked down the street was of a high chain-link fence topped with barbed wire, cameras mounted above the windowless doors, and three vehicles big enough to hold five people each parked close to the loading dock of the sprawling warehouse.

"Time to move," Clive said, nodding to the tech who was already typing away, preparing to black out the cameras.

Tank threw open the door, and six FBI SWAT agents jumped onto the street. As Grant fell into the front of the line, his adrenaline picked up. His regular position on VCMO was interesting and challenging, but SWAT—most of the time—was downright fun. Yeah, it was serious, but anyone who tried out for a SWAT team had to get a thrill from this kind of work.

As he took off down the street, he imagined anyone who happened to be in the decrepit building across the street looking outside and getting a shock. Normally, this area was pretty deserted after business hours, and for good reason. Even during the day, it wasn't the sort of place you'd want to wander into accidentally.

Just about every building on the block had been raided by FBI or local police or both at some point. But for every criminal they pushed out, another seemed to take his place. Gunshots weren't uncommon around here, but rarely did anyone call for help when they happened.

But six FBI agents decked out in combat gear, carrying heavy weaponry and a battering ram, running at full speed, had to make anyone with half a brain pray the targets were arrested quickly and without a fight.

Over his radio, the tech's tinny voice came through. "The target's cameras are down…now!"

Almost before he'd finished speaking, Clive was using bolt cutters on the lock keeping them on the wrong side of the fence. Then they passed through single-file and moved for the entry on the corner, the one with the least visibility for the occupants inside, and the best coverage for the agents, according to the blueprints they'd accessed.

As Clive fell to the back of the line, Maggie came up beside Grant, her MP-5 submachine gun up to cover him as he lifted the battering ram.

One solid hit, and the door flew inward, bouncing off the wall and almost closing on them again, until he smashed it back open with his foot. His night vision equipment lent an eerie green glow to the short, dark hallway, but it didn't illuminate any targets as Maggie stepped in first, moving past him quickly and off to his right.

Grant dropped the battering ram, raising his own primary weapon as he came up beside her. Then they were moving together, in a choreographed entry that felt like a thousand practice runs.

The rest of the team came in behind them, their combat boots clomping on the concrete floor as they moved quickly down the hall as a unit.

"Clear," Maggie's confident voice came through his headset as she opened a closet door on her side and checked it. Then they came up to the wide, open area that was the main part of the warehouse.

The agents began splitting off in twos, each into their own sectors. Much of the open warehouse space was filled floor to ceiling with boxes, providing plenty of places for targets to hide, and lots of places to clear. The area in his and Maggie's sector was open until it branched off down a separate hallway leading to offices.

Checking his peripherals because his teammates wouldn't be able to clear their sectors as quickly, Grant was surprised not to see anyone in the main area. Either the targets hadn't heard the entry—which they should have, with a battering ram—or they were hiding. Or everyone was in one of the two offices.

"Quiet," Maggie's voice whispered through his headset.

Too quiet was what he knew she meant.

He nodded once to acknowledge it, and then jutted his chin toward the door straight ahead. It was closed, but there was a light on inside. As they got closer, he could just make out a voice, and he strained to listen. It sounded like a scream, only turned down to almost nothing, as though it was coming from a TV.

"Possible target," he whispered as they both lifted their NVGs.

Maggie reached for the door handle with her left hand, keeping her weapon sighted with her right.

She turned the handle slowly, nodding as it moved on its own—meaning it wasn't locked. Then she shoved it open, giving him a view of one corner of the room, but no angle on the rest, as the muted scream became a high-pitched wail, full of pain. The soundproofed walls registered in his brain as a charred smell instantly filled his nostrils.

He watched Maggie's left hand go back to her weapon almost before the door opened, then watched her jaw go slack and her eyes go abnormally wide before her whole body froze.

Grant stepped sideways quickly, the rest of the room coming into view. The filthy, half-dressed woman on the floor, a man's knee pressed into her back as he held a lighter to her. Another man standing beside him, looking bored. And a third behind them, surprise on his face as he yanked up a pistol.

Grant heard himself screaming at the target to put it down, even as he lurched sideways, shoving Maggie out of the doorway and trying to sight his weapon at the same time.

He pulled the trigger, then something smashed into his chest, and he flew through the air as a pair of gunshots filled his ears. He slammed into the ground with enough force that it would have knocked the air out of his lungs, if he could actually breathe. His head hit the ground, and his vision dimmed as he gasped for oxygen and groped with his left hand for the source of the pain exploding in his chest.

From what seemed like a long distance away, he heard Maggie's voice screaming his name, and two more gunshots in rapid succession. Then a dark figure filled his vision, and he tried to blink it into focus, tried to lift the weapon he was pretty sure was still clutched in his right hand, as his fingers finally grazed over his chest and dipped into the bullet hole.

"Grant!"

Panic filled Maggie's chest as she slung her MP-5 over her back, dropped to her knees and reached for the hand Grant had clasped over his chest. His eyes were rolled back in his head, but he kept blinking as though he was trying to focus, and gasping for breath.

Please let him be okay, a voice chanted in her head, as she tried to remember all the training that had become second nature over the past four years in SWAT. Never in those four years had she watched a teammate take a bullet.

"Where are you hit?" she yelled, even though she knew he couldn't answer her.

She didn't wait for him to try. Instead, she pushed his hand aside, relief flooding through her as she saw the bullet lodged near the top of his Kevlar vest. But that didn't mean it hadn't caused damage.

Forcing her hand underneath his vest, she searched for any sign the bullet had gone through. But there was no blood.

Still, it was possible he had a collapsed lung, or broken ribs, or...

"I'm okay." Grant interrupted her fears as he finally seemed to catch his breath and started to push himself up.

"Stay there," Maggie said, but he ignored her, getting to a sitting position and looking around, already back on task as he checked for new threats.

"Status? Maggie, status?"

Suddenly realizing the question was coming from both Grant beside her and Clive over her headset, Maggie replied, "Grant was hit in the vest." Her heart still raced as she tried to get it together, tried not to think about what could have happened, tried not to think about *why*.

She'd never let anything distract her from a mission before. Never let her history prevent her from doing her job. Until today.

There'd be plenty of time to berate herself later. Right now she needed to get her mind back on the mission.

"Three targets down. One victim needs an ambulance."

"And Grant?" Clive pressed.

"I'm okay," Grant told them both.

Maggie glanced at him where he sat on the floor, still wincing as he braced a hand against his chest. "Grant, I'm sor—"

"Not now," he said, getting to his feet with a lot more effort than it should have taken.

"Are you sure you don't need—"

"It'll be a nasty bruise. Nothing's broken. Let's check the room." He slung his own MP-5 over his back, grunting at the movement, and grabbed the Glock strapped to his thigh then moved toward the room.

Reluctantly, she unholstered her own Glock, better for close quarters than the MP-5, and followed, looking into the office.

Inside, the three men who were listed on their warrants were down for good, one from Grant's bullet and two from hers. The three traffickers had only gotten two shots off, the one that had hit Grant and another that had gone wide, passing over her right shoulder.

There was nowhere in the office to hide. The only other person in the room was the woman who'd picked herself up off the floor and was cowering in the corner, rocking back and forth. Surely one of the trafficking victims.

The smell hit Maggie as soon as she entered. Not the blood. The burning.

She fought back the urge to gag, fought the memory that tried to incapacitate her a second time. The same memory that had surged forward the instant she'd opened the door. A memory she hadn't even realized she possessed.

A memory that had very nearly gotten Grant killed.

She glanced at him, checking the pulses on the three men on the floor, even though they were clearly gone. It chilled her how close he'd come to dying outside this room.

He looked back at her, concern and a hint of pain in his deep brown eyes, and she couldn't hold his gaze.

"Our sector's clear," Grant said into his mic, and within the next few minutes, the rest of the team announced the same.

"We've got ERT, an ambulance and the coroner on the way," Clive told them. "They're less than a minute out. We're coming to you now."

Before the team made it into the room, Grant had checked the woman over for any serious injuries—and weapons, because you could never assume—and Maggie had cuffed the three perps with the zip ties looped on her belt. Dead or not, it was procedure.

The whole time, she tried not to breathe too deeply.

"You okay?" Clive asked Grant as he joined them in the office, the rest of the team behind him, looking shaken. This was first time anyone on the team had been shot since before Maggie had joined four years ago.

"I'm good," Grant replied easily, already beginning to move around as if he hadn't taken a bullet to the chest.

Vest or not, at this range, that had to *hurt*. A few inches higher, and it could have been much, much worse.

Was he playing it down because that was a SWAT agent's way? Or because of her?

"What happened?" Clive asked.

Grant opened his mouth, but Maggie cut him off, not wanting to know what he was going to say. Not wanting him to tell Clive she'd frozen at a critical moment, but not wanting him to lie for her, either.

"It was my fault," she said, watching her teammates'

eyes widen behind Clive as they looked back and forth between her and Grant and the dead men on the floor.

Grant frowned, his attention darting to the woman in the corner of the room, and Maggie realized he'd put it all together.

Of course he had. He'd read all the details from her case file. He knew exactly what had happened to her a decade ago, every terrible detail. Including the brand on the back of her neck.

It had smelled the same today as it had ten years ago, when she'd heard a voice whispering in her ear, telling her something would hurt. As she'd struggled toward consciousness to find her head pressed against a cold, hard surface. A hand against the back of her head. A disorienting, numb feeling over her entire body, and complete confusion as a room slowly came into focus around her. A room she didn't recognize. And then a sudden, fierce pain at the back of her neck, and the smell of her own skin burning.

She tried to force back the memory, then looked up at Clive and blurted out words she never thought she'd say. "I need to leave the SWAT team."

Chapter Six

"I'm so sorry."

Maggie blurted the words as soon as Grant opened his door. The door she'd finally gotten the courage to knock on after standing on his front stoop for ten minutes in the glow of the porch light.

She'd never been to his house before, but she'd told Ella and Scott not to come over tonight, because she was going out with her SWAT friends. There'd be plenty of time to break the news to them later about her sudden career change.

Instead, she'd looked up Grant's address and made the surprisingly short drive to his house.

Grant opened the door wide and stepped aside. His voice was somber when he said, "Come in, Maggie." He sounded as if he'd expected her, as though maybe he'd been waiting up for her.

Nerves, guilt and regret mingled as she stepped inside, glancing around. His tidy little row house looked similar to hers on the outside, but inside it was very different. Hardwood floors instead of carpet, beige walls instead of the muted blues and greens and yellows she'd chosen. More sparsely decorated, but somehow it still felt cozy.

She followed him into the living room, and her eyes

were immediately drawn to a row of pictures over his fireplace. She couldn't stop herself from stepping closer.

One was clearly him in high school, because he was wearing a letter jacket. He'd been muscular even as a teenager, and he had his arms around two smaller boys, a tired-looking black woman behind them. The younger boys took after their mother where Grant, who seemed to have some strong Mediterranean heritage, probably resembled his father. Still, there was something so similar in their expressions, marking them as siblings. The pictures on either side were of those boys grown up, married, little kids on their knees.

Grant stood next to her, his shoulder brushing hers. "My younger brothers." He pointed to the pictures on the outsides of the little boys, pride in his voice. "And this is them now, with my nephews."

She looked back at the young boys, his brothers' kids, who looked like miniature versions of Grant, and an ache settled somewhere inside that she didn't want to acknowledge. She'd never really let herself think about kids, because she'd never been able to get anywhere near the point of wanting to have them with someone.

"And your mom?" Maggie asked, looking at the center picture again, the one where Grant's expression said he'd grown up fast. Too fast. Even as a teenager, the protective instinct nearly screamed from him. The same way it did now, on SWAT.

"Yeah. Not the greatest picture of her, but it was one of the first family photos we have from after my dad took off. I need to get something more recent up there before she comes to visit and gets mad at me for choosing that picture to put up."

He grinned at her, and she couldn't help it. There was something about the way he smiled, the way it made his eyes brighten, the way he seemed to grin with his whole face, every time, that always made her smile back.

But it faded fast. "Grant, I owe you—"

"Nothing." He cut her off, actually sounding as if he meant it. "You owe me nothing."

"I owe you a lot more than just an apology. I wish I could go back to the day Clive asked me if I wanted to take time off from SWAT and—"

"Stop it," Grant said, and it wasn't his words, but the fact that he actually put his finger over her lips that made her quiet.

The touch sent a tingling feeling outward over her face, and his expression changed, too. The serious veneer was gone, replaced with a mixture of emotions she couldn't begin to unravel. But worry and desire were definitely part of the mix.

His gaze dropped to her lips, and instead of moving his finger, he traced it slowly over her mouth.

Every pore on her body seemed to suddenly come alive as the tingling swept outward, down to her toes. She stepped back fast. "What are you doing? I got you *shot* today!"

He walked over to the oversize leather couch on the far wall and sat down. "You're human. Everyone makes mistakes, Maggie."

She stared down at him incredulously. "You can't be serious!"

"I've messed up clearing a room before."

"Did you get someone else shot?" she demanded.

"No. I got lucky." He leaned forward, taking his arms off the back of the couch where he'd rested them as though he was settling in for a long argument. "Ask any guy on the team, and I bet you'll hear the same thing."

She frowned. Maybe that was true, maybe not, but it

was irrelevant. Her actions had gotten a teammate shot. And it didn't matter that he was okay. It didn't matter that it had happened because of a memory she couldn't have predicted would rear its ugly head at exactly the wrong time. What mattered was that it had happened.

"If I hadn't quit tonight, I would have been off the team, anyway."

"You would have been talking to OPR," Grant countered. The Bureau's Office of Professional Responsibility, who would investigate tonight's incident, got involved whenever a firearm was used. "Just like you're doing now. But you'll come through this, and you need to *fight* for your spot on the team, Maggie. You belong there, and we all know it. Besides, I'm fine. No harm, no foul."

She gaped at him. "How can you be this calm about getting shot?"

"It hurt less than being stabbed."

A burst of laughter escaped. "You should be pissed at me right now. What's wrong with you? You should hate me!"

"It wasn't you who shot me," Grant said, still so calmly it was starting to piss *her* off.

"No, it was me who *got you* shot!"

"And I'm glad it was me who was hit." He leaned toward her and held out his hand. "Come here."

"What?" She shook her head, not moving. "Why?"

He rolled his eyes, stood up and peeled his T-shirt off, tossing it aside. "Look." He put his hand up at the top of his chest, where a huge purple bruise spread outward from a dark center to a lighter bluish color snaking toward his neck.

She'd seen him without his shirt on before, but always in training, surrounded by a group of other FBI agents, including herself, all keeping in shape for missions. Times when she'd purposely avoided looking. Nothing like the sudden intimacy here, alone with him in his home.

Her mouth suddenly felt dry. She couldn't stop her eyes from wandering over football-player shoulders, down biceps that bulged with muscle without even being flexed, to what should have been a six-pack but looked more like a twelve-pack.

Her fingers pulsed with the need to reach out and stroke the bruise, or the shiny, jagged scar that ran along his side—a present from the Manhattan Strangler. From there, she could trace her fingers up to the ridges of muscle on his abdomen. She could glide her hands over him until he truly forgave her for what had happened in that warehouse tonight.

"Maggie." He sounded amused, but when she forced herself to look up, heat lit his eyes.

"Sorry," she whispered.

He strode toward her, and common sense told her to flee, but he was standing in front of her before she could move, so close she could feel the heat from his body.

She bit her lip as she felt his hand close around hers, lifting it up. He placed it over his bruise, and just as her fingers started to open, he moved her hand back toward her.

In an instant, she realized why he'd told her he was glad it had been him who'd gotten shot. It had happened because she'd frozen, but if he hadn't shoved her out of the way, she'd have been the one with a bullet hole.

Her fingers drifted over the base of her neck, neatly lined up with the bruise on the top of Grant's chest. No vest would have saved her.

The knowledge left her suddenly cold. The cold intensified as Grant turned and walked away, grabbing his T-shirt off the couch and slipping it over his head.

When he settled back on his couch and gestured for her to join him, this time her feet moved slowly until she was sitting next to him. "That doesn't make me feel any better."

"Well, you're going to have to deal with it. And you have enough to focus on right now, so stop worrying. I'm fine. You're fine. And once you go through all the OPR stuff, we want you back. *I* want you back."

Maggie shook her head, but he insisted, "Don't decide now. But just so you know, everyone on the team agrees."

She was touched by their loyalty, and surprised. Because on SWAT, decisions about teammates had nothing to do with friendship, and everything to do with ability. But it didn't matter how they felt. She had to do what was right for the team, whether they saw it or not.

"I'm a liability." It killed her to admit it, but right now, it was true. And she didn't remember much at all from her attack, so how could she predict if that would happen again, some other memory getting triggered at the wrong time?

Grant took her hand in his. "Once this case is closed and you've got your focus back, you'll change your mind."

"You're too nice for your own good. You know that, right? You know it's not normal to ask the person who just got you shot to come back and cover you?"

"I'll let you cover me anytime you want."

More laughter snuck out at the completely out-of-character remark, and she shifted to face him on the couch. "Are you actually hitting on me right now? Because your pickup lines could use some work."

"Really?" He turned slightly, moving a little closer and

stroking his fingers over the palm of her hand, igniting her nerve endings with the simple touch. "The way you were drooling before, I thought it'd be okay."

"I was *not* drooling," she said, even as she felt heat in her cheeks. But she found herself smiling back at him.

How did he always do that to her? Even on a day like today, with everything going on, with the shooting and the memories and the guilt she was feeling? How could he still make her feel this ridiculous, giddy happiness?

"Maybe you're right," she whispered, suddenly desperate to feel his lips on hers the way they had been in the parking lot of the WFO a week ago.

She leaned toward him, fast, before she could change her mind. Moving in close, she pressed her mouth to his.

And just like the last time they'd kissed, all rational thought fled her mind, and she could only focus on Grant. The bunching muscles underneath her hand, the tiny rasp of stubble from his chin, the ridiculous softness of his lips.

She moved even closer, until she was plastered against him, and could slide both her arms around his neck. Until she could open her mouth, inviting his tongue inside.

He didn't hesitate, and the first brush of his tongue against hers left her desperate for more. She tried to lean even closer, and felt his hands slip underneath her thighs and lift her up onto his lap as though she weighed nothing.

She tried to wriggle closer still, and felt the rumble of his laughter as his hands locked on her hips and held her still. She thought she heard him mutter something about his self-control—or maybe it was hers—and then he was kissing her again, flooding her entire body with need.

She ran her hands down over his arms then underneath his T-shirt, wanting to feel his bare skin again, this time wanting to caress her fingers over all the muscles she'd seen earlier.

He sucked in a breath as her fingers followed the lines of muscle in his abdomen up to his chest, stopping just short of his bruise, and she flattened her hand there, loving the feel of his heart thumping madly underneath her fingers. She wanted more.

Wrenching her mouth from his, she panted, "Bedroom," then leaned back in, hoping he'd just stand up and take her there.

Instead, his hands moved up to her waist, skirting around the gun at her hip, and he didn't let her close the distance to his lips again. "Maggie," he whispered, his voice even deeper than usual. "Maybe this isn't a good idea."

Surprise and embarrassment flooded. What was she thinking? She'd gotten him shot, then tried to sleep with him in the same night?

She tried to move off his lap, but his hands were still tight on her waist, holding her in place.

Of course this wasn't a good idea. Now that Grant knew everything he knew about her past, it was only a matter of time before it colored the way he looked at her. And she wasn't the type to sleep with someone without being in a relationship. Not anymore. Not in a long, long time.

"I'm sorry," she muttered, dropping her hands off his shoulders. "Let's forget this ever happened."

GRANT CURSED AS Maggie flushed deep red, trying to get off him.

"I just meant the timing, Maggie. Not that I'm not interested." Which should have been pretty obvious.

She still looked mortified—and as if she didn't quite

believe him—so he slid one hand up her back until he could pull her toward him and capture her mouth with his again.

He'd intended to kiss her fast, just once more, then convince her that they should wait until after her case was solved. Because a relationship between them was complicated enough already, with work, and especially now, with the inevitable OPR investigation into today's SWAT call. But add in her flashback and everything happening with her case, and he didn't want to screw things up for later by jumping in at the worst possible time.

But as soon as his lips found hers, longing rocked through him, a reminder of everything he'd been wanting for the past nine months. Everything he'd been looking for since before he even met her. *Maggie.*

He must have said her name out loud, probably sounding as desperate as he felt, because she mumbled something in return, then brought her mouth to his again. A second later, she shifted, until he could feel her whole body against his.

And he knew right then that it would take way more willpower than he possessed to say no to her again. But he pulled away from her long enough to whisper, "How about you take this off?"

She blinked back at him, and he patted her holster so she'd know what he was talking about.

She looked a little disappointed, so he added, "I'd prefer to take the rest off myself."

She smiled, but he didn't miss the brief indecision in her expression before she unstrapped her holster.

As she leaned over to drop her weapon on his side table, he forced himself to say, "Maggie, we can—"

"Shut up, Grant," she replied, wrestling his shirt off and tossing it on the floor. Then she sat there staring at him, eyebrows raised, as if she was waiting for him to make good on his promise.

Remembering how she'd responded before when he'd stroked his fingers over her palm, he reached for her hand and pressed it to his lips, tracing a circle on her palm with his mouth and his tongue until she relaxed toward him. Then he stroked his other hand up underneath the back of her T-shirt, marveling that someone who could handle an MP-5 the way she did had such silky, soft skin.

She squirmed on his lap and took her hand from his lips, hooking it onto his shoulder as she leaned into him again.

Tilting his head, he kissed her harder, drawing her T-shirt up. Then he stopped kissing her long enough to slip it over her head. He got a brief glimpse of a blue satin bra the same shade as her eyes, and then her bare skin was against his, and he groaned.

She smiled back at him, a pleased smile that told him she knew exactly what she was doing to him right now, and then she dipped her head, and he felt her lips on his earlobe. As her tongue slid across his neck, he felt his self-control slipping further and further out of reach.

Frantic with the need to kiss her again, he slid his hand up her back, so he could glide his fingers through her hair and tilt her head back to his. Just before his fingers reached the back of her neck, he realized what he was doing. A jolt hit him at his mistake, and he froze.

He tried to recover and skip over her neck to just palm the back of her head, but it was too late.

Hurt showed in her eyes as she stood up. She bumped his coffee table hard enough that it was probably going to leave a bruise, but she didn't seem to notice as she grabbed her T-shirt off the floor and pulled it over her head.

"I'm sorry." He got to his feet, too, dread pooling in his stomach.

"And you said knowing about my past didn't change anything."

He shook his head, genuinely bewildered. "It doesn't."

"Right." She turned away from him, picking up her holster and strapping it back on.

"Maggie." He put his hand on her arm, and felt her muscles tense. "It doesn't change how I *feel* about you. I just didn't think you'd want me touching you there. That's all."

She looked up at him, hurt and frustration written on her face, but he could see the truth of his words register there, too.

She wore her hair short enough that it wouldn't be a hassle in SWAT, but long enough to cover the entire back of her neck. It was a logical assumption she wouldn't want any man touching the brand there.

She stepped backward, making him drop her arm. "If it really didn't matter, you wouldn't be thinking about that at all. You'd be focused on me. On us. On right now."

"That's not fair," he countered. "After what happened today—"

She cut him off, swearing. She was practically yelling, but she sounded more frustrated than angry when she said, "I'm so sick of this. Every year. Every single year, I'm just sitting around waiting to see who's next." She dropped onto his couch, something defeated in the hunch of her shoulders he'd never seen before. "And this year, it's me again."

He sat next to her, wrapping an arm around her shoulder even as she tensed up at his touch. "It's *not* going to be you again. This is all going to be over soon."

"It'll never be over." She turned her head, looking

away from him, then admitted, her voice cracking, "I *don't* like anyone touching my neck."

He could feel her arms trembling as she said, so quietly he had to lean in to hear, "I had to go back six times before I could manage to get the tattoo over it."

"But you did it."

"Yeah, well, I wasn't going to let him win. No way was I leaving that mark on my body."

She turned away from him even more, lifting his arm off her shoulder. But when he'd expected her to stand up and leave, she tilted her head down and lifted her hair.

He'd seen the pictures from the case file, when the brand was new. Red and angry, an ugly raised hook on her delicate neck.

Now the damaged skin underneath was still evident if you looked closely enough, but she'd had a tattoo—some Chinese letters—put directly on top of it. Something that must have been incredibly difficult to do, but that was Maggie. She never backed down from any challenge.

"What does it mean?" he asked, as she dropped her hair back down to cover the deep black symbol inked on her neck.

"Strength," she answered, getting to her feet.

"Good choice," he said as she turned to face him. It was probably the most appropriate thing she could have chosen. She was one of the strongest people he knew.

She nodded, and from the raw look in her eyes, he suspected she very rarely showed it to anyone.

"Can you tell me what you remembered today?" he asked. He'd planned to do it tomorrow, but he suddenly didn't want to make her talk about it at the office.

"I figured we'd get to that eventually," she said then sat back down at the far corner of the couch, away from him. She glanced at him briefly, then away. "Can you put a shirt on?"

"Okay." He picked up his T-shirt from the floor and put it back on, then settled in the center of the couch, giving her the distance she obviously wanted.

"It was the smell." She was looking straight ahead, not at him, but he could tell she was wearing her SWAT-ready expression.

"I figured," he said softly. Scent was one of the most powerful triggers for memory.

"I thought I'd remembered everything I'd ever get back about that day—which wasn't much," she said, then shook her head, and her voice was stronger, more detached when she continued. "But today I remembered a room. I'd never been there before. It was…fancy. My head was on a table, a really cold table." She frowned, looking pensive, and then finally nodded, adding, "I think it was marble."

A marble table? Definitely not a pay-by-the-hour type motel or in a vehicle. Which lent credence to his theory that the person who'd done this had actually lived in DC when he'd attacked Maggie, and that he hadn't just been passing through searching for a victim.

"The room was blurry. From the drugs."

Grant tried to ignore the fury that rose up as Maggie talked, at the idea of anyone drugging her, hurting her. But it rose up like bile in his throat.

"I'm not sure I'd recognize it if I saw it today. But there were pictures on the wall, big ones, nice frames. And carpet under my knees. Thick carpet. I think it was a large room." She shuddered when she added, "When I screamed, it echoed."

"Do you remember anything about him?" Grant asked, trying to keep the anger out of his voice.

But she must have heard it, because she turned and looked at him. He thought she was going to say something—not about the case, but about his reaction—but after a long pause, she just shook her head.

"He was behind me. With the—with whatever he used on my neck. I think I passed out again after that." She paused. "I still don't remember him."

"Well, this could help," he told her. "These are new details. And I think…"

"What?" she demanded when he cut himself off before he blurted out his case theories.

"It could help."

"I told you all that, and that's all you're giving me?"

"You know I'm not supposed to—"

"What?" she interrupted. "Make out with a teammate?"

Even though he knew she was pissed, he couldn't help smiling at that. "Well, yeah, that, too."

"Come on. You already know I'm investigating. We have twenty days." She looked at her watch "Make that nineteen. I may not be VCMO, but I spend my days investigating some nasty stuff, too. Don't waste resources. Tell me what you're thinking."

Despite the voice screaming in his head that this was a really bad idea, screaming that she was using his feelings for her to get case information she'd never have access to otherwise, he told her. "I think he started in DC. I think you were the first one he marked, but not his first victim."

She frowned back at him. "Yeah, Ella thinks that, too, about him having a history of rape. Not necessarily about DC."

"Well, I think whoever he started with was someone in his life, and that her attack is why the date is significant."

She stared back at him, nodding slowly. "Maybe."

"If I'm right—"

"There could be a way to track him," she finished.

Chapter Seven

Maggie was sitting up in bed, her hand already gripping her gun, before she'd even identified what had woken her. Her heart thudding, she glanced at her alarm clock—6:00 a.m.

Below her, from outside, a car door slammed. Her bedroom faced the street, but there wasn't a lot of traffic quite this early, not where she lived.

Getting out of bed, she moved beside the window, lifting the slats on the blinds to peer outside. She saw Grant walking up her drive at the same moment she heard movement from inside her house, on the first floor.

Where her overprotective brother had spent the night on her couch. He'd been there, half-asleep, when she'd gotten home from Grant's house last night. For once, she'd managed to avoid his questions and go straight to bed.

She doubted Grant had already been to work, or had a break in the case, which meant he was probably stopping by on his way to the WFO. And that meant he either wanted to talk about her quitting SWAT or what had happened between them last night.

She felt momentarily frozen watching him stride up her driveway, until she heard another thud from downstairs. Probably Scott preparing to confront any approaching threats.

Cursing, she let the blinds drop and ran down the stairs. "Scott, it's just—"

Before she'd finished speaking, her brother had swung open the front door and tucked his gun into the waistband of his pants. "Grant."

"Scott, hi." Grant held out a hand for her brother, looking surprised.

"Scott and Ella alternate staying with me until this whole thing is over," Maggie reminded Grant, her words coming out too fast, and she felt herself flush as his gaze locked on hers. After last night, even his eyes on her gave her goose bumps.

Scott gave her a questioning look as he shook Grant's hand, and she remembered she hadn't told him that Grant was working the case.

"Come on in," Scott said, stepping back and rubbing his eyes. "You guys have a call or something?"

Grant frowned as he walked inside. "No. Didn't Maggie tell—"

"Is there something new with the case?" she asked, willing him not to tell her brother she'd left SWAT.

"No. I'm sorry. I just, uh—"

So he'd come by to clear the air about last night. After she'd told him the details of her flashback, things had suddenly felt awkward in a way they never, ever had with Grant. Not until he'd started investigating her case. She'd had a desperate need to get out of there, so she had, quickly, with barely a goodbye.

She'd known seeing him in the office today was going to be uncomfortable. She should have figured Grant would do this.

"Sorry I ran out on you last night," she said, hoping her

brother would assume the "you" she was talking about was plural—the whole team. "It was a long day."

"Sure, that's okay," Grant said slowly.

Maggie tried to appear nonchalant when Scott looked at her.

Grant was terrible at deception. He'd be an awful undercover agent.

It was a good thing he'd gone into VCMO and SWAT, where he could use his size and pissed-off expression to terrify the criminals, and his easygoing, contagious smile to reassure the victims, or charm his way into a tight-knit SWAT team. Or into her affections.

"I'm going to grab a coffee," Scott said in an obvious move to give them privacy. "Nice to see you, Grant." As he walked past Maggie, he raised his eyebrows, and she knew she'd be getting grilled as soon as Grant left.

"You, too," Grant called after him, then quieter, to her, "You haven't told him?"

"No," she whispered back. "But now I'll have to, because it's pretty obvious something's up." She shook her head at him, moving closer so her brother wouldn't overhear. "You're a terrible liar."

"He caught me off guard."

"I told you he was staying with me." Suddenly conscious of the fact that she was wearing pajama pants and a snug tank top without anything underneath, she crossed her arms over her chest. Instead of asking him why he was there, she said, "Can we talk later?"

"Yeah, I wasn't thinking about your brother being here. I totally forgot. I just wanted to see you, to—"

"To clear the air about last night," she said, staring at the collar of his T-shirt, where a hint of his bruise was visible. "I get it. But things are fine between us, okay?"

"No, I came by to apologize."

Surprised, she looked up at him, and he stepped closer still, close enough that she could smell his citrusy after-shave. She resisted the urge to breathe deeply, resisted the urge to lean into him the way she had last night. She'd gotten him shot, and now *he* wanted to apologize? "About what?"

"My timing."

She could feel herself gaping at him as he continued, "I waited nine months to do that. I could have waited an-other three weeks, until this case was over. I'm sorry."

"You waited nine months," she said slowly, "to—"

"To kiss you."

The flush she'd felt the second he walked through her door doubled. "We *met* nine months ago."

He grinned at her. "Yeah, I know. I walked into that first SWAT meeting, and you introduced yourself, and that was it."

"Introduced myself? I flipped you."

It was standard ops to prank the new guy. And since she'd joined the team, one of her teammates' favorite ways to initiate the newbies was for her to walk up, hold out a limp hand for them to shake, then promptly flip them to the ground.

In the three years before Grant joined that she'd been part of the team, she'd gone along with it because she found it was a good way to stop any preferential treat-ment before it could start. Drop a guy on his very first day on SWAT, and he wasn't likely to go easy on her just because she was a woman.

The four guys she'd flipped before Grant had been pissed off and embarrassed, but they'd gotten over it and become her friends. Grant had actually pulled her down with him. When they'd landed, with her braced on top of him, he'd looked stunned for a second, then offered her a hand as he'd gotten to his feet, laughing.

Oddly enough, that was the moment she'd fallen for him.

"Yeah, well, I like a woman who knows how to be in control. Besides," he said, leaning close to whisper, just as she heard her brother walk back into the room behind her, "I'm okay with you being on top."

She stammered something unintelligible as he backed up, nodded at her brother and walked out the door.

"What was that about?" Scott asked.

"Nothing," Maggie answered, but her voice came out way too high.

"Uh-huh," Scott said, "nice try. What's going on?"

Hoping she wasn't still blushing furiously, Maggie turned around. "Work stuff."

Scott snorted. "Come on. What's happening? And while you're telling me what's up with Grant, you want to fill me in on what you told Nikki?"

"Nikki? What are you talking about?"

"She called. Asked me about coming to visit in a few weeks. She wanted to be here September 1. I thought maybe you'd said something—"

"No way," Maggie said. "I didn't tell her about the letters. Did you?"

"No. And I told her to stay home, obviously. I said she should focus on her new job and getting settled in her new place. But I was surprised she volunteered."

"She's growing up." It *was* surprising, though, not because Nikki was insensitive, but because they'd always tried to keep her far away from their horrible September 1 ritual. And Maggie wanted to keep it that way.

"Okay, well, she'll probably call you. I told her not to come, but I don't think she was ready to give up."

"I'll handle her," Maggie said.

"Okay, and what about Grant? I don't know the guy all that well, but he was acting unusually cagey. And he knows about the Fishhook case? What didn't he want to say in front of me? If there's something about the case you're keeping from me—"

"It's not that. I mean, yes, I remembered something new about what happened to me, but it doesn't help with the case."

"You remembered more?" Scott sounded surprised. "Are you sure it won't help us? Because whatever it is, I don't want to be in the dark on this, Maggie. I can't help if I don't know everything."

"He wasn't here about the case. Although he's been assigned to it."

Scott's eyes narrowed with suspicion. "Is there something going on between you two?"

"I'm off SWAT," she blurted, not needing an overprotective brother to mess up her already rocky love life. And she definitely wasn't ready to talk about whatever was happening with Grant.

"What?" Scott set his coffee down, his face going pale. "What happened yesterday? Are you okay?"

"I made a mistake. It was bad, and I'm going to have to answer for it with OPR." Before he could dig for details, she added, "I quit the team."

She tried not to think about what that meant. Sure, she was dedicated to her regular work on the civil rights squad, but she *loved* SWAT. She had from the moment she'd been accepted onto the team.

"What? Maggie, what happened? I'm sure you can—"

"I'll give you the awful details later, okay?" She dreaded the idea of telling him about those ten crucial seconds when she'd frozen. HRT training was even more intensive than SWAT, and her brother had never made the kind of error she'd made today. On top of his ever-present worry about her, she didn't want to see disappointment on his face.

She ducked her head as he stared at her as if he could read the answer on her face if he looked long enough. Suddenly wishing Ella were here instead of her brother, Maggie sighed. At least with Ella, if she said she needed a little space, she'd get it. With Scott, *not* telling him something just made him even more persistent.

But for once, he backed off. She could tell he had a hard time getting the words out as he said, "Okay. Just tell me if you need anything. Ella, too." He squeezed her arm. "We're here for you. We always will be."

Tears stung the backs of her eyes as she nodded. They'd stuck by her for a decade, changing the whole course of their lives and joining the Bureau because of her. Every September 1, they dropped everything to be by her side. Now they were secretly investigating the Fish-hook Rapist case with her because she couldn't leave it to the case agents.

Meanwhile, she was making errors at work she'd never, ever allowed herself to make before. Errors that would threaten not only her place on SWAT, but if she wasn't careful, her place in the Bureau, too.

And if she let Scott and Ella, they'd go down with her, like a sinking ship.

"What do you want?"

The woman peering suspiciously at him looked nothing like the picture Grant had in a police file from thirteen years ago.

She'd only opened her door an inch or two, so he held his badge a little closer to her, and repeated, "I'm with the

FBI. I wanted to ask you a few questions about a crime you reported a long time ago that might be connected to a current investigation."

She shook her head, limp peroxide-blond hair swinging. "I never reported any crime."

"It was a sexual assault report."

"Oh." Her shoulders slumped, and she glanced quickly behind her, then opened the door wide. Instead of inviting him in, she came outside, shutting the door behind her. Folding her arms, she said, "I don't want my kids to hear this." Then she squinted at him and asked, "What do you want to know about that? It was a really long time ago." Her shoulders lifted. "They never figured out who did it."

"Is there anyone *you* suspected?" Grant asked hopefully.

This was his third stop this morning. It would have been more, but only a handful of the possible matching cases had victims still in the area.

It was actually a little scary how many rape cases in the five years prior to Maggie's assault happened on or around September 1 in the DC area. He'd been able to narrow it down to the Fishhook Rapist's victim type— women in their late teens to early twenties, with long, dark hair. Which had given him three possibilities.

So far, no one he'd talked to had been able to give him anything new. Shana Mills, the woman standing in front of him now, was his most likely option, but even she was just a slim possibility. Given how under-reported rape was, chances were that even if his theory was right, and the Fishhook Rapist had assaulted women before he'd gotten his media name, they probably wouldn't have a police report for it.

"I don't have any ideas," Shana replied. "Not any more than I did back then. I was drugged. To be honest, I wasn't even totally certain what had happened until the doctors confirmed it."

"So you don't remember anyone?"

"No."

He glanced at the notes he'd jotted from the police file. Three years before Maggie's assault, Shana Mills had been drugged and raped. He'd almost missed it when he'd been digging through the DCPD's files, because she hadn't gone to the hospital until September 2, and the official police report hadn't been filed until later.

The investigation had been almost nonexistent, because the police had little to go on. Shana didn't remember her assailant; he'd worn a condom, and Shana had woken up in the basement of a frat house the morning after a big party. Lots of possible suspects, lots of potential witnesses, but no one had seen a thing, and the evidence hadn't been there.

"What can you tell me about Jeffrey Hoffmeier and Kevin Sanders?" Those were the only names listed in the police report who were possible suspects in his current case, since they were the only ones with a personal connection to Shana. That was assuming Grant's attempt at a profile of the Fishhook Rapist was right. It wasn't his specialty, but he'd put together a solid profile before, with the Manhattan Strangler, so he had to trust his gut.

He also had to hope for a break soon, because they were running out of time. There were exactly two weeks left until September 1, and with every day that passed, Grant got more anxious.

Shana shrugged at his question, and Grant tried to imagine her the way she'd looked in the police file. Back then, she'd had long brown hair, blue eyes and a lean frame. Even though to him she hadn't really resembled Maggie, he had to admit the basics were the same. For a serial rapist, the women definitely fit a "type." Now they looked nothing alike.

Shana's overdyed hair hung around an unremarkable face, and she seemed wrung out, with none of the energy and determination that practically seeped from Maggie.

"Jeff was my ex. We'd broken up a few weeks before."

"The police report says you saw him that night? He was at the party?"

"Yeah, he showed up, begged me to take him back. I refused. Again. He left, I think with some other girl."

"You see him after that?" Grant asked.

"A couple of times. We actually got back together, real briefly, about six months later, but it didn't last long at all. Maybe a week or so."

"Why didn't it work?"

Her face twisted with distaste. "He was cocky, obnoxious. Rich-kid syndrome, my roommate called it. I'm not even sure why I went out with him in the first place, except he was cute."

"What about Kevin?"

Shana scowled. "*That* guy creeped me out. I tried to get a restraining order against him, but police said they needed some kind of threat or something first."

"He was stalking you?"

"Yeah. He was angry that I wouldn't go out with him. And his daddy was some kind of big deal, so he seemed to think if he bragged about that enough, I'd suddenly go out with him."

"Was he still hanging around after your attack?"

"Oh, yeah. He hung around until I graduated and moved away. Then I guess he moved on to someone else."

Grant looked up from jotting notes. "You know who?"

"No. I just assume he did. That's how those guys work, right?"

"Usually." Grant shut his notebook and gave her his full attention. "Anything else you can tell me about that night? Anything at all?"

"I told the police everything. Everything I could remember, anyway. I don't even know how I got the drugs. My drink, I guess, but I always got my own."

"At a frat party, it could have been in the keg, or with whoever was mixing drinks or—"

"Canned beer," Shana said. "That's what I was drinking. I wasn't stupid. Friend of mine had been dosed a few weeks before."

That was news to Grant. "What was her name? Did she file a report?"

"She didn't get raped. I was with her when she started feeling weird. We took her to the hospital."

"They figure out who drugged her?"

"No. It happened at another party. But she was drinking whatever was handed to her."

Grant frowned, wondering if there could be a connection, and wondering how Shana had been dosed. "Anyone else hold your beer for you?"

"I don't remember. It was more than a decade ago. I've been married, divorced, married again, and had two kids since then. Not to mention gotten my degree, worked for four different companies, lived in two other states before I came back here. I don't remember who might have held my drink thirteen years ago."

Grant nodded, not really surprised. "Have you seen Kevin or Jeff in the last ten years?"

"No." She studied him more intently. "What happened to me back then sucked, but how could it possibly be connected to a current case? I mean, it was probably some frat guy who took advantage of the fact that I was unconscious in his basement, right?"

"I'm just running a theory," Grant said, handing her his card. "But if you think of anything else, or if you have any other ideas about that day, can you give me a call?"

"Yeah, okay," Shana said. She tucked his card in her pocket, where Grant figured she'd forget about it within the hour, and probably toss it in the wash with her jeans. Without a backward glance, she disappeared inside.

Grant probably would have forgotten about most of his chat with Shana, too, except something nagged him until he got back to the office and opened Maggie's case file again. He skimmed over the details of what she remembered from her assault.

College party. She'd been there with friends and a boyfriend. Her friends had left early, then she'd fought with the boyfriend, so she'd headed back to the dorm alone. It was on that walk back when she'd been taken.

Grant kept reading, then his heart rate picked up when he read the details about her being drugged. The only thing she remembered drinking at the party was canned beer, beer she'd opened herself.

Just like Shana.

Chapter Eight

Maggie rubbed her eyes, trying to focus on the report she'd been filling out for the past few hours. She should have been able to knock it out in half an hour, but her vision kept going unfocused; her mind kept wandering to the Fishhook Rapist case, and then suddenly another hour had passed.

At least the office had mostly emptied out, and there weren't a lot of agents there to witness her struggling over simple paperwork. Her civil rights squad supervisor had finally left, after asking her no fewer than three times if she needed some time away.

She'd told him no just like she had last week, and last month, when he'd first learned about the letters. But if two more weeks passed and they still had no idea about the identity of the Fishhook Rapist, maybe she should do it. The FBI would offer her protection, of course, but maybe she should just take off, head somewhere far, far away.

Hide. Go to ground, and pray he wasn't savvy enough to follow.

Gritting her teeth, Maggie closed the file and turned off her desk light. As appealing as the idea sounded, she knew she'd never do it.

Because no matter how much the thought of facing

her attacker again terrified her, she wasn't twenty-two anymore. She wasn't drugged and helpless. If this guy really planned to come for her again, he'd be facing down a trained SWAT agent armed with every weapon the FBI had issued her.

And come September 1, there was no question she'd be surrounded by Ella and Scott like always. She suspected that Ella's fiancé, Logan, a seasoned police detective and Scott's girlfriend, Chelsie, an FBI negotiator, would be there, too. Knowing Grant, whether she asked him or not, he'd show up with a small arsenal and plant himself directly in front of her.

What chance did the Fishhook Rapist really have?

Maggie sighed, getting up from her desk. It didn't matter how much she told herself that; it didn't even matter how logical it was. Because every time she so much as thought about September 1, her hands started to shake.

Even the idea of walking into the parking garage right now—despite the fact that no one who didn't possess FBI credentials could get in there—made her irrationally nervous.

Get it together, she told herself.

Her phone trilled, and she jumped, instantly chastising herself for letting her fear override common sense. "Maggie Delacorte," she answered.

"Hey, Maggie, it's Nikki."

Nikki. Maggie closed her eyes and tried to make her voice cheery. She didn't want her little sister worrying about her. She'd tried hard for so long to keep this from touching Nikki, and she didn't plan to stop now. "How's the new apartment? And when do you start your job?"

"The apartment's great," Nikki said. "And I start in a few weeks. So I was thinking I have time to come and stay with you and Scott for a little bit. I figured maybe the three of us—and Ella, of course—could go out on September 1." Her voice turned hesitant. "You know, do something fun."

It was sweet of her sister, especially since the whole family babied her, and she probably could have gotten away with acting completely spoiled. But she never had.

Still, Maggie didn't want her anywhere near DC right now. She also didn't want her worrying. "That's nice of you, Nikki, but work is really busy right now. For Scott, too. The timing won't work, but I'm going to make a trip home next month. See your new place."

"Okay," Nikki said slowly. "Well, I would stay out of your way. I just thought—"

"Thank you. Really. But another time, okay?" Maggie said, knowing the strain was starting to come through in her voice.

"Okay," Nikki conceded. "Is everything all right?"

"Just busy," Maggie lied, and she had a feeling her sister could tell. "I'm actually still at work. Can I call you later?"

"Sure." Her sister sounded disappointed. "Let me know if you change your mind."

"I'll talk to you soon," Maggie said, feeling relieved as soon as she hung up the phone.

A hand clapped her on the shoulder as she put the phone in her purse, and she turned, startled.

"Sorry," Grant said, and put a steadying hand under her elbow.

"It's okay," Maggie said, easing her arm free. "I'm just a little jumpy tonight."

He frowned at her, looking worried, but all he said was, "Can I ask you some questions?"

"Okay." She studied him more closely, the dark circles under his eyes, the rolled-up sleeves on his dress shirt that showcased muscular forearms. Even though she was used to seeing him in his office clothes, he looked more natural in his SWAT getup. Maybe because he was built like a linebacker, khakis and a button-down never looked quite right on him.

Looking back to his face, she noticed the tight line of his lips, as if he was about to do something he didn't want to. "It's about the Fishhook Rapist case, isn't it?"

"Yeah. I'm sorry. I'm just trying—"

"No, it's fine." She tried to keep the exhaustion out of her own voice, knowing that Grant had been working more hours than anyone in the office since he'd been assigned to this case. Knowing that it was for her. "What is it?"

"The night you were drugged, your report says you were drinking beer out of a can. Is that right?"

Maggie gritted her teeth and nodded.

"Do you remember if you had anything else? Or if anyone could have—"

"You're wondering how I was drugged?" When he nodded, Maggie shook her head. "I'm not sure. Back then, I didn't know the things I do now, but I was relatively street smart. I didn't take drinks from people at parties, or let anyone I didn't know hang on to it, or leave it anywhere. I opened it myself. Best guess is that someone dropped the drugs in without me noticing."

Grant frowned. "Hmm. Okay. Are you sure no one got it for you?"

"Well, my boyfriend did, but I opened it."

"Do you know the names Jeff Hoffmeier or Kevin Sanders?"

"No. Why?"

He seemed disappointed, but not surprised, by her answer. "Just running some theories. Thanks."

As he turned to go back to the conference room, Maggie grabbed his arm and felt his muscles tense at her touch. "Are they suspects?"

"Not right now." She thought he was going to say more, but Kammy walked into the bullpen, her eyes narrowing when she saw them standing close together.

"Maggie," Kammy said, nodding at her, then she looked pointedly at Grant.

"Back to work it is. Thanks, Maggie."

When Kammy turned and headed off to the coffeepot, Maggie touched his arm again before he could follow. "Grant."

"Yeah?"

She stared up at him, not sure what she'd actually planned to say. She saw him in the office every day, but lately it had felt different. Even standing in front of him now, doing something as impersonal as touching his forearm, felt intimate.

She had a sudden flashback to the feel of his hands clutching her thighs as he lifted her onto his lap, the feel of his body pressed tight to hers, his heartbeat thundering against her palm. Heat spread through her.

It must have shown on her face, because his pupils suddenly dilated as he stared back at her.

Her voice came out huskier than usual when she blurted, "Uh, why don't you come over after you finish here? We can talk."

"Sure," he said, sounding surprised. He glanced at his watch, and when he looked up at her again, there was anticipation in his eyes. "Probably an hour or two?"

"Whenever," she said, then watched him hurry back to the conference room, knowing he'd thought she wanted to talk about what had happened between them last night. Or maybe start right back up where they'd left off.

She tried not to feel guilty as she walked to the parking garage. Because he was in for quite a surprise when he did arrive at her house, and that's not what she was after at all.

WHEN IT CAME to work, Grant had never been able to do anything but go all-in. He couldn't help himself. With his cases, it was all or nothing. It had gotten him in trouble a time or two, namely during the Manhattan Strangler case.

If he'd waited for backup the way he'd been told to, he probably wouldn't have ended up in the hospital getting stitches for a nasty stab wound. He wouldn't have ended up with the censure in his Bureau file, or ultimately decided it was time to transfer to a new field office for a fresh start.

Then again, if he'd waited for backup, the victim surely would have died. And the Manhattan Strangler probably would have gotten away yet again.

So he'd never been able to regret his actions. Not on that case, and not on any job where he went in strong, the way SWAT let him do as their designated door-kicker.

But in his personal life, he was a little more restrained, particularly when it came to relationships. He'd had a few that had approached serious, but he'd never felt that all-consuming need to dive in, the way he did with his cases. Not until Maggie.

Which was probably why he was standing on her doorstep right now, instead of home in bed. Because she might have been purposely vague about why she wanted to talk to him tonight, but he'd realized exactly why she'd invited him over.

She wanted to grill him for details about the case. Details he was supposed to keep confidential.

Swearing, Grant lowered his fist from the door instead

of knocking, but it opened, anyway. And suddenly the cars in the driveway made sense, because it wasn't Maggie who answered, but her friend Ella Cortez.

A feisty profiler in the Bureau's Behavioral Analysis Unit, who'd shown up with Maggie a few times at O'Reilley's. He didn't know her particularly well, but he'd seen her name in Maggie's police file from a decade ago. Ella was one of the friends who'd left the party, thinking Maggie was safe with her boyfriend. She'd been the one to call the police the next morning when Maggie had stumbled back to their shared dorm room, bleeding and branded on the back of the neck.

"Ella, hi," he said.

It almost seemed that she could read what he was thinking, but she just said evenly, "Grant."

Then she stepped backward and led him toward the living room, where Grant saw a group of people gathered. "Come on in. We've been waiting for you."

His eyebrows rose. "I didn't realize it was going to be a party."

"Sorry about that," Maggie said as she came toward him, dodging an open pizza box on the floor.

She'd changed out of the dress pants and stiff, short-sleeved blouse she'd worn at the office into curve-hugging jeans and a well-worn T-shirt that looked more *Maggie*. His fingers itched to touch the soft cotton, to caress the skin underneath.

As he stared at her, probably broadcasting his every thought for the entire room, she lowered her voice. "I figured if I told you—"

"I knew what you wanted to talk about." He was trying to stop staring at those gorgeous blue eyes of hers, but ever since he'd realized her attraction to him might actually come close to how he felt for her, he seemed to have lost all his willpower. "I just didn't realize you expected me to break protocol in front of a crowd."

She turned red, but Scott came up behind her and said, "You don't have to worry about that. Nothing you say leaves this room."

The serious, massively protective, big-brother expression on Scott's face made Grant get his act together. He stood a little straighter and ripped his attention away from Maggie. "Quid pro quo?"

"Absolutely," Scott answered. "We'll share everything we're thinking. But I've got to tell you, it isn't much. We don't have the access you do. But you know we're not going to sit idly by on this one."

"Neither will I," Grant said, and he knew his conviction—and probably the strength of his feelings for Maggie—rang in those words. "I'll do whatever it takes to get this guy."

Scott stared back at him a minute, then simply nodded, but Grant could see in that minute he'd won Scott's approval.

"Let's get going, then," Scott said.

Ella had already sat down in a chair in the corner, beside a guy who looked about Grant's age. He had gruff, hard features, dark, close-cropped hair and the intuitive stare that immediately labeled him as law enforcement.

"Logan Greer." The man stood and introduced himself with a hint of a drawl. "I'm Ella's fiancé and a detective with the DC PD."

"Nice to meet you," Grant said.

"Hi, Grant," the last person in the room called from the floor, where she was jotting notes in a legal file with one hand and holding a slice of pizza in the other.

"Chelsie," he replied. Chelsie Russell was a willowy blonde who worked in the WFO and had an ancillary position as a negotiator. When he'd first met her, she'd seemed stiff and quiet, but she and Maggie were friends, so he'd learned she actually had a pretty good sense of humor and a decent break at the pool table.

"So we've got a couple of tactical agents, a profiler, a negotiator and a detective," Grant summed up. Not to mention his experience on the violent crimes division and Maggie's work in civil rights cases. "Let's see what we can come up with here."

He tried to ignore the voice buzzing in the back of his brain telling him this was going to end like the Manhattan Strangler case, with yet another censure in his file for disobeying orders.

He glanced at Maggie and found her looking gratefully at him. Suddenly, he didn't care what the case did to his file, so long as the other part of the Manhattan Strangler case didn't come back to haunt him. Because he couldn't bear to watch Maggie get hurt.

Just the thought of it made his chest tense up until his breathing felt unnatural.

Forcing himself to focus, he found a spot on the floor, helped himself to a slice of pizza and told the group the details of the Shana Mills case. "She didn't show up at the hospital until September 2, but she was assaulted on the first, thirteen years ago."

"Okay." Scott sounded skeptical. "What happened in the two years in between, then? Other victims who he didn't brand? On the same date?"

"Maybe, but none of the other cases I looked at had any similarities. And if there was no branding, I'm not sure the date matters."

Ella started shaking her head and leaned forward, so Grant cut her off. "Look, I'm no profiler, but the date is significant for a reason, right? Don't you think there's a good chance it was the date he assaulted the person he actually *knew*, the one he really wanted to hurt? Originally?"

Ella frowned, grooves appearing between her eyebrows. "My theory is that the date is important because it's when he finally took the step he'd fantasized about for years. It's when he finally abducted someone, and everything that came after that. And he wanted to keep doing it. That's why he's coming back for her. Ten years have gone by. Ten years to build up the sick obsession of his first target. Ten years, and suddenly he's not having such an easy time fitting in around these college students. He's looking for a replay of when it all worked for him."

Her voice was strained, and as her fiancé put his arm around Ella's shoulders, Grant realized how hard it was for her to profile Maggie's case.

"I think you're wrong."

Everyone stilled and stared back at him at the announcement, probably because Ella was a heck of a profiler. Even he knew it, and he'd never worked with her.

"You were there when it happened. You're too close to see it clearly."

She jerked back as though she'd been insulted, and he quickly added, "I'm sorry. I just think the date has to be more significant. Otherwise, why wait so long? If it was really just about when he started, why not make it the first of every month? Or every six months? There's still a pattern in that, and then he's not forced to wait a whole *year*. It's got to be more. It's got to be *personal*."

Silence greeted his argument, and Grant cursed himself for his word choice. The September 1 a decade ago was extremely personal to everyone in this room.

It was Chelsie who finally spoke up. "Why this case? Why Shana Mills?"

"She's pretty sure someone drugged the beer she was drinking. Beer in a can, that she opened herself."

"So what?" Ella said, then held up a hand when he started to continue. "Yeah, I know that's what happened to Maggie, but what does that tell us? That both perps were savvy enough to get close to their victims without being noticed. Doesn't make it the same person."

She was right, but something about this file brought his investigative instincts to life.

"Then there's this." He handed Ella the copy of Shana Mills's picture he'd taken from the case file.

Her eyes went from the picture to him and back again. "Okay," she admitted, "there's a certain type here. Same basic look as all the Fishhook victims."

Maggie, who'd been mostly silent and still during the exchange, reached over from where she'd been standing, arms crossed in the corner, and took the picture. She frowned. "You think she looks like me?"

The truth was, he didn't. Not in the ways that mattered. But when it came to the basics—the long, dark hair with the off-center part, the light blue eyes, the slender, toned figure—the similarities were definitely there.

"It's a type," Ella spoke up. "The kind of similarities this guy might be looking for." She looked at Grant. "It's still not a sure thing. Scott's right about the two-year wait."

"You think he would have started the branding the very next year, if my theory is right?" Grant pressed, genuinely wanting Ella's opinion. She knew this kind of killer better than he ever would, regardless of how close she was to the case.

She fiddled with the diamond on her finger, seeming to have an internal argument, before she finally said, "Not necessarily. You could be right about there being more victims who weren't branded in between, and then the date might not be as important. Or it's possible he waited, put together his plan, found a location, did practice runs."

"Practice runs?" Logan asked, sounding as if he wasn't sure he wanted to know what that meant.

"Victims he killed. Or victims he didn't think would ever report, even with a brand. Prostitutes, for example."

"So what do we do with this?" Scott was tapping his foot incessantly, which made him seem desperate to move, and move now.

"It's just a theory," Grant said. "Two names came up in Shana's file. I'm going to run them down."

"Jeff Hoffmeier and Kevin Sanders," Maggie said.

"Yeah." He squinted at her, surprised she'd remembered the names he'd mentioned at the office. "*I'm* going to run this down," he emphasized. "If it leads anywhere, I'll loop you in."

Maggie looked as if she was going to argue, but Scott cut her off. "We're trying to go at this from the traveling angle. How does he move around so much, and what does that mean for his occupation? We're considering trucker, contractor, independently wealthy—"

"Wealthy," Grant interrupted. "The marble table."

"What marble table?" Chelsie asked, setting her pen down and staring up at him.

Grant swore as he looked over at Maggie, then started to apologize.

"It's fine," she said. "I haven't had a chance to tell them all the details. I had a flashback. I remembered room details. I wasn't thinking about what it meant for the profile, but the room I was in was nice. It wasn't some dive hotel. It was someone's house."

Ella stood. "Maggie, that's huge. That means he *did* live here ten years ago. When he talked about *home* in his letter, it wasn't a figure of speech. We need to start looking at anyone who lived on or around campus back then who moved within the year."

Maggie sighed loudly. "That's been done several times over the years. Besides, the number will be huge. With all the colleges around here, the population shift is enormous. And if he left in the summer right before the following September, it would be when a whole graduating class left."

"Yeah, but he was older," Ella said. "He wasn't a college student. That I'd bank on. Although…"

"What?" Scott demanded.

Ella looked at Grant. "If you're right about Shana Mills, he could have been a student *then*. Probably not an undergrad, but maybe a grad student or a teaching assistant or something."

"Okay." Grant's energy level, which had been hovering around zero when he'd arrived, suddenly spiked. This was the best lead he'd had yet. And if it wasn't the ex-boyfriend or the stalker, it was probably someone in Shana's life. Someone who'd been in DC thirteen years ago, and who'd been here ten years ago, but had left sometime after September 1 of that year.

Even though he didn't have any solid evidence to back up the connection to Shana Mills, he knew he was onto something.

He glanced at his watch—9:30 p.m. Kammy would probably still be at the office. "I need to go. Let me know if you come up with anything. And I'll tell you what happens on my end with the interviews of those two guys."

Maggie nodded, but there was something in her expression…

Grant looked at Scott. "Can I talk to you in private for a second?"

Maggie didn't seem happy about that, but Scott nodded. "Yeah, okay."

"I'll be in touch," he promised everyone as he followed Scott down the hall and to the front entryway, where there was a modicum of privacy.

"We're sticking close," Scott told him before he could say a word.

"Good." Grant pulled a card out of his pocket and handed it over. "Just call me if you need help. I'll be here. The same is true of any of the guys on the team. They all love your sister."

As soon as the words were out of his mouth, Grant felt as if someone had sucker punched him.

"You okay, man?" Scott asked.

"Yeah, fine." He tried to shake off the realization that had just hit him, but the knowledge rattled around in his brain even as he tried to focus. "Look, this perp knows Maggie is SWAT. He must."

"Which makes him an idiot," Scott spat. "I mean, believe me, I'm not leaving her alone, but she doesn't need me. You should know—you see her working on SWAT."

"That's the thing," Grant countered. "He's *not* an idiot. He has to be really intelligent to have pulled this off for a decade."

"So you're thinking, what? That he doesn't actually plan to get close again? You thinking a long-distance shooting?"

Grant swore at that idea, which had never occurred to him. "No. Talk to Ella, because she knows this stuff better, but I don't think so. But he's *obsessed* with Maggie, fixated on her in a way he's never been on any of the others. So he must have a plan to get near her. Unless maybe his plan is purely psychological? Break her down by giving her reason to believe he's coming after her, then stick to his normal pattern and grab someone else?"

Scott nodded, looking grim. "Well, we're going to assume he's serious. But you could be right. Every year, waiting for a new report…" Scott shook his head. "It's really hard on her. If she's focused on this threat against her, and that's where the manpower is, and then he hurts some other woman…"

"I know."

"Thanks for helping out," Scott said.

"Of course."

Scott slapped his arm and walked back toward the living room, his steps slow, as if he didn't want to talk to Maggie about the possibilities Grant had suggested.

Grant stepped outside but before he'd made it off the stoop, Maggie ran out, closing the door behind her.

"I just told your brother—"

"To keep an eye on me," Maggie said, interrupting him. "I get it. Look…" She trailed off, studying him. "Are you okay?"

A smile slipped out as he stared back at her. "Yeah, I'm okay." He stepped forward, until they were standing close to each other.

He didn't know how deep her feelings for him ran. She was attracted to him, and they were friends, and at least to some extent, she was using his feelings for her to get his help on this case. But was there more?

He lifted his hand, stroked the side of her cheek, and she leaned her face into his palm. He moved a little closer, until he could feel her breath on his chin. Until he could lower his lips and press them lightly to hers, try to show her what he'd realized, what he wasn't ready to say out loud.

He was in love with her.

Chapter Nine

When Maggie walked back into her living room, everyone was staring at her. Everyone but Logan, who was staring resolutely at the wall, obviously wanting no part of whatever was about to happen.

"What?" she demanded.

"What's the deal with Grant?" Ella asked, a smirk on her face that Maggie recognized all too well.

"Nothing," Maggie answered, knowing her voice was giving her away. "We're friends. You know that."

"I also know when you're lying to me," Ella answered, still looking smug. "I've known you way too long. You really think you can keep secrets from me?"

"I like him," Scott put in, and Maggie gaped at him. "What? I do."

Over the years, Scott had taken his big-brother role with both her and Ella a little too seriously, especially when it came to guys, and even more so since her attack. He'd gone easier on Ella, and he'd approved of Logan, but Maggie didn't think anyone had ever passed his test for her.

"Well, that doesn't matter," she started, but Ella cut her off.

"I wondered how long that was going to take."

"What are you talking about?"

Ella leaned forward, grinning, and in the chair beside her, Logan made "sorry my fiancée is nosy" gestures so animated that Maggie couldn't help but laugh.

Ella glared briefly at him, then continued, "The times you invited me along with your SWAT team to O'Reilley's, I could tell you were interested. And so was he." She looked pleased with herself when she added, "I wondered how long it would take for you two to finally admit it."

"Well, it doesn't matter," Maggie said again, settling back on the couch beside her brother and crossing her arms over her chest to signal that the discussion was over.

"Why? Because he's a teammate?" Chelsie asked.

"He's not a teammate anymore," Maggie said, and stopped Scott before he could jump in as she knew he wanted to, telling her she'd get back on SWAT. She definitely didn't want to get into that discussion. "Grant's investigating my case, so that's the end of it."

"He's trying—" Ella started.

"I don't want to talk about it," Maggie blurted, and her friends went silent, because she rarely refused to discuss anything. "It's not happening, so just leave it alone."

Scott and Ella shared a glance that Maggie purposely ignored, and then Logan spoke up, clearly trying to change the subject. "Look, this isn't my specialty, but given what Grant was suggesting about that Shana Mills case, if the perp actually knew her, is there any chance he knew Maggie, too?"

Ella sat straighter beside him, instantly serious, and started shaking her head, then paused, looking pensive. "He wouldn't have been someone in Maggie's life. But if she was the first one he didn't know, it was a change in tactics, so it's possible he was around the periphery."

"What do you mean?" Scott demanded, leaning forward, the muscles in his arms bulging.

Ella looked at Maggie. "The thing Grant said about your drink. We know this guy stalked you. He would have done that with all of his victims. If he got close enough to slip drugs into your drink while you were holding it, maybe he talked to you. Maybe you knew him in some way—not well, maybe not even well enough to know his name, but enough to recognize him when he walked past you."

Numbness started to fill Maggie, and she recognized it as the coping mechanism she'd adopted whenever the discussions turned to areas she didn't like. Usually it happened when talking to investigators about specific details, not with her friends. But the idea that she might have known the person who had hurt her, even in some small way?

The numbness evaporated, and cold swept over her in its place, a light-headed feeling she tried to replace with anger. "So you think I could recognize him now?" she asked, and her voice sounded as though it was coming from far away.

Concern wrinkled Ella's face, but she nodded. "It's possible. I think you should ask Grant to take a look at pictures of any of his suspects."

Maggie nodded, even as discomfort overwhelmed her. It was bad enough that Grant was investigating, and hard enough to discuss the case with him—as though it didn't hurt her to think about him digging into the worst day of her life. She really didn't want to dig through it with him.

But if it meant catching the Fishhook Rapist, she'd do it. Because no matter how hard she tried not to dwell on it, she knew exactly how long she had left. Thirteen days, two hours and six minutes until it hit September 1.

And then the Fishhook Rapist would be back for her.

MAGGIE COULDN'T WAIT any longer.

She'd been sitting at her desk, staring at her files, for over an hour, waiting for Kammy Ming to finally call it quits and head home. So she could talk to Grant alone. But the WFO had pretty well cleared out, and Grant and Kammy were still cloistered in the conference room, going over the case.

Her stomach rolling at the idea of what she was about to do, Maggie stood, moving through the dark and empty bullpen toward the conference room fast, before she could back out.

When she opened the door, Grant and Kammy stared back at her with surprise. They were sitting across from each other at a long conference table that was covered in open case files, boxes and laptops. A whiteboard at the far end of the room was inked up with notes, and a map pinned next to it had red circles and writing that Maggie didn't need to get close to to read. She recognized the locations instantly. The nine credited attacks of the Fishhook Rapist, scattered across the country.

She tried not to look at the files as she headed for the far end of the room where Grant and Kammy sat. Grant stood as she approached, and she couldn't help herself from glancing over the contents on the table. A box full of information on the fishing industry. Stacks of college attendance records from all across DC from a decade ago. Victim case files.

Over the years, Maggie had been tempted to try and reach out to the other victims, try to piece together what they knew. Try to get answers. But she'd resisted. Not just because it would have been completely against protocol, but also because she didn't want to go over every tiny, insignificant thing she could remember, or the big hole in her memory. So how could she ask someone else to do it?

As she reached Grant's side, Maggie forced herself to look away from the case files before she spotted her own. She knew what was in it, and she didn't want or need to see it. She had enough memories.

"We're doing everything we can," Kammy told her, sounding worn-out, and beneath the seasoned investigator's voice was something that sounded an awful lot like defeat.

"What is it, Maggie?" Grant asked, as he closed the file next to him, which had to be hers.

She tried to keep the emotion out of her voice as she told him, "I want to look at pictures."

"What pictures?" Grant asked, just as Kammy said, "You need to leave the investigation to us."

How was she going to do this without letting Kammy know Grant had been sharing information with her? Frustration filled her, because she couldn't wait around to talk to Grant in secret. Keeping her personal investigation segregated from their official one was limiting resources. What if not working together prevented them from finding the Fishhook Rapist in time?

"If there's a chance this guy started with someone he knew before me, maybe he hung around me when he was stalking me. Maybe I could recognize him."

Kammy glared at Grant. "I know James talked to you about confidentiality—"

"It's not him," Maggie said. "I'm an agent, too. I can't sit back and leave this to someone else. I'm looking into it myself."

For a split second, Kammy looked furious, but Maggie

could see her making a concerted effort to rein it in as she said, "There's a reason you weren't assigned this case, Maggie. You're too close to it, and you know it."

"I can help," Maggie snapped. "I want to look at the pictures. I don't want to be sitting in my house, hoping this guy won't come back for me in thirteen days, because you were worried about bureaucratic procedure!"

Kammy stood, and even though Maggie had eight inches and probably thirty pounds on her, she suddenly understood why Kammy had a reputation as someone not to cross. The full force of her glare was intimidating.

But Maggie was SWAT—or at least she had been—and she glared right back.

Grant held his hands out and said calmly, "Look, this is on me. I told Maggie my theory. I asked if she recognized the names from the Mills file. No sense in spreading our resources thin if she knew them. She didn't, but let's see if the faces ring any bells. Okay?"

Kammy turned on Grant again and gave one curt nod, and Maggie knew her outburst had just put a dent, not in her career, but Grant's.

Ashamed, she opened her mouth to apologize, but Grant held out a file before she could speak.

"Here," he said. "This is the stalker, Kevin Sanders. He look familiar?"

Her hands shook as she took the file from him, and she braced herself. But when she stared at the picture of Kevin Sanders from thirteen years ago—blond hair, cocky smile, college sweatshirt even though he'd already graduated—she felt nothing. No sudden burst of recognition, no painful memories. Nothing.

She looked harder, willing something forward. They already knew he was a stalker, and if Shana Mills was the original victim, he had to be first in the suspect line. If it was him, they would have a name, a person to hunt down.

Finally, she looked up at Grant and shook her head. "I don't recognize him."

"That's okay." Grant closed the file and set it down. "We're still going to check him out." He handed her a second file. "The ex-boyfriend, Jeff Hoffmeier."

She opened it fast, expecting nothing, but hoping for... something. But just like Kevin Sanders, he didn't look familiar. He was scowling slightly, which made what would have otherwise been a good-looking face seem ugly and angry. His dark hair was buzzed close to his head, and his eyes were strikingly blue. He had apparently already graduated a few years earlier when he'd been dating Shana, but he still looked like a college kid in the picture. A typical college kid.

She started to shake her head and hand back the file when a voice from her past whispered in her head, *What are you drinking?* The same voice that she remembered from one other time, telling her, *This is going to hurt.*

She gasped, and the file slipped from her hands, spilling its contents all over the floor.

"Hey." Grant's hand locked on her arm, and the voice in her mind faded. "You recognize this guy?"

Kammy leaned toward them across the table, looking expectant, a phone already in her hand, as if she was ready to call in the rest of the team.

"Uh, I don't know." Her voice shook, and Maggie tried to get it together. She reached down for the file, and Grant stopped her.

"I got it." He set the file on the table. "Did he look familiar?"

"Let me look again."

"You want to take a break?"

"No, I'm fine." She gritted her teeth and opened the file on the table, taking out just the picture. She focused hard, studying Jeff Hoffmeier more closely.

He had a strong, angular face, an aristocratic nose and a strong jawline. He'd probably had an easy time getting dates, if he didn't scowl the way he was doing in the picture. But no matter how intently she stared at him, willing the memory back, she didn't recognize him.

So why had that memory rushed forward when she'd looked at his picture?

Was it even a real memory? She had no recollection of the Fishhook Rapist ever talking to her before the abduction, no recollection of him asking her about her drink, even though he'd obviously dosed it. Had the investigation created false memories?

She knew it could happen. She'd seen it firsthand in her own cases. The further back an incident was, the harder the memories were to access. The more details a victim had about the possible suspects, the more likely she was to talk herself into believing something just because she needed answers.

Was the same true of Maggie, despite her FBI training?

"Do you know him?" Kammy asked, and Grant said, "Give her a second." Their voices seemed distant as she kept staring desperately at Jeff Hoffmeier.

Finally, she set the image down and shook her head. "I'm not sure. He gives me a bad feeling, but he doesn't look familiar."

"What does that mean?" Kammy asked, sounding frustrated. "You think this is him or not?"

Grant glared at Kammy, but when he turned back to her, his expression was even and calm. "What about him gives you a bad feeling?"

"I'm not sure. I think I had a memory when I looked at his picture, but it was just a voice. And I can't be certain…" She sighed heavily, infuriated that she couldn't say more. She'd always been grateful that she couldn't remember much from the attack itself, but suddenly she wished she did.

"I'm not sure *why* that happened. Maybe it's him, or maybe something about him just reminds me of the guy. I don't know." She heard the anguished frustration in her voice and tried to even it out, like the professional she was. "Maybe when you talk to this guy, I should go with you."

"No," Grant barked.

"If it's him, and he sees me, he might—"

"No," Grant cut her off. "We'll look into him more closely, see if he's even a possibility. If he looks good for it, we'll bring him in, and if there's a reason for you to get involved, you can do it through the glass."

"That's not—"

"It's not happening," Kammy said softly, and Grant looked as though he might burst an artery.

"Okay, look—"

"We're not tipping our hand on this." Grant seemed to be working hard to keep his voice calm. "Once we narrow in on a name, there's going to be a pattern, and it might take a little time to dig up, but it will be there. We're not letting anyone know they're on our suspect list until we show up at their door to slap the cuffs on, got it?"

Maggie frowned, unable to deny the logic there. She definitely didn't want him running, if it was him. "Okay, then why haven't you started digging into information on these two already?" They had to be at the top of the list, if Grant's theory was to be believed. "I can—"

"We had some other leads today that looked good," Kammy said. "But they didn't pan out."

"What were they?"

"They didn't pan out," Kammy repeated tightly. "But Grant is right. If Hoffmeier is the guy, then he's lived in all the locations on the board." She gestured vaguely behind her at the map with the bright red circles. "And we'll find that."

Maggie nodded. Their plan made sense. "Okay." She pushed a stack of files aside and settled into the chair next to where Grant had been sitting until she walked into the room. "I'll help."

"No way," Kammy burst out.

Maggie crossed her arms over her chest and gave Kammy her best SWAT stare, the one that said she wasn't backing down. "You want me out of here, you're going to have to drag me. And I've got to warn you, you're not going to have an easy time of it."

"Are you kidding me?" Kammy let out a stream of curses more creative than Maggie thought the uptight woman knew.

"I'll track locations," Maggie insisted as she tried not to look at Grant. She could see him out of the corner of her eye, staring at her with an expression she couldn't quite read.

Anger? Worry? Disappointment? Probably all three, and she didn't want to think about what her actions were doing to his reputation within VCMO, or how they were going to impact his feelings for her.

"Fine," Kammy said tightly. "But you research what we hand over, and nothing else. Any more than that, and I don't care about your personal stake in this. The rules exist for a reason, and you step any further over the line, and I'm putting it in both of your files. Got it?"

Maggie nodded, the fear of harming Grant's career weighing on her more than the chances of hurting her own. And from the perceptive look in Kammy's eyes, she knew it.

"You take Sanders," Grant said, handing her the file.

"I want—"

"I'll deal with Hoffmeier," Grant interrupted. "Kammy was already digging into other people in Shana's life who might be involved."

Maggie looked up at her, where she was still standing, looking irate. "You find anyone?"

"No." She dropped into her seat, wrestled her jet-black hair streaked with gray into a knot and added, "I'm still looking, though."

"Thank you."

Kammy frowned at her. "I respect your work here, Maggie, or I wouldn't let this—" she gestured around her at the files "—slide. But watch your step. If you want to be involved with this in any capacity, you need to stop your side investigation. I don't want you running across this guy unprepared."

Maggie nodded, hoping she looked convincing. Kammy's argument was logical, but no way were Ella or her brother stopping, which meant she wasn't, either.

Kammy's eyes narrowed suspiciously, so Maggie grabbed the Kevin Sanders file and started working.

It didn't take long before her heart rate picked up, and she began to wonder whether her reaction to Jeff had actually been a delayed response to seeing Kevin Sanders's picture. He'd served two stints in jail in the past five years, both for sexual assault.

Neither were in states where Fishhook Rapist victims had appeared, but they were in between attacks, so they could have been en route to a new state. She sat straighter, sifting through information faster, looking for a connection.

An hour later, she sank back in her seat and shook her head, trying not to dwell on her disappointment. "It's not Kevin Sanders."

Grant looked up from his own laptop and rubbed his eyes. "Why not?"

The dejection sounded in her voice when she told him and Kammy, "At the time of the third victim's attack, he was in lockup for drunk driving. Thirty days. There's no way it was him."

"I haven't come up with any other likely possibilities from Shana Mills's life," Kammy said, slumping back against her chair. "How's your luck, Grant?"

Maggie turned toward him expectantly, but one glance at the weary slump of his shoulders and her hope for a break in the case faded, especially as he shook his head.

"Jeff Hoffmeier is a real possibility."

"What?" Maggie sat straighter, grasping his arm before she realized what she was doing. She quickly pulled her hand back. "What do you mean?"

"He was living in DC ten years ago. After that, I have no idea."

Maggie frowned. "You can't track him? He has to have owned property, or gotten a driver's license or—"

"I can't track him," Grant said. "It's as if he just disappeared. And it happened sometime after September, ten years ago."

Chapter Ten

Grant had finally lain down in bed when the doorbell rang. He stared up at the ceiling in the darkness, sighed, then threw on a T-shirt and went to the door, feeling every step. It had been a very long, frustrating day, and the verbal warning from James—who'd had a call from Kammy about him and Maggie—had capped it off.

He opened the door, already knowing who was standing on the other side, and turned around, telling her, "Come on in."

"I'm sorry—"

"Stop apologizing," he told Maggie as he led her to the living room, squinting as he flipped on a light.

He turned around and faced her, discovering that she looked more worn out than he felt.

"I didn't mean to wake you. I just wanted to apolo—"

"Maggie," he said. "If you're going to start every visit to my house with an apology, it's going to get old fast. You want to come by, then come by because we're friends, and you want to see me. Come by because we're—" he paused, then settled on "—more than that, and you just want me." He grinned to let her know he was at least partly teasing, and finished, "Just don't say *sorry* one more time."

She fiddled with the hem of her blouse, stuck her hands in her pockets, took them out again and crossed them over her chest. "Okay. Sure." She glanced over his T-shirt and boxers, and added, "I didn't think you'd be sleeping."

It was still early evening, but he'd put in so many late nights during that past two weeks, he'd finally crashed.

"Long day," he said, settling onto the couch and gesturing for her to join him. "You're here to find out where we are on the case, I assume." He'd leaned his head against the back of the couch and closed his eyes, so he didn't know if she nodded or not as he felt her sit down next to him, but he continued, "Jeff Hoffmeier's name pops up a few times, but it's sporadic, and it's not giving us places of residence."

"What about his family? They're still in town."

Slowly, Grant opened his eyes and looked at her. She'd sat closer than he'd realized, and he could see the strain on her face that got worse with each day closer to September 1.

"I thought you were going to stay away from this." That had been their agreement, after she'd helped them the night before at the office. Kammy had insisted she stay away from Hoffmeier, and she'd agreed. Grant had known she wouldn't stay away from the investigation entirely, but he'd thought she'd conceded to focus on her safety, and let them run down the lead. Apparently, he'd been wrong.

Before she could reply, he swore. "Maggie, please tell me you didn't talk to them."

"I didn't give my name. I called, claimed to be from the alumni association, asked for contact information for him."

Grant sat up, suddenly wide-awake and furious. "Are you kidding me? Are you trying to sabotage this investigation?"

She leaned toward him until they were mere inches apart, looking furious herself. "You know me. You know I wasn't going to leave this to anyone else."

"I was checking into Hoffmeier," he growled. "I told you to leave it alone."

"Yeah, well, you're not my boss."

"Your boss told you to leave it alone, too."

"Too bad," she said. "I called. It's done. And they gave me the runaround, said he wouldn't want to be in the directory listing, even when I pushed for just a phone number to ask him myself."

Grant rubbed his forehead, where a headache was rapidly forming. "You're going to get yourself hurt," he said quietly, trying to keep the anger out of his voice. And he was successful. Because what came through was worry.

He felt her hand close on his, and even though he'd seen up close in SWAT what she was capable of doing with those hands, all he could focus on was how tiny they were, compared to his.

"I didn't go anywhere near him, and I don't plan to, even if I'd learned where he was. I made a phone call. If anything had come of it, I would have…"

"What?" he pressed when she paused. "Called Scott and taken him over there?"

"No," she replied. "I would have called you. I understand that I have a target on my back. I'm not going to put anyone else in danger by going near a possible suspect who's out to get me, and probably willing to take other people down to get to me. But that doesn't mean I'm going to sit home, boarding up my windows and praying someone else finds him, after a decade of dead ends. Come on!"

Grant tried to forcibly keep the words in that wanted to burst from his mouth. When he felt he had it together, he told her, "I'll pay the family a visit tomorrow."

"What about not tipping your hand?"

"If Hoffmeier is living in DC right now, he doesn't have his name on any lease. Which means he's either off the books somewhere, or his family is putting him up. They've got some serious political connections, and they're not going to scare easily, but they're also not going to want bad press attached to the family name. I'm going to use that."

"How?"

"Maggie, trust me, okay? I've run a lot of investigations like this. I understand why you can't back away, but just let me run with Hoffmeier."

"We've got twelve days, Grant," she said softly, nervousness in her eyes that he hadn't seen on even the diciest of SWAT calls.

He stroked her hand. "If we don't have someone in custody by August 31, the FBI is putting you in protective custody. And I'm taking a break from the case to be on the detail." That last part hadn't been approved, but it didn't matter. Whatever it took, he planned to be there for her.

She gave him a forced smile. "That's sweet of you, Grant, but I've got SWAT training. If he gets anywhere near me…"

"I know." He made sure he put conviction in the words, wanted her to know he believed them. "But this guy is smart, and I'm not willing to take chances. Neither is anyone in the Bureau. I didn't even need to request this. The word came down from way above me."

She was silent a minute, and he wasn't sure if she was digesting that, or trying to come up with an argument, but he spoke up first.

"Even if it wasn't an official order, Maggie, you know every single guy on our team would have taken personal time to stand by you on September 1. This SOB would have had to go through an entire team of SWAT agents to get anywhere near you."

Tears welled in her eyes—something he'd never once seen—and he finished, "But it's not going to come to that. We're going to get him."

She nodded. Then she reached up and put her hand on the back of his head to pull him to her, and softly kissed him. She leaned back again before he'd really registered what was happening. "Thank you."

She'd never let go of his hand, so he used it to tug her closer, until he could wrap his arm around her shoulder. He knew she cared about him, and she was attracted to him, but beyond that? He really had no idea. And now was the wrong time to find out, but when she rested her head in the crook of his arm and relaxed against him, it felt right, like something a girlfriend would do.

"When I was a teenager, my dad left."

Maggie shifted, apparently surprised by the change in conversation, but he kept his arm around her shoulder and drew her back against him.

"It was sort of out of the blue for all of us. My parents never had the most solid marriage, but they never argued, either. There was just this…distance. Then my dad just left. Middle of the night and everything. Packed up one suitcase and bolted. Left everything else behind, including his family."

Maggie's fingers tightened around his, telling him

she was listening carefully, even though he couldn't see her expression.

"I get postcards and phone calls every so often, but for all real purposes, he just washed his hands of us. Never got an explanation, either. I think that's the part that eats my mom up most. But the timing…" He sighed, remembering the changes that had come swift and unforgiving during his sophomore year of high school.

"We lived in the city. New York. We were already struggling, but without the second income, we had to move, and where we ended up was bad. Real bad. With a big gang presence."

"And they took one look at you and wanted you to join," Maggie guessed, reminding him she'd seen the picture on his mantel.

Even in high school, he'd looked like the kind of muscle a gang might want to use. "Yeah. My younger brothers weren't quite my size, but they tried to jump all three of us in. I worked hard to keep us all out of it."

"And what happened?"

The memory made him tense. "Vinnie was okay. It wasn't easy, but he genuinely wanted nothing to do with it, so even though it wasn't exactly simple to keep them off our doorstep, at least we were only fighting on one side there. But Ben—he's the baby of the family, in seventh grade then—he was interested. I honestly thought we were going to lose him to them. I'd all but given up, when one of his friends was killed in a drive-by. It scared him straight."

"They seem to be doing pretty well now," she said. "From your pictures, I mean."

"Oh, yeah. Vinnie's still in New York, but way up north now, and Ben moved out to Chicago a couple of years back."

"And you stayed in New York."

"Well, that's where the Bureau assigned me."

She twisted to look at him. "You requested it, though, didn't you? As your office of preference?"

Once an agent made it through the FBI Academy, they got to request the field office where they wanted to be placed. It was considered sort of a joke, because rarely did anyone seem to actually get their office of preference, but he had. "Yeah. Well, at the time, my family was still there, and I wanted to…"

"Make a difference," she finished.

"Sounds a little corny, I know, but—"

"It doesn't sound corny at all," she said.

"Well, I didn't get gangs, which honestly, I'm kind of glad about—I'd had plenty of that—but I've been in VCMO my whole career so far. I wanted to try for SWAT in New York, but there was never an opening. So when I came here and a place opened up right away, it seemed like it was meant to be."

"Maybe it was."

He stared down at her, looking back earnestly, and he knew he'd probably never get a better opening. "I feel the same way about meeting you."

She jerked backward, eyes wide, and dread overtook him. He'd pushed too much, too soon.

"Grant, you know…" She sighed, cutting herself off. "There's been something…more than friendship… between us all along."

"There has?" She'd felt it right away, too?

"Yes. But things have changed."

"Why?"

"You look at me differently now," she said softly, slipping out of his grasp and standing.

He got to his feet, too. "Maggie, that's just not true."

"I know you don't want it to be, but it is. I could feel it, before, when you kissed me."

Because of his mistake with her neck. He tried to argue, but she talked over him.

"That one day has affected *everything* in my life ever since. I joined the FBI because of it, I take a personal day every September 1 because of it, and every relationship I've ever had has tanked in one way or another because of it."

Her voice wavered, but there was certainty in her eyes as she said, "It's been ten years. I need to get to the other side of this. And I can't do it with you. Not with everything you know, with everything you've seen in my case file. I'm sorry," she finished quietly, then she turned and headed for the door.

MAGGIE SQUEEZED HER eyes shut and pressed a hand against the ache in her chest as she opened her car door.

From behind her, another hand reached out and slammed it shut.

As she whipped around, a woman out jogging paused and let out a cat call, then raced on past as Maggie realized Grant had followed her outside, in boxers, a T-shirt and bare feet.

She blinked, hoping Grant couldn't tell she was seconds from crying, and tried to turn her back on him. Just get in her car and drive home. Put this whole day behind her.

He took her arm and spun her around, something fierce in his expression as he told her, "The only thing that's different now is my feelings for you have gotten stronger, Maggie. If you're not interested, fine," he said, although his voice broke on the last word. "But if you're really worried I see you as somehow *less* because of what happened to you, that's just not true."

She pulled angrily out of his grip. "Look, Grant, maybe I've been giving you mixed signals, because I *am* interested. You know it. But it doesn't matter! What happened before—"

"When I almost touched your neck and I froze?" he asked bluntly.

"Yes." Some part of her actually wished he'd done it, that she'd had her inevitable panicked reaction. Maybe then she'd be able to admit to herself, once and for all, that it wasn't going to ever matter how the guy responded to learning about her past. That it was *her*. That she was never going to be cut out for a normal relationship.

She gulped and hung her head, not wanting him to see that fear in her eyes. Because if anyone might, it was Grant.

"I just didn't want to hurt you," he said softly.

"You saw me as damaged," she said, and preempted the response he was trying to give, adding, "Maybe I do, too."

"Maggie." He put his hand under her chin, forcing it up so she was looking at him. "I don't think that. You're one of the strongest people I know. And you must know that about yourself, or you'd never have had the confidence to go out for SWAT."

"That's different."

"It's no different—"

"Yes, it is. Romantically, men find out and they look at me as if I'm…tainted." She hated even saying the word, hated believing it was true. But decent men, men she'd been interested in enough to go out with, had suddenly changed when she told them. They'd begun looking at her as though she was a victim, and worse, as though she was somehow a different person than before. Unintentionally, she was sure, but to her—being on the other end of it—that didn't matter.

"Oh, Maggie," Grant sighed, and he sounded so sorry for her, she just wanted to leave.

She reached for her door handle again, but he drew her hands to his chest.

"The only person tainted by any of this was him. You came out of that stronger." His face was as serious as she'd ever seen it as he told her, "That's my theory on why he's threatening to come back for you, and not any of the others."

"I was first," Maggie said, feeling her shoulders slump with sudden exhaustion.

"Sort of," he said. "The first with the brand, anyway. But I don't think that's really why. I said from the start that it's because he couldn't break you. It's why his sick little obsession with you didn't end that day. You were too strong for him. You always will be."

She stared up at him, the anger and weariness fading underneath hope and fear that mingled together in equal measure.

He must have seen it, because he insisted, "What happened to you changes *nothing* about how I feel about you."

She blinked at him, her pulse beginning to race. "Prove it."

He went completely still for a few seconds that seemed to stretch out forever, then he peeled the keys out of her hand, hit the lock button and put his hands on her face, leaning in.

A car driving by honked, and Maggie jumped. "Not here."

"Okay." He bent down and with one smooth motion, picked her up and tossed her over his shoulder.

She was so surprised, she let out a burst of laughter, and suddenly the tension that always seemed to fill her broke apart. But nervousness quickly settled in its place.

They were back inside before she had a chance to figure out how to handle her anxiety. Then he was setting her down and bringing his hands back up to cup her cheeks, his thumbs caressing her skin before his lips slowly descended on hers.

Just like the other times he'd kissed her, she marveled at how soft and gentle his lips were. It was such a contrast to the hard muscles in his arms that she felt as she ran her fingers upward to tangle around his neck.

They stood there for a long time, his mouth pressing softly and sweetly against hers, his tongue teasing the seam of her lips, until she couldn't take it anymore, and she pushed up on her tiptoes and wound her leg around his.

Finally, he slid his hands down her back, pausing just long enough to unstrap her holster and set it on the mantel. Then his hands drifted lower, gripping her thighs. Pinpoints of pleasure danced over her skin where he touched her, and he lifted her up. As soon as she wrapped her legs around his waist and thrust her tongue into his mouth, he turned, heading straight for the couch.

Ripping her mouth from his, she panted, "Bedroom," then stared back at him, waiting, hoping he wouldn't stop the way he had the last time she'd made that request.

Instead, he smiled at her, one of those huge grins she'd always been drawn to, and strode down the hall as though he couldn't get there fast enough. He flipped on the light in his bedroom, and she had a brief impression of framed art on the wall, an open closet filled with suits on one side and cargos and T-shirts on the other, and a king-size bed.

She expected him to place her back on that bed, but

he turned around and sat on the edge, so she was sitting on top of him. He didn't give her time to decide if that was because he was afraid she wouldn't like someone over her; his hands slipped underneath her blouse and started stroking the curve of her waist. He ran his tongue along the outside of her ear, and need pulsed through her.

"Grant," she moaned, shocked at how desperate she sounded as she grabbed fistfuls of his shirt and tugged it over his head.

"Mmm," he responded, then turned back and fused his mouth to hers, simultaneously unbuttoning her blouse and sliding it off her arms.

As soon as it was off, she arched into him, loving the feel of his skin against hers. His hands started to head back to her waist, so she took hold of them and directed them to the button on her pants.

He undid them fast, then flipped her over onto her back, standing up and pulling the pants slowly down her legs, his gaze traveling the same path.

She propped herself up on her elbows to watch him there in nothing but his boxers, and when his eyes met hers, the pure desire she saw made her smile. In that instant, she was absolutely certain he wasn't thinking of anything in her past. Only her. Only right now.

She crooked her finger at him, and he smiled back at her, a smile full of anticipation and want and something else, something powerful that told her this was going to be more than a fling between friends. That maybe she'd found something much, much stronger.

Her breath caught as he lowered himself slowly on top of her, until she couldn't wait any longer. She had to wrap her arms and legs around him and arch up to meet his mouth.

Practically the instant his lips touched hers, a sudden ringing jolted her out of the moment.

He swore and glanced at the phone lit up on his nightstand, then down at her, then back again. Letting out a few more curses, he rolled over, bringing her with him so she was lying on top of him and making her laugh as he whispered, "Shhh," and picked up the phone.

"Work," he said, his voice suddenly serious and grim as he answered. "Grant Larkin."

Maggie could hear just enough to tell it was Kammy, but not enough to know what was happening. But there was no mistaking the all-business expression that wiped away the desire that had been on Grant's face seconds before. "Okay, I'm heading there now," he said, and hung up.

"What is it?" Maggie asked, propping herself up on her elbows so she could look down at him.

"The Hoffmeier family is taking a little impromptu vacation. There's a flight plan scheduled on their private jet leaving in less than an hour. I've got to go meet the plane." He pressed a fast kiss to her lips, then sat up, lifting her with him. "I've got to go."

Chapter Eleven

Grant was pissed off as he bullied his way onto the private airfield, using his Bureau credentials, his badge and his best SWAT scare tactics. What timing that the Hoffmeiers had to suddenly decide to leave DC. Really, really bad timing for him. And particularly suspicious timing for them.

"Heading to Florida, are you?" Grant called as he approached the midsize Cessna private jet being loaded with baggage as a man and woman stood beside it, looking impatient.

They both turned as he approached. The man was late sixties, with a shock of white hair and the kind of grimace on his face that looked as if it was permanently embedded there. Despite the warm August weather, he was wearing a lightweight suit. Beside him, the woman looked a few years younger, but she'd clearly tried to stave away the years with plastic surgery and dye. The result was too-plump lips, too-high eyebrows and unnaturally blond hair. She'd topped the look off with a candy-pink skirt suit, a floppy hat and oversize sunglasses.

"It's so lovely this time of year in Naples," Lorraine Hoffmeier replied, while her husband just scowled.

"I thought this was the rainy season," Grant said as he reached them and held out a hand. "Grant Larkin, FBI."

Lorraine took his hand limply, looking sideways at her husband, Frederik, who ignored it entirely.

"This is a private airstrip," he snapped.

"Not to me," Grant said, glancing over at the pair of men loading up the Hoffmeiers' luggage. It was going to take a while. "Long trip?"

"We're—" Lorraine started, but Frederik cut her off.

"If you have a business question, you can go through my office," Frederik said, peeling off a shiny business card and handing it over.

Grant pocketed it without a glance. "I don't. I have a family question."

Lorraine shuffled on tall heels that couldn't have been comfortable in the eighty-degree heat, and Frederik snapped, "I don't know what you think you're doing, harassing my family, son, but I know people over at the FBI. Whatever you're here for, it's not sanctioned, and your supervisor will be hearing about it."

Grant gave him a hard smile in return. "My supervisor is aware that I'm here. The Hoffmeier name has come up in connection with a case. I have a few simple questions for you, so that *I* don't have to kick this up to the next level."

Frederik turned to face Grant, leveling him with a look that had probably served him well in boardrooms for the past forty-five years. But this wasn't a boardroom, and Grant didn't intimidate easily.

"I know my rights. I don't have to answer a thing," Frederik said.

Grant shrugged, as though it didn't matter to him either way. "You don't. I can reach out to your employees, business associates and other family members next. Maybe they'll be more willing to cooperate in our investigation. Especially when they learn what we're investigating."

"I keep an attorney on retainer, son. I don't think you or the FBI wants a slander suit." His voice was hard and steady, but his jaw quivered.

Beside him, Lorraine had hunched down, and she'd crossed her arms over her chest.

"It's only slander if it's not true," Grant reminded him, then shrugged again and started to turn. "I'm surprised you don't even want to know what the investigation's about."

"What's it about?" Lorraine burst, like he'd gambled she would.

He turned slowly back around. "It's a serial rape case."

Lorraine turned so pale Grant thought he might have to catch her if she fell over, and Frederik sounded insulted when he said, "This is outrageous!"

"Obviously, you're not suspects," Grant said with the friendliest smile he could manage. "But your son has a connection to one of the victims, and we think he might be able to help us identify the person who did it."

Frederik's lips thinned into a straight line, but it was Lorraine who stiffened and said, "Jeffrey would not associate with a rapist. And I'm afraid he's unavailable. He's been living abroad for many years."

"Oh, I didn't say Jeffrey associated with him," Grant said, choosing his words carefully. "But he might have some key information to point us in the right direction."

Lorraine shook her head. "He's not here."

"That's okay. I just need some contact information." Grant took out a pen and notepad. "Phone number, address. I won't take much of his time."

Frederik and Lorraine stared at one another, seeming to have a silent communication, until Frederik gave one brief nod, and Lorraine pulled out her phone with shaking hands. "All I have is a cell phone number." She read a number off to him, which he jotted down.

"What about an address?"

Lorraine shook her head. "He moves around a lot. You know how some kids backpack across Europe?" She waved a still-shaky hand, encrusted with rings, in the air. "He never got over it."

"Where was he living the last time you talked to him?" Grant asked, trying to keep the annoyance out of his voice.

"I really don't know," Lorraine said, a long-simmering frustration in her tone. "He told me he was in Europe. That's all. I gave up trying to get more from Jeffrey a long time ago. The boy likes his privacy."

"Is he planning to come back to DC this summer?"

"Summer's about over, son," Frederik said, seeming to get his equilibrium back.

"I know. But September seems a perfect time to visit DC."

Lorraine's eyes narrowed, but confusion knitted her brow, as if she suspected there was more to his words, but she didn't know what. Beside her, her husband just frowned.

"You have the number," Frederik spoke up. "Now we need to get on our way." He turned toward the two men who'd almost finished loading the plane. "Let's get moving!"

The pilot who'd just come over from the closest building in time to overhear Frederik's demand, looked at them, then at his clipboard. He held out a hand to Frederik. "Just the three of you, sir?"

"Not him," Frederik said.

"I thought there were three passengers?" the pilot asked.

"Sorry I'm late!" someone called from behind him,

and before Grant turned around, he saw Lorraine smile widely and Frederik's scowl deepen.

The woman walking toward them in an expensive-looking skirt and blouse made Grant feel light-headed.

He must have been gaping because she tilted her head, gave him a perplexed look and asked, "Are you working security for my father?"

"Claudia Hoffmeier," he said. He'd known the Hoffmeiers had a daughter, younger than Jeffrey by six years, but he'd never seen a picture.

"That's right." She stood there, giving him an obvious appraisal.

He was probably staring right back, although his expression had to be a little more of the just-seen-a-ghost variety.

Claudia Hoffmeier had dark hair that hung halfway down her back, sky-blue eyes and a trim, athletic figure. Her gaze was direct, her stance assured, and her neck long and elegant, although he doubted hers sported a hook on the back. But she looked a lot like Maggie. A lot like eight other pictures stapled to case files.

He did the math in his head, realizing she was the same age as Maggie, too.

Various scenarios ran through his head, and he wasn't happy with any of them. It seemed pretty doubtful that Jeff Hoffmeier's name would come up in connection with a rape case, and his sister just *happened* to look like the victims. But what sort of deranged personality raped women who resembled his little sister? What would the motivation be? Some misplaced revenge for a sibling rivalry? An inappropriate attachment? Both?

"What?" she asked, sounding amused. "We know each other?"

"No," he said, his voice not quite right. "But I think there's someone in common we both know."

"Oh, yeah?" she asked, just as Frederik stepped forward and grabbed her arm. "Who's that?"

"Maggie Delacorte," he said, taking a chance and wishing he'd done more background on Claudia.

The smile instantly dropped off her face, and she stumbled, though he couldn't be sure if it was his question or her father yanking her away.

"Uh, sorry, no," she said, shaking her head. "I don't think so."

"Does Jeffrey know her?" he asked, getting louder and following as Frederik dragged Claudia toward the plane.

Lorraine moved more slowly, looking between them.

"I don't like this line of questioning, son," Frederik said, spinning and holding his hand up.

"Dad," Claudia said. "It's fine. Who are you, exactly?"

"Grant Larkin, FBI."

Her forehead furrowed as she studied him for a moment, and then she reached into a purse that probably cost more than he made in a month and handed him a card. "I have no idea if Jeffrey knows this woman, but I doubt it. He's lived abroad a long time. But whatever this is about, we're happy to help."

She tapped the card he was holding, and he finally glanced down at it. Claudia Hoffmeier, Attorney-at-Law, General Counsel for Hoffmeier Financial.

"Go ahead, Dad," she said, ushering him toward the jet, then looking back at Grant. "You have questions, feel free to give me a call, Mr. Larkin."

Then she and her parents boarded the plane, and Grant moved back, heading numbly toward his own vehicle, still staring at the card and pondering Claudia Hoffmeier's reaction.

Did she recognize Maggie's name? Did her parents know their son had done something they should be worried about? *Was* Jeffrey really living abroad?

Putting the card away, Grant doubled his speed. He needed to go to the office, call the number Lorraine had provided for Jeffrey and see if he could get a lead on where it pinged to, and check out the entire Hoffmeier family.

GRANT CURSED AS he hung up his cell phone, wishing he was using a landline he could slam down, maybe a few times. "Out of service," he told Kammy.

She looked unsurprised as she nodded at him from across the conference table at the WFO.

He'd called her back there after visiting the Hoffmeiers, and he could tell she'd been planning to make it an early night, just like him. She'd swapped the suit she seemed to own in every shade of black, blue and gray for linen pants and a T-shirt, and scrubbed her face clean of makeup. It should have made her seem more approachable, but somehow she still looked every bit the harddriving FBI supervisor.

"You think Lorraine Hoffmeier gave you a dead number on purpose?" Kammy asked.

"I don't know. When I asked about Jeff coming back to visit in September, she gave me this look that said she knew I was alluding to something, but she didn't know what. The father and sister, on the other hand…"

"You think they're knowingly covering up for a serial rapist? That would make them accessories. If she's a lawyer—"

"I think they suspect. And I think they're trying to distance themselves from him, protect their family name.

It's why I was hoping they'd cooperate, so if it *does* turn out to be him, they'll look like they have clean hands."

Kammy braced her elbows on the table and leaned forward. "Let me ask you a question, Grant. Something here stinks, that's for sure, but we've only really connected Jeff Hoffmeier to Shana Mills. What if she's the only victim? Maybe the family found out and suggested he take to backpacking in Europe."

Grant swallowed his instant reaction, which was to argue, and thought about it. "Well, assuming we're talking first-degree sexual assault, statute of limitations in DC generally runs out after fifteen years. But he didn't leave right after Shana's attack. He left DC ten years ago, after Maggie's."

"Maybe the family found out later?"

"It's possible, but that's some coincidental timing."

"Unless he really is in Europe. In which case, he's not a possibility at all. If he's here, he's stayed way below the radar. You think the family's supplying him with wads of cash? He'd have to stick to places that weren't running credit checks. That means no house rentals, nothing. You think a kid with his background is living that low to ground?"

"Or the family money supplied him with forged documents," Grant suggested, then he did pound his fist on the table. "I should have pushed harder, not let them get on that plane."

"We had no reason to compel them to stay," Kammy reminded him. "And the sister is a lawyer, so she knew that, even if the parents didn't."

"Oh, Frederik Hoffmeier knew. That's the other thing. He handed me a business card, tried to kick me off the airfield as soon as I showed up. Had no interest in even hearing what case I was investigating."

"He owns a big, successful business," Kammy said. "I'm not sure that's a smoking gun. This guy has been investigated before."

"Yeah, I know," Grant said. "Securities fraud. It might not have stuck, but you'd think going through an investigation again would worry him. You'd think he'd want to at least *pretend* to cooperate. Besides, even after I told him it was family-related, he didn't want to talk to me."

"Again, that's not a cry of guilt. You're suggesting that this man knows—or at least suspects—his son has abducted, raped and branded nine women in the past decade. That's some pretty strong family loyalty."

"I've seen it before," Grant said. "I'm sure you have, too."

She sighed and nodded. "Yeah. But for something this serious and long-running? I'd say he'd be the exception. And what about the sister? An intelligent, high-powered lawyer who's willing to keep her brother's sick secret? Especially when it involves him attacking other women, ones who look like her?"

"A high-powered lawyer who works for the family business," Grant reminded her. "A thirty-two-year-old woman who reacted when I said Maggie's name."

"Who reacted when you said my name?"

Grant looked toward the door of the conference room as Maggie strode in, wearing the gray dress pants and short-sleeved blouse she'd shown up in at his house. But his mind instantly flashed to how he'd seen her last: stretched out in his bed in nothing but a dark blue bra and panties. Her hair haloed out behind her on the bed, her lips swollen from kissing him.

Maggie flushed, and he realized his thoughts must have been showing, so he quickly looked away, before Kammy saw, too.

Kammy glanced back at him suspiciously, but Grant fiddled with the file in front of him until he was sure he had control of his emotions, then he looked up, all business, and told Maggie, "Claudia Hoffmeier."

The very next call he'd made after talking to Kammy on his drive over to WFO had been to Maggie. She'd still been waiting at his house, and he'd fought the instinct to call Kammy off and just go home to Maggie. The idea was so appealing, even the thought of her waiting in his house made his body heat up.

But the case was too important, and he was onto something with Jeff Hoffmeier. He was sure of it.

Maggie frowned as she walked around the long table and sat down next to him. "The name doesn't sound familiar."

Grant reached for Kammy's open laptop and turned it toward Maggie. "This is her." The picture was from the Hoffmeier corporate website, and for the millionth time that night, Grant wished he'd looked it up on his phone on the drive over to the airport.

Maggie studied Claudia's photo, either not noticing or not commenting on the similarities between them. Finally, she shook her head. "I don't recognize her. What's the connection?"

"She's your age. And look at her bio. She went to your college at the same time you were there."

"So did thousands of other students. She said she knew me?"

"She claimed she *didn't* know you. But she definitely reacted when I said your name. And it hasn't been in the papers, so there's no reason for her to recognize it."

"And you think, what?" Maggie asked. "That she knows her brother is the Fishhook Rapist?"

"I think she suspects," Grant said, just as Kammy mused, "The Fishhook Rapist."

"What?" Grant glanced over at her.

Kammy dug through the file in front of her, then set the picture of Jeffrey Hoffmeier on the table. "How does a rich kid get a name like that?"

Maggie paled a little, but she said, "You mean why the brand of a hook?"

"Exactly," Kammy said, clearly uncomfortable as she stared back at Maggie. "What connection does he have to the fishing industry?"

"Maybe it's random," Maggie suggested. "Something to throw investigators off track?"

"No," Kammy said adamantly. "The profiler we had look at this a few years back said this hook is his signature. You know what that means, right?"

"It's the thing he's compelled to do. It matters to him," Maggie replied, her tone professional, as though it wasn't her own case they were discussing. "So it must mean something. There has to be a connection. You're right." She looked questioningly at Grant.

He frowned. "We can search for a connection, but I think we should put our resources into finding this guy. Let's talk to Interpol."

"We need more than your gut to get Interpol involved," Kammy said.

"Okay, fine. I don't think he's in Europe, anyway. I think he's here."

"And what if you're wrong?"

The question came from Kammy, but Grant looked at Maggie. If this were any other case, he'd push to follow his instincts, but it wasn't any other case. For him, this one was all about Maggie. And he'd never be able to forgive himself if they let the Fishhook Rapist slip through their fingers because they were following his stubborn lead on the wrong guy.

"What if I tried calling Claudia?" Maggie suggested.

"She's on a flight to Florida," Grant reminded her.

"Yeah, but it's a private plane. She could have her cell phone on."

"What are you hoping to gain from that?" Kammy asked.

"Shock value. See if we can figure out how she knows me."

"She's a lawyer," Kammy reminded her. "I don't think—"

"A lawyer," Maggie repeated, looking pensive.

"What is it?" Grant asked.

"See if you can find a picture of her from college."

"I'll try," Grant said, dragging the laptop toward him again and starting a search.

"I took a prelaw class right before my senior year. There was a girl in my class—I can't remember her name—but we did a project together. We weren't friends or anything, so I don't remember a lot about her, but I do recall we did well on that project. She suggested I could intern at her family's company—that I should apply once I finished my undergrad degree. It was so long ago, and after…what happened…I decided not to go to law school, anyway, so I totally forgot about it."

Maggie had once planned to go to law school? Grant glanced sideways at her, surprised. He knew her decision to join the FBI had come because of her assault, but he couldn't imagine her doing anything else. She was such a natural on the SWAT missions, and he assumed she ran case investigations with the same intense, focused tenacity.

"You think this girl was Claudia?" Kammy asked. "Did you ever meet her brother?"

"It's possible it was Claudia." Maggie shook her head. "I just don't remember. It was only a weeklong project. And it was ten years ago. It was the very end of the summer semester and I didn't end up taking more prelaw classes my senior year, so she fell off my radar. But as for meeting her brother? If I did, it wasn't through her. We never talked outside of class. I was surprised when she mentioned the internship thing."

"So you never interviewed for it?" Kammy pushed.

"No."

"I've got her," Grant said, turning the computer so Maggie could see the grainy yearbook image. It was amazing what you could find on the internet.

He pointed to the girl at the end of the dorm picture. "That's Claudia, from ten years ago."

Maggie squinted at it, her teeth catching her bottom lip, and Grant forced himself to stop staring before Kammy suspected there was something between them— if she didn't already.

"Is that her?" Kammy pushed.

"It could be," Maggie said slowly, not sounding certain. "This picture looks sort of familiar."

"What about the company? Hoffmeier Financial?" Grant asked.

"Hoffmeier Financial? That's what their family business is called?" Maggie's eyes drifted upward, and he could tell she was trying to remember. "You know, it might be her, then. I remember the company didn't sound like a typical law firm, so I asked about it, and she said it wasn't a law firm at all. But she said they had a lawyer on staff, and that she had the position lined up as soon as she graduated."

Grant nodded at Kammy. "Claudia has been working for her father's company since she graduated from law school."

"What about Jeff?" Kammy asked. "They promised Claudia their general counsel position, but nothing for him?"

"Well, he obviously hasn't worked there in the past decade," Grant answered. "Before that, I don't know. He would have been twenty-eight a decade ago, so it's possible he worked for the company before he left for Europe, assuming that's what he did."

"And if he didn't actually go to Europe, maybe he quit when he dropped off the map a decade ago." Kammy nodded. "It's worth checking out."

"When exactly did he disappear?" Maggie asked, her hands clutched too tightly in her lap.

"December is the last time his name shows up on ownership documents," Grant said, "So a few months afterward."

"What did he own?" Kammy asked. "A house?"

"An apartment."

"Not a likely spot to bring his victims, then," she concluded.

"What about the parents' house?" Grant suggested.

"That would be risky," Kammy said. "But worth looking into, I suppose. Maybe they were away. Let's dig deeper on Jeff and see what we can find."

"Thanks for coming back in," Maggie said softly.

"Whoever it is, we're catching him. And if it is Jeff, and his family knew, I don't care how connected they are. We'll make sure they pay for it, too."

Grant nodded at Kammy, pleased by the intensity in her voice. "Let's get to it." He tried to sound confident, but he'd already spent time hunting for Jeff and hadn't come up with any solid leads.

Praying tonight they'd find the break they needed, he told them, "I'll check into his connection to the company."

An hour later, he stared at what he'd found, surprised. "Jeff *did* work for Hoffmeier Financial. He went to college out of state—where he apparently spent most of his time partying—and then moved back and started working for his dad. I've got some buried arrests from that time period, and from when he was at school. Apparently Dad kept having to bail him out of trouble."

"What kind of arrests?" Maggie asked.

"A couple of DUIs, some resisting arrest and assaulting a police officer charges related to cops breaking up a party at his college fraternity house back in Palo Alto when he was still a student. Plus a handful of other charges, mostly minor stuff, but a few assault charges that got pushed under the rug once he moved back to DC after he graduated. Not sexual," he clarified. "Mostly seems to be him getting into bar fights."

"So what happened? Why did he leave the family business?" Kammy asked.

"It seems that Frederik Hoffmeier got sick of his son's work ethic and kicked him out of the company."

"What was his position while he was there?" Maggie wondered.

"Vice President," Grant replied. At her raised eyebrows, he added, "Hoffmeier Financial had three back then, and from what I can tell, Jeff's was mostly in name only."

"So he got kicked out of the family business and left DC," Kammy summed up.

"No," Grant said, "He got kicked out of the family

business, and hung out in DC for another year, dating college girls and blowing through his trust fund."

"What's that?" Maggie said just as he was about to tell them more about Jeff's wastrel lifestyle.

"What?" Grant asked, glancing at her.

Her whole face had tightened as she leaned toward his computer.

"I found an old archived image of the Hoffmeier website, listing executives."

"In the corner," Maggie said, her voice as tense as her expression.

Grant leaned closer, too. "The logo. That's weird," he realized. "It looks like the current logo was cut in half from this original one." He clicked to enlarge it and then felt his jaw drop.

"It's him," Maggie choked out.

"How do you know?" Kammy asked, standing up and moving behind them to see the screen.

Grant pointed. The current Hoffmeier Financial logo resembled the top half of a family crest, but the original logo had been the entire thing. And the bottom half of the crest contained three distinct fishing hooks.

Chapter Twelve

Maggie glanced around her at the near-empty WFO office and then opened the picture of Jeff Hoffmeier on her computer screen. Except for the initial reaction she'd had to him, she still didn't recognize him.

Yet for her, the hooks on the family crest—and Hoffmeier Financial's sudden logo change about a decade ago—cinched it. Jeff had to be the Fishhook Rapist.

Kammy and Grant were theorizing that he might have actually used something with the family crest on it to make the brand. On her own, Maggie had told Ella about it, and she agreed, saying it was a good bet Jeff had used the crest because he harbored hatred toward his family for cutting him out of the business.

From an investigative perspective, the fishhooks had led them off track, because the FBI had long theorized the rapist was in the fishing industry. The reality was that the Hoffmeier family *had* been in fishing—but centuries ago, back in Germany.

From a psychological perspective, Ella had told Maggie that Jeff had probably used the hook as a way to try to implicate his family. Not that he was trying to get himself—or them—caught, but that he got a sick thrill out of branding something so intimately connected to the family that had rejected him onto the women he was trying to mark with a type of ownership.

Ella had also been the one to point out that Jeff's firing from the company business had happened only two years after Shana Mills's attack. He'd gotten away with that assault, giving him the confidence that he could do it again, and a plan had started to form in his mind. At least that was Ella's theory.

She'd continued to profile that he probably particularly resented his brunette, blue-eyed sister, for getting the place he thought he deserved as the firstborn son. That, too, would have happened within a year of Jeff's being pushed out.

So Maggie already fit his "type." She looked like both Shana Mills and Claudia Hoffmeier—the two women he simultaneously loved and hated, in different ways. And the rest of the known Fishhook Rapist victims fit, too. But Ella thought Jeff might have targeted her specifically because he learned his sister had offered her a job at the company that wanted nothing to do with him.

It made her sick just thinking about it, especially if Claudia knew—or suspected—what he'd done to her afterward, and said nothing. And there was a good chance she had, since the Hoffmeiers had cut the family crest in half, using only the top part for their company logo, after he'd begun his attacks.

Grant and Kammy had been back to talk to Shana Mills, to see if she had any idea where Jeff might be, and to get more insight into that relationship. Grant had returned from the visit convinced that Shana had been his first rape victim, and that he'd gotten power out of the fact that drugging her prevented her from realizing it was him. He hadn't told Maggie that; she'd overheard it.

It had instantly made her think about what else she

knew about Shana and Jeff's relationship: that they'd dated again after Shana's rape. Maggie's whole body chilled at the idea that Shana hadn't realized she was going out with the same man who'd hurt her.

It was bad enough that Jeffrey Hoffmeier was a rapist, but what kind of sociopath dated the woman he'd assaulted, secretly feeling empowered because she didn't know? The answer was the kind of sociopath she wanted behind bars for the rest of his sorry life.

But when she'd pushed to find out everything else Grant and Kammy knew, she'd learned that with only three days left until September 1, it wasn't enough. It wasn't anywhere near enough.

Staring at Jeff's picture all the time wasn't telling her anything new, either. Because just like Shana, she didn't remember the person who'd hurt her. And it wasn't doing her any good obsessively staring at him, hoping a memory would surface. The reality was that even if one did, it probably wouldn't help them find him now.

Closing the image, Maggie shut down her computer and headed for the conference room. It had become her last stop of the day. Sometimes the whole team working the case was there, but often Maggie stayed late, waiting until everyone had gone home except Kammy and Grant, who were working later and later each night as the deadline drew closer.

Her own supervisor had already approached her and told her that in two days, if they didn't have Jeff under arrest, they were putting her in protective custody. Even though she was officially off the team, she still felt like a SWAT agent, and she hated the idea of needing protection. But she wasn't about to turn it down.

Before she reached the conference room, Maggie's phone rang. Halting midstride, she checked the readout, then turned the other way, down the hall where the coffeepot was situated, for a little privacy from the few remaining agents in the bullpen. It was the investigator from OPR.

"Hello," she answered, hearing her nerves come through in the single word.

"Agent Delacorte, this is John from OPR. I'm sorry to call you in the evening."

"That's okay. I'm still at the office," she said, trying to calm her voice. OPR calling her meant they'd made a decision about the incident that had caused her to leave SWAT.

"I wanted you to know that we came to a decision. The incident will go in your personnel file," he began, but she'd expected that.

It was the least of her worries.

When she didn't say anything, just waited, her breath stalled, he continued, "Your teammates think very highly of you. Every one of them spoke up on your behalf."

Her eyes got watery at the idea that all the guys still wanted to work with her, that they still trusted her in a firefight after she'd frozen at such a critical moment. That included Grant, even though he was the one who'd paid for her error, but she realized that part didn't surprise her. Grant always stood by her.

The thought stuck with her even as John continued, "Until the investigation into the Fishhook Rapist is concluded, you're to stay on only your civil rights squad duties. However, after that time, you're free to rejoin SWAT."

They'd cleared her.

Maggie gasped, then stuttered, "Th-thank you."

"Don't thank me," John said. "Thank your teammates. They were very convincing that you're an asset to SWAT.

Between them and your excellent record there over the past four years, we agree."

Relief washed over Maggie stronger than she'd expected as John hung up, and she doubled over with the knowledge that she hadn't let the Fishhook case destroy her SWAT career.

It didn't mean she'd be going back, though. When the Fishhook case was over, there was going to be another stumbling block: Grant.

She had no idea how to define their relationship, but there was no question they had one that went beyond the scope of teammates. She wasn't willing to give up whatever was developing between them, which meant one of them would have to leave SWAT.

Maybe a spot would eventually open up on another team, but it was rare. And it wouldn't be the same. Her SWAT team had become like family.

The very idea of leaving left a knot in her chest, but Maggie straightened, vowing to worry about it later. Right now, she needed to find out the status of the case.

She hurried through the bullpen, past the only two agents still cloistered in their cubicles, and into the conference room. The room was an organized mess. The files and documents covering every surface seemed to have tripled in the past week as they tried to hunt down Jeff Hoffmeier.

Grant and Kammy sat in their usual seats at the far end of the room, and both looked up at her with bloodshot eyes as she entered.

"What happened?" Grant asked, standing.

"Nothing. I just heard back from OPR."

"I'll give you a minute," Kammy said, getting tiredly to her feet. When Maggie started to protest, she added, "I need caffeine, anyway, or I'll be down for the count."

She headed out the door, closing it behind her, and Grant was instantly at Maggie's side. "How did it go?"

"They told me you spoke for me."

"Of course."

"You're not worried—"

"What?" Grant cut her off. "That you'll have another flashback to a memory you didn't even know you had, when responding to a SWAT call? What are the chances of that? Probably as slim as my MP-5 misfiring."

"That could happen," Maggie said.

"Exactly. Or Clive could have a heart attack on a call. But the chances are much higher that none of those things will happen, so why lose one of the best members of the team?"

"You think I'm one of the best members on the team?"

"And the cutest," he teased, then got serious. "I do, but it was Clive who told OPR that part."

Wow. Her team leader thought she was one of his best agents? That was high praise from Clive. "Well, it's official, but I'm not sure what I'll do. You know, with everything between us…"

She stopped as Kammy came back in the room, practically gulping from a coffee mug.

"We'll figure it out," Grant said, pressing his hand against her upper arm before he returned to his seat.

Maggie followed more slowly, more torn than ever. She'd felt vindicated to hear she was still on the team, then conflicted because of Grant, and now even more conflicted hearing how her teammates viewed her. She couldn't deny whatever was happening with her and Grant. If they were going to be serious, one of them had to leave the team. She'd been there for four years, so it seemed only fair that it be his turn on SWAT now. But how could she leave the team after their vote of support?

Pushing the worry to the back of her mind, Maggie focused on the more immediate problem. "Do you have anything new?"

"A new reason September 1 is Jeffrey Hoffmeier's date of choice," Kammy said.

"What do you mean?"

Kammy gestured to Grant, and he said, "I kept digging for old information about Jeffrey from eleven years ago, when his family pushed him out of the company, and I found a press release. It announced that Jeffrey was leaving the company as VP and named some other guy who was taking his place. It was dated September 1."

She felt a wave of hot anger, "So he's using part of the crest to punish them, and that—plus Shana Mills's attack—is why he picked September 1? Because it's a date that ties to both Shana and Claudia and his family?"

"Looks like it," Grant said.

"Have you been able to track him?"

"Well, we've confirmed that he had a pretty sizable trust fund, although what happened to it all is questionable," Kammy said. "We think at least some of the money went into foreign banks and was hidden under shell companies. We've got some of our White Collar agents digging around, but they're not likely to be able to untangle that mess in the next three days."

"Claudia Hoffmeier isn't answering at the number she gave us, and neither are her parents," Grant said, clearly frustrated. "And we're trying to get some warrants to get the family property information—whatever we can't dig up on our own—but it's not happening."

Maggie nodded, angry but unsurprised. She was sure it was Jeff Hoffmeier now, but what did they have, evidence-wise, really? A lot of conjecture, some suspicious timing and a family crest with an element that, while it wasn't typical, definitely wasn't unique to the Hoffmeiers.

"What about the property we do know about?" Maggie asked. "He must be in DC at this point."

How close had he gotten to her? Maggie shuddered, thankful Grant was looking at Kammy and didn't notice.

Kammy set her empty coffee mug down, seeming significantly more awake. "The Hoffmeiers have a house in the city, and another in horse country in Virginia. Claudia has one here and an apartment in Maryland, where her boyfriend lives. Beyond that, we don't know, but we've already found a couple of shell companies with Frederik's name on them, so we're digging deeper there."

"But even if you find something, you can't get on the property," Maggie summed up.

Grant glanced at her, and the expression on his face told her that if the deadline hit and they hadn't caught the guy, procedure was going right out the window.

She started to shake her head at him, then realized there was no way he'd be kicking down doors on September 1, because he'd be wherever *she* was, standing beside her. Or, really, knowing Grant, he'd be standing in front of her, wearing Kevlar and holding a Glock.

A smile quivered on her lips, and he looked back at her questioningly, but she didn't get a chance to say anything, because her phone rang again.

She glanced at the readout and rolled her eyes. "Scott," she told them. "I'm running late. He probably expected me at the house two minutes ago and is panicking."

She stood and hurried out of the conference room to answer, not wanting to distract them any more than she already was by constantly seeking out updates. "Hey, Scott, I'll be leaving the office in a few minutes, I promise. I just—"

"Don't leave," Scott said, panic in his voice that made fear creep along her nerve endings.

"What's wrong?"

"I'm not at your house," Scott said, and it was so obvious he was trying not to worry her that it was making it worse.

"Why not? What happened?"

"There was a break-in at my house," Scott said, and his voice got choked up as he finished, "Chelsie was shot."

Shock made her go rigid, then pain seemed to explode in her chest. Her voice came out too high when she asked, "Is she okay?"

"I'm driving to the hospital right now. I'll call you with an update. All I know so far is that she's in surgery."

Maggie ran over to her cubicle and grabbed her purse. "I'm on my way to meet you."

"No," Scott replied. "Call Ella. Ask her to come over tonight and stay with you, okay?"

"Scott, I want to—"

"I can't stay with you every second at the hospital, Maggie. And that place is busy. I don't want someone coming in with a weapon and walking you out of there—"

"It's not September 1," Maggie reminded him. "That date *matters* to him. A lot. How would he even know about Chelsie, anyway?" Her legs wobbled and she sank onto her chair. "Did—"

"It's not him. They got a description from my neighbor, who happened to be out running at the time." Scott lived quite a distance from his closest neighbor, out in the country in Virginia. "The person who broke in was black. Not this Hoffmeier guy."

"Is it connected to what happened a few months ago?" Maggie asked. Chelsie had been targeted by some men with major resources, and Scott had been shot in that house protecting her. But she'd thought that nightmare was over.

"No. Local police called me, and they're pretty sure they know who it is. It looks like he was after money. He's a known druggie, and this isn't his first offense of this type."

"So let me come—"

"No," Scott said, his tone harsh and final. Then he said more calmly, "Please don't make me worry about you, too. I know my hospital scenario is me being overly paranoid, but humor me. Just call Ella. Promise me you won't go anywhere until you hear from her, and I'll let you know when Chelsie's out of surgery."

She heard Scott's tires squeal and then his car door slam and realized he must have arrived at the hospital.

"Okay," she promised. "Please call me when you know anything."

"I will," Scott said and hung up.

Maggie's hands shook as she did the same, then immediately dialed Ella. It went straight to voice mail, so she left a message telling Ella to call her, then walked slowly back to the conference room.

Grant lurched to his feet. "What happened?"

"There was a break-in at my brother's house. Chelsie was shot."

"Is she okay?" Grant reached for the holster he'd set on the cabinet behind him. "You need me to drive you to the hospital?"

Beside him, sympathy and frustration warred on Kammy's face.

"She's in surgery," Maggie said, walking to the end of the table and taking a seat. "Scott's going to call me when he knows anything. But I'm going to stay here until I hear from Ella."

"Good idea." Grant, who knew about Scott's and Ella's

determination not to let her out of their sight unless she was with other FBI agents, nodded approvingly. Then, ignoring Kammy, he slung an arm around her shoulders and gave her a hug. "Chelsie's almost as stubborn and strong as you are. She'll be okay."

"I hope so," Maggie said, then straightened, determined to distract herself. "I don't suppose anything new came up while I was on the call?"

"Actually," Grant surprised her, "I was running down a hunch, and I did find something."

"It's good," Kammy said, leaning toward them. "This might be enough to get us a warrant on the properties, if we follow the trail far enough."

"Or maybe some new places to look," Grant suggested. Maggie's heart rate spiked. "What is it?"

"Since we weren't having any luck with Jeff's name showing up in any of the cities where the attacks occurred, I started checking into other family members." He leaned back in his seat, looking proud. "I got a hit. Another name that showed up in every city, at all the right times."

Shock pulsed through her. Had they been wrong? Had she been unable to recognize Jeff Hoffmeier because it wasn't actually him? Had her reaction to his picture been because he resembled the actual perpetrator, some other member of his family?

"Who is it?" Maggie choked out.

"Jeff's cousin. Different last name, which is why Hoffmeier didn't come up for us."

"What's his name?" Maggie asked. "Do you have a picture?"

"Yeah." Grant typed away on his computer, then turned it around.

A picture labeled Jasper Grimes filled the screen, and

he looked a lot like Jeff Hoffmeier. Slightly more angular features, bigger nose, not quite the same bright blue eyes. But close enough that it would explain her reaction to Jeff. Except...

She looked over at Grant. "I don't recognize him."

"No." Grant shook his head. "It's not him. Sorry, I should have been more clear. Jasper Grimes was in a car accident eleven years ago. He was badly injured. He made it through, but with severe brain trauma. He'd been living in a medical facility in Maryland ever since. It's not him using that ID."

"It's Jeff," Maggie realized. "He hasn't been in Europe. He's just been using his cousin's ID to stay under the radar."

"Exactly," Grant said. "Credit checks were fine, because Jasper's still alive—his ID is still good. And Jeff looks similar enough. So that's why we see Jeff popping up randomly in the states every few years. He uses his own ID to access his trust fund in some in-between state where there's no connection to the Fishhook cases, then keeps traveling and goes back to Jasper's ID."

"So," Maggie asked the most important question, "does Jasper Grimes own property in DC?"

"Let's find out," Grant said.

He and Kammy started searching, while Maggie tried not to think about how Chelsie was doing.

Finally, Grant sighed and glanced over at Kammy, who shook her head.

"Either he's not using Jasper's name here, or he's buried it under one of his dad's shell corporations. I can't find him."

Maggie tried not to feel discouraged. The information could still lead them to him. She had to think positive.

But all she could think of was the anniversary looming

over her. Three days from now, she wouldn't be gathered with Scott and Ella, praying no other victim would show up in the news reports.

She'd be surrounded by federal agents, in some undisclosed location, under protective custody.

If Jeff Hoffmeier couldn't find her, who would he go after instead? And how would she ever forgive herself when she heard that name?

Chapter Thirteen

"Come home with me."

Grant's request was met with silence from Maggie, as she stared up at him, seeming to only half comprehend.

They were still at the WFO, an hour after Kammy had gone home. An hour after the rest of the office had completely emptied out. Grant had promised himself he'd wait until she heard back from Scott about Chelsie before suggesting it, but it wasn't doing either of them any good being at the WFO.

The office was dark except for the conference room, which looked as though a tornado had hit it, dropping Fishhook Rapist detritus everywhere in its wake. Not exactly what Maggie needed to be surrounded by while she waited to hear the status of her friend's condition.

And although Grant was still searching for leads on the Jasper Grimes ID, he was heading rapidly for a wall of exhaustion, and he knew it.

"What about—" Maggie started, but jumped when her phone rang. She grabbed it, stress in her voice as she answered. "Scott? How is she?"

Grant tapped her arm, and Maggie hit speaker.

"She made it out of surgery." Scott's weary voice came over the speaker sounding tinny and far away.

"Thank goodness," Maggie said.

"There were no complications. The bullet went straight through, so she lost a lot of blood, but it didn't nick anything vital on its way. She got lucky."

As lucky as anyone who got shot could be, Grant thought, taking Maggie's hand in his.

She gave him a shaky smile, her eyes watery, then looked back at the phone. "She's going to be okay?"

"Yeah," Scott said. "But I'm staying with her here overnight. Not exactly protocol, but the FBI credentials are good for something."

"Good," Maggie said. "Did they catch the guy who did it?"

"Not yet." Scott's voice was instantly hard and angry. "But the police chief stopped by the hospital personally, and he tells me they're running down all of this guy's haunts. He's supposed to call me as soon as they have him in custody."

"Okay," Maggie said. "Let me know. And tell Chelsie I'm thinking about her, when she wakes up."

"I will," Scott said. "Am I on speaker? Is Ella there?"

"Uh, no," Maggie said. "I'm still at WFO. I called the BAU office and was told Ella's in a late meeting, so I'm waiting until she gets out to go anywhere."

"Do you need me to—" Scott started.

"No," Grant said. "I'm here with Maggie. If we don't hear from Ella soon, Maggie can come back to my house. I won't leave her alone."

"Thanks, man," Scott said, relief obvious in his voice. "Call me if you need anything."

"Don't worry," Maggie said, squeezing Grant's hand. "Just focus on Chelsie."

She hung up the phone and turned toward him. "Let me try Ella one more time."

He nodded at her, taking in the tension of her jaw, the

deep shadows under her eyes that hadn't been there six months ago. He stroked his fingers over hers, silently praying that they'd catch Hoffmeier and end this all for good.

He missed the light that used to come into her eyes when they did SWAT training, the easy way she'd joke with them at O'Reilley's after a call. He hated watching this weigh on her, and ten years was far too long.

Worry filled him, the fear that even having identified Hoffmeier, they wouldn't be able to catch the guy. He realized after a moment that he'd squeezed Maggie's hand even tighter.

She looked questioningly at him, and he lifted her hand to his lips, pressing a kiss on her knuckles that made a smile lift her face and a little of that light he loved come into her eyes.

"Go ahead and call Ella," he said, instead of telling her what was on his mind. "See if her meeting is over."

She dialed, then shook her head a minute later, looking frustrated as she set her phone down. "She's still not picking up." Nerves strained her voice when she said, "Do you think something's wrong?"

"I think her meeting is going late. Or maybe the profiler you called forgot to give her the message. She thought Scott was with you, right? She was planning to just go home. Maybe she's there, and she's got her phone in the other room or something, and can't hear it."

"Yeah, but maybe I should call Logan. Just to make sure." She checked her watch, then looked at Grant. "He's at work now. I didn't realize it was so late. You're probably exhausted."

He was, but that didn't matter. "I'm fine. Come on." He stood, pulling her up with him. "You can just as easily call Ella again from my house."

He'd expected her to drop his hand, but instead, she turned it and threaded her fingers through his as she tucked her phone in her pocket. "Okay. Getting out of here—" she gestured around her at the case information "—sounds really good."

"Let's go," he said, heading for the conference room door, their linked hands swinging between them making him ridiculously happy even with everything that was happening.

They'd almost reached the parking garage when Maggie's cell phone rang. She whipped it out of her pocket. "Ella," she said, pressing the phone to her ear.

Then she ground to a sudden halt. Her face went unnaturally pale as a stream of what sounded like gibberish to Grant burst from her phone.

"What is it?" he asked, wrapping an arm around her shoulders in case she was going to fall.

She held up her hand, listening to whatever Ella was telling her, as foreboding traveled up Grant's spine, raising goose bumps along the way.

"No, no," she finally spoke into the phone. "Scott's at the hospital with Chelsie. Break-in at their house. Chelsie's okay." There was a pause, then she sobbed, "I'm so sorry."

He watched her trying to get it together as Ella said something else, then Maggie assured her, "I'm with Grant at WFO. I won't leave his side. We've got three days. We know September 1 is too important to him, and the FBI is putting me in protective custody the day before. Go. Check on Logan. Call me when you know."

"What happened?" Grant asked as soon as she hung up.

Maggie's voice was barely above a whisper as she told him, "Ella is on her way to the hospital. Logan and his partner were called to the scene of a crime, where they were ambushed. Logan was hit." A sob escaped as she said, "They don't know if he's going to make it."

"This isn't random," Grant realized.

"It's my fault," she sobbed, and before Grant could argue, she finished, "It's the Fishhook Rapist, trying to take away the people who've always been beside me, so I'll be isolated. So I'll be all alone when he comes back for me in three…" She glanced at her phone, and he saw that it had just hit midnight. "Make that two days."

Chapter Fourteen

Maggie crossed her hands over her chest, a stubborn tilt to her chin Grant recognized from SWAT calls. "I'm not putting you in danger, too."

"Well, I'm not leaving you alone," Grant said, "and you know it. Would you feel better if I called the rest of the team? We can all camp out at my house. Or we can get the FBI to start the protective custody now."

"No," she responded instantly, standing her ground at the dark entrance to the WFO parking garage, where she'd halted as soon as she realized what Ella's call meant. "I'm not going into hiding, not with Logan and Chelsie in the hospital. Scott or Ella might need me."

"There's nothing you can do for them right now," Grant said, but he knew that trying to make her go anywhere while her brother and best friend were in trouble wasn't going to happen. Especially not when she was this angry.

At least she was furious and not terrified. Or at least, that's what she was letting him see.

"I've got two days until he comes for me," Maggie reminded him.

"I'm not sure we can count on that," Grant said. "Maybe he anticipated the FBI putting a detail on you, and he's trying to strike early. Why would he go after

Logan and Chelsie today if he wasn't coming after you for another two days?"

"They were both shot," Maggie burst out. "They'll be in the hospital at least that long. And it's the psychology of it. He's been playing mind games with me for months, with those sick letters. This is more of it. He's drawing everyone I love away from me, and I'm not letting you put yourself in harm's way, too."

"You don't have a choice," Grant said softly, folding her hand into his. Her slim, pale fingers looked so small and delicate next to his bigger, darker hand.

"Ella and Scott have been beside you for ten years. They're long-term staples in your life he would obviously anticipate. But Hoffmeier doesn't know about me. And look, I think we should assume the worst, but honestly, I agree with you about the date. We know September 1 is symbolic to him. I'm not sure why he went after your friends early, but I think he's tied to the date. I think he'll wait for it. Assuming the whole thing isn't one huge mind game."

Which he wasn't going to count on, but he couldn't rule it out. He'd wondered from the very beginning how the Fishhook Rapist planned to overpower a trained FBI SWAT agent. Maybe he never planned to do that at all. Maybe he was hoping to break her from a distance.

"So then—" Maggie started.

"So nothing," Grant said. "We prepare for the worst, just in case. Let's call the rest of the team and at the very least, put them on standby."

He could tell she was in the middle of an internal debate. Finally, she conceded, "Okay, let's just text them and tell them we might need them. I don't want to call everyone out of bed on a false alarm."

"Done," Grant said. "In the meantime, we're not going

anywhere near your house. And on second thought, in case for some reason I'm on his radar, we're not going to mine. We'll go to a hotel. Even if he can find us, he won't risk getting himself caught by trying something with that many people around."

Maggie nodded slowly, her shoulders relaxing a little, but worry was still written all over her face. "That makes sense."

"Logan and Chelsie will pull through." Grant tugged her toward him until she put her arms around his back and rested her head against his chest. "You have to believe that."

"If they don't, it will be my fault."

"Bull," he said. "What happened to them was *not* your fault. And there's no way you could have predicted this. Not even Ella predicted this, and that's part of her profiling gig, figuring out what these guys will do next."

"Yeah," Maggie said, "But I should have—"

"What? Not let anyone close to you because some psycho fixated on you?" He hugged her tighter, and emotion seeped into his voice, all the worry and anger and love he was feeling right now. "Even if you'd tried, Maggie, that never would have worked. Not with Scott or Ella and not with me."

She lifted her head and told him, "Just don't get yourself shot for me again. Got it?" Her tone was lighter, as if she was trying to make a joke, but it didn't hide her concern.

"You need to stop worrying about that. It happened. It's over. And I'm fine."

As she stared up at him, looking unconvinced, she was so close, he couldn't resist. He tried to tell himself he was reassuring her as much as himself as he bent his head and brushed his lips softly over hers.

Her arms moved from his waist to his neck as she kissed him back. Unlike the previous times they'd kissed, where it quickly turned passionate and sent his libido rocketing out of control, she seemed as content as him to let their mouths linger, slow and tender.

Even after a full day in the WFO bullpen, she smelled fresh, a faintly gingery scent he associated solely with Maggie. She tasted like the best coffee he'd ever drunk, and her body fit against his with no space between them, like a puzzle piece.

When he finally eased back, the stress on her face had faded a little, and she even gave him a hesitant smile. "Let's get to that hotel."

If only circumstances were different right now, those words would have him running for the door.

She must have sensed it, because she shook her head at him, took his hand and led him into the empty parking garage.

Even though it was connected to an FBI building and there was no way Hoffmeier could have gained access, Grant's eyes swept over the open space, lingering in the dark corners, as they approached his car. Then he checked in the backseat before hustling her into the car and climbing in beside her.

"Not taking any chances," she observed, and she was glancing around the lot, too, as he put the car in gear and pulled out onto the street.

It was after midnight, but the streets were still clogged as he drove through the tourist district. He picked an expensive high-rise hotel near the Virginia border he knew had solid security, because they'd helped with the detail for a government function shortly after he'd joined the team.

Beside him, Maggie smiled approvingly as he bypassed the valet, taking a ticket and parking the car himself. They didn't have luggage, but he usually kept a duffel bag with extra clothes in the trunk, and he took the spare weaponry from his lock box and added it to the duffel.

There was no way Hoffmeier could have followed them from a nonpublic FBI building all the way to the hotel, but still, Maggie kept glancing around nervously until they'd checked in—under his name—and settled into their room on the thirtieth floor.

Grant dropped his duffel bag in the corner as Maggie sat down on the oversize chair by the floor-to-ceiling window. She kicked off her combat boots and leaned back in the chair, closing her eyes.

If it weren't for the stress radiating from her and the horrible reason they were here, this was a page out of Grant's dreams. Alone with Maggie in an absurdly decadent hotel room.

As though she could read his thoughts, her eyes opened, and she studied him. "Let me ask you something serious."

"Okay." Grant sat on the very edge of the king bed close to her, suddenly realizing it hadn't occurred to him to get a room with two beds. He hadn't even noticed it until just now.

"How can you get over what happened in that SWAT call so easily?"

"Maggie, we don't—"

"Seriously, Grant. I need to know. I mean, I'm glad it hasn't ruined things between us, believe me, but getting shot is a big deal. You just shrugged it off as though it was a blank in a training exercise."

"Well, I figure with all the crap life throws at you,

you can either choose to let it drag you down, or you can focus on the good stuff."

She leaned forward, propping her chin in her hands. "Really? And it's that easy?"

"If it's not, I hit the gym and get some sparring in. An hour in the ring kicking the heck out of a substitute—or a punching bag—also does the trick." He grinned at her.

"Now, that I can see," she said, glancing at his biceps. "So you hit the gym after that warehouse bust?"

"Nope."

She looked surprised, and maybe a little pleased, so he clarified, "Didn't need to. I meant what I said before, Maggie. You froze. It was a mistake, and an understandable one, given the situation. It was, what? Ten seconds? It just happened to be the wrong ten seconds. Honestly, I was just relieved that I got you out of the way."

She attempted a smile, but couldn't quite do it, so he added, "And then I went home and bought more stock in Kevlar."

She gave a small laugh, which he'd hoped for, and he said, "But when you asked if it was that easy? Yeah, most of the time it is. The stuff with my brothers was hard. It was so much work, every single day, trying to keep the gangs off our steps, trying to keep Ben from going to them. Not to mention just being in that house. Everything was falling apart, the rats were so bold they came out in the daytime, my mom was a mess, my dad was gone."

His shoulders tensed, remembering those days. "I spent a couple of years just mad all the time, and it got old. It probably helped with the gang stuff, and keeping my brothers in line, but it got to the point where *I* didn't like being around myself. And that's just not who I am. I'm not that pissed-off guy, angry at the world."

Maggie got up and sat beside him on the bed, leaning against him until he put his arm around her shoulder. "You do have a pretty good angry face, though," she teased.

"I do?"

"Yeah. You should see the way you glare when we go into a SWAT call. I wouldn't want to be the crook on the other side of that. This big, buff guy running toward them with an MP-5 after he's smashed the door in? No way."

"Buff, huh?"

"Like that's news," she said, nudging him. "So tell me. What happened? You got tired of being mad, so you just stopped?"

"Close enough. Things started turning around my senior year of high school. Mom got it together, got a better job. We moved somewhere a lot safer. I stopped worrying about Vinnie and Ben and started worrying about getting into college. And I just made up my mind that I might not be able to do anything about the hardships life throws at me, but I can control how I react to them."

He stopped, suddenly embarrassed. "I sound a little bit like a public service announcement, don't I?"

"Maybe a little," she joked. "But it's a good outlook. It's one of the reasons I fell for you, you know?"

His pulse picked up. "That first day I walked in to meet the SWAT team, you mean?"

She turned so he could see her clear blue eyes gazing up at him. "That's when it started." Her tone got more serious, quieter. "It's just gotten stronger."

He stared back at her, and even though he knew this was the wrong time, he couldn't help himself. "It's gotten stronger for me, too, Maggie. If I could, I'd go to the Bureau right now and tell them I can't be on your team anymore because we have a relationship that's way more than professional. If I could, I'd tell everyone I know that we'll never be able to work on the same squad again, because it would break the rules. Because I'm in love with you."

She stared at him, surprise in her eyes, and her mouth opened soundlessly.

He put his finger over her lips before she could figure out what to say. "You have other things to think about right now. I don't need you to say anything. I just wanted you to know."

She closed her eyes, as though she was working it out in her head, and he prayed he hadn't just blown it. "I realize it's too soon—"

"Shhh." She grabbed the front of his shirt and drew him toward her. She kissed him softly, twice, then leaned back to stare at him, looking so serious. Then she leaned in and pressed her lips to his once more.

Certainty flooded him in that moment. She might not feel as strongly about him, yet, but she'd already told him she'd fallen for him. He just had to give her more reasons to keep falling. And that would be easy, since he'd do anything for her.

Maybe she knew what he was thinking, because she grabbed his hand and pulled it up and around.

Realizing what she was doing, he let his hand go limp, so she could control it completely.

Her chest rose and fell faster as she placed his hand on the back of her neck, then slid her fingers down his arm until they were resting at his elbow.

He could feel the raised and puckered skin beneath his palm, but he could also feel the silky smooth skin on either side. He kept his touch light, skimming his fingers upward into the base of her hair then back down, under the edge of her blouse and back again.

She had such a soft, delicate neck, but like everything else about Maggie, there were strong muscles underneath.

Pain and anger that someone would dare do this to her flooded him, and he tried to shove it aside, because he knew it wasn't what either of them needed to focus on in this moment. Instead, he thought about what it meant for her to let him do this, and the wonder of that.

Her hand dropped off his elbow onto his knee, and she raised her head, unshed tears in her eyes as she looked at him, but with relief on her face.

He slid his hand from around the back of her neck to cup her cheek and touch his lips once more to hers, then she whispered, "I think we *are* going to have to talk to the Bureau."

It wasn't exactly a declaration of love, but it was close.

SHE WAS IN love with Grant Larkin.

She smiled and snuggled closer to him in the ridiculously huge hotel bed, feeling lighter than she had any right to feel with everything that was going on. She knew the heavy weight pressing on her would return as soon as she emerged from the dreamlike half sleep she was still in, and so she resisted wakefulness.

It wasn't hard with Grant next to her. She wasn't exactly small, but he made her feel tiny and protected. His head was barely an inch from hers on the pillow, his body seeming to somehow surround her with one hand tucked around her waist, holding her close.

Exhaustion had hit her last night so hard and fast, she'd barely gotten under the covers before falling asleep fully dressed. Apparently, Grant had shed his button-down, and the heat from his bare chest warmed her, keeping her in that sleepy haze even after she opened her eyes.

She studied his features as he slept—from the thick eyebrows, the big nose, the generous lips, to the sandpapery scruff coming in on his chin. He had a strong, hard profile, but in sleep—just like when he grinned at her in a training exercise—he didn't look intimidating.

Instead, he made her feel safe. He made her feel happy. He made her want to move forward with her life, to start a new chapter where the past no longer haunted her.

It would always be there. It had defined her for so long, in ways both good and bad. But last night, when his hands had skimmed over her neck, and all she'd felt was *Grant*, she'd realized that he was right about her. She *wasn't* broken. And she was ready for more, with him.

His eyes opened slowly, something intimate in the depths of his deep brown eyes as he smiled sleepily at her, and she knew. This was exactly how she wanted to wake up every day.

Her hands were tucked up between them, one of them clutched in his hand. She let her other hand drift down, over the bare skin of his chest, where the bruise from that bullet was just a splotch of yellow now. It was barely visible against his light brown skin. Another day or two, and it would be gone entirely.

Another day or two...

The comfortable, sleepy haze lifted, and Maggie's body tensed up. "Where'd I put my phone?"

He brought the hand resting at her waist around, and she saw he had her cell phone clutched in it. "It'd been a long day," he said, his voice rumbly with sleep. "I was worried we wouldn't hear it unless it was close."

He handed it to her, and she moved just enough to look at the readout. No missed calls. But it was earlier than she'd thought, barely 5:00 a.m. She'd only slept a few hours, and somehow she felt more rested than she had in weeks.

"I should call the hospital, check on Logan and Chelsie."

When she just stared at the phone, not moving, Grant asked, "You want me to make the call?"

"No." Chelsie was supposedly stable. And whatever Logan's status right now, Ella deserved to hear from her. "I can do it."

Before she could dial, the phone rang, startling her.

The readout just read "Private Number." Probably the hospital. "How are they?" she answered.

"They?" a voice came over the phone that locked her muscles and sent fear racing through her.

She must have looked panicked, because Grant leaned in close, propping up on one elbow and leaning down so he could hear, too.

Her hands trembled, but she turned the volume up and tilted the phone a little so he could listen.

"You mean *her*, don't you?" that voice from her nightmares continued. "Or are you talking about Logan and Chelsie? Tsk, tsk."

"What do you want, Hoffmeier?" Maggie demanded, and her voice came out stronger than she'd expected as Grant took her hand in his.

There was a pause, then he responded, "You figured that out, did you?" A hint of unease sounded in his voice, but it was gone when he said, "Too bad you didn't figure out my plan sooner, isn't it?"

"You're not going to get away with this," Maggie said, wondering how he'd even gotten her cell phone number. Was he close?

She couldn't help looking at the huge window across from the bed, behind Grant. The thick, heavy curtains were drawn, no way for Hoffmeier to get line of sight if he was across the street peering down a rifle scope.

Hoffmeier laughed, a nasty, ugly sound that seemed

to skitter over her skin, making her feel dirty. "I already have."

"What are you talking about?" she asked, her dread swelling. Had Logan died?

"You have forty minutes," he told her, his voice eerily calm and confident as he gave her an address that sounded vaguely familiar.

"His parents' country house," Grant mouthed.

"You come to me, alone," Hoffmeier said.

She wanted to laugh back at him, to scoff and call his bluff, except he sounded too confident, too certain she'd agree. And she knew, deep in her gut, that he'd found a way to win again.

"Aren't you going to ask why you'd do that?" he mocked.

Grant's jaw tightened, and Maggie could tell it was taking everything in him to stay quiet, to let Hoffmeier believe she was alone right now.

"Why?" she asked, and her voice shook.

"Because I have something you want."

There was a brief shuffling noise, then her sister's voice came over the line, high-pitched, scared and speaking at warp speed. "I'm so sorry, Maggie. I came to DC, anyway. I knocked on your door, and you weren't home and then I was on my way back to the hotel and he grabbed me. I didn't—"

"That's enough," Hoffmeier said, and Nikki was gone.

Maggie sucked in a breath that didn't seem to contain nearly enough oxygen and choked out, "Leave her alone! I'll be there, I promise. Just please don't hurt her."

"Come alone," he repeated. "I even *think* you have backup, and she's dead. *After* I give her a token on her neck to match yours."

Maggie's hand tightened around the phone, panicked

for the baby sister she'd always tried to protect from this evil. "Don't touch her," she barked, terrified that it was too late.

"Forty minutes," he reminded her, then hung up.

Chapter Fifteen

"Hang on," Grant said as Maggie leaped out of the bed, tangling in the covers and almost pitching herself to the floor.

She righted herself, tossed him her phone and ran for her boots, lacing them up fast. "Look up the address, would you? Get me directions." She checked her watch, and there was panic in her voice when she choked out, "Forty minutes! I can't make it in forty minutes, not even if I speed the whole way."

Grant pulled his shirt on, punching the address into her phone as he groped for his own shoes with his other hand. "Just wait a second, Maggie. Let's call Clive, have him get the rest of the team on the move."

"There's no time! That's the whole point. They can't gear up and get out there that fast, either. And it's in the middle of nowhere, that much I know. We have no time for a tactical plan, and he'd see them coming from a mile away. This is Nikki's life. I'm not risking it."

"Maggie," Grant pressed. "We train for this."

She strapped on her holster, then raced over to his duffel bag, unzipping it. Ignoring his comment, she asked, "You have an ankle holster? Something I can take as a backup?"

"Nothing that won't show," he said. "But I'm your backup."

"No," she answered, the way he'd known she would. She was in full-on panic mode, desperate and not thinking straight.

He yanked his shoes on, then hurried to her side and grabbed her arm, making her pause.

"Grant, I have to *go*."

"Just hang on a second, okay? You can't run right into his trap. That's going to get both you and Nikki hurt."

She froze at his words, and her arm tensed under his hold.

"It's going to be okay," he reassured her, but she shook her head.

"I don't think it is," she whispered. "I have to play by his rules. I can't let him do to Nikki what…what he did to me."

It was unspoken, but hung in the air, that it might already be too late.

"We need to treat this like a SWAT call," he said, trying to reason with her, but the truth was, they *didn't* have a lot of options. Not on that timetable, and not with the location he'd provided.

Even if they called the rest of the team, the houses—estates, really—where the Hoffmeier family had their second home was deep in Virginia horse country, where neighbors were miles apart. Worse, land there was flat enough to see for miles. The team would only be able to drive in so far, and they'd have to hoof it from there. By the time they arrived unseen, it would probably be too late.

Still, if everything fell apart, it would be good to know they were on the way.

Maggie stepped back and yanked her blouse down

over her gun, her movements jerky and panicked. "I'll call them on the way."

"Okay." He strapped on his own Glock, then took out his MP-5. He dumped out the contents of his duffel, then stuffed the gun back in, zipping it up. "But I'm going with you."

Her head swiveled toward the door and back, desperation still in her eyes, her body twitching with her obvious need to move. "You heard him—"

"I'm not a full SWAT team. It'll be easier for me to sneak in with you."

She shook her head. "I have to *go*."

"Fine. We can argue on the way," he said. "Let's move."

"WATCH THE LIGHT," Grant warned.

Instead of stopping as the light at the intersection turned from green to yellow, Maggie slapped Grant's siren on the roof of his car and flew through it. Honking and the squeal of tires filled the air, and she just pushed down on the gas, taking the corners dangerously fast.

She called on every bit of the special defensive driving training she'd taken at the FBI's training facility at Quantico as she raced through the outskirts of DC. It wasn't even 6:00 a.m. yet, but here, commuters were already out, ladder-climbers getting an early start, and political assistants prepping for the day ahead.

"You can't stay there once we get close," Maggie said, keeping her attention totally on the road, watching the sidewalks in her peripheral vision for jaywalkers.

Panic threatened, like a river about to burst through a levee. How had he gotten close enough to her house to spot Nikki? And how had no one noticed Nikki had left Indiana for DC?

Sitting beside her, Grant said, "When we're close, I'm going to get down in the backseat."

"He'll see you!"

"No, he won't," Grant replied, sounding calm. "You'll stop the car far enough away. He's not going to be looking in the backseat. To do that, he'd have to get close enough to have his back to you, and he's not stupid. He's going to make you come to him. So you leave me in the car. I'll come after you."

There was such confidence in his voice, such certainty. She'd heard it plenty of times in SWAT calls, and he'd always been able to back it up. But today was different, in so many ways.

"Maybe you should just get out before we drive close enough for him to see the car," Maggie suggested. She knew the area where Hoffmeier had called her to was nothing but open spaces and gently rolling hills. For her to stop where he couldn't see the car would be too far away for Grant to help.

"No," Grant replied. "But that's where Clive will be."

"Don't call Clive," she burst when Grant started to dial his phone. "Hoffmeier knows what I do. What if he's sending me here as a test? What if he's not there at all? I could show up and find a note on the door, sending me to some other property his parents own under that shell company. Meanwhile, he's got a camera set up there and knows I've brought backup and he kills Nikki!"

"That's really elaborate," Grant reasoned. "Most criminals think basic."

"Well, it was pretty elaborate to hire a druggie to break into Scott's house and shoot Chelsie. It was pretty elaborate to hire a couple of guys to open fire into a crime scene with police detectives there. Who knows who else he's hired? Who knows who else he's got with him, watching the area!"

"Your sister said she came to DC on her own. She couldn't have been here long, which means this wasn't his original plan. Not this part. So he's working at least a little bit on the fly here. He hasn't had a lot of time to work all the details out."

"Yeah, but this guy has gotten away with it for a decade! He's not stupid." Maggie whipped around another tight corner, then finally, finally, she was on the I-66 West freeway heading out of DC. It was an hour's drive to the location he'd named, in the best traffic conditions. Even speeding like a maniac, she wasn't sure she'd make it in Hoffmeier's forty-minute time line.

She knew that was the point. He wanted to give her no time to react, no time to come up with a counterplan. He wanted to make her panic, so she wasn't thinking clearly when she arrived. So he'd have the upper hand.

It was working.

"No, Hoffmeier isn't stupid," Grant agreed, still sounding calm; he might've been in the WFO office, planning SWAT details. "But his goal is to get you there. And I bet those guys he hired were purely about throwing cash at people who already had records. There's no way he'd invite strangers into this part. This is about him. And it's about you. He's counting on you to react emotionally."

"I know," she told Grant. "But what choice do I have? This isn't just another SWAT call. This is my sister. I'm not taking any chances."

"Our team is the best," Grant said, still sounding way too calm, as he put the phone to his ear. Then she heard him talking to Clive, going over the details, warning Clive to stay at a distance until they'd checked the place out.

The truth was, Clive and the team wouldn't make it until past the deadline, anyway. The hotel had been a solid twenty minutes closer to Virginia than Clive and her other teammates, who lived on the opposite side of DC. By then, she'd know for sure if Hoffmeier's plan was more involved than it seemed, if he was planning to send her somewhere else. By then, she'd have eyes on Nikki. By then, hopefully, it would all be over.

If it wasn't, there was a good chance she'd need the team. She couldn't risk bringing them too early and alerting him, but thinking like a civilian and playing entirely by his rules could get everyone hurt. She had to have a contingency plan in place, and besides Grant, Scott and Ella, she trusted her SWAT team the most. If she didn't make it, she wanted Nikki safe.

Before she knew it, Grant had put his phone back in his pocket. "The team is coming," he said calmly as she picked up her speed even more. "It's going to be okay."

She bit back her instant response. There was no reason to take out her fear and anger on him, not when he was putting his life in danger for her and Nikki. Not when she cared about him the way she did.

What if she never got the chance to tell him?

"Grant, I need to tell you…" She took a deep breath, wishing she could actually look at him when she said she loved him for the first time. But she couldn't. She was going ninety-five on the freeway, racing around the other vehicles with her siren blaring.

"Tell me later," Grant said, and from the tone of his voice, she could tell he knew it was about their budding relationship.

"But just in case—"

"You don't need a *just in case*. We're both coming out of this, and you can tell me when your sister is safe, okay?"

"Okay," she said, because right now, she needed both of their attention focused on saving Nikki.

But the words sat heavy on her tongue. She prayed he was right, and she would get the chance to say them.

The reality was, she'd do whatever it took to get Nikki away from Hoffmeier. And if she had to trade her own life to do it, she wouldn't hesitate.

Her hands gripped the wheel even tighter, and the farther they got from DC, the lighter the traffic got, giving her room to increase her speed even more. Beside her, Grant had one hand braced on the door handle, but he didn't say a word as she picked it up to over a hundred miles an hour.

He got his duffel bag from the backseat and removed his MP-5, then crammed the empty duffel under the front seat. He set the MP-5 in the backseat, where he'd be climbing before too long.

"You have any other weapons?" she asked, even though she shouldn't need them. Chances were, Hoffmeier would try to get her to lay her gun down. But all she needed to do was get close enough. Her training with the FBI's SWAT team meant her hands were deadly weapons. Assuming she didn't freeze the way she had in the warehouse the second she saw Hoffmeier with her sister.

"I've got the obvious," Grant said. "Wrench for changing a tire, pen knife."

"Pen knife," Maggie said. "Can you put it in my pocket?"

Grant reached into the glove box and took out a small folding knife, then slid it into the pocket of her slacks. "He'll probably search you."

"He gets that close, and I won't need the knife," Maggie said darkly, praying it was true. Praying that if she got the chance to pull her Glock on him, her trigger finger wouldn't shake the way her entire body did every time she so much as thought about seeing Hoffmeier face-to-face.

"That's my girl."

"You're right about that," she said seriously, taking her eyes off the road for just a second to look his way, hoping he understood the subtext. He wanted her to wait to tell him she loved him, fine. But at least this way, if the worst happened, he'd know.

He squeezed her knee as she took the exit onto M-50 and glanced at the dashboard clock. If she could keep her speed up on the country highway, they might actually make it.

Just as that thought hit, Grant's phone rang.

"It's Clive," Grant said, picking it up and talking to their team leader a minute. Then he told her, "I'm leaving the call open," and he stuffed the phone under the middle seat. "He'll be able to hear us," Grant explained to her. "If he has to, he can call HRT, and they can come in by helicopter."

Maggie nodded mutely. If Chelsie hadn't been shot, Scott would have been with HRT right now, armed with a sniper rifle that could take out Hoffmeier from half a mile away. All assuming he'd have been able to mobilize and find an unseen location by then, and assuming Hoffmeier came out into the open.

But the deeper into the country they traveled, the more she realized how smart Hoffmeier had been in choosing his location. A distance shot wasn't going to happen here.

If he was going to be taken down, it would have to happen up close. And she was the only one who'd be able to get close enough without endangering Nikki.

"This is the road," she finally said, terror settling

deep inside as she followed the GPS onto a smaller country road.

The scenery was gorgeous: deep green, rolling plains dotted with grazing horses and the occasional estate. It was also the perfect place to hide a kidnap victim. Even if a scream echoed here, who would hear it?

"I'm getting in the back now," Grant said.

She slowed her speed a little as Grant unfastened his seat belt and climbed into the backseat, settling down on the floor, where there was no way Hoffmeier would see him without standing close to the car. She glanced over her shoulder and saw he had one hand lingering near the holster, holding his Glock, and his MP-5 clutched in his other hand.

"Here we go," she said, turning onto a driveway so long it could have been its own private road. She slowed even more, rolling down her windows so she could hear as she passed large, empty fields meant for horses.

She studied two huge outbuildings as she drove past, but continued on toward the looming main house straight ahead. It was ridiculously ornate, lined with perfectly groomed shrubbery, columns highlighting the entryway. An empty truck was right up front.

Maggie squinted at the house, still a solid five hundred feet away up the drive. "I don't see him," she whispered.

The boom of a voice—*Hoffmeier's* voice—startled her so badly she jerked the wheel, almost veering off the drive.

He was using a bullhorn, she realized, even though she still didn't see him. But he was here.

"Stop the car," he ordered, so she did, planting her foot on the brake, but not putting the car in park.

Her hands shook around the wheel as she waited for more, as she squinted at the house, trying to see any sign of where he was. Something glinted in a front window, and she stared until her eyes hurt, but she couldn't tell what it was.

"Toss your gun out the window," he said, and his voice made the nerve endings in her neck fire to life, almost as if they were preparing for the pain of another brand.

When she hesitated, he snapped, "Don't make me ask again."

Maggie undid her seat belt and unholstered her Glock, holding it out the window so he could see, then dropped it.

"Good," he said, sounding pleased and confident, as if he'd always known it would come back to this, to him in charge. "Now, your backup weapon."

She held up her hands and shook her head, assuming he was staring at her through binoculars.

"Of course you brought a backup gun," he said. "Let's motivate you."

A pained scream echoed through the bullhorn, bringing tears to Maggie's eyes, and Grant's whisper barely penetrated her fear.

"Under the seat."

Reaching down, she picked up his Glock, then held it out the window and tossed it as tears tracked down her cheeks. She didn't bother to wipe them away. He wanted to be in charge, and as much as everything in her resisted, she needed to show him he was. She needed to let him think this would break her. Needed to get him to let her close enough to bring him down. Her hands clenched into tight fists on her lap, where he couldn't see them.

"Very good," Hoffmeier said, and there was that flicker again, in the front window.

Was it open? Maggie wondered.

"Now there's just one more thing," Hoffmeier continued, "and then you can drive up to the house. You follow all my instructions, and I'll let Nikki walk out of here. You know it isn't her I want."

Maggie stared at the house, her jaw trembling, and not because she was trying to let him see fear, but because she couldn't control it. Because she knew exactly who he did want. And she knew exactly what he wanted from her.

"You don't follow my instructions, and I'll shoot her right now, you understand?"

All she could do was nod desperately and wait.

"Tell Grant to get out of the car," his voice boomed.

Maggie froze, terror lodging in her throat. What was he going to do to Grant if she told him to do it? What was he going to do to Nikki if she didn't?

"Tick tock," Hoffmeier mocked.

Before Maggie could figure out what to do, she heard the back car door open.

"Grant, don't," she warned, and her voice came out a desperate whisper, but she was too late.

A flash of light exploded at the front window, with a sharp crack that sent birds flapping from a grove of trees behind the house. Next to her car, Grant dropped to the ground, and dark red spread across his chest.

"Now you can come get Nikki," Hoffmeier said, opening the front door and stepping outside, a pistol pointed at her sister's head.

Chapter Sixteen

"Grant!" Maggie cried, her foot automatically lifting off the brake. The car rolled forward, and she stamped her foot back down, glancing over her shoulder. "Grant," she pleaded again through the open window.

On the ground, Grant lay flat on his back with his right arm splayed out beside him, completely still, not responding. Maggie knew the amount of blood seeping through his shirt meant if he wasn't already dead, he would be soon.

Panic raced through her, the desire to leap out of the car and check his vitals. To press her hands into the wound and try to stop the bleeding.

"Tick tock," Hoffmeier called, startling her.

She looked back at him, where he held a bullhorn in one hand and Nikki in front of him. Then she glanced once more at Grant and gulped back a sob. This time, he wasn't wearing any Kevlar. This time, there would be no "do overs."

"Now!" Hoffmeier screamed. "Or Nikki pays, too!"

Praying Grant was still alive—and that Clive had heard them over the open phone line in the car and was coming—Maggie pressed on the gas, stopping right in front of the porch.

Up close, she could see that Nikki's hands were bound

together in front of her. She was wearing shorts and a T-shirt, and although she was clearly terrified, she was alert, and Maggie didn't see any obvious injuries. She hoped there were none she couldn't see, no brand already seared into Nikki's neck.

Nikki's lips moved, and although Maggie couldn't quite hear her, she read the words. "I'm so sorry."

Hoffmeier dropped the bullhorn on the ground, drawing her attention to him. He looked older than the pictures she'd seen of him, and the years hadn't treated him well. If the idea that people's psychology eventually showed up on their faces was true, he was a prime example.

He still had the good bone structure, but there were more lines on his face than he should have had at his age. The smug, vile smirk that looked stamped on his face overrode any charm he might have once possessed.

But he was still in good physical shape. Maybe more so than he'd been a decade ago, judging by the muscle outlined on his bare arms. Even if she could get close, he wouldn't go down easily.

"Get out of the car, slowly," Hoffmeier said, "and don't try anything."

She turned off the engine and stepped out, her hands up over her head, an overriding fury surging inside.

He waved the hand holding the gun at her, and Maggie's calves tensed the second his weapon left Nikki's temple, but he was too far away to rush.

His eyes narrowed, and he pressed the gun back to her sister's head before he demanded, "Lift your shirt. Are you wearing a holster?"

Every time he spoke, she had to resist the urge to cower. Even with him right in front of her, no flashbacks raced forward, but his voice was imprinted on her memory like a brand of its own.

"Yes. For the gun you made me toss." Her voice came out shaky, and she moved slowly, lifting the side of her blouse so he could see her holster was empty. The weight of the pen knife in her pocket seemed abnormally heavy, and she hunched a little, hoping he couldn't tell she had something there.

"Good," he said, not seeming to notice. "Let's go inside, then." His tone was suddenly jovial, as if he was inviting her to brunch. He backed toward the house, dragging Nikki inside with him.

Her sister's gaze locked on hers as she was yanked inside, such guilt and regret there, the same things Maggie felt herself whenever she thought about the Fishhook Rapist.

She cast one more desperate glance over her shoulder, but in the distance, she could see that Grant was still prone on the ground.

She looked farther down the road, but there were no SWAT vehicles barreling down on them. She needed them right now, for Grant. Yet, if they showed up, Hoffmeier would surely kill Nikki.

Her vision clouded with tears, Maggie followed them inside.

Hoffmeier and Nikki backed through a long entryway into a formal living room, and Maggie walked a few paces behind, her hands up by her ears. The second she entered the room, her eyes were drawn to the elaborate painting on the wall, inside a gilded frame. Then they were pulled to the antique coffee table with the ball and claw feet and the beautiful marble top.

The place where he'd forced her to her knees and branded the back of her neck, tying them together forever. On top of the table was a circular piece of metal attached to a short pole, and as Maggie squinted at it, she realized what it was. A modified family crest, one hook soldered to raise above the rest.

Her whole body shuddered, and Hoffmeier's lips slowly spread. "You remember," he whispered.

This is going to hurt. This is going to hurt. This is going to hurt.

The words chanted like a record set too fast that she couldn't turn off, until she wanted to curl into a ball and slap her hands over her ears. Only it wouldn't help, because the voice was in her head.

"I hoped someday you'd remember what we had," he said, and Nikki suddenly stiffened and snapped, "Stop it!"

Hoffmeier drew the pistol away from her temple then slapped it across her cheek, making Nikki's head whip sideways and blood trickle from her lip.

It snapped the world into focus for Maggie, and she straightened her spine. "I'm here. Time to let Nikki go."

Her voice sounded stronger, and Hoffmeier's smile faded. "Not yet. I know what you do for the FBI, Maggie."

He shifted to the side, yanking Nikki with him, and behind them, Maggie realized there were two mahogany chairs in the middle of the room. "A place for us to talk," he told her. "You sit in the one on the right. There are ties there to make sure you do as you're told."

"Don't do it," Nikki burst out.

Maggie shook her head at her sister, willing her not to antagonize him. "What assurance do I have you'll let Nikki go once I do what you want?"

His eyebrows lifted. "You'll just have to trust me. What choice do you have? Don't do what I say, and I pull the trigger." He tapped the gun barrel against Nikki's head.

"And then I kill you," Maggie vowed, her voice dark and so ominous even Nikki's eyes widened.

"Oh, I probably won't shoot her in the head," Hoffmeier said conversationally. "But a kneecap maybe. Somewhere really painful, that'll never heal right."

He swept his free hand grandly toward the chair, as though he was presenting something at auction, and Maggie moved slowly toward it.

If she could just get close enough, get him to lift his gun away from her sister's head…

But as she stepped toward them, Hoffmeier yanked Nikki off to the side, away from the chairs. So they were both out of striking range.

Nikki mouthed, *No.* But what choice did she have? Maggie picked the zip ties off the chair and sat down.

"Loop it around your wrist and the chair arm," Hoffmeier instructed. "Hurry up."

It was awkward, but Maggie managed to get one arm fastened to the chair, then she held up her free hand with the other zip tie and shook her head. "I can't do this with one hand."

"That's okay," he said cheerfully. "Nikki will finish it." His tone turned menacing. "And you'll sit still. If I could hit your boyfriend in the heart from five hundred feet, I can hit your sister in the head from three." He smiled, a crazy glee in his eyes as he added, "Dad taught me to shoot skeet when I was five, but it never interested me until recently."

Pain wrenched through her at the mention of Grant, and Maggie pushed it aside. She had to focus on Nikki now.

She had to watch for any chance to escape, because yes, Hoffmeier really wanted her. So he might well just let Nikki go once he had her immobilized. By the time

Nikki could get help, he could plan to knock Maggie out with something, load her in the trunk and be long gone.

Yet it was equally likely he'd keep Nikki right here, use her to make Maggie tame, to get her to do whatever he wanted.

Maggie tried to numb herself, tried not to think about what he might want, as Nikki approached. Maggie kept her eyes on Hoffmeier, looking for any moment that his gun might move away from Nikki. If she had the chance, it didn't matter that the chair was attached to her wrist. She'd bring it with her when she tackled him. It was awkward, but it weighed less than her fifty pounds of SWAT gear.

Nikki reached her side, and her own hands, already tied together so tight her wrists were raw, fumbled with the second zip tie. Her fingers trembled as she closed the zip tie around Maggie's other wrist. The whole time, Hoffmeier just stared back at her, barely blinking, his bottomless blue gaze unnerving.

"You okay?" Maggie whispered, and Nikki nodded.

"Enough sisterly love," Hoffmeier said. "Take the other seat, Nikki."

"No," Maggie burst. "Let her go!"

"I will," Hoffmeier said, then waved Nikki over. "Eventually. Right now, I need her here to keep you in line. I know you, Maggie," he purred. "You were always a fighter."

She wrenched at the ties, bile rising up in her throat. She didn't remember the assault; did that mean she'd fought him back then? Or was he just referring to her using his attack as motivation to join SWAT?

Nikki's head moved back and forth between them. "Leave my sister alone."

"Listen to that," Hoffmeier said. "I guess Nikki here

is getting a backbone. I like that in a woman." He sighed dramatically. "Too bad for her that I'm already way too obsessed with her big sister to bother with the knockoff version."

Maggie scowled at him, then glanced at Nikki and hoped she wasn't making an irreversible mistake. "Do what he says." Instinct told her he would only hurt Nikki to force her hand, that he was being honest about wanting to hurt Maggie, not her sister.

"No," Nikki said, and her jaw jutted out as she stepped in front of Maggie. "My sister has her team of SWAT agents on the way and they're going to—"

"Now!" Hoffmeier bellowed.

"Nikki, please. Just do it," Maggie begged, and with one last worried glance at her, Nikki sat in the other chair.

Hoffmeier kept his gun aimed at her, and he stayed carefully away from Maggie as he walked to the far side and secured an extra zip tie to the one around Nikki's wrists, so she was latched to the second chair.

Only then did he turn his gun on Maggie and move closer, murmuring, "I've been waiting so long for this."

Maggie fought off the panic building inside her and prepared herself. Keep coming, she willed him, hoping that if he gave her the chance, she wouldn't freeze up.

But the nearer he got, the faster her breath came, the louder her heartbeat thudded in her eardrums, the more terror clouded her vision. Was this the end for her and Nikki both?

GRANT GROANED AND rolled to his left, uninjured side, trying to push himself off the dirt. His right arm hung limply at his side, blood dripping steadily down it.

He'd waited until Hoffmeier had disappeared inside with Maggie and Nikki to try to move at all, not wanting

Hoffmeier to realize he'd survived. The way his shoulder throbbed and pumped blood, that survival was still in question.

Fighting dizziness as he got to his knees, Grant managed to get his button-down off. He swore as he slid the shirt off his damaged right arm and got a good look at the injury.

As a SWAT agent, he had basic medical training, the sort of thing a soldier learned for the battlefield. But he didn't need it to know his injury was bad. Really bad.

His shirt was soaked through with blood, and so was the ground below him. He had to stop the flow, or he was going to die of blood loss way before backup arrived.

Awkwardly, he managed to wrap the shirt around his shoulder, getting it above the bullet hole. Using his good hand and his teeth, he tugged the knot tight enough that the blood slowed to a stop.

His right hand immediately started to tingle and as he pushed himself to his feet, he swayed and almost fell. Realizing he didn't have a weapon anymore, Grant stumbled as he looked around, finally spotting his Glock a few feet away in the dirt. He walked unsteadily over to it, a wave of dizziness sweeping through him as he bent down to grab it off the ground.

His hand shook around the handle, and he knew the gun wasn't going to do him any good. His body was already shutting down from the blood loss. The likelihood of being able to pull the trigger with Hoffmeier standing close to either Maggie or Nikki and actually hitting Hoffmeier wasn't strong.

Nerves rose up, for Maggie, for Nikki, for himself, and he tried to think the way he would on a SWAT call. Stay calm and focus.

He shoved the gun in his holster, clenched his teeth

against the pain and headed for his car, up by the house. If he could just get to the cell phone, he could tell Clive to call HRT, get them airborne immediately. If he was really, really lucky, Clive and the rest of their team were already close, and they'd arrive in time to stop Hoffmeier from carrying out whatever plan he had for Maggie and Nikki.

New pinpricks of pain skittered up his arm as it began reacting to the blood flow being cut off. It meant he'd successfully tied off the wound, which would buy him some time, but it also meant that arm was completely useless.

Reaching the car, Grant braced himself against it. He reached for the door handle, then moved his hand away. He'd have to get down on the floor and reach under the seat to search for the phone, and if he bent back down, there was a good chance he wouldn't get up again.

Normally, Grant would have skirted the front entry of the house and moved around the side, peering into the windows and getting a lock on the subject and the hostages before he made a move. But with Maggie inside and knowing his time of being any help at all was fading fast, he climbed onto the porch and looked into the house. The door was open, and he could see a long, ornate entryway, but not Maggie or Nikki. Not Hoffmeier.

He had to get to Maggie now, while there was still something he might be able to do. Hopefully, she wouldn't even need him, but since he'd come up close to the house, he hadn't heard anything from inside.

He was careful with every step because he was feeling clumsy from blood loss, and he didn't want to stumble, make noise and give himself away. But fear skyrocketed as Maggie's anguished voice screamed out, "You said you wanted me! Leave her alone!"

Flattening himself against the wall, and vaguely registering that he was smearing it with blood, Grant peered around the corner and into the large living room. At the far end of the room, Hoffmeier had his back to Grant. Maggie and Nikki were each tied to a chair in front of him. Hoffmeier was leaning toward Nikki, running the hand not clutching his gun over her face, but his attention was entirely on Maggie.

Maggie's eyes suddenly widened, and he realized she'd spotted him. He ducked his head back around the corner just in case her reaction gave away his presence.

Dizziness hit again, and he closed his eyes briefly. Was he going to be able to help, or would he just get them all hurt?

Grant willed his body to hold out a little longer and carefully peeked around the corner again. There was no way he could use a gun right now, but he didn't need his arm for pure, brute force. He tried to signal Maggie, but had no idea if she knew what he was telling her.

"I don't want her," Hoffmeier told Maggie. "And now that you're here—" he gestured to her, tied up in the chair "—I don't need her."

Instead of the terror Hoffmeier had probably expected to see on Maggie's face, fury raced over her features. "What do you want?" she barked. "I'm here. But it sure seems like you're too scared to get close, even with me tied up."

"Maggie," Nikki whispered, but Maggie ignored her, her eyes lasered in on Hoffmeier.

Grant couldn't see his face, but his whole body visibly stiffened. "I didn't think you'd have figured out my name, but it was going to come out. It was always going to come out. I had everything planned out perfectly," he bragged, his gun hand drifting down as he talked to Maggie.

Although Maggie just continued glaring, Grant knew

her. She was waiting for him to get more distracted, to move the gun a little bit more away from Nikki.

"Your sister doesn't matter. She wasn't even part of the original plan, but she sure did make it easier when she showed up at your door. She really looks like you, you know? I was just going to leave her here, tied up, until someone came and got her. She would have been fine, but she's unimportant. Expendable, if you didn't follow my instructions, if I needed her to make you behave. Your boyfriend doesn't matter, either, although him I kind of wanted to kill. You belong to me!" He bellowed the last part.

"After ten years, I knew it was time. The perfect time." He laughed. "I never actually planned to wait until the first to come for you, but I needed you to believe that. We were going to have two perfect days together, and then I was going to call your brother on the first, tell him where to find us. On our anniversary."

In that instant, Grant realized the rest of Hoffmeier's plan. From the look on Maggie's face, so did she. This was his end game.

"We were going to be together forever, Maggie," Hoffmeier purred, and he moved a little more, obviously wanting to revel in Maggie's reaction to that news.

It was a huge mistake. And Grant knew Maggie. He knew she would take advantage of that error.

So the second he saw it, he didn't wait for her signal. He just raced as hard and as fast as he could into the room.

He watched Maggie's feet shoot out and lock around Hoffmeier's knees the instant he moved the gun off Nikki. She used her legs to yank him down hard.

Hoffmeier flew backward, his arms lurching up, and

his head smacked the floor as the gun blasted a hole in the ceiling, dumping plaster on top of him.

Tied up, Maggie didn't get her feet clear fast enough, and her chair slammed down, too, rolling sideways, right after Hoffmeier. He swore and swung his gun back around fast, looking furious and only a little disoriented from the fall.

Grant had a brief vision of Nikki uselessly fighting her bonds, of Maggie scrambling to right herself, before he pushed off and dived the final distance straight at Hoffmeier.

Chapter Seventeen

Grant landed on top of Hoffmeier, and he heard the air whoosh out of Hoffmeier's lungs. Then the gun blasted off again, with deafening effects, right beside Grant's ear.

His right shoulder screamed in pain as Grant reared back and smashed his left fist into the space between Hoffmeier's shoulder and his chest. Hoffmeier's eyes went wide with pain, but the gun didn't fall, so Grant hit again, swallowing back nausea at the movement.

This time, the gun dropped out of Hoffmeier's hand, but Hoffmeier got smart and twisted underneath Grant, smashing his own fist into Grant's wounded arm.

Searing pain raced down his arm and across his chest, and he was pretty sure something in his shoulder tore. Trying to ignore it, Grant flung his right arm wide, knocking Hoffmeier's pistol out of reach.

Blackness threatened at the edges of his vision, and something damp that had to be blood escaping his make-shift tourniquet splattered like big raindrops onto Hoffmeier. He willed his body to keep going, to stay conscious long enough to get rid of the threat, to get Maggie free.

Beside him, on the ground, he could hear Maggie frantically trying to get her arms unhooked from the chair, without success. Then she seemed to give up on it and

just spun, pushing the chair backward so her feet were
pointed toward him.

Grant used his good arm to propel himself up off Hoffmeier enough to give her a target, and she didn't hesitate. His whole body was wrenched sideways along with
Hoffmeier as Maggie kicked up and out, meeting Hoffmeier's chin with her foot.

The strike effectively knocked both of them out of her
reach, but it slowed Hoffmeier down, and Grant pushed
up to his knees, trying to get another hit in.

Before he could, Hoffmeier recovered, shoving Grant
off him. He scrambled to his feet, glanced at the gun in
the corner, then back at Grant, who was hauling himself
up on Nikki's chair.

It felt as if Grant was moving in slow motion, inch by
painful inch, but he must still have seemed like a threat
to Hoffmeier as he finally hauled himself to his feet.

Because instead of running for the gun, Hoffmeier
glanced desperately at Maggie one last time, then swore
and ran the other way, out the door.

"GRANT! GRANT!" MAGGIE SOBBED.

He was staring in the direction Hoffmeier had disappeared, but it wasn't until he looked back at her that her
fear subsided. His arm looked bad, but when Hoffmeier
had hit him and the wound had opened up again, she'd
thought he was going down for good.

He looked steadier on his feet now, and his shoulder
had stopped bleeding. "How hurt are you?" she asked.

"I'll make it," he said, and dropped to his knees beside her.

"I didn't know if you—" she started.

"I know," he said, and his words slurred a little, then

he seemed to make a conscious effort to sharpen them. "I'm sorry. I couldn't let Hoffmeier see I was alive."

"My pocket," she said, moving closer so he could get access. "The knife."

"Got it," he said, and fumbled for it, finally getting the knife out and open.

As he cut awkwardly at the zip tie, she studied his face, looking for signs he was worse than he was telling her. Then she glanced at Nikki, still tied to the chair, who had silent tears running down her face.

"You okay?" Maggie asked.

"I'm fine," Nikki answered. "He didn't hurt me, he just hit me the one time to make me scream when..." She choked back tears. "I'm so sorry. And then he fired the rifle and..."

"It's okay," Grant told her. "I'm tougher than I look."

Nikki actually laughed a little through her tears, probably because Grant looked pretty tough. Then she stared at Maggie. "Are *you* okay?"

"I'm fine," Maggie said. It was Grant she was worried about. And Hoffmeier getting away, disappearing for another decade.

As soon as Grant got the zip ties sliced open, Maggie lurched for the landline, knowing that Grant needed help soon. Instead of calling an ambulance, she called Clive. "Where are you?"

"Two minutes out, max," he answered.

"Go faster," she begged. "Grant needs medical attention now. He was shot, and I need you to get him airlifted out of here to the closest hospital."

"I'll make it," Grant told her, giving her a weary-looking smile as he shuffled over to her sister on his knees and set the pen knife against her zip ties.

"Where's Hoffmeier?" Clive asked.

"He ran." She glanced at Grant, cutting her sister free, and then at the doorway. Could she wait for Clive? Or would Hoffmeier get away again? With his resources, would they ever find him?

She looked at the marble coffee table where he'd pressed her head a decade ago, and at the metal brand he'd made, still lying there.

Would he get away again, make a new brand? Keep trying to punish his family for their perceived wrongs against him? Keep hurting young women, to try and give himself some kind of sick power?

"Go," Grant said. "Get him. End this for good."

Over the phone, Clive said, "Here we come. We're at the drive."

"Go now," Grant said. "Don't let Hoffmeier get away."

The squeal of tires sounded outside, and Maggie jumped to her feet. She heard Grant's voice call after her, "Be careful," as she ran as fast as her feet would carry her out the door.

The living room opened up on the other side into an expansive kitchen, and the back door was hanging open. Maggie might have thought it was a trick, except the wide, flat land that had been a challenge before was now a benefit. She spotted him, running flat-out across the expansive field behind the house, away from the SWAT agents' vehicles descending on the front where his truck was parked.

He glanced back at her, and in that instant she realized she'd left her gun behind, that it was just her and Hoffmeier again. The way it was ten years ago.

She pushed down her emotional reaction and tried to think like the SWAT agent she'd become. She had the upper hand this time.

She took off as fast as she could after him, her combat

boots smashing through the thick, immaculately groomed grass. Her lungs burned as she pushed herself harder, and the distance between them began to close.

He looked back again, stumbled when he saw how close she was getting, and then turned, heading in the other direction, around the back of the house, toward an enormous man-made pond.

Maggie followed, and just as Hoffmeier looked as if he was going to change direction again, Maggie realized she was close enough. She pushed off and flew through the air toward him, landing hard and taking him down with her.

They crashed into the muddy ground at the edge of the pond, Maggie on Hoffmeier's back, and she scrambled to get to her knees. To push him down flat and get his arms behind his back. It occurred to her in that moment that she'd left her handcuffs back in the hotel room, but it didn't matter, because he suddenly flipped over, getting her beneath him.

"It's not finished," he panted, sounding out of breath and injured.

He was heavier than he looked, and with the back of his head pressed against her face, Maggie got a whiff of his expensive cologne, and it took her back ten years. The same smell, the same voice, the same man.

Instead of immobilizing her, it filled her with fury. "Yes, it is," she swore, pushing right back, trying to shove him off her. She thought she'd succeeded, but he managed to grab hold of her, and they both flipped over the edge of the pond.

She'd expected it to slope slowly downward, but instead it abruptly dropped off, and it was much deeper than she'd thought. Together, they sank down, and kept going, toward the muddy bottom.

Maggie twisted, trying to pull out of his grasp, but his other hand closed desperately around her arm, dragging her down with him. Her lungs screamed for air, and her eyes opened, filling instantly with water and grit.

She could make out Hoffmeier, not fighting to get back to the surface at all, just letting himself sink, trying to hold on to her.

Wrenching her legs in front of her body, she kicked hard, her feet connecting with his stomach. Air bubbles flooded all around her as his grip slipped, and she got free.

Knowing he wouldn't want to go down without her, Maggie swam hard for the surface, her muscles shaking now since she'd gone into the water without getting a breath. Finally, finally, she broke the surface.

She sucked in air over and over, coughing as she swam for the edge of the pond, not sure how they'd drifted so far so quickly. In the distance, she saw Clive running toward her.

She was close to the edge when he surfaced, gasping for air and grasping for her. His flailing arms gripped her hair, then slid down to the back of her neck as he pulled her under.

Maggie twisted frantically, turning to face him, and jammed her fist as hard as she could into his throat.

His eyes bulged, and his limbs thrashed as she watched him breathe in a mouthful of water.

She pushed for the surface, looking back in time to see his limbs slow then stop, and then he sank toward the bottom of the pond, his eyes and mouth wide and unmoving.

It was over. Maggie burst to the surface and gratefully drew in more air. She swam hard for the shore, until finally, her fingers dug into the dirt at the edge of the pond, and Clive was hauling her out of the water.

"Where's Hoffmeier?" he asked.

She blinked grit from her eyes and peered over the huge pond, toward the spot where he'd sunk. "He's gone."

"Good," Clive said. "Then we need to get back to the house. The medical helicopter is coming. Grant's in trouble."

"What?" She whipped her attention back to Clive.

"He lost a lot of blood. He needed a surgeon—and maybe a transfusion—ten minutes ago."

Maggie ran as fast as she could toward the house, still gasping for breath. Clive ran alongside her, and she could tell by his strides that she wasn't at her usual speed. She pushed harder, frantic to get back to Grant. She heard the roar of blades as the helicopter landed on the Hoffmeier estate's lawn.

Maggie watched two of her teammates race toward it, carrying an unconscious Grant between them. Nikki ran out after them, looking around until she spotted Maggie, then gestured for her sister to hurry.

Maggie ran faster, and Nikki gripped her arm, pushing her into the helicopter with Grant before it lifted off. The huge house faded below her, the forty-foot-wide pond soon becoming nothing more than a speck.

But Maggie barely noticed as she took Grant's limp hand in hers and sobbed, "You need to fight. I have something important to tell you, and you promised I'd get the chance as soon as this was all over."

Grant didn't move, his face and lips abnormally ashy, and Maggie held on tighter. "I love you," she said just as the monitor beside him let out a long, flat, final-sounding beep.

Epilogue

Maggie paced back and forth in the hospital waiting room until Nikki pushed her into a plastic chair.

"I should have stayed," Maggie said for what felt like the millionth time since they'd been in the Hoffmeier house two days ago. She'd gone over and over it in her mind, that moment she'd chosen to chase after Hoffmeier instead of staying beside Grant.

"He told you to go," Nikki reminded her. "So stop beating yourself up."

"She's right," Scott said, and Maggie glanced over at him, his hand clutching Chelsie's.

"You need to stop beating yourself up about all of it," Chelsie ordered. "And don't look at me like that. I'm fine."

Chelsie had been discharged a few hours earlier. She was moving more slowly, and she'd be off work for two weeks, but doctors didn't expect any lasting problems from her injury.

"Logan's fine, too," Ella put in, probably seeing guilt still on her face.

Maggie glanced from Ella to Logan, sitting close together on the uncomfortable hospital couch.

Logan nodded his agreement. "My injury just looked bad. But head wounds always bleed like crazy. And hey, we caught the three guys Hoffmeier paid off for those hits."

Maggie couldn't help smiling a little. Only someone in law enforcement could make light of having a bullet graze his head. But he was right—the injury itself had been minor, and he'd actually been released within a few hours.

"And it really worked out for me," Chelsie joked, wiggling her left hand, where a brand-new diamond sparkled.

Next to her, Scott rolled his eyes. "I already had the ring. But seeing you in the hospital, I just couldn't wait."

"See?" Nikki said. "Everyone is fine. And it's finally over."

"It will be," Maggie agreed.

Local police had dragged the Hoffmeier lake and found Jeff's body. And his family had been forcibly returned to DC to answer questions.

Apparently, Lorraine had been completely ignorant of her son's criminal activities. She'd simply thought he was spoiled and difficult. She'd had no idea he'd left DC ten years ago at her husband's insistence. She was back home in DC, cloistered alone in her house and avoiding the press camped out in her yard.

Frederik and Claudia were in custody, awaiting a hearing on bail. Clive predicted it would be denied, because of their resources and the amount of money they'd thrown at Jeff ten years ago, to make him go away. They were being charged as accessories in nine sexual assaults, and four assaults on law-enforcement officials, along with obstruction of justice, and a slew of other charges. Even if only some of them stuck, they'd pay.

Both had initially insisted they really thought Jeff had been in Europe the past ten years. But the Hoffmeiers were well-known in DC, and the story had broken quickly in the press. A witness had come forward, a friend of Claudia's from college, who'd said Claudia had tearfully confessed that she suspected her brother had raped Maggie. She'd confessed to telling her father, who'd changed the family logo and paid Jeff to stay away from them. Apparently, Claudia had gone back to that friend a few days later and said she was wrong, and that police had caught the real offender.

Back then, since Maggie was the first to be branded, and there were no other known victims, the friend had believed the story. Since Maggie's full name had always been kept out of the press accounts, she claimed she'd forgotten all about it until she saw the recent news.

Whether it was true or not, her going to police had broken Claudia's silence. There was some question to how much the Hoffmeier family actually knew, and how much they'd only suspected, but they'd known enough. They should have turned Jeff in a decade ago, and they could have prevented eight other women from going through what Maggie had. Instead, they'd changed the Hoffmeier Financial logo to get rid of the hook images that matched the brand on her neck. Instead, they had tried to protect the family business, and the family name.

Nikki squeezed her hand. "I talked to Mom and Dad this morning at the hotel. Apologized for telling them I was spending the week with friends, instead of letting them know I was coming here. I know they told you when they got here, but they are really proud of you, you know? For getting through this. For finding the guy and stopping him for good."

Maggie smiled back at her, but her feet tapped nervously on the floor of the surgical area waiting room. What was taking so long?

"He'll be here," Scott said.

Then the door to the waiting room opened, and he was. Maggie sensed everyone getting to their feet, but she couldn't be certain, because she was already running across the room. She stopped just in front of Grant, resisting the urge to throw her arms around his neck and just hang on and never let go.

He looked awful. His skin was still a little ashy, and pain was etched on his face, his right shoulder looking lumpy under his hospital gown from the bandages. The nurse pushed his wheelchair into the room and as soon as she left, he scolded, "Don't look at me like that. If all goes well, they'll release me tomorrow. I'll be kicking down doors with SWAT again in no time."

He winked at her, and Maggie felt a grin break free, then she did lean down and throw her arms around his neck, only lightly, barely touching him.

He squeezed back, with more strength than she'd expected after having his heart shocked back into rhythm on the helicopter, then being rushed here for a blood transfusion and surgery to repair his shoulder.

"How long?" she asked him, leaning back to look at his face.

"Probably six months," he replied. "The shoulder is going to need some rehabilitation."

Most SWAT agents would be furious at that much time away from the team, at the prospect of that much work to get back into fighting shape. But this was Grant, and he said it not only like a guarantee he'd do it, but with his typical good-natured attitude.

Nothing ever kept him down. It was one of the things she loved best about him.

At that moment, she realized he'd never even heard her say it. He'd almost died for her and Nikki, and he didn't really know how she felt about him.

She must have gone pale, because he said, "It's okay. I have a plan."

"What's your plan?" Scott asked him. "You taking some time off to heal, and having Clive hold the spot for you on the team?"

"Not exactly," Grant said, looking up at her.

He patted the chair next to where the nurse had left his wheelchair, and Maggie sat, as he folded her hand in his. It was funny how natural that already felt.

"You're not leaving SWAT?" she asked. "Because I—"

"No." He twisted a little in his chair so he was facing her. "But I talked to Martin two weeks ago." He was the leader of the second SWAT team at WFO. "One of his guys is transferring to the LA field office in April, and I asked about taking that spot."

"No," Maggie said. "You waited so long to get on a team. It's not fair that you be the one to—"

"I talked to Clive last week, too," he said. "I told him I wasn't going to be able to stay with the team. I didn't say why—I figured I'd wait until you and I talked about it first—but he knew."

Maggie blushed at the idea that the team already knew what was happening between her and Grant before she'd had the chance to tell them, but they were practically family. It shouldn't have surprised her. "Did Martin guarantee you a spot on his team?" She held her breath.

"No."

"Then I should be the one—"

"But he'll give it to me," Grant insisted. "As soon as I get through rehab and can prove to him my shoulder's back to one hundred percent." He brought her hand up to his lips and pressed a kiss to it. "It's perfect timing, Maggie. I should be through the rehab right when a spot opens up. I'll get it."

She grinned at him, not believing they might actually be able to date and still both have a place in SWAT. Although she'd miss running into missions with him by her side. "Are you sure?"

"I'm determined," he said. "I don't give up on something I want." He smiled back at her and asked, "It worked on you, didn't it?"

"Oh, yeah." She leaned in to kiss him, and just before her lips met his, she corrected, "But I think it was me who went after you until you couldn't resist any longer."

His mouth covered hers, showing her that determination. When he kissed her like that, she could almost forget he'd been shot. She could almost forget all of it. When he kissed her, there was a lightness in her soul that she'd never had before.

"Mmm," she mumbled against his mouth a few minutes later. "Don't ever stop that."

He smiled back at her, a glint in his eyes that promised he'd do more than that as soon as he healed up.

Suddenly remembering where they were, Maggie glanced over her shoulder and saw that everyone had cleared out to give them a little privacy.

But she didn't need it. She was ready to tell everyone, including the Bureau, that she and Grant were forming their own team now.

Before she could say it to him, he stroked his hand down her cheek and asked, "How are you doing?"

She knew exactly what he was asking. Four hours had passed while she'd waited frantically to hear about Grant's condition. Another two days had gone by while she sat in this waiting room with Scott, Nikki, Ella, Chelsie and Logan for Grant to be well enough to leave ICU.

Now it was September 1. A day she'd never thought

would be anything but painful, even after they'd finally caught Hoffmeier for good.

She squeezed his hand and told him honestly, "It's a good day today. A really good day."

He leaned down to kiss her again, and she pressed a finger to his lips. "You haven't let me finish what I was trying to tell you before," she told him softly.

Realization washed over his features, then a slow smile spread across his face, even before she said, "I love you, Grant."

Then he did kiss her again, and his lips were full of promise.

Today was the first day of a new start for her. A fresh new life with Grant, and she was going to grab hold with both hands and never let go.

* * * * *

He felt a driving need to protect her.

He tried not to speed on his way back to the cabin, but he didn't like leaving McKenna alone so long. She was making a good show of being stronger, but he'd seen the circles of fatigue under her eyes, the pale tone of her skin. She was still weak, still vulnerable.

About three miles from the turnoff, a glance in the rearview mirror made him sit up straighter. That black SUV about three cars back had been with him since he'd left The Gates, hadn't it?

He took the next turnoff and drove at a steady pace down one of the small feeder roads that led toward Warrior Creek Falls. Only one vehicle behind him followed, keeping a steady distance back. The black SUV.

He was being tailed.

KILLSHADOW ROAD

BY
PAULA GRAVES

MILLS & BOON

Published in Great Britain 2015
by Mills & Boon, an imprint of Harlequin (UK) Limited,
Eton House, 18-24 Paradise Road, Richmond, Surrey, TW9 1SR

© 2015 Paula Graves

ISBN: 978-0-263-25303-0

46-0415

Harlequin (UK) Limited's policy is to use papers that are natural, renewable and recyclable products and made from wood grown in sustainable forests. The logging and manufacturing processes conform to the legal environmental regulations of the country of origin.

Printed and bound in Spain
by CPI, Barcelona

Paula Graves, an Alabama native, wrote her first book at the age of six. A voracious reader, Paula loves books that pair tantalizing mystery with compelling romance. When she's not reading or writing, she works as a creative director for a Birmingham advertising agency and spends time with her family and friends. Paula invites readers to visit her website, www.paulagraves.com.

For Jenn,
who shares my love for all things Darcy.

Chapter One

Tablis, Kaziristan, baked beneath the August sunshine, and no amount of joking about it being a dry heat could make the place feel any cooler to the soldiers and diplomats assigned to protect the US Embassy against the rising unrest in the no-man's-land beyond the city walls.

For Nick Darcy, who'd spent most of his childhood in the cool, mild south of England, the brutal summer heat in the Central Asian republic was a shock to the system. The dress code for his job with the Diplomatic Security Service—suit, tie, holstered weapon—didn't help.

But the escalating tensions in the Kaziristan countryside had driven considerations such as climate and comfort from the minds of everyone tasked with the embassy's protection.

Something was building. Something bad. Darcy could feel it as if it were a living creature writhing beneath the dusty earth, making the very ground beneath his feet feel unsteady.

Trouble was coming. Fast and hard.

A harsh squawk of static from his handheld radio jangled his nerves. "BOGART on the move."

Darcy acknowledged the signal and watched from his post for the ambassador's car to emerge through the slowly opening gates. The dusty black sedan moved safely through the opening and onto the four-lane boulevard in front of the embassy. The sedan made it down the road about thirty yards before all hell broke loose.

A rocket-propelled grenade slammed into the ambassador's car and sent pieces flying through the air. One slab of metal debris slammed into the stone column next to Darcy, fragmenting the stone and sending a large chunk slamming into his forehead.

Staggered by the blow, he held on to the column to stay upright and tried to see through the blood pouring into his eyes. The road in front of the embassy was suddenly teeming with armed men and even more young men throwing rocks and swinging clubs.

The embassy was under siege.

Darcy managed to get his pistol out of his holster, but his movements felt slow and awkward, as if he couldn't quite convince his limbs to do what he asked of them.

A pair of small but strong hands wrapped around his arm and pulled. "Move it, Darcy! We're under siege!"

He turned to look at the speaker, tried to focus on her small, freckled face and her sharp green eyes, but the world seemed to be spinning out of control, around and around until black spots started to appear in his vision.

She muttered a profanity and started yelling for help in that hillbilly accent of hers that always made him smile. He tried to smile now, but his face felt paralyzed.

Nothing made sense. Not anymore.

His world fragmented into a thousand shards of light, then faded into nothing.

Nick Darcy woke to the sort of darkness that one found miles from a big city. No ambient light tempered the deep gloom, and the only noise was the sound of his heart pounding a rapid cadence of panic against his breastbone.

Only a dream.

Except it hadn't been. The embassy siege had happened. People had died, some in the most brutal ways imaginable.

And he'd been unable to save them.

He pushed the stem of his watch, lighting up the dial. Four in the morning. As he sat up and reached for the switch of the lamp on the table beside him, he heard a soft thump outside the cabin. His nerves, still in fight-or-flight mode, vibrated like the taut strings of a violin.

Leaving the light off, he reached for his SIG Sauer P229 and eased it from the holster lying on the coffee table in front of the sofa.

The noises could be coming from a scavenging raccoon venturing onto the cabin porch or the wind knocking a dead limb from one of the blight-ridden Fraser firs surrounding his cabin.

But between his years with the DSS and the past year he'd been working for Alexander Quinn at The Gates, he knew that bumps in the night could also mean deadly trouble.

As he moved silently toward the front door, he heard another sound from outside. A soft thump against the door, half knock, half scrape.

There was no security lens set into the heavy wood front door of the cabin, a failing he made a mental note to rectify as soon as possible. He improvised, edging toward the window that looked out onto the porch and angling his gaze toward the welcome mat in front of the door.

The view was obstructed by the angle, but he thought he could make out a dark mass lying on the porch.

He checked the SIG's magazine and chambered a round before he pulled open the front door.

A woman spilled inside and crumpled at his feet.

Fearing a trick, Darcy swept the porch with his gaze and his SIG until reassured the woman at his feet was his only visitor. Crouching next to her, he didn't touch her at first, looking for any signs of a booby trap or some sort of body-worn explosive.

Instead, he found blood. A lot of it, seeping through the woman's dark sweater and leaving a smear on the hardwood floor of the cabin.

In the dark, he couldn't make out much more about her except that she was small and slimly built, with a mass of curly hair that seemed to wrap itself around his fingers like a living creature as he pushed it aside to take a look at the face hidden beneath.

Even in the gloom, there was no mistaking the belligerent round chin or small, slightly snub nose.

"Rigsby?"

She stirred at the sound of his voice, her eyes opening enough for him to catch the slight glitter of reflected moonlight before her eyelids fluttered closed.

He pushed to his feet and flicked the light switch by the door, squinting against the sudden brightness. Illumination only made things seem more dire, he observed as he knelt beside McKenna Rigsby's still body and checked her vitals.

Her pulse was stronger and steadier than he'd anticipated. Good sign. The blood on her sweater, while sufficient in quantity to be alarming, seemed limited to only that one spot near her rib cage. He eased the sweater up and away from her skin, revealing a pair of bullet holes in the soft tissue of her left side, beneath the rib cage but above the curve of her hip. Not a large caliber, he saw with relief. The bullet had gone in and out without leaving a large exit wound.

Still, she needed medical attention, and soon.

Well, as soon as EMTs from town could get out to this stretch of wilderness in the Smoky Mountain foothills.

What was McKenna doing here? Had she come here looking for him after all these years?

Questions can wait. Find the phone. Call 911.

As he started to rise, McKenna's hand snaked out and

grabbed his, keeping him crouched beside her. Her eyelids opened to reveal bright green eyes dark with pain. "Don't trust anyone."

"What?"

"Don't trust anyone. Don't call a doctor." Her grasp weakened, her hand slipping away to fall with a soft thud to the floor. Her eyelids shut again, and she was out once more.

At any other point in his life, he'd have ignored her whispered commands and called 911 anyway. But the past few years had taught him a hell of a lot more than he wanted to know about treachery. He was on suspension from The Gates because of someone's treachery, with no access and no way to find out who was trying to destroy his life.

Tugging the sweater up again, he looked more closely at the bullet wounds, trying to remember everything he knew about field triage. Her pulse was still strong and steady, and the blood on her sweater, while a gory mess, wasn't more than a couple of pints. As long as no vital organs or blood vessels had been hit, she could survive that much loss of blood if he could stop the bleeding and rehydrate her.

The bullet holes in her side were only a half inch or so from the curve of her abdomen, so it was possible the bullet had gone through flesh only, missing any organs.

But why was she unconscious?

He checked her head, ignoring the way her curls tangled around his fingers as he gently probed her skull for any sign of a head injury. He felt no bumps, no cuts or abrasions, nothing to suggest she'd taken any sort of blow to the head. He sat back on his heels and observed her for a second.

She appeared thin. Thinner than he remembered, certainly. Her skin was naturally fair, but the darkened shadows beneath her eyes gave him an uneasy feeling in the pit of his stomach.

"Rigsby?"

Her eyelids fluttered open. "Hi."

He smiled. "Hi. Can you stick around this time and tell me what happened?"

"I'm tired." Her eyes started to close again.

He gave her a light shake, earning a grimace of displeasure from his patient. "If I'm going to do what you asked and not call a doctor, I need you to give me a good reason for my restraint."

Her eyes snapped open again, meeting his steadily for the first time. "Darcy."

"Rigsby."

Her lips curved slightly at his dry response. "Of all the cabins in all the Podunk little mountain towns…"

"You had to fall headfirst into mine."

"I knew you lived here." She made the admission as if she was a little embarrassed. "I didn't know who else to trust. Not even sure I can trust you, but I need help, so…"

"How bad are the gunshot wounds? Can you tell?"

"I don't think it hit anything major." She tried to rise, grimacing with the effort.

He helped her into a sitting position. "Define *major*."

She looked up at him through a tangle of auburn curls that had fallen over her forehead. "No internal organs or major blood vessels compromised."

"Are you certain?"

"I've been running through the woods for six hours and I haven't bled out yet."

Six hours? She'd been in this condition for six hours? "Do you know who shot you?"

She shook her head no. "Not a clue. Which is why I can't trust anyone." She pushed her hair back with one shaky hand, meeting his gaze. "I'm hoping I can trust you."

"You can," he said firmly. "We need to stop the bleeding."

She looked down at her side, her lips curling in dismay. "That's gonna leave a scar."

"Never knew you to be vain, Rigsby."

She looked at him from beneath a furrowed brow. "Been so long out of the DSS that you've forgotten what battle-field humor sounds like?"

He didn't feel like smiling. "Why would someone be shooting you, McKenna?"

She made a face at his use of her first name. "I was looking into something. For the FBI. I guess I got too close."

"Too close to what?"

She looked down at her bloody hands. "Do you think we could get me cleaned up a little before I undergo the post-mission debriefing, Agent Darcy?"

"I'm not with the DSS anymore."

She slanted him a look of pure irritation. "Yes, I know."

"Keeping up with my career, Rigsby?" He helped her to her feet, keeping his hands on her arms until he was sure she wouldn't topple over if he let go. "I'm touched."

She pulled her arms free of his grasp and took a stagger-ing step back before she regained her balance. "Purgatory is in my new jurisdiction," she said coolly. "I was assigned to the Knoxville Field Office a few months ago."

"After the incident at the Tri-State Law Enforcement Society conference?"

"As a matter of fact, yes." She tugged the edge of her bloody sweater down to cover her wounds, wincing. "I really need to sit down."

Muttering a soft curse, he crossed to where she stood and picked her up, tightening his grip against her weak strug-gles. "Stop fighting me and I'll let you go soon enough."

He carried her through the narrow hallway into the cabin's main bathroom and set her on the counter of the long double-sink cabinet. She looked around the spacious room, one ginger-brown eyebrow cocking upward. "Nice digs."

"It came with the job." Most of the men and women who

worked for Alexander Quinn had no idea that he owned about half the real estate in the foothills just east of Purgatory, including almost fifty rental cabins that brought in a generous income beyond his profits from The Gates. While the security and investigation agency was doing remarkably brisk business for a new company, the kind of high-tech services The Gates offered weren't inexpensive. But Quinn was a wealthy man in his own right, and if he had chosen to funnel his own money into the company, who was Darcy to question his wisdom?

"Looks like one of those tourist-honeymoon cabins." She nodded at the ridiculously large claw-foot tub. "Is your bed heart-shaped?"

"You'll see for yourself once you've cleaned up and re-hydrated."

"I could kill for a strong cup of coffee." She winced again as he tugged the hem of her sweater up to take another look at her wounds.

"We'll start with water and see how that goes." He opened the drawer of the sink cabinet and pulled out a clean wash-cloth. "First, we need to clean your wounds and get them disinfected."

"Don't suppose you know a crooked pharmacist we could bribe for some antibiotics?" she asked as he turned on the hot-water tap and let the water soak the washcloth.

"Sadly, no, though I could probably throw a stick in any direction and hit a methamphetamine dealer."

"We call 'em 'meth mechanics' or 'meth cookers' around here," she said, a smile in her voice despite the obvious pain creasing her forehead. "I will say you've lost a little of your accent since the last time I saw you."

"Perish the thought." He wrung some of the excess water from the washcloth before adding a dollop of antibiotic hand soap to the rag. "Not quite Betadine, but—"

"Ow!" She sucked in a harsh breath, making him feel like a brute.

"Sorry," he murmured, trying to take it easier on her.

"No, don't be gentle. The cleaner you get it, the less likely I'll end up in a hospital on an IV." She twisted to give him better access to her injury, moaning a little as he washed the ragged edges of the bullet wounds.

"You're likely to end up hospitalized no matter what I do," he warned as he rinsed blood from the used washcloth and dug into the drawer for a fresh one. "Why is it that you think there's no one you can trust?"

Instead of answering his question, she leaned forward, resting her forehead on his shoulder. Her low alto drawl came out weak and strained. "Hold off a second, okay?"

He put his hand on the back of her head, his fingers tangling in her curls. Her skin was hot and damp, and her breath burned against his throat when she turned her head toward him.

"I was so afraid you wouldn't be here," she murmured.

"I'm here." He stroked her hair, fighting against an old familiar ache of longing. McKenna Rigsby had twisted him into knots once, a long time ago, and it had taken years to untangle himself.

"I know you have every reason to be mad at me, Darcy," she whispered against his collarbone. "I wouldn't blame you if you tossed me back into the woods to fend for myself."

"I would never do that."

She lifted her head, gazing up at him with pain-dark eyes. She lifted one bloodstained hand to his face. "I know. That's why I came to you."

He couldn't stop himself from bending to touch his forehead to hers. Her breath came out in an explosive little whoosh, mingling with his ragged respiration. "You'll be the death of me yet, Rigsby."

"I never wanted to hurt you, Darcy. That's why—" Her

words ended on a soft sigh. "I don't like to need people. You know that."

All too well. "But you need me now."

She pulled back, her gaze intense. "I do. I need your help."

"You have it."

To his surprise, tears welled in her eyes. She brushed them away with her knuckles. "Ready to give this torture another go?"

He reached for the hot washcloth and the hand soap. "Are you?"

She stripped her sweater over her head, tossing the bloody garment onto the floor, revealing her bra and a holster on her right hip the sweater had hidden. She tugged the holster free and laid it on the counter, the Glock 27 gleaming.

Bending to expose her side to him, she told him, "Finish it."

He cleaned the wounds a second time, making sure to remove anything that looked like debris from the raw skin. The bleeding had nearly stopped, he saw with relief. If he could get a few pints of water into her, she should recover from the blood loss soon enough.

He washed the blood from his own hands and opened the cabinet over the nearest sink. He had a prepackaged first-aid kit stored there, though he wasn't sure the maker had planned for a medical emergency that included bullet wounds. There were better kits stocked at The Gates, but he was on paid leave from the agency at the moment. He could hardly sneak in and spirit out supplies without someone taking notice.

Pulling out the best tools available—antiseptic wipes, antibiotic ointment, sterile gauze pads and some surgical tape—he treated and bandaged the wounds as quickly and efficiently as he could. "The sweater is a loss, I fear."

"Just lend me a T-shirt." She slanted an amused look at him as she picked up her weapon and holster. "You do own one, don't you?"

"Several, actually." He helped her down from the sink counter, trying to ignore the silky heat of her bare skin beneath his fingers. She wobbled a little, and he slipped his arm around her shoulders, keeping her upright as they left the bathroom and headed down the narrow hall to his bedroom.

As he dug in the large chest of drawers in the corner for a clean shirt for her, she eyed his large bed with a hint of dismay. "Not heart-shaped."

"Sadly, no." He handed her a black T-shirt and a long-sleeved fleece jacket. "It'll get cold in the night."

"Where are you going to sleep?" She eased the T-shirt over her head with a grimace.

"The sofa in my study is comfortable."

"I should take it." She swayed a little, her face paler than usual.

He caught her before she collapsed, easing her down to the bed. "Let's get you under the covers." He pulled back the blanket and helped her slide between the sheets. Tucking the blanket up around her, he added, "We need to get some fluids back into you. Think you could handle soup or some broth as well as water?"

She caught his hand as he started to rise. "Wait. First, I need to tell you something." Her voice faltered, and her eyes began to droop again. "There's a reason you can't trust anyone. You can't let anyone know I'm here. Not even someone you trust."

"What the hell is going on, Rigsby?" He cradled her

face between his palms, not liking the flushed heat rising in her cheeks. "Who is after you?"

"I'm not sure exactly," she admitted, her eyes fluttering to stay open. "But I know it's someone I work with."

He frowned. "Someone you work with?"

Her gaze steadied, locking with his. "Whoever shot me was working with someone in the FBI."

Chapter Two

McKenna could see the wheels in Nick Darcy's mind turning at turbo speed. Despite his recent clashes with hide-
bound bureaucracy, she knew there would always be a part
of Darcy that tried to play by the rules. He'd grown up in
a Foreign Service household, where protocol and diplo-
macy reigned, and not even the past few months of work
as a private security contractor had freed him from those
constraints.

"Someone in the FBI?" He dropped his hands away from
her face and rose from the bed.

"You say that as if you'd never seen government cor-
ruption." Her whole left side was beginning to ache like a
bad tooth, and her throat felt dry and scratchy. "I don't suppose we could discuss this further over a gallon of water
and some ibuprofen?"

"Of course." He disappeared through the bedroom door
as if a horde of rogue FBI agents were after him.

She fell back against the pillows of his bed and stared
up at the exposed beams of the ceiling, trying to pretend
she didn't feel like one big bloody wound. She was in a
safe place, for now at least, which was a hell of a lot better
position than she'd been in just an hour ago.

Only a handful in the FBI knew the dangerous game
she'd been playing for the past three months. One of them

had put her in the crosshairs of a deadly group of domestic terrorists and given them the go-ahead to pull the trigger. Literally.

But who?

Darcy returned to the bedroom carrying a wicker basket. When he set it on the bed and opened the latch at the top, McKenna saw it was exactly what it looked like—a picnic basket containing a large bottle of water, a metal thermos and a bottle of ibuprofen tablets.

"I didn't think you'd want anything heavy, so the soup is just chicken broth. I packed a few crackers in there if you want them." He set the water bottle on the bedside table next to her. "How long since you last ate?"

She rubbed her gritty eyes. "Yesterday. I had a protein bar around dinnertime, I think."

He went still, his hand closed around the top of the vacuum flask. His dark eyes slanted to meet hers. "How long have you been running, Rigsby?"

"Two days."

Slowly, he withdrew the thermos and sleeve of crackers from the basket and set them on the night table beside the water. He picked up the bottle of pain-reliever tablets and set the basket on the floor before he sat down beside her.

"You've been running for two days."

She tried to push up to a sitting position, biting her lip at the hard arc of pain that rushed down her side in response.

Darcy leaned forward and wrapped his arms around her, pulling her upright until they sat in an approximation of an intimate embrace.

Except, it didn't feel like an approximation. It felt right. So right.

Darcy's arms fell away too soon, and he sat back, his eyes fathomless. "What sent you on the run?"

"It's a really long story."

His eyes narrowed slightly. "One you don't intend to share with me?"

"I didn't say that."

"Here." He leaned forward, his chest brushing against her shoulder as he picked up the thermos. As he removed the top, the fragrant steam of hot broth drifted past her nose, igniting a storm of hunger in the pit of her empty stomach. "Eat. Then sleep. We can talk when you're stronger."

Watching him pour broth into the cap of the thermos, she sighed. "I will tell you everything I know, Darcy."

His gaze angled to meet hers. "Yes. You will."

The firmness of his tone should have irritated her. Instead, it sent a flutter of relief rolling through her, as if she'd finally reached the solid shore after an endless battle with a raging sea.

He gave her the thermos lid that doubled as a mug. "Drink."

She drank a few swallows of the hot broth, trying not to shiver as warmth spread through her insides and started to warm her chilled bones. Darcy picked up the bottle of ibuprofen, shook out a couple of tablets and handed them to her. "Want the water or can you swallow them down with the broth?"

She took the tablets and washed them down with a couple of gulps of broth. "Thank you."

"You are safe here, Rigsby. You know that, don't you?" There was a soft tone to Darcy's voice that she'd rarely heard in all the time she'd known him. She looked up to find him watching her from beneath a furrowed brow.

"As safe as I am anywhere," she agreed.

His hand moved toward her, just a few inches, before falling back in his lap. She felt an answering tug low in her belly, a sensation so familiar it made her want to cry.

How long had she been fighting against the pull of him? As long as she'd known him?

The siege in Kaziristan had happened almost eight years ago. She'd been a rookie FBI agent, fresh out of law school and the Academy. Her first overseas assignment had landed her in the middle of a brewing civil uprising, working as an assistant in the FBI Legal Attaché Office in Tablis—the legat, in bureau parlance. The legat's primary missions in Tablis had been to train the local police forces in counter-terrorism strategies and to aid in the investigation of crimes against US citizens, especially embassy personnel.

She'd gotten a quick and brutal lesson in both during her time in Kaziristan. So had Nick Darcy.

"Do you still see people from Tablis?" she asked as she reached for the sleeve of crackers he'd set on the nightstand.

He got there first, pulling open the airtight packaging and holding it out for her to retrieve a couple of crackers. "Sometimes. I ran into Maddox Heller a few years ago in the Caribbean."

"Wow, that's a blast from the past." She nibbled the edge of one of the crackers. "Y'all so shafted him after the siege."

Darcy's expression tightened. "I had nothing to do with it."

"Right. It was all Barton Reid, I guess?" She grimaced. Marine Security Guard Maddox Heller had saved dozens of lives during the siege in Tablis, but the State Department had made him a scapegoat for the security mistakes made at the embassy.

"It wasn't all Reid's doing. But he was the instigator, yes."

"I knew he was a snake. Didn't shed a tear when I heard he got life for his crimes." She sipped some more broth. "How was Heller when you saw him?"

"He was living life as a beach bum."

She winced. "That bad?"

"*Beach bum* is perhaps an exaggeration." Darcy's lips curved, almost forming a smile. "He'd inherited a good deal of money and invested well. But he dressed atrociously, worked questionable jobs and frequented shady establishments, so—"

"The horror."

His lips tilted farther upward. "He's married now. Moved back to the States to be with the woman. Has a young daughter." There was more to Maddox Heller's story he wasn't sharing, she saw, but she didn't push. Another lesson she'd learned from her year in Kaziristan—some secrets needed to remain unspoken. Lives could depend on it.

"Good for him." She made herself swallow the remaining broth in the thermos cup before she set it on the nightstand next to the flask. "How's Quinn?"

"Largely unchanged." A hint of irritation edged his voice.

"He's the one who put you on administrative leave?"

His gaze snapped to meet hers. "How do you know about that?"

"We're the FBI. We hear things."

The annoyed expression that came over his face was so familiar she could barely suppress a smile. "There's an internal investigation into an information leak."

"Right. A leak about what?"

He arched an eyebrow. "I'm not the leak."

She reached across the space between them and put her hand on his arm. His gaze darkened, but he didn't look away. "I know you're not."

He pressed his hand over hers briefly, then moved her hand away and stood. "I'll leave everything here in case you get thirsty later. Call out if you need me. I'll be listening."

"Thank you." A sense of calm reassurance swamped her suddenly, making tears of relief prick her eyes. She hadn't been sure, even to the last second before Darcy opened the door, that she'd made the right decision coming here. But now she knew her instincts had been correct.

Nick Darcy might not like her very much these days. He probably didn't trust her, at least on a personal basis, at all.

But he was still the only person she trusted to have her back in a crisis.

HE WAS HARBORING a woman with bullet wounds in her side. An FBI agent, to be exact, a woman who now claimed that someone in her own agency had targeted her for murder and nearly succeeded.

"Bloody hell," he murmured, dropping onto the sofa in his study and sinking into the comfortable cushions, his mind racing a mile a minute.

His first instinct, he realized with some surprise, was to call Alexander Quinn. Only a few years back, his instinct would have been quite the opposite.

The trill of his cell phone sent a jangle of nerves jarring their way up his spine. He grabbed the phone from the nearby desk and shook his head as he saw the name on the display. "What is it, Quinn?"

"I've received notice of an APB out for an FBI agent suspected of aiding and abetting a domestic terrorist group."

Darcy went still. "And you're telling me this because?"

"We know her. From Kaziristan."

There had been only one female FBI agent in the legat in Tablis. "McKenna Rigsby?"

"That's the one."

"Aiding and abetting a domestic terrorist group how?"

"The information I received didn't say, and I didn't ask." Quinn's voice deepened. "She attended that law enforcement conference the Blue Ridge Infantry infiltrated a few months ago. Maybe they had more people on the inside than we realized at the time."

"And you're telling me all of this now because?"

"Because the last time anyone saw her, she was crossing Killshadow Road, about a mile from your place."

Darcy tightened his grip on the phone, his skin prickling with alarm. She was spotted so near? It must have been a recent sighting. Searchers were probably close by.

Would they want to search his place?

"I haven't seen her since Kaziristan," he lied. "And I doubt she'd care to see me again, considering how strained our acquaintance had become by the time we parted ways."

"You never told me what happened."

"No, I didn't."

"You will contact me if you spot her?" Quinn asked.

"You're first on my speed dial."

If Quinn noticed his reply was hardly an affirmative answer, he didn't respond. In fact, he said nothing else before he disconnected the call.

Darcy released a pent-up breath and set the phone on the desk as he rose and crossed to the window. Killshadow Road was the only regular road leading into this part of the woods. Gravel and dirt roads branched off the paved road for a stretch of five or six miles, some leading to occupied cabins, while others ended in grown-over plots of land where cabins had once stood.

Back during the boom period for the area, when the Smoky Mountains became a tourist destination for people in the southeastern United States, entrepreneurs had tried to capitalize on the desire for short-term mountain living, and tourist cabins and resorts had begun to dot the landscape for miles just outside the national park's perimeter. Some of those resorts had thrived, especially those easily accessed from the interstate and major highways.

Others, like Purgatory, Tennessee, had never caught the imagination of the tourists.

It was a shame, Darcy thought, because there was a lot to recommend the little town in the middle of nowhere.

"Was that Quinn on the phone?"

The sound of McKenna's faint voice sent a little thrill

of awareness rushing up his spine to spread like tingles through his brain. He turned and saw, with dismay, that she was as pale as a winter sky and barely upright, leaning against the door frame.

He crossed quickly to her side and wrapped his arm around her waist, taking care to avoid the site of her wounds. "What are you doing out of bed?"

"He told you, didn't he?" Her breath warmed his neck and stirred the hair behind his ear, sending a different sort of tingle coursing through him. He ignored the bad timing of his libido and helped her back to the bedroom.

"If you mean he told me you're wanted by the FBI, then yes. He did."

She slumped back against the pillows, looking defeated. "You told him I'm here. Didn't you." It wasn't a question.

He tucked the covers up around her. "I didn't. I should have, God knows. But I don't think he wanted to know."

Her brow furrowed. "What do you mean?"

"If Quinn wanted to know if you were here, he'd have stopped by to see for himself. Instead, he wanted to get me some information I needed, in case you *were* here."

"That's ridiculously convoluted," she muttered.

"That's Quinn." He smoothed the blanket beside her. "He believes you're being railroaded. And he wants me to do anything possible to protect you."

She levered herself upward to a half-sitting position, grimacing. "What do *you* believe?"

"I believe you're in trouble."

Her eyes narrowed, and he saw his halfhearted answer had struck a blow. She looked away and finished sitting up. "I can go." She plucked at the hem of the borrowed shirt. "Can I keep the tee? My sweater is a loss."

He closed his hands over her arms, holding her in place when she started to edge toward the other side of the bed. "Don't be stupid."

"Don't be insulting." She shook off his hands.

"I don't think you've hooked up with a domestic terror group."

"Wow, thanks for that vote of confidence."

"But I know how little you care for the rules if you think they'll stop you from getting the outcome you want." He kept his tone gentle, though there was an edge of bitterness he couldn't quite keep out of his voice.

"And I know how piously you worship them," she shot back.

"We had to follow the evacuation protocols."

"And Cameron died!" Her voice rose to a point before dropping to a hoarse half whisper. "He died because we left him behind."

He pushed down a surge of guilt and kept his voice as even as he dared. "I know that. I never, ever forget that."

"We could've—" Her voice broke, and he knew she was thinking the same thing he was. If they'd stayed to save Cameron from the fire, they'd have died, too. That part of the embassy had collapsed seconds after they cleared the area. Lingering one minute more would have been certain death for all three of them.

"No, we couldn't. And I know you'll never forgive me for pulling you out of there. I can live with that." He put one finger under her chin and tipped her face up, willing her to look at him.

Her eyes drifted closed, refusing to comply.

He dropped his hand away. "I know that whatever you've done, whatever you're doing now, is something you believe is right. Whatever rules you've broken, whatever orders you've defied, you've done it with good intentions. That's what I believe."

Slowly, she opened her eyes and looked at him, fire in her expression. She spoke slowly and carefully, her accent disappearing with her precise pronunciation. "I broke the rules, Darcy, because someone in the FBI was aware I was getting close to discovering their link to the Blue Ridge Infantry and their hodgepodge of associates. Those people have gone beyond meth dealing and planting pipe bombs. They are up to something huge. Mass-casualty huge. And someone in the FBI is facilitating their plans."

"And you don't know who?"

"Six people in the FBI knew I was trying to infiltrate the Blue Ridge Infantry. One of them set me up. I just don't know which one."

She looked even paler than before, he realized, except for the bruise-like purple shadows beneath her haunted eyes. He hated what he was about to say but he had no choice. Quinn's call had been a clear signal.

"I know you're tired. Clearly you need rest."

"I'm okay—"

"No, you're not." He reached over to the nightstand and picked up the thermos. He checked to make sure the seal was tight before he put it in the wicker basket on the floor at his feet. "But this can't be helped."

"What are you doing?"

"Packing," he said as he reached for the water bottle and checked the top, as well. "We have to leave this cabin now. Before the people out there looking for you realize you came here."

Chapter Three

"How are you holding up?"

Darcy's low voice rumbled like thunder through her pain-hazed mind, stirring her from a jumble of disjointed dreams. All she could remember of those fractured images was the loamy smell of decaying leaves on the forest floor beneath her nose as she hid from a horde of faceless shadows chasing her through the woods.

She twisted her head to look at him. "How do you think?"

"You look like bloody hell."

"You're so free with the compliments, Darcy. People will talk." She realized they weren't moving. Looking up, she saw they were in a line of cars waiting for a stoplight to change colors. "Where are we?"

"Just south of Bitterwood."

"Where's that?"

"Just south of Purgatory."

"And where's that?"

"Somewhere north of hell." Darcy's lips quirked at the corners. "I think you'd be safe to take some acetaminophen now if you think it'll help with the pain. Your ibuprofen dose was nearly two hours ago."

She shook her head. "No more pain relievers. They're making me feel loopy and that's worse than the pain."

He pressed the back of his hand to her cheek, catching her off guard. She slanted a questioning look toward him and he dropped his hand away. "Over-the-counter pain relievers shouldn't be making you feel loopy. You're a little warm for my liking."

She shifted in her seat, sucking in a quick gasp at the ache in her injured side. "You think I have a fever?"

"Maybe. I don't have time to get the first-aid kit out." Ahead, the light had turned green and they started moving again. "We'll be there soon and I'll take your temperature and see where we are."

"Where is 'there'?" She fought to keep her eyes open, weary of the nightmares that chased her through her dreams when she drifted off.

"It's a cabin. Belongs to someone I work with."

"Quinn?"

"No. Someone else. He's out of town for a week. Took his sister and his fiancée to the beach to celebrate. His cabin is empty for the next few days, and it's deep in the woods, far enough from here that no one should bother us."

Even through the haze of pain, mention of a trip to the beach caught her attention. "Are you talking about Hunter Bragg?"

He angled a sharp look toward her. "You know Bragg?"

"I know his fiancée. She's my cousin. I talked to her a couple of weeks ago, before everything in my undercover op started going belly-up." She quirked one corner of her mouth. "Pear-shaped, I think you Brits call it."

"Not a Brit," he murmured, but his lips curved upward. It was an old joke between them, one she hadn't been certain he'd remember after all this time.

He was technically as American as she was. He just sounded like his British-born mother after spending his formative years in England.

"Did you tell Hunter what's going on?" she asked after his smile faded.

"Of course not."

"So we're breaking in and staking out squatters' rights for a few days while he's away?"

"Yes."

"That sounds a whole lot like breaking the rules, Darcy."

"I like to live life on the edge." His dry tone made her laugh, which she instantly regretted.

"Ow," she moaned, shifting to find a more comfortable position.

"We're close," he promised her, and sure enough, within a few minutes he had turned the Land Rover off the main highway onto a one-lane road that twisted and turned deep into the woods.

The one lane ended abruptly in the middle of nowhere, and for a second, McKenna thought they'd taken a wrong turn. But at the last second, Darcy steered the Land Rover onto a narrow dirt road the woods seemed to swallow whole.

The road twisted and climbed until they appeared to be a long way from anything approaching civilization. Then the dirt road disappeared, and Darcy stopped the Land Rover and turned off the engine.

McKenna gazed into the dense thicket of trees in front of them, her heart sinking. "Where's the cabin?"

"Through those trees."

She felt sick at the thought of trudging through the woods again so soon. "Don't suppose we could just stay here? Bunk down in the back?"

"I promise, it's not far." He unbuckled his seat belt and got out of the SUV, walked around the front and opened the passenger door. His dark eyes met hers steadily. "You can do this."

Gritting her teeth, she unbuckled her own seat belt and eased her legs toward the open door, trying to ignore the burning ache in her side. "If anyone ever says 'It's just a flesh wound' to me again, I swear I'm going to belt them right in the mouth."

He held out his hands. She took them and let him help her to the ground. Her legs felt like noodles, but she willed herself to stay upright, not wanting to show any weakness in front of Darcy. If she couldn't convince him she was on the mend, he would ignore her wishes and follow his own instincts to call in help.

And if he did that, they both might end up dead.

McKENNA HAD GONE from pasty white to a sickly gray color by the time the evergreen trees gave way with shocking suddenness to a narrow clearing that housed a small, rustic-looking cabin. Darcy slid his arm around her shoulders and felt her tremble under his touch.

"Thank God," she murmured, leaning her head briefly against his shoulder before she started to move again.

"It's hardly the Waldorf," he warned as he helped her up the three steps to the cabin porch and settled her in one of the two cane-bottom rockers that sat to the right of the door.

"Whatever."

He wasn't sure she'd be so blasé about the cabin's primitive comforts. The owner, Hunter Bragg, didn't live there full-time, but it was apparently a favorite getaway for him and his new fiancée, if office scuttlebutt was anything to go by.

There was no easily discovered spare key to be had, Darcy was certain. The Gates trained their agents not to be careless.

But the agency also taught their agents to be skilled and

resourceful. Darcy pulled a lock-pick kit from his backpack and made quick work of the dead bolt on the front door.

"That is so illegal," McKenna murmured, sounding impressed.

He shot her a quick smile. "I am not the man you knew in Kaziristan."

"I'm beginning to see that." She pushed herself up from the rocker, wobbling a little when she gained her feet.

He caught her elbow in his firm grasp and led her into the dark cabin.

The power was running, though all the lights and appliances had been turned off, leaving the cabin's interior shadowed in the early-morning gloom. Darcy flicked the light switch on, and the overhead lamps revealed a small, cold front room furnished with an old but sturdy-looking sofa, what looked like an old Army footlocker doubling as a coffee table, and a couple of mismatched armchairs that sat across from the sofa to create a shabby but cozy conversation area.

"Are you cold?" he asked, nodding toward the fireplace.

She followed his gaze, one eyebrow arching as she saw that, instead of logs, the width of the hearth was filled with a large electric space heater. "Well. *That's* different."

"Apparently the point of this backwoods haven is maximum seclusion and secrecy. I suppose smoke rising from the chimney would negate that effect." He took her arm and eased her over to the sofa. "Sit. I'll retrieve the rest of the supplies from the Land Rover."

By the time he returned with the two large duffel bags he and McKenna had stuffed full of supplies they might need, McKenna had curled up into a miserable-looking knot on the sofa.

"You look ill," he commented as he set the duffels on the floor.

"You're such a sweet talker, Darcy. I bet all the ladies love you."

He ignored her soft gibe and crossed to her side, placing the back of his hand against her cheek. She was definitely warmer than she'd been in the car. And she'd been quite warm then.

"I need to take a look at your wounds."

She managed a grimace of a smile. "Is that a proposition?"

"It's a statement of fact. You appear to be feverish. If your wounds are infected, we need to alter our plan."

"We had a plan?" she asked through gritted teeth as she plucked the hem of his T-shirt away from her side.

Blood had oozed through the gauze bandage, he saw, though not a lot. He eased the bandage away from her torn skin and took in the two holes in her flesh. The skin around them was reddened and warm to the touch. "I'm afraid infection may be setting in."

"Clean it again," she said. "Just give me a bullet to bite first."

"You need antibiotics. We need to get you to a physician."

"Can't do that," she said with a firm shake of her head. "Any other ideas?"

One, but he didn't particularly like it. "I could break into the free clinic in Bitterwood and steal some antibiotics."

She stared at him in stunned silence for a moment. "You are definitely not the man I knew in Kaziristan."

He wasn't. He hadn't been for a long time.

"Is there an option between those two extremes?" she asked when he said nothing else.

He nodded. "I can call on someone I trust for help."

"He hasn't made contact again, has he?"

Alexander Quinn looked up from his laptop computer

and found Olivia Sharp standing in the doorway of his office, her shoulder leaning against the door frame. Her bare, shapely legs seemed to rise for miles before disappearing beneath the charcoal pencil skirt of her lightweight summer suit. She was a tall woman who didn't need to wear heels to be imposing, but today's footwear sported four-inch heels and open toes that displayed the impertinent bright green of her toenail polish.

"He has not," he answered her question. "Have you anything new to report?"

She shook her head as she entered the office and closed the door. "Anson Daughtry has taken advantage of his administrative leave to drive down to Atlanta for something called The Mixed Magic Tour. Five alt-punk bands on one stage, lots of alcohol and girls with rainbow-colored hair." She shrugged. "Are you sure he's thirty-two?"

Quinn tamped down a smile. "Almost thirty-three."

"Either he's not concerned about the internal investigation or he's trying very hard to appear unconcerned." Olivia shot Quinn a shrewd look. "I'm leaning toward the latter."

Quinn concurred. "What about the agent you assigned to him?"

"He can hardly follow him to Atlanta. Daughtry would spot him." Olivia sat in the chair across from Quinn's desk and crossed one long leg over the other. "I take it Darcy hasn't sent out a distress signal to the other agent?"

"Not yet."

"How did he sound when you talked to him earlier?"

"Worried. And wary."

She nodded. "To be expected."

"You haven't told me which man you most suspect of being the mole."

"I consider everyone a suspect at the moment." She arched one honey-brown eyebrow. "Even you."

He smiled at that. "Anything new on the FBI angle?"

"I'm not exactly the bureau's favorite former denizen."

"Still, you worked for the FBI for almost eight years. Surely there's a contact left you can exploit."

Her brow furrowed, and he realized he'd touched a nerve. "I've put out some feelers."

He frowned at her wary tone. "What aren't you telling me?"

"I've told you everything I know pertinent to this case."

"The next time you bother to come to my office to talk, I expect you to be the one supplying information. Clear?"

Her full lips thinned with annoyance. "Yes, sir." She rose like a waterbird taking flight, all long legs and soaring, restless spirit. She stalked to the door in three long strides, then turned at the last moment to look at him.

"I'm going to find out who's leaking information from this agency, Quinn. No matter who it is. How's that for a little useful information?" Before he could respond, she was out the door, letting it shut with a loud snap behind her.

Quinn sat back in his chair, regarded the closed door and unsuccessfully tried to stifle a smile.

His intercom buzzed. Line four—Dennison. He felt a flutter of anticipation as he picked up the phone. "Tell me you've got something."

Cain Dennison's gravelly voice held a hint of irritation. Quinn knew the agent didn't care for spying on one of his own, even in an attempt to clear his name. "He called two minutes ago."

"What did he want?"

"He wants a few minutes alone with my grandmother."

"SHE'S A WHAT?" McKenna stared at Darcy, certain she'd misunderstood.

"A sort of mountain healer, if the stories are true." Darcy checked the magazine of his SIG Sauer and slid the pistol into the pancake holster behind his back. He shrugged a thin plaid shirt over his T-shirt and jeans, leaving the buttons open in the front. "Do I look like a local?"

She took in his day's growth of beard and broad, muscular shoulders, the casual clothing and the baseball cap he pulled low over his forehead. "As long as you keep your mouth shut."

"I shouldn't have to speak to anyone but Lila Birdsong."

"Pretty name."

"She's an interesting lady, if her grandson's stories are anything to go by." He checked his watch. "I have to go soon."

"Are you sure you can trust this Dennison guy you called?"

"As much as I trust anyone." She could tell from his tone that he wasn't as certain about Dennison's motives for helping him as she'd hoped.

"You know the protocol for internal investigation is to use an agent's closest friends against him."

He nodded. "I'm pretty sure Dennison's the agent Quinn has assigned to keep an eye on me. So might as well let him. I have nothing to hide."

"Except me."

"Quinn already knows about you. He's already made his choice which side he's on—yours."

"How does he know I haven't gone to the dark side since we all last worked together?" she asked curiously, resting her head against the sofa cushions as she watched him pace a tight circle next to the coffee table.

"I suspect he knows more about your career than almost anyone but your supervisor." Darcy stopped in front of her, his brown eyes narrowing. "He knows more than I do, certainly."

"Do you think I've gone to the dark side?" she asked, curious.

His smile made his eyes sparkle. "I always thought you

were on the dark side, Rigsby." His smile faded. "Are you
certain you're going to be all right here alone?"

She patted the holstered Glock 27 sitting on the sofa next
to her. "Mr. Glock and I will be just fine."

He took the portable phone off its cradle and set it in
front of her on the footlocker coffee table. "You have my
cell number memorized?"

"You've spent the last hour drilling it into my brain."
Her achy, tired brain. "Just go see what the witch woman
has for us. And if you don't like what she has to say, you
have my permission to rob a pharmacy."

"Duly noted." He opened the front door and turned to
look back at her. "You sure you're okay to stay here alone?"

"I'm fine. Go. Hurry back."

She forced herself to remain upright until he was out the
door. But as soon as the lock clicked shut, she slumped back
against the sofa cushions, gazing at the holstered Glock by
her side. It looked far away and heavy.

She hoped the next time the door opened, it would be
Darcy returning. Because she was anything but fine—and
in no shape to fight for her life.

Lila Birdsong lived near the top of Mulberry Rise, below
the craggy face of Miller's Knob, in a small cabin surrounded by dense evergreen woods. Darcy had been there
once, with Cain Dennison and a few of the other Gates
agents, for a cookout in the brick barbecue pit behind Dennison's old silver Airstream trailer. From Darcy's cabin, the
drive had taken five minutes.

From Hunter Bragg's cabin in the middle of nowhere,
however, the winding mountain roads and sharp switch-
backs took almost twenty minutes to navigate.

Twenty long minutes for something to go terribly wrong
back at the cabin where McKenna waited for him to return.

Her temperature had been elevated when Darcy checked

it before he left, but not high enough for immediate concern. McKenna had downed a couple of ibuprofen and told him to go meet with Lila Birdsong, although he could tell she was skeptical that Cain Dennison's grandmother could provide anything useful to stop her wounds from becoming any more infected.

He would normally be as skeptical, but Quinn himself had consulted with Lila Birdsong about herbal remedies that could work as stopgaps in the field, when prescription medications weren't readily available.

Maybe she wouldn't be able to come up with anything to help him. But the alternative was getting antibiotics by deception or outright theft.

The road up the mountain topped off suddenly, giving Darcy a good look at the small clearing where Lila's cabin sat. The Airstream trailer that had been home to Cain Dennison was gone.

But in its place sat a Ridge County Sheriff's Department cruiser.

Chapter Four

The FBI legal attaché in Tablis, Kaziristan, had been a cramped office located at the back of the slightly shabby embassy building. Only one small window, set high in the back wall, let any natural light into the room, but the men and women who'd crowded into the tight space hadn't had much time for gazing out windows.

Eight years ago, Tablis had simmered in the harsh summer heat, close to boiling.

McKenna had been twenty-four years old, law school and twenty weeks of FBI Academy training behind her and a whole new career ahead of her. She'd been shocked and happily surprised by the assignment to the embassy legat. Even though it was largely grunt work, an embassy placement was a plum assignment for a green agent. Her superiors had assured her it was a sign that the bureau had high hopes for her career advancement.

Then everything had gone to hell in a firestorm of rocket-propelled grenades and brutal al Adar terrorists on a mission of death and chaos. She'd been lucky to get out of the embassy alive. Several other Americans hadn't fared as well, including three of her legat office associates.

She pushed herself up from the sofa, not liking the trembling weakness in her knees as she crossed to the front window to look out at the woods beyond the small cabin clearing. Morning was giving way to midday, the light moving inexorably toward the west.

Darcy had been gone almost twenty minutes.

Letting the curtains swing closed, she leaned against the windowsill, feeling achy all over. She felt hot and grimy, in desperate need of a shower and about a week of sleep, but she didn't trust her shaky limbs to hold her weight long enough to take a shower. Plus, the hot water might reopen her wounds and start the bleeding again.

Damn it.

She stumbled her way back to the sofa and sank into the cushions, hating how weak she felt. She'd worked so hard to stay fit, stay strong, keep up with the men in her FBI unit, and one stupid bullet—one that hadn't even hit any vital organs—had her as wobbly and weak as a newborn calf.

The last time she'd felt this shaky, she'd been huddled with several other embassy employees in a curtained alcove, watching an al Adar rebel named Tahir Mahmood slit the throat of one of the embassy's translators, helpless to do anything in case it alerted the other armed terrorists swarming the embassy to their hiding place.

She'd grown up just over the state line in North Carolina, until her family had moved to Raleigh when she was a teenager. Life in the Appalachian Mountains could be both beautiful and hard, and she'd experienced both sides of that life. But nothing she'd seen or heard in the hills, during her FBI training or during the first ten months of work at the US Embassy in Tablis had prepared her for the raw brutality and utter disregard for human life she'd witnessed during the embassy siege.

It had changed her. Her outlook on life. Her career goals. Her hopes.

We have to go back for him!

Her own voice rang in her mind—younger somehow, more naive and trusting than now. She'd thought they could save Michael Cameron, one of her fellow legat agents, when rockets had set their section of the damaged embassy ablaze. She'd wanted to dig through the rubble a little longer, try to reach him before the flames could, but the back section of the embassy had been crumbling around them.

Darcy had grabbed her arms and forcibly removed her from the area, hustling her, even dragging her to other parts of the embassy that had remained structurally stable during the onslaught of rocket fire.

They'd eventually met up with several other embassy employees being herded to safety by one of the embassy's Marine Security Guards, a Georgia boy named Maddox Heller. Heller had sneaked them into the alcove in the formal dining room to hide when al Adar rebels had stormed that section of the embassy.

Teresa Miles, a pretty young interpreter in her first Foreign Service assignment, hadn't been so fortunate.

A trilling sound made her nerves jangle. The phone was ringing.

She picked up the receiver and glanced at the digital display window. Darcy's cell-phone number.

Should she answer? What if something had gone wrong? What if it was a trick?

Quelling a surge of fear, she pushed the answer button and lifted the phone to her ear. But she didn't speak.

"Rigsby?" Darcy's voice was low and soft on the other end.

"Yes," she breathed. "Are you okay?"

"For the moment." Even over the phone, she could hear the tension in his voice. "When I arrived at Lila Birdsong's cabin, there was a sheriff's cruiser there. I think I know who it is, but she knows me. I can't risk going inside yet until she comes out."

"Won't she see the Land Rover?"

"Not unless she's looking. I've hidden in the woods off the road."

"Darcy, this is crazy. Just get back here. We'll figure out something else. I'm feeling better already," she added, wondering if he could discern the lie on his end of the line.

"No, you're not," he growled, answering her question. "I've been searching the internet on my phone while waiting, and I encountered some options for us to try before we start breaking into pharmacies."

"Don't take any stupid risks, Darcy."

She could almost hear his smile. "I never take stupid risks, Rigsby. Only smart ones. I'll be in touch." He hung up before she could respond.

She hung up and set the phone on the coffee table, her hand trembling and her pulse pounding in her ears.

THE SHERIFF'S CRUISER passed slowly on its way down the mountain road, the midday sun glinting off the chrome and briefly obscuring the driver as the vehicle approached Darcy's hiding place in the woods. He'd left the SUV behind and walked closer to the road for a better view.

The glint faded as the cruiser rolled past, giving Darcy a good view of the driver's shoulder-length bob of dark hair and pretty profile. Sara Lindsey. Cain Dennison's girlfriend.

Darcy knew that Sara and Cain's grandmother had become close a few months earlier, when Sara had returned home to Ridge County after several years as a Birmingham, Alabama, police officer. Maybe her visit to Lila Birdsong had been entirely unrelated to the call he'd made to Cain Dennison.

Or maybe it had everything to do with it.

He pulled out his phone and punched in Dennison's phone number. The Gates agent answered on the third ring. "Darcy?"

"Did you tell anyone besides your grandmother that I was going to visit her?"

"No." Cain sounded curious. "Did something happen?"

"Your girlfriend was at your grandmother's place when I arrived."

"So?"

"So, I didn't expect to see a Ridge County sheriff's deputy as part of the welcoming committee."

Cain sounded confused. "It's not like you don't know Sara, Darcy. You're a friend, not a suspect."

On the contrary, Darcy realized with a gut-twisting wrench. He didn't have any friends. He couldn't afford them.

Not with McKenna Rigsby's life hanging in the balance.

THE RATTLE OF the doorknob sent a hard shudder down McKenna's back. Groping for the Glock, she knocked the pistol and holster to the floor.

Damn it!

The thought of bending down to pick up the fallen weapon was almost more than she could contemplate, but she forced herself into motion, retrieving the holster, grabbing the grip of the pistol and sliding it out smoothly just as the cabin door swung open.

Darcy froze in the doorway, raising his hands, one of which held a large plastic sack. "It's me. Don't shoot."

She lowered the pistol, her hands shaking. "You could have called to warn me."

"I thought you might be sleeping. You need rest, and I didn't want to risk waking you." He locked the door behind him and looked around the room. "Have you been here the whole time I was gone?"

"I took a bathroom break about thirty minutes ago." She didn't tell him that walking down the short hallway to the bathroom had sapped most of her strength. Nodding at the plastic bag, she asked, "What's that?"

"Some things I found at the compounding pharmacy in town."

"So you didn't make it to see the witch woman."

"Nope. Didn't think the risk was worth it." He sat in the armchair across from her and emptied the bag onto the foot-locker between them. "This is something called Dragon's Blood. Tree sap of some sort. Said to have strong antibiotic, antiviral and antifungal properties. Plus, anti-inflammatory and analgesic."

"Overachiever," she muttered, eyeing the dark red liquid in the small bottle with skepticism. "Does it do windows, too?"

Darcy's lips quirked as he pushed another small bottle toward her. "Eucalyptus oil. Also supposed to be antibiotic, if the articles on the internet are anything to go by."

"Because everything you read on the internet is true."

He slanted another amused look at her. "This is good old fashioned aloe vera gel. I figure it can't hurt."

"And that?" she asked, pointing at the bottle that sat behind the rest.

"Betadine. If hospitals use it, it must be effective, yes?"

"Works for me." She leaned forward to pick up the bottle of Betadine and gasped at the burning ache in her side. "Ow."

Darcy was up from the chair and by her side in a second. "Sit back. You're doing too much."

To her horror, hot tears stung her eyes. She blinked them back. "I'm fine."

"You're far from fine. You're injured and probably haven't had a good night's sleep in days. Have you?"

"What I'd really like is a shower," she blurted before she could think better of it.

"That can be arranged." Darcy's dark eyes met hers.

Despite the pain in her side, despite the weakness in her limbs, she felt a flood of pure sexual heat flow between them, and her breath stilled in her lungs. The intensity of his regard overwhelmed her, but she couldn't drag her gaze away.

He broke the connection first, moving away and turning his attention to the bottles sitting on the coffee table. "A bath might be the better option."

He was right about that. Her legs would never hold her upright long enough to finish a shower. "That would be lovely."

"Stay right here." As he passed her on the way to the bathroom, he brushed the back of his hand briefly against her cheek. As much as she might have wanted to believe it was a simple show of affection, she had a feeling he'd been surreptitiously checking her for fever.

"Am I burning up?" she called after him.

"Didn't even singe my fingers," he called back, his tone light. But she heard worry lurking just beneath the surface.

She'd been running around in the woods for six hours, forced to ignore her pain and weakness. The wounds had remained untreated, open to any sort of airborne pathogens that might have found their way to the bloody holes in her side.

She'd spent a lot of time zigzagging to throw off her pursuers, and for what? They'd still spotted her less than a mile from Nick Darcy's cabin. She'd still had to run for her life.

Darcy came back a few minutes later. "Your bath is ready," he intoned in his plummiest accent.

He watched with hawk-like intensity as she gingerly inched her way toward him, though he kept his hands to himself, letting her pull her own weight, as if he sensed that she needed to make that small, unconvincing show of strength.

In the warm, cozy bathroom, the fragrant air smelled

like crisp green apples. She turned in the doorway to look at Darcy. "Green apple is Susie's favorite."

He smiled, his eyes crinkling at the corners. "Explains why Bragg always smells so nice."

Steam rose from the foamy bathwater. "I think I can take it from here."

"Call out if you need me." With a long, narrow-eyed gaze that sent a shiver skittering down her back, Darcy backed out of the bathroom and closed the door behind him.

She stripped off the borrowed T-shirt and, gritting her teeth, tugged the bandages away from her bullet wounds. Using the small oval mirror over the pedestal sink, she took a look at the injury. There was distinct redness and inflammation around the entry and exit wounds, but she didn't see signs that infection had spread. That was good, wasn't it?

After she finished undressing, she headed over to the tub. She had to grip the sides of the tub to keep from falling over as she stepped into the bubble bath. The water was deliciously hot against her skin, and for a second, she thought the bath might turn out to be more enjoyable than she expected.

Then the water hit her wounds, and she couldn't hold back a sharp yelp.

A couple of seconds later, the bathroom door slammed open and Darcy filled the doorway, his dark eyes alert.

She ducked down until the foamy water covered her naked breasts, shooting him a baleful look.

The concerned expression faded into a ridiculous smirk. "Hot water hit the wounds?"

"Yes, as a matter of fact."

"Are you all right?"

She nodded.

"I can stay in here. In case you need help." His lips curved a little more, and for a second, she was tempted to splash water on him. Then it occurred to her what he was doing. He was trying to distract her from the pain still slicing through her ravaged side.

"I'm fine," she assured him. "Really, I am. Not pretending to be stronger than I am."

"Are you certain you want me to leave?"

"Positive," she answered, mocking his accent.

His quirked lips made it all the way to a smile. "I'm told I'm excellent at scrubbing backs."

"I'm sure you are. But I think I can reach my own back." She almost believed she could, although she wasn't in a hurry to test the theory.

"You know, maybe we should consider conserving water, since we're borrowing the place from someone else—" He reached for the top button of his shirt.

"Out, Darcy."

He dropped his hands and grinned. "Call if you change your mind."

"I won't," she vowed as he headed out of the bathroom again.

At least, she hoped she wouldn't. The mental image of Nick Darcy's big, soapy hands moving over her body was already making her feel weak.

And weak was the last thing she needed to be around him.

ABOUT TWO MINUTES before Darcy was ready to barge back into the bathroom to see what was taking so long, McKenna emerged wrapped in a fluffy terry-cloth robe. "I found this in the bathroom. Must belong to Susie."

"Right."

"Kind of hoping she has more clothes around here. She's a little taller than I am, but we wear close to the same size." She tugged the garment more tightly around her. He saw a spot of blood beginning to appear and spread on the side of the robe.

He rose quickly to reach her. "You're bleeding again."

She looked down at the bloodstain. "Oh. I don't think it's a lot." But as she looked back up at him, she began to sway a little, her eyes drifting unfocused.

He scooped her up and carried her back to the bedroom, depositing her on the bed. Her hands dropped away from the lapels of the robe as her eyes struggled to focus, and the robe gaped open, revealing the shadowy curves of her breasts. They were milky pale, one apricot-colored nipple just visible under the edge of the lapel.

Desire lanced through him, but he quelled it ruthlessly, tugging the edges of the robe closed before he realized he needed to remove the robe entirely if he wanted to take a look at her wounds.

"I'm okay," she murmured, sounding anything but.

He checked her pulse and found it fast and a little weak. Her skin felt dry and loose. "Rigsby, did you drink any water while I was gone?"

"I ran out, and I didn't feel like getting up to get more."

"Damn it, Rigsby, you're dehydrated. We must get some fluids into you before you pass out." He brushed her hair away from her face, not liking how warm she was. Maybe the hot bath had been a bad idea.

He crossed to the closet door and pulled it open, hoping he'd find some of Susannah Marsh's clothes hanging there, but there were very few hanging clothes, only a couple of jackets and what looked like an Army dress uniform stored in a plastic garment bag.

"Try the drawers," McKenna suggested, her words weak and slurred.

He hit pay dirt in the dresser at the foot of the bed. Two drawers contained women's underwear and a variety of shorts, jeans and T-shirts.

"She likes to dress down these days." McKenna had pushed herself up on her elbows and was looking at him through a tangle of ginger curls. "She can be herself here, again. She was always a tomboy. Hated heels and skirts and all that girlie stuff, as she calls it."

"She's gone blond-haired and blue-eyed again."

"I know." McKenna's eyes followed him as he returned to the bed with a bra, panties, a light blue T-shirt and a pair of navy running shorts. They were a murky green color at the moment, like a mountain pool. "You gonna dress me, Darcy?"

"Don't tempt me," he murmured, handing over the clothing. "I'll be in the kitchen getting you something to eat and refilling your water bottle. Call me if you need me."

He took several deep, bracing breaths as he refilled the water bottle, adding a little ice this time in hopes of helping her fight the fever. It was utterly ridiculous that he found himself thinking of stripping her naked now, of all times, considering her weakened condition.

But she'd always had that effect on him, hadn't she? Even in the high-stress atmosphere of the US Embassy in Tablis, McKenna Rigsby had been a constant temptation to him.

It wasn't just that she was beautiful in that fresh-faced, natural way of hers. It was also her sharp mind, her blazing intellect and her dogged determination to reach her goal in any situation, despite any obstacle.

He might have saved her from sacrificing her life in a lost cause to save her colleague that fateful day in Tablis, but she'd saved him first, dragging his concussed and woozy ass back inside the embassy before the terrorists blew up the gates and surged inside.

As he set the water bottle on the table, he heard the sound of footsteps behind him, moving at a quick but unsteady pace. He turned to find McKenna standing in the kitchen doorway, her face sickly white. She'd managed to put on the T-shirt, but she wore only panties beneath, and blood was trickling down her left leg.

As he took a step toward her, she grabbed his arm, her green eyes wide with fear.

"What is it?" he asked, his gut tightening with alarm.

Her voice came out in a raspy whisper. "Someone's outside."

Chapter Five

He was so warm. So solid. Right now, McKenna felt like a mass of cold jelly, shivering and wobbling as she followed Darcy back to the bedroom. He turned suddenly, catching her as she stumbled into him and easing her onto the foot of the bed. "Stay right there. I need to find you something a little warmer to wear."

Resisting the temptation to drop back onto the soft mattress, she watched him search the dresser drawers until he found a pair of jeans. "May be a little long for you, but we'll have to make do. Can you get them on?"

It was going to be hell wriggling into jeans, she realized, but she took the pants from him and did her best, biting back a deep groan.

He moved to the window and took a quick peek out the curtains. "Nobody's there."

"I swear, there was."

"I don't doubt you." He left the window and crossed to where she sat. "Do you need help?"

She could tell from the impatient tone of his voice that he didn't want to be slowed down by having to aid her in dressing herself, so she shook her head. "Do whatever you need to do."

He touched her face briefly, his fingers cold against her

skin. His brow furrowed as he dropped his hand away. "I'll be right back."

She finished tugging the jeans over her hips and slumped back on the bed, feeling as if she'd just run a marathon. She was still sitting in that position when Darcy returned a few minutes later with a large backpack and a medium-size duffel, both olive drab and well used. "I've packed supplies in the backpack," he told her, setting it on the floor by her feet. "Food, water, flashlights and tools. In case we have to bug out."

"How can we bug out?" she asked. "If someone's out there, they already know we're here."

"There's another way out," he said cryptically as he held his hand out to her. "Let's get those pants zipped and see if we can find you some socks and a jacket."

She let him pull her to her feet, not even protesting when he caught the tab of her zipper and pulled it up to close the fly of the jeans. But the slight curve of his lips as he snapped the button closed on the waistband sent a flood of heat pouring straight to her core. "That's rather the opposite of what I'm used to," he murmured.

A flare of jealousy snaked through her, catching her off guard. "How used to it are you?" she asked before she could stop herself.

His dark eyes snapped up to meet hers, a hint of humor dancing in their depths. "Gentlemen never unzip and tell."

"Tease," she murmured, dropping back to the edge of the bed while he went in search of socks.

He found a pair and brought them over to her, bending to put them on her feet.

"I can do it," she protested.

"I'm sure you can, but there's no point in your expending any extra energy. If we have to leave, you'll need all the strength you can muster." He slipped the second sock on her other foot and reached for the shoes she'd been wearing that morning when she showed up at his door. They were a sturdy pair of cross trainers, built for support, and they'd probably helped keep her going long after her stamina had begun to fail her.

Right now, however, they felt like two stone blocks tied to her feet. She wasn't sure how she was going to walk across the room, much less go on the run.

As Darcy turned back to the bed holding a corduroy jacket that clearly belonged to her cousin, a rapping sound came from the front of the house, and they both froze, staring at each other.

"Not a sound," he murmured, touching his hand to her face. "Stay put."

Then he turned and was gone.

She heard his footsteps all the way down the uncarpeted hall, then moving across the front room. The door opened, and she heard the soft murmur of voices. Then, with a click, the door closed again, and the cabin fell silent.

What was going on? The curiosity that had been a characteristic part of her life since she was a tiny child kicked in with ferocity, tempting her to ignore Darcy's order to stay put.

But her weary, aching body wouldn't comply with her mental order to start moving. She felt as weak as a newborn kitten, and just about as useful.

To her dismay, she started to cry.

"WHAT THE HELL are you doing here?" Cain Dennison's gray eyes narrowed as Darcy hustled him out of the doorway and back onto the porch.

"Checking on the place for Bragg," Darcy lied. "What are you doing here, following me?"

Dennison raked his fingers through his dark hair, looking suspicious. "You didn't show up at my grandmother's place earlier."

"Yeah, changed my mind."

"Why?"

Darcy ignored the question. "How did you know to look for me here?"

"Your vehicle's still fitted with a company GPS tracker." Dennison arched one dark eyebrow. "Why'd you change your mind?"

"I found what I wanted to know on the internet."

"What did you want to know?"

Darcy crossed his arms, noting his fellow agent's sudden inquisitiveness. Cain Dennison had never been the talkative sort, and while Darcy considered him one of his closer friends at The Gates, it was more a matter of his not really having any close friends to speak of. He'd grown up in the spotlight as the son of an American ambassador, and his parents had drilled into him warnings about the folly of letting down one's guard to the wrong people.

What they'd failed to teach him was how to tell the wrong people from the right people. So he'd ended up trusting almost no one at all.

"Research for a book," he answered. "Since I'm not allowed to work for my pay, I thought I should start doing something constructive."

"And you're doing it here at Bragg's primitive cabin?"

"Was your only purpose in tracking me down to ask me why I didn't show up at your grandmother's place? Because I've answered that question."

"Are you sure it wasn't because you got there and saw Sara's cruiser?"

Darcy grimaced. "You were assigned to watch me, weren't you?"

For a moment, he thought Dennison wasn't going to answer. Then the other agent gave a brief nod. "Yes."

"Quinn seriously believes I'm the mole at the agency?" He shouldn't have felt hurt, but he did, he realized. While

Darcy might not have many close friends, Alexander Quinn was one of the few people in the world he'd come to trust— for the most part. He certainly trusted Quinn to do what he thought was the right thing for the most people involved, at least.

But clearly, Quinn didn't return that trust.

"I don't think he does," Dennison said quietly. "I know I don't. You don't have that sort of treachery in you."

"You don't really know me, Dennison."

"I guess not. Because you're lying to my face right now, and I sure didn't expect that of you."

Guilt pricked Darcy's conscience, but it wasn't just his own life at stake. McKenna Rigsby was waiting inside, ill and feverish, entirely dependent on his ability to protect her. His loyalty to Cain Dennison, to Alexander Quinn and The Gates, had to come second to her.

She was relying on him. He couldn't let her down.

"Is there anything else you need?" he asked Dennison in a cool, imperious tone he'd learned from his father.

Dennison's eyes widened slightly and he took a step back. "No. I don't need a damn thing from you." He turned and descended the porch stairs.

Darcy was tempted to call him back, but he quelled the urge and watched until Dennison had disappeared into the woods. He took a deep breath, filling his lungs with cool mountain air, then turned and went back inside the cabin.

He found McKenna sitting where he'd left her, slumped forward with her chin on her chest. "He's gone."

She lifted her head slowly, and the look of sheer misery on her tearstained face made his breath catch. "For how long?"

He crouched in front of her. "What's wrong?" He caught her face between his hands, alarmed at how hot she was. "You're burning up."

"I don't feel so great."

"Let me see your wounds." He tugged gently at the hem of the T-shirt to expose her open wounds. Though the entry and exit wounds were puffy and red, he'd seen worse, he realized with relief. But if the infection was strong enough to cause McKenna to run a fever, it was still a source of concern.

"We need to clean your wounds out and get some of these treatments started," he told her in a firm tone.

"No, please. I can't take it right now."

Her teeth were chattering, he saw with alarm. Was her fever increasing?

"Rigsby, you have to." He crouched in front of her, taking her hands. Her fingers were icy cold; he rubbed gently to warm them. "I know you're tired and you're hurting, but we may need to leave here, sooner or later."

"Who was at the door?"

"One of my colleagues." He told her about Dennison's visit as he continued to warm her hands between his. "I think he suspects I'm up to something strange."

"You told him you were checking on the place for Hunter?"

"Yes, but I don't think he believes me."

"What do you think he'll do?" Her teeth had stopped chattering, he noticed, and her eyes seemed a little clearer than before.

"Nothing for now," he answered. "Possibly report my presence here to Alexander Quinn."

"Is that good or bad?"

He thought about the question for a moment. "Neutral, I suppose. He's not going to interfere as long as we're safe."

"Are we?" she asked quietly as he released her hands and started to rise. "Safe, I mean."

He cupped her hot cheek with his palm. "As much as we can hope to be at the moment." He dropped his hand away and opened his backpack to retrieve the first-aid kit he'd packed in case they needed to evacuate quickly.

Feeling her gaze on him, he turned to look at her. The tears were back, trembling on her lower lashes. "I'm sorry."

He made himself look away, knowing pity was the last thing she wanted. "For getting shot? I doubt you chose that option willingly."

"For going weak-kneed on you."

"That's the infection and dehydration. Speaking of that—" He reached in the backpack and pulled out a bottle of water. He twisted the cap open and handed the bottle to her. "Drink up."

She did as he asked, blinking back the tears that had formed in her eyes, not letting them fall. This was the Mc-Kenna Rigsby he remembered, the tough, gutsy redhead who'd taken the US Embassy in Tablis by storm. "Hurricane Rigsby," some of the guys in security had called her, for she'd had a way of blowing into a room and blowing out again, leaving everything and everyone upended behind her.

He finished gathering the supplies he needed and carried everything to the bed where she sat. "Do people still call you Hurricane?" he asked as he lifted the hem of her T-shirt again to check her injury.

"Not to my face," she said bluntly, flashing him a pained smile.

He smiled back. "No, never to your face."

"I'm not the same person, Darcy." Her voice darkened. "A lot has happened since I walked into the embassy almost nine years ago."

"A lot happened in the time you were there."

"No kidding."

He poured Betadine onto a cotton ball and pressed it to the entry wound, eliciting a soft hiss from her lips. "Sorry."

"Don't dally."

"Wouldn't dream of it." He applied the antiseptic liberally to both wounds and the skin surrounding them. "Do you stay in touch with anyone from the Tablis legat?"

"No." She grimaced as he dabbed the excess Betadine with a clean cloth. "I don't think many of us wanted reminders."

"Is that why you never answered my calls?"

Her gaze flicked up to meet his. "Mostly."

"Mostly?" He applied aloe vera gel to the wounds, taking care to be gentle.

"My reasons for not responding to your calls were complicated."

"Meaning, you were still furious at me but didn't want to have to admit it?" He tried to keep his tone light, but the words he uttered stung, even coming from his own lips. "You clearly haven't forgiven me for what happened to Michael Cameron."

She shook her head. "I haven't forgiven myself."

"For listening to me?"

"For not figuring out a way to get to him before the fire did." A hard shudder rippled through her body. "They drummed it into us, over and over—know the layout. Know where the exits are, where the escape routes lie. And I should have known the place better, figured out another way to get to him—"

He wiped his hands on a towel. "There was no other way, Rigsby."

McKenna shook her head. "There had to be."

"There wasn't. If there had been, I'd have taken a chance on trying to get him out of there." He put his hands on her upper arms, forcing her to look at him again. "I did have the layout memorized. Completely. Backward and forward. The problem was, the wall took a direct hit. It blocked any outlet entirely. It would have taken heavy equipment to dig Cameron out, sweetheart. But there wasn't enough time."

She bent forward, and for a moment, he thought she was about to lose consciousness. But she pressed her forehead against his, lifting her hands to cradle his face. "Promise me that's the truth?"

He closed his hands over hers. "I promise."

She pulled back, gently tugging her hands away. Leaning sideways, she pulled her T-shirt hem up again. "Let's get this over with."

He bandaged her wounds as quickly as he could and put the excess supplies back into the first-aid kit. He pulled out a packet of ibuprofen and ripped it open. "Need more water?"

She looked at the empty bottle of water she'd set beside her on the bed. "I guess I need to get more fluids in me."

"You'll feel better if you do," he assured her, pulling a second bottle of water from the backpack and opening it for her. "Take these ibuprofen. It will relieve your pain and bring down your fever."

She took the tablets, washing them down with a long swig of water. "Be honest, Darcy. How badly infected are my wounds?"

"They're infected," he admitted, "but I've seen much worse. You're in good health otherwise, aren't you?"

She nodded.

"And we've been aggressive about cleaning out the wounds and treating them. What you need most is to get fully rehydrated and get some rest." He stood up. "I don't think we need to go on the run again quite yet."

"What about the visit from your friend?"

"He's suspicious, but Quinn will keep him from going off half-cocked," Darcy replied, wishing he felt a little more confident. "I'll worry about Dennison. You worry about getting some sleep. Would you like another cup of soup before you rest?"

She shook her head, her tangled curls dancing around

her face like living things. "I just want to sleep for about a week."

"You can sleep as much as you want." He couldn't resist wrapping one of those coppery curls around his finger.

She looked up at him, her eyes liquid and as dark as the dusk falling outside the bedroom window, only a faint rim of green showing. "Where are you going to sleep?"

The question was innocent, but he couldn't stop his body's quick, fierce reaction. He tugged his hand from her hair. "I'll be on the sofa. Call out if you need me. I'm a light sleeper."

She caught his hand as he turned to go, her fingers no longer cold. The heat of her touch burned all the way to his core. "Darcy, thank you. For everything. I know this can't be much fun for you."

"On the contrary," he said, entirely sincere. "I've been bored senseless for the past week. A rogue FBI agent falling wounded on my doorstep? I can hardly contain my excitement. So, no, Agent Rigsby. Thank *you*."

As he'd intended, she smiled. "Anytime, Darcy."

In the hall closet, he found a blanket and an extra pillow, to his relief. He might not have turned out quite as pampered and privileged as his parents had reared him to be, but he liked his creature comforts as much as the next man, particularly when he knew he might have to rough it soon enough. At any moment, they might have to run for their lives.

He knew Cain Dennison wouldn't be a problem. Quinn would make certain of it. But someone was out there, looking for McKenna. Maybe several someones.

And until they figured out exactly who and why, they remained in grave danger.

Chapter Six

The wound on Nick Darcy's forehead had finally stopped bleeding, but the previously unstanched flow had made a mess of his face and the front of his formerly snowy-white shirt. McKenna had gotten him as far as the embassy ball-room before he stopped short and looked around him as if trying to make sense of the chaos.

The staccato cadence of gunfire, punctuated now and then by booming rocket blasts, couldn't drown out the cries of fear and pain that echoed through the embassy halls.

"Darcy?" She spoke in a whisper, but the sound seemed harsh and loud to her ears.

His unfocused gaze slid toward her but didn't quite connect. "The ambassador—"

"Can't be helped now." She caught his hand in hers, ignoring the sticky warmth of his blood against her palm. At least he was alive. They were both alive. So many others weren't. They'd already passed three dead embassy employees to get this far. "Darcy, we have to find a way out."

"No way out," he murmured.

"I know there's an underground exit. I've heard people talk about it. We just have to find it."

"It's beneath the west wing." His gaze met hers, finally focused. "It's covered with rubble. We can't get to it."

Her heart skipped a beat. "So we're trapped?"

His fingers tightened around hers. "I didn't say that. We simply must think our way through this." He lifted his free hand to his forehead, wincing as he touched the bloody lump the flying shrapnel had left over his right eye. "Unfortunately, thinking isn't coming easily to me at the moment."

"That's why you have me." She tugged his hand, moving toward the ballroom exit. This area was too exposed, too easy a target for the rebels. "Let's find a place to hunker down and think."

He didn't resist, following her from the ballroom into the narrow corridor that led toward the events kitchen. Once there, they found three of the embassy food staff huddled in the corner. One of them rose at the sound of their footsteps, brandishing a large meat cleaver. It was Jamil Guram, she saw, the embassy's sous chef from Punjab—the one in India, he was always quick to specify, not Pakistan. His dark eyes locked with hers and the cleaver clattered to the floor. "Agent Rigsby," he breathed.

"Just the three of you?" she asked.

"Yes," he answered in his lightly accented English. "Will you be able to get us out of here? The terrorists are not far away. I have heard them shouting nearby."

She couldn't promise him anything, she realized with dismay. She wasn't sure any of them would get out of here alive.

Behind her, she felt Darcy move closer to her, the heat of his body spreading across her back, seeming to imbue her with added strength. She straightened her spine. "We'll do our best," she promised Jamil.

But before the final word escaped her tongue, hell descended in a roar of fire and brimstone.

McKenna sat up with a gasp, her ragged breath loud in the darkness, joining the cacophony of her hammering pulse and the throbbing agony in her side. She was surrounded by darkness so deep and impenetrable that she thought for a moment she was still dreaming.

Then, as her eyes began to adjust to the gloom, she made out the shapes of ordinary things—a dresser, a closet door, a window where the faintest of ambient light trickled past the barrier of curtains.

She was holed up in Hunter Bragg's cabin in the Smokies, she remembered, her pulse still racing. She had been shot by someone in the woods, someone in cahoots with one of her FBI colleagues.

And Nick Darcy was sleeping on the sofa in the front room, playing the role of her protector after eight years of silence and distance between them.

She slumped back against the pillows.

Why had she really come here? Was it what she'd told Darcy—that he was the only person in the area she felt she could trust? She supposed there was some truth in that statement, but it wasn't the whole truth, was it?

She'd come to him because she'd been afraid she might be dying. And she wanted to see him again, one more time.

He was so not her type. If her high school friends had been around at the embassy in Tablis, they'd have been shocked if she'd admitted to finding buttoned-up, very formal Nick Darcy attractive. Her tastes had always run more toward the sweet-talking, hard-living country boys she'd grown up with, all brazen flash and Southern charm.

Darcy was nothing like those guys, but still, there had been something about him, some dangerous gleam in his dark eyes, that had piqued her curiosity and made her want to know him better.

And then his quiet competence and courtly manners had sucked her in completely, even though he was so off-limits to her it wasn't funny. Their relationship—if you could even call it that—had been carried out in lingering gazes and furtive touches, stolen conversations and one near kiss that had left her aching for days.

She knew he'd grown up in London for the first eighteen years of his life, with the occasional summer in his father's native Virginia. His mother was a British citizen, a lesser peer whose name had once been bandied about as a potential bride for the royal family—a fact that had been a source of amusement to Darcy, who described his mother as a down-to-earth horsewoman better suited for hunts than balls.

"My mother's rustic leanings used to drive my father crazy," he'd shared over a quick lunch one day in the embassy kitchen. "Until he figured out that she knew where all the skeletons were hidden because of all that time she'd spent as a girl, wandering about on the country estates of some of England's most influential parliamentarians."

That he loved his mother had been obvious. That he'd respected his father had been equally clear. What had most intrigued McKenna, however, was how distanced he seemed to feel from both of them.

"You're awake."

The sound of Darcy's voice in the dark sent a delicious shiver sliding down her spine. She turned her head to find his dark silhouette in the bedroom's open doorway.

"Just woke." Her voice sounded raspy. She cleared her throat and spoke again. "What time is it?"

"A little after midnight. Time for you to take some more ibuprofen." He flicked the switch on the wall and light flooded the room, nearly blinding her. "Sorry."

Her eyes adjusted quickly to the brightness, quickly enough that she could enjoy the sight of Darcy's slow, long-limbed approach to the bed. Barefoot, wearing a pair of worn jeans and a rumpled gray T-shirt, his hair mussed and longer than she remembered from his time at the embassy,

Darcy looked a hell of a lot more like one of those redneck boys she'd always favored than he ever had before.

But when he sat beside her and spoke, the illusion disappeared, and the cool, competent former DSS agent she'd known in Tablis reappeared. "I thought I heard you call out."

She tried to remember her dream, but it was a tangle of images and snippets of memory she couldn't seem to make cohere. "I think I was dreaming about Tablis," she murmured as he pressed the back of his hand to her cheek, then her forehead.

"Your fever seems to have subsided." He reached down and pulled his backpack onto the bed beside him. "Let's check your temperature."

She caught his hand as he started to unzip the bag. "I know you made the right decision in Tablis. I do."

His dark eyes lifted to meet hers. "I wasn't going to let you get killed for nothing. And without heavy equipment and a full extraction crew, we weren't going to get Cameron out of there."

"I lost my head. So much death—"

He brushed his fingertip against her cheek, and she felt the wetness of tears she hadn't been aware of spilling. "You were brave. And strong. I wouldn't have survived the siege without you."

"Back at ya," she murmured.

He pressed the temporal artery thermometer against her temple and waited for the beep. "Ninety-eight point eight," he murmured. "That's good."

"I feel better," she admitted.

"Also good." He shook two ibuprofen tablets from the plastic bottle and handed them to her. "Finish off that water washing these down and I'll get you a fresh bottle."

She did as he asked and handed over the empty bottle. "Have you gotten any sleep?"

"Some."

She wasn't sure she believed him. "Don't make yourself sick trying to take care of me. I'm better already, I promise."

"I'm fine," he insisted.

"Is the sofa uncomfortable? Maybe you should be in the bed—"

His eyebrows ticked upward. "You want to share?"

His tone was light, but the look in his eyes was sultry and serious, and despite her still-weakened condition, despite eight years of separation and a million very good reasons why giving in to lust was a bad idea, she was sorely tempted to call his bluff.

She managed to resist. "I could take the sofa."

He made a face. "That's no fun."

"Seriously, Darcy. I'm feeling better, and I've slept on so many office sofas so many times I've lost count. Bragg's sofa can't be worse than those."

"It's not. It's quite comfortable. Truly."

He seemed sincere, and now that she'd found a position on the bed that seemed to be mostly pain-free, she wasn't in a hurry to change her accommodations. So she didn't argue further. "Any more unwanted visitors? Threatening phone calls from the boss?"

He shook his head. "Silent as the tomb."

She winced. "Lovely metaphor."

"Simile," he corrected with a twitch of his lips.

"Still an insufferable grammar scold, I see." She softened her words with a smile.

"It's part of my charm."

Her smile widened. "Sadly, it's most of your charm."

He laughed. "I see some things haven't changed in eight years. You can still smart off with the best of them."

"Lots of practice, working for the government." Before she could quell the urge, she caught his hand in hers. "I was surprised to hear you'd left the DSS. I thought you'd be a lifer."

Looking down at their hands, he curled his fingers over hers, his thumb rubbing lightly against the back of her hand. "After the siege, a lot of things changed for me."

"You stayed on for seven more years."

He nodded. "I did."

"But your heart wasn't in it?"

He grimaced. "It wasn't that, exactly."

"Then what was it?"

He let go of her hand and stood up. "Let's table any long stories until we both get some sleep."

"Darcy—"

"We'll talk in the morning." He left quickly, closing the door behind him.

She slumped back against her pillows, frustrated. He'd always been careful and self-protective, she remembered, and if anything, the passing years had made him more so.

But she needed to know she could trust him. And how could she trust him if he was hiding things from her?

DARCY WOKE TO light filtering through the curtains of the front windows. Rubbing his bleary eyes, he checked his watch. Almost seven. He'd overslept.

Grimacing at the ache in his back from a night on the unfamiliar sofa, he pushed to a sitting position and stretched his arms and legs, trying to get some of the kinks out.

"Good morning."

McKenna's voice, close behind him, gave him a start. He twisted to look at her and found her looking surprisingly alert, considering how weak she'd been by the time he'd tucked her into bed. "You look better."

Her lips curved just short of a smile. "I feel a lot better."

"That could change quickly," he warned as he rose and

turned to face her. "You hungry? I think we can come up with something from the pantry."

"Yeah, I've already been scoping it out. There's frozen waffles in the freezer and some syrup and peanut butter in the pantry."

He grimaced.

"You'd prefer kippers, I suppose, Prince Charles?"

"Not a Brit."

That time her lips made it all the way to a smile. "Good, because we're fresh out of kippers."

He followed her to the kitchen and waved at the small table by the window. "You sit. I'll see what our options are."

"I'm telling you, I looked. No milk or eggs. Just a few frozen things and nonperishables." She sat at the table and watched while he poked through the cabinets and refrigerator for a few moments before having to concede she was right.

"I could run into town later for supplies," he said.

She looked up sharply. "What if you're followed back here?"

"Would you rather starve?" His words came out more sharply than he'd intended, thanks to his edgy nerves.

She slumped in her chair. "I shouldn't have gone to your cabin in the first place. I knew it might put you in danger."

He felt a sharp stab of guilt as he closed the refrigerator door. "I'm glad you did. You couldn't have gone on much longer with those wounds untreated."

"But you would be back at your cabin, not breaking and entering and avoiding your colleagues."

He crossed to her, crouching in front of her chair. "Stop, Rigsby. If you hadn't shown up when you did, I'd still be fuming about my suspension and feeling sorry for myself. I needed the distraction."

One corner of her lips curved. "I live to be a distraction."

He barely kept himself from pushing back the auburn

curls that had fallen to frame her face. "You're quite good at it, you know." He pushed to his feet. "Waffles?"

"With peanut butter and syrup," she said, her tone brighter.

He grimaced again. "Hillbilly."

"Not a hillbilly," she retorted with a grin.

As he struggled against an answering smile, heat coiled low in his abdomen, reminding him that friendship with McKenna Rigsby might be more dangerous than conflict.

He found a jar of strawberry preserves in the refrigerator and spread the treacly berries over his toasted waffle, while McKenna slathered peanut butter and syrup over her own. She ate with a gusto that made him feel hopeful that they'd managed to turn the tide of her infection.

She seemed stronger and clearer-eyed, as well, when she helped him wash and dry their plates and put them away. "You weren't lying about feeling better, were you?" he asked as he took the dishrag from her hands and folded it.

Taking a step closer, she took the dishrag from his hands and set it on the counter. Heat from her body swept over him like a wave, setting off tremors low in his abdomen. "Maybe you missed your calling, Darcy. Although your bedside manner could use a little help."

He took a step back before realizing he was trapped against the counter.

McKenna's eyebrows arched a notch. "Last night, you said we'd talk this morning. Well, it's morning, Darcy. So talk."

"I could ask the same of you, Rigsby." He pushed away from the counter, closing the space between them to inches. "You told me a little about what you've been doing, but you know what you haven't told me? What you did to make the FBI put out an APB on you."

She sighed and took a step backward, bumping into one of the kitchen chairs. She reached back to steady herself before lifting her chin and meeting his gaze. "I ignored a direct order from my SAC."

He frowned. Special Agents in Charge, or SACs, were direct superiors in the FBI chain of command. If her SAC had given her an order, disobeying it was a big violation of the rules. "Why?"

"Because he told me to meet another agent at a staging point for extraction."

"He wanted you to bug out."

"He wanted me to meet someone I had reason to believe might want me dead." Her clear green eyes met his steadily. "I overheard a discussion between a man named Calvin Hopkins and an anarchist who goes by the name Komodo. Don't ask—I have no idea why he goes by that name. But Hopkins told Komodo that he'd gotten a tip from the Fibber."

He frowned. "Komodo and the Fibber? Sounds like a comic book."

She took a step toward him again, and the fierce look in her eyes sent him backward again until his hips hit the edge of the counter. "It may sound comical to you, but the Fibber, as they called him, is apparently someone in the FBI, because he blew my cover completely. I barely got off the BRI compound without being caught. Then I got the call from my boss to meet an agent named Cade Landry for extraction."

"And you don't trust Landry?"

"I don't trust anyone!" Her voice rose with frustration. "Not a damned person in the FBI or anywhere else." She took a deep breath and lowered her voice. "I want to trust you, Darcy. I need to trust you."

"You can," he said.

Her gaze searched his, looking for God only knew what. Some secret sign that he was worthy of her faith, he supposed. He didn't know how to reassure her. Either she believed in him or she didn't.

"Okay. I believe you." Her lips curved and she took a step closer, placing her hands on his shoulders. She smelled good, the scent of green-apple bubble bath lingering on her skin. "Thank you. For the way you've taken care of me. And for believing me."

His pulse ratcheted up as she rose to her toes and pressed a soft, lingering kiss against his cheek. Desire tore through him like a bullet, and he took a quick, deep breath.

McKenna's fingers tightened over his shoulders, but she didn't move away. Her lips brushed against his jawline.

He pressed his hand against the small of her back, tugging her closer. She moved fluidly toward him, her hips sliding against his, the friction delicious and hot. One slender hand curled around the back of his neck, tangling in his hair.

"You've let your hair grow," she murmured against his chin.

"I told you. I'm not the man you knew."

"Maybe that's a good thing." She lifted her gaze to meet his. "Maybe it's a good thing neither of us is the same person we were eight years ago."

"I'm not sure you're right about that," he murmured, his head dipping toward her. "But I find I don't care."

Her hand tightened on his neck, drawing him down to her. Her nose brushed against his as he slanted his head and closed the distance between them.

They had never done this, not once. There had been moments between them in Tablis when the sexual tension had been pure torture, moments when he'd wanted her with a ferocity that he'd never known with any other woman.

But they'd never closed the gap between them, never crossed that line.

Well, here he was. Here was the line, awaiting one more step.

His breath escaping his throat in a trembling sigh, he crossed it.

Chapter Seven

She'd wondered for a long time what it would be like to kiss Nick Darcy. Though she normally tried not to dwell on things that would never happen, she'd sometimes dreamed about kissing Darcy, imagined the feel of his mouth on hers during sleepless nights and even fantasized about what might happen next, whenever she wanted to distract herself from the stresses of her work.

Fantasies had seemed harmless enough, given the years and miles between her and the object of her unfulfilled desires. But mouth to mouth, body to body, drowning in the masculine scent of him, the heat of his hands sliding over the curve of her spine to settle low on her back, tugging her closer—he overwhelmed her utterly.

She felt hot all over. Hot and restless and rapidly losing control. He slid his hand beneath the hem of her T-shirt and up her back, his palms rough against her skin. Wrapping her arms around his neck, she pressed closer, flattening her body against his as he touched his tongue to hers, demanding a deeper response.

He pulled her closer, his arm tightening around her waist. His fingers dug into her side.

Her injured side.

Pain raced through her at his accidental touch, and she couldn't stop a sharp cry from escaping her lips.

He jerked back, releasing her, a stricken expression on his face. "Oh, God, I'm sorry."

"It's okay." Her voice came out a little breathless as she waited for the pain to ease.

"Let me take a look—I might have reopened your wounds."

"I think they're okay," she said as the pain settled down to a moderate ache.

"I am a complete idiot." His mortified tone tweaked her funny bone and she had to struggle against laughing.

"No, you're not." She caught his hand. "I'm fine."

"I should check to make sure it's not bleeding."

She arched her eyebrows. "Admit it, Darcy. You just want to get me naked."

He looked affronted. "Not at all!"

"Not even a little?" she asked with an exaggerated pout.

His expression softened. "You're having me on."

"I was trying to have you on. Me, that is. But then you freaked out like a virgin." She made a face at him. "Is that why you never put any moves on me all those years ago, Darcy? Performance anxiety?"

He smiled at that. "Now you're trying to bait me."

She took a step closer, knowing she was playing with fire. If she were a wise woman, she'd take advantage of this interruption and retreat to her corner. But not when Darcy looked so damned rumpled and sexy.

"Is it working?" she asked, her tone as sultry as she could manage.

"Am I tempted?" He dipped his head toward her, his breath warm and sweet against her cheek. "Absolutely."

"But?" she prodded, hearing the hesitation in his tone.

"But the last thing we need right now is a distraction. You're in danger, and we don't know from whom, exactly." He placed his hands on her shoulders, gently pushing her backward, putting distance between them. "Are you certain I don't need to check your wounds?"

"They're not even hurting anymore," she assured him, trying to quell her disappointment. He was right. She knew he was. The last thing either of them needed to do right now was drop their guard.

She was safe for the moment. Her wounds seemed to be healing, and so far, their efforts were keeping infection at bay. She was warm, dry, reasonably well rested and no longer completely alone.

It was time to stop running, she realized. Time to hunker down and come up with a plan other than "run as fast and far as you can."

"What are you thinking?" Darcy asked.

She looked up and found him watching her through narrowed eyes.

"You had a look on your face—" His lips quirked. "I've seen that look before. You've made a decision about something."

Her own lips curved in response. "I was just thinking that I've grown very weary of running."

"I'm sure you have."

"It's time to stop, don't you think?"

His eyebrows notched upward. "What do you have in mind?"

"I think," she said slowly, "it's time we sat down and devised a plan."

"A plan?"

She nodded. "I'm sick and tired of being the prey. I think it's time I became the hunter."

"Calvin Hopkins took over after the Ridge County Sheriff's Department arrested Billy Dawson and his crew after they attempted the mass poisoning at the Highland Hotel and Resort." McKenna sat cross-legged on the sofa across from him, her fingers playing with the fringe of the sofa pillow she held in her lap.

Taking in the rise in her color and the return of strength and steadiness to her limbs, Darcy let himself begin to relax. They would have to remain aggressive with the fight against infection, but he was beginning to believe they might have caught it in time.

"Do I need to recap any of that part of the story?" she asked with a twitch of one eyebrow. "Or are you familiar with it?"

"I know about it," he assured her. He hadn't been directly on the Billy Dawson case, but everyone at The Gates knew how it had gone down. One of his fellow agents, Hunter Bragg, had infiltrated the Blue Ridge Infantry in time to uncover a plot to poison a convention full of federal, state and local law enforcement officers. Three hundred lives had been in danger before Hunter and the hotel's events planner, Susannah Marsh, had figured out the plot and found a way to foil it, despite the grave threat to their lives.

The same Susannah Marsh who'd turned out to be McKenna's cousin.

"Susannah told Quinn you and your mother helped her when she had to leave Boneyard Ridge to escape the Bradburys," he said.

She grimaced. "Sick bastards. One of those inbred monsters tried to rape a sixteen-year-old and she's the criminal because she shot him in self-defense?"

"She said she'd have never made it without you."

"She's family." McKenna shrugged.

It must be nice, he thought, to have family upon which to rely without question. In his own family, there had been love, of course, but also inflexible expectations. His father had been displeased by his choice to enter the security side of Foreign Service, dismissing his DSS position as nothing more than "a glorified security guard."

And his mother had been unhappy he'd chosen Foreign Service at all, hoping instead that he would stay near her in their Yorkshire country estate and help her raise and train racehorses.

"But you're good with the horses," she'd protested when he'd told her of his new career. "Do you realize how rare that really is? How many men and women in racing would kill for your natural talent with those beasts?"

He'd left England and his family behind, and most days, he had no regrets. Even now.

But sometimes—

"Hopkins had learned from Billy Dawson's mistakes. He was very careful who he let into the group. I knew I was never going to get into the inner circle as a woman. They're sexist pigs to the core."

"Then how did you propose to do it?"

"All I had to do was get inside once to set up the listening devices."

"And how did you accomplish that?"

"How does any woman infiltrate a group of men?" She smirked a little. "I showed them a little skin."

A cold, squirmy sensation jolted through him, settling in a queasy mass in the center of his stomach. "Which means?"

"One of them had a fortieth birthday coming up. So we started spreading flyers around Ridge County advertising private strip parties."

Another chill darted through him. "You stripped for them?" She let strange men—morally bankrupt reprobates—watch her undress?

Her lips curved in a smart-ass grin. "Oh, you thought I was the one who stripped? Hell, no. You know I'm the shy, retiring type. No, we hired a couple of girls from the go-go bar over in Barrowville, and they only stripped to their bikinis. I supervised the music, which included running wires and setting up the speakers—"

"And planting listening devices all about the room." Darcy started to relax.

"Yes. We knew the BRI had taken over the old lodge on Killshadow Road as their meeting place. We knew they'd held parties there before, even events like a community fundraiser for one of the BRI members who'd lost a leg in a car accident. We figured if we could get the place wired up, we might be able to find out exactly what they've got up their sleeve."

Darcy nodded. "But something went awry?"

"Not then. But a few days later, they had a couple of their anarchist hacker buddies in for a powwow and the hypervigilant nerd brought along a bug detector. They found the device and it didn't take long to narrow down the list of suspects to the maintenance crew they'd hired to clean up after the party or—"

"Or you," he finished for her.

"The maintenance crew was made up of family and friends. They shook them all down, scared the hell out of them and quickly figured out none of them was smart enough—or stupid enough—to pull off that kind of betrayal."

"Which left the strippers."

"And their DJ. The strippers were pretty well-known around town, and neither of them knew a thing about electronics, so it didn't take long to concentrate on me instead."

"Did you know your bug had been discovered?"

"The FBI did. I wasn't part of the listening crew. I was working other angles when it went down."

"Surely they warned you."

"They should have."

"But they didn't?"

She passed her hand slowly over her face. "There were

six people in the FBI who knew what I was doing, but only four count. The director himself and his deputy director signed off on everything, but they're not really in the day-to-day loop, so I'm not sure I should count them as suspects."

"Okay, who are the other four?"

"The Knoxville SAC, Glen Robertson, of course, and the SSA in charge of my unit, Darryl Boyle," she answered, glancing at him as if to gauge whether he knew what the acronyms meant.

He did, of course—working in a federal agency himself, he'd had contact with the FBI on numerous occasions. The SAC was the head of the field office where she'd worked, Knoxville in this case. The SSA was the Supervisory Special Agent directly in charge of her work as a special agent.

"Then there was Pete Chang, head of the Johnson City RA," she added, referring to the smaller resident agency located in a town northeast of Knoxville. "He assigned another special agent, Cade Landry, to work with me, since the BRI's territory in Tennessee straddles both jurisdictions."

He jotted the names down in the notebook app on his cell phone. "Okay, I can do a little digging around on these guys. Who was assigned to contact you about the discovery of your surveillance equipment?"

"SAC Robertson said he contacted both Agent Boyle and Agent Chang. Agent Boyle tried to reach me, but I was in a part of the mountains where cell reception was nil. Chang reached Landry, or so he said. Landry swears he didn't get any call from Chang about anything."

"Do you believe him?"

She frowned, clearly giving the question serious consideration. "I don't know," she said finally. "Landry—I think maybe he's a burnout. He does his job competently enough, but his heart's not in it."

Darcy knew the type. He'd gotten dangerously close to being one of those burnouts himself by the time he'd resigned from the DSS and taken Alexander Quinn up on the job offer with The Gates. "Apathetic, then? Or openly hostile toward being ordered around?"

"Not hostile," she said quickly. "If anything, he was too much the opposite. Nothing fazed him. Or interested him. He did his job because it was required of him, but there was no joy. No anger. No fire for justice. No fire at all."

"And you say he works out of the Johnson City RA?"

"Right. I think he was with the Richmond, Virginia, field office before that."

So, he'd moved from a bigger office to a resident agency, Darcy thought, jotting a note for himself. Sounded like a step down, not up, the bureau career ladder.

"Someone at The Gates was in the Johnson City RA before taking a job with us," he murmured. "I might be able to get her alone, away from the office, and pick her brain about Landry."

"You're talking about Ava Trent, right?"

"You know her?"

"I met her once or twice. Never worked with her. But yeah, I think she and Landry worked together on a couple of cases before she left the FBI."

"Before the BRI discovered the listening device, did you learn anything about their plans? You said the FBI believes they're plotting something very large and very deadly, yes?"

Her eyes narrowed at his tone. "You know something about that, don't you, Darcy?"

He gave himself a mental kick for not being more guarded with his thoughts and expressions. Despite eight years apart, he'd easily fallen back into the camaraderie he and McKenna had shared with the other "glorified security guards" watching over the US Embassy in Tablis. Despite the traditional interagency rivalries, people tasked with protecting America's diplomats in dangerous places had learned the hard way that working as a cohesive team was the only way to survive the challenges.

But was it a good idea to trust her with some of the secrets he and the other agents at The Gates had uncovered during their recent investigations into the criminal nexus between the Blue Ridge Infantry, an elusive group of black-hat anarchist hackers, and a loose confederation of methamphetamine manufacturers? A lot of good people had put their lives on the line for the information they'd helped gather. He wasn't going to betray their trust just to get on McKenna Rigsby's good side.

"You don't trust me?" She sounded both hurt and angry.

"I have to be careful. Some of the things I know are volatile."

"A lot of what I know is volatile. But I need your help, so I have to tell you what I know." She slanted a considering look at him. "Maybe then you'll tell me what you know and we'll both be better equipped to handle whatever kind of storm is blowing our way."

"Maybe." It was as much of a concession as he intended to offer until he heard more.

She blew out a breath, exasperation edging her expression. "Okay, fine. We think they're planning a domestic terror attack."

"Tell me something I don't know."

Her eyes narrowed. "So you do know more than you've said."

"I haven't said anything, so of course I do."

She narrowed her eyes further at him. "We don't think they'll try to repeat their plans from the attempted attack on the Tri-State Law Enforcement Society convention."

"No more poisoned béchamel?"

"Exactly. They're going for something bigger. I do know there's something up, something specific that they're planning. We were able to glean that much from their discussions before they discovered the bug."

"Just no details? No idea of the target?"

"Only that it will be big and very public."

"Of course," Darcy agreed. The point of any terrorist attack, domestic or foreign, was to incite fear and panic in the populace. "I suppose the more pertinent question is, what do they hope to accomplish? Do they have a goal beyond creating chaos?"

"That's the question, isn't it?" She unfolded her legs, stretching them out in front of her. She flexed her bare feet, pointing her toes, then curling them up toward her shin, as if stretching her calf muscles. For a moment, her concentration centered entirely on stretching and contracting her muscles, and Darcy found himself watching the bunching muscles of her calf with almost as much focus, imagining how those toned legs would feel beneath his touch.

When she spoke again, the sound of her voice sent a jolting ripple along his nerves. "There has to be something they hope to accomplish, but apparently nobody at the FBI can agree on what that could be." She looked up at him. "How about y'all? Anybody have a theory?"

"When our happy band of mismatched criminals was working for Wayne Cortland, figuring out what they wanted was easy enough," he said. "Cash."

"Which funded their individual projects, whatever those might be." She agreed with a brief nod. "That makes sense."

"But to stick together now, without that unifying entity, there has to be something else animating them. Something beyond cash."

"They all seem to hate the government."

"Many perfectly law-abiding people think ill of the government."

"But they don't conspire to poison a convention full of cops." She grimaced as she clasped her hands together and

stretched her arms over her head. "There has to be something more specific than just some nebulous dislike for
government."

"Unless they're planning to cripple the government in
order to create the sort of chaotic conditions necessary for a
revolt." Darcy knew firsthand how close the BRI had come
to doing something just that massive only a month before.

"Cripple the government? You know as well as I do
how many safeguards are in place to prevent governmen-
tal collapse."

"A month ago, the BRI was conspiring with hackers
to shut down power to the eastern half of Tennessee, remember?"

"Creating trouble for half a small southern state is not the
same as bringing down the federal government." She shook
her head. "And that was really about Albert Morris and his
greed, wasn't it? Morris was banking on the power failure
to send state governments rushing to Cyber Solutions for
help hardening their infrastructure against hacking—that's
why he invested in so much of their stock."

"Morris was also trying to sell the federal government
on Cyber Solutions," Darcy pointed out. "Which suggests
he knew bigger attacks were on the horizon."

"But Morris was arrested and Cyber Solutions is under
enormous scrutiny. What good would it do anyone to attempt another infrastructure attack?" McKenna shook her
head, morning sunlight slanting through the cabin windows
setting off sparks in the auburn curls dancing around her
face. The urge to bury his face in those soft curls hit Darcy
like a gut punch.

He dragged his gaze away, looking down at his clenched
hands. "The only thing the BRI, their hacker mates and the
drug dealers that help fund them have in common is a desire for chaos. So perhaps the more pertinent question is,
what's driving the traitor in the FBI?"

McKenna's gaze snapped up to meet his. "That's a damned good question, isn't it?"

He nodded. "What benefit could someone in the FBI receive from letting a terrorist attack play out?"

Chapter Eight

"You told him about the GPS tracker?" Sunlight angling through the large window in Alexander Quinn's office set Olivia Sharp's face aglow and turned her eyes to a dazzling turquoise. Right now those turquoise eyes flashed angry fire at the occupant of the chair in front of Quinn's desk.

"I did." Cain Dennison sounded unapologetic. "I've also removed the one I found in my own truck," he added, looking away from Olivia and meeting Quinn's steady gaze. "And warned as many other agents as I've been able to talk to. If that's a problem for you, then I'll resign. But I'm not going to work for a company that treats me and the rest of the agents around here as if we're criminals who need to be tracked at all times."

"Fair enough," Quinn conceded. "I'll send out a memo to the other agents who'd like to have their trackers removed, as well."

"You're making my job twice as hard," Olivia protested.

"Work it out," Quinn said bluntly, his gaze leveling with hers until she looked away. He turned back to Dennison. "Have you informed Anson Daughtry, as well?"

Dennison nodded.

By the window, Olivia muttered a soft curse.

"I would have preferred that you had come to me first,"

Quinn told Dennison, "but I do understand your sense of violation."

"Why did you do it, then?"

Quinn folded his hands in front of him, not sure how to answer. Old habits died hard, true, but he should have known better than to play games with his agents' lives. One of the reasons he'd left the CIA after so many years with the agency had been his increasing disgust with the way the government viewed its agents as pawns in a high-risk game. It had ever been so, of course, and probably would be so for as long as a dangerous world required spy games to keep the planet from going up in flames.

But people used to matter. They had value beyond their usefulness. The spy game had never been fair or above-board, but the players used to be more than just human chess pieces.

He'd almost forgotten that himself, more than once. Had let the game control him when he should have been controlling the game.

People had died. People who shouldn't have.

"I forgot who I am," he said finally, meeting Dennison's gaze without flinching. "I forgot why I'm here."

Dennison's eyes narrowed but he gave a short nod. "We all do, sometimes."

"You're right." Olivia walked away from the window and dropped with casual grace into the seat next to Dennison, crossing one long leg over the other. "One of the reasons I left the FBI was to get away from this sort of game-playing. I'm sorry."

"Look, I know we all want to find out who among us is leaking information. But if we're all going around suspicious of everybody, it's going to kill our ability to work as a team." Dennison stood up. "For the record, I don't think for a second Nick Darcy is the mole. He doesn't have a treacherous bone in his body."

"We have to do the investigation," Olivia said. "We can't assume anything."

"I know that. But I don't think he's going to listen to anything else I have to say." Dennison pulled a well-worn baseball cap from the back pocket of his jeans and pulled it over his head. He tipped the brim toward Olivia, then shot a long, hard look at Quinn. "If you want someone spying on him, you'll need to find another agent."

Olivia's gaze followed Dennison from the room. "Perhaps I made a bad choice with that one."

"You were looking for an agent Darcy considers a friend," Quinn said. "Dennison is as close as it gets."

"Darcy's quite a loner."

Quinn shot her a pointed look.

Her lips curved slightly. "Touché. But I have good reasons for my curmudgeonly ways."

"As does Darcy." Quinn leaned back in his chair, steepling his fingers over his stomach. "For the moment, he and Agent Rigsby are safe. He'll protect her because he knows I want him to. And because he has a connection to her."

"A connection?"

"An old one. But he's the one she went to when she was in trouble." Quinn had seen signs that the pretty FBI agent and the quiet, serious DSS agent were forming a special connection, though he'd never detected any sign that they'd crossed a line. Wouldn't have been his business if they had, though knowing all the secrets inside the embassy had been part of his job as a CIA operative.

"What do we know about her problems with the bureau?" Olivia asked, curiosity sparking behind her bright eyes.

"The only word we're getting is that she's gone rogue. She disobeyed an order from her superiors and is now considered a compromised asset."

"And we have no idea what that order might have been?"

Quinn sat up straight. "She was asked to meet a fellow agent for extraction from an undercover assignment."

"Undercover doing what?"

"That's the question."

Olivia was silent for a moment, her gaze lowered to her folded hands. When she looked up again, Quinn didn't miss the worry in her eyes. "There's something you're not telling me, isn't there? Is it about Landry?"

He'd wondered when she would get around to asking that question. "Landry was assigned to the same investigation Agent Rigsby was on."

"But he's out of Johnson City. You said Rigsby was working out of the Knoxville Field Office."

"Joint operation."

Olivia's fingers threaded together, her grip so tight that her knuckles began to whiten. "Has he gone rogue, as well?"

"Not to my knowledge."

She relaxed visibly. "Do you want me to try to find another agent to replace Dennison on the Nick Darcy investigation?"

Quinn shook his head. "Dennison was the best you were going to get. I'll cover it myself. I think he still trusts me enough to stay in touch if he needs help."

"You don't think he's responsible for the leaks, do you?"

"I don't." Quinn looked up at her. "I don't think Daughtry is responsible, either. But they were the only other agents who knew about Mallory Jennings and her work here. Someone leaked that information to some very bad people. So we have to look closely at both Darcy and Daughtry."

"If you don't think it's one of them—"

"I don't think either of them would leak the information intentionally."

"But you don't know whether it might have been an accident," Olivia finished the thought for him. "So maybe I should be looking at the people around them?"

Quinn opened his desk drawer and pulled out a folder. "I've surveyed three months of security video and compiled every contact between Darcy, Daughtry and other agents and support staff. The notes are here." He handed the folder to Olivia. "Have fun."

She took the folder, her eyes narrowing. "You want me to do background checks on all the people those two have come into contact with for the past three months?"

"Yes."

She released her breath on a long, slow sigh. "Can I have some agents to help me out?"

"Sure." Quinn waved his hand at the folder. "Anybody who's not working another case and isn't on that list of contacts."

She shot him a hard look. "You've got to be kidding me. Everybody in the office is probably on this list."

"I culled the list to support staff. If none of those pan out, then we'll start looking at field agents."

"Fine." She slapped the folder against her hip and stalked out of the office, looking like a pissed-off swan as she floated out the door, slamming it behind her.

Quinn couldn't hold back a smile.

"I DON'T THINK it can be either the FBI director or his deputy, so we can mark them off the list." Darcy came back from the kitchen with a bowl of soup for each of them. He set the bowls on the coffee table between them and pulled spoons wrapped in paper towels from the pocket of his jeans. "Here you go."

McKenna took the spoon and dipped it into the thick broth. "What is this?"

"Hearty beef and vegetable, or so the can said." He pulled the armchair closer to the footlocker doubling as a coffee table. "It's fluids and nutrition, both of which you need, so eat up."

The soup was pretty good for something out of a can, and she was hungrier than she'd thought. She'd consumed almost half the bowl before she realized Darcy was watching her.

"What?" she asked, wiping her mouth with a napkin.

He smiled. "Glad to see your appetite is coming back. You used to eat like a horse when we were working at the embassy."

"Yeah, well, that was eight years ago. Oh, to be young again."

"You still look great."

A flutter of pure feminine pleasure darted through her. "Back at ya."

"There are more cans in the kitchen if that's not enough."

"This should be plenty." She put her spoon down for a minute, not wanting to eat so quickly she made herself sick. She hadn't had a decent meal in a couple of days, so she'd have to ease her stomach into being full again. "I don't think my SAC would betray me," she said, playing with the corner of her napkin. "So that leaves my supervisory special agent, Darryl Boyle, the head of the Johnson City RA, Pete Chang—"

"And Cade Landry."

Something about Darcy's tone made her sit up straighter. "Do you know something about Landry I should know?"

He shook his head. "Just that he worked a case recently that The Gates ended up getting involved in."

"Was it Susie's case?" She didn't remember her cousin mentioning any involvement with the FBI, but there was a lot about her life that Susie—Susannah—hadn't told McKenna.

"No. It was earlier than that. He was assigned to a case involving a married couple ambushed and abducted from their motel room—"

"Oh, right. That's the case where it came out that Sin-

clair Solano was still alive. And not really a traitor." Some
of the people she worked with hadn't been happy about
learning they'd spent years and resources hunting a fugitive that the CIA knew was one of the good guys. "Let me
guess—Quinn was the CIA agent who failed to inform all
the other pertinent government agencies that Solano wasn't
actually a terrorist."

"Not only that, but Solano is working for Quinn now.
And recently married Ava Trent."

"Wow. Didn't see that coming."

"They both joined The Gates around the same time, and
though they tried to be circumspect about it, it's difficult to
hide when one is madly in love." Darcy's smile was close
to a grimace. "Confirmed singles are dropping like flies
around that office these days. I'm beginning to wonder if
Quinn has slipped something into the water."

"You're such a romantic, Darcy."

His smile faded. "Romance is folly. Better to join one-
self to another, if that's what you choose, with your eyes
open and your heart intact."

"Is that what your parents did?"

He made a face. "God, no. Well, my father did, I suppose. He weighed my mother's qualities and assets and
found her an appropriate mate for a man in his position."

"But your mother fell in love?"

"She did. Just not with my father."

"Oh."

"Nothing came of it. Nothing ever could have. He was
married and a peer. She was married to an American diplo-
mat." Darcy pushed his half-empty soup bowl away. "Love
is a mercurial bitch."

"So that's why—" She stopped, not sure she cared to
hear the answer to her unspoken question. "Never mind.
So you think Ava Trent could help us find out more about
Cade Landry?"

"Maybe. Probably could give us a pretty good bead on whether Pete Chang is the sort of man who'd leak information to the BRI, as well."

A flicker of excitement burbled in her chest at the thought she might be one step closer to finding out who had put a target on her back. "Do you think you could risk giving her a call and picking her brain?"

"I'd prefer to meet face-to-face," Darcy answered. "She may suspect more about one or the other of them than she's willing to share on the phone. I can press her for more information if I see she's holding something back."

"Can I go with you?"

He slanted a quelling look at her. "No."

"She doesn't have to know who I am."

"I'm fairly sure Quinn will have passed along the FBI all-points bulletin. It's standard procedure at the agency when such information comes our way. If he didn't, and someone discovered the omission, it would raise questions about why he failed to do so."

"Questions Quinn wouldn't want to answer."

"Exactly." He nodded at her mostly empty bowl as he picked up his own and rose to his feet. "Are you done?"

She pushed the bowl toward him. "Yes, thanks."

When he returned from the kitchen, he picked up the leather jacket he'd left draped over his chair. "I'll drop by the office and see if I can track down Ava. You should lie down and get some rest."

"I'm not tired," she protested.

"Doesn't matter. Your body needs rest if you're serious about speeding up your recuperation time." He arched a dark eyebrow at her. "You are serious about getting better soon, aren't you?"

She controlled the urge to hurl one of the throw pillows from the sofa at him. "Of course I am."

"Find a book to read." He waved his hand at the built-in

bookshelves that flanked the hearth. "Or find a radio and listen to some music, if you can find a station around here that plays anything other than hillbilly anthems. Oh, wait, you are a hillbilly—"

"Not a hillbilly, Jeeves."

Shrugging on the jacket, he shot her a grin. "Not a Brit, Elly May."

She managed to hold back her smile until he was safely out the door.

THE VISITOR'S BADGE clipped to the waistband of his jeans flapped as he walked down the corridor to the agents' bull pen, a nagging reminder that he was no longer one of them. Not in any meaningful way.

There were only a handful of agents in the office at this time of day. Fortunately for Darcy, Ava Trent—Solano, he amended mentally—was one of them.

She looked up at him, her hazel eyes brightening. "Darcy!"

"Hey, Ava." He pulled a nearby metal-and-vinyl chair up to her desk and sat. "Where's Sin?"

"Out on a case." She lowered her voice. "Quinn still won't let us share a case. I think we'll probably be celebrating our twentieth anniversary before he trusts us not to get distracted by each other."

"I've seen the two of you," Darcy said with a smile. "Quinn's probably right, you know."

She laughed. "Probably. What brings you here? Quinn's reinstating you, I hope?"

"Not yet," he said with a sigh. "Actually, I'm looking into something that's sort of fallen into my lap. A personal issue, I guess you could say, regarding someone I worked with several years ago."

Ava twisted her wavy brown hair into a knot and stuck a pencil through the twist to hold the makeshift chignon in place before she bent closer. "A personal issue? Do tell."

"Could we take a walk?"

She shot him a puzzled look but stood and grabbed her jacket from the back of her chair. "If Quinn asks, tell him I'm taking my break," she told the nearest agent, a tall blonde who had come on board a couple of days before Quinn had put him on administrative leave. Olivia Sharp—he finally placed her as she turned to give Ava a quizzical look.

"We get breaks?" she drawled.

Ava just grinned and looked at Darcy. "So, you have a personal problem? You need a woman's viewpoint? Advice?"

What was it with people in love? They couldn't seem to bear it if the rest of the world didn't find a way to pair up, two by two.

"It's not that sort of personal issue," he said, quickly shoving the memory of kissing McKenna Rigsby to the back of his mind. "It's a former colleague who's run into some trouble with the FBI."

Ava looked faintly puzzled. "And because I used to work for the FBI you thought—"

"Actually, you used to work with the Johnson City resident agency, and that's why I'm here. What can you tell me about a special agent named Cade Landry?"

A loud thud behind him made him jump. He turned in time to see Olivia Sharp crouching to gather up a stack of files she'd dropped.

"I didn't work with Landry for long," Ava said, drawing his gaze back to her. "Really only a month or two before I left the bureau to come work here. Why do you want to know something about Landry?"

He took the jacket from her hands and helped her into it. "Let's walk," he said.

Ava led Darcy out of the bull pen and down the hall, where he relinquished his visitor's badge to the receptionist.

Outside, the sun was dipping toward the west, taking with it most of the day's heat. Ava kept pace with Darcy's longer legs as they headed east on Magnolia Drive.

"What do you want to know about Landry?"

"Have you seen the APB from the FBI regarding a rogue agent?"

Ava's eyes narrowed. "I have. You think Landry might be involved with this missing agent?"

"Something like that."

Her lips tightened to a tight line. "I don't like to speak ill of people when they're not here to defend themselves."

"But you know something?"

She lowered her voice. "If you're asking me if I have any proof that Cade Landry is a crooked agent, no. I don't."

"So what *do* you know?"

"I know that he has an impressive job jacket. Great scores at the Academy, commendations out the wazoo from his first weeks and months on the job. He was going somewhere. Fast. And then—"

"And then?" he prodded when she fell silent.

She released a deep sigh. "About a year ago, he started going downhill quickly. Went from a blue-flamer heading up the ladder in the Richmond Field Office to a glorified grunt in the Johnson City RA. He was actually junior to me, even though he had more years of experience. That doesn't happen unless something has gone very, very wrong."

"But you have no idea what?"

She shook her head. "I didn't stick around that long, and it wasn't like I was looking to become his confessor."

"What was he like to work with?"

Ava's brow creased. "Apathetic. He went through the motions, did the work adequately enough, but I could tell he really didn't have any heart for the job. I know there are some agents who try to maintain a certain distance from the work—it's probably smart, since I've seen a lot of agents get too close to their cases and end up in long-term therapy before it was all over—but with Landry, it wasn't even about keeping his professional distance. He really didn't seem to care about anything at all."

"Any theories as to why?"

"Like I said, I didn't ask any questions and he didn't offer any answers. I'm pretty sure that whatever went wrong went wrong when he was in Richmond, though. Because before Richmond, he was fast-tracking it to the top. And then his forward progress just seemed to stop."

"Do you know if it could have been related to his personal life? A broken marriage? Death of a loved one?"

"He was never married. That much I got out of him on a stakeout once." Ava shook her head. "As for a family member dying? I don't know. He didn't mention any family at all while we worked together in Johnson City. I wish I could tell you more."

"That's helpful, truly." He could do some digging into Landry's public records, see if he could find something about the man's family. An emotional upheaval could lead an otherwise stable man off the deep end, and deep ends were exactly where a crew of parasites like the BRI and their criminal comrades could do a lot of damage.

"Is that all you needed?"

"Just one more question. What can you tell me about Pete Chang?"

Ava's expression darkened. "He's a jerk. A total brown-noser trying to move his way up to a better assignment. He's an FBI man through and through."

"Could he be compromised? Could he be corrupted?"

"Chang? Not by anyone outside the FBI, no." Her lips flattened. "Now, if someone in the FBI gave him a shady order, and he thought it could give him a boost up the bureau ladder? He'd be tempted. But I don't know that I think he'd even do something corrupt then. He'd probably think it was a test or a trap and report the overture up the chain of command."

"Ah, one of those."

Her lips quirked. "I imagine you had dealings with that type of bureaucrat working at State."

"I did indeed." He managed a smile, hoping it didn't appear too much like a grimace. "Thank you for the information."

"Anytime." She started to turn toward the old Victorian mansion Quinn had turned into The Gates, then stopped and looked back at Darcy. "This is about that FBI agent on the run, isn't it?"

He didn't answer. He could see in her eyes he didn't have to.

"Do you trust her?"

He didn't answer that question, either, but whatever Ava saw in his expression seemed to satisfy her.

"Be careful." Her smile held considerable concern.

"Always am." He watched her walk back down the sidewalk to The Gates, wishing he could go with her, not as a visitor but back at his desk, working the job he hadn't realized he'd come to enjoy so much until he'd been barred from doing it.

He tried not to speed on his way back to the cabin, but he didn't like leaving McKenna alone so long. She was making a good show of being stronger, but he'd seen the circles of fatigue under her eyes, the pale tone of her skin. She was still weak, still vulnerable.

And he felt a driving need to protect her.

About three miles from the turnoff, a glance in the rearview mirror made him sit up straighter. That black SUV about three cars back had been with him since he'd left The Gates, hadn't it?

He took the next turnoff and drove at a steady pace down one of the small feeder roads that led toward Warrior Creek

Falls. Only one vehicle behind him followed, keeping a steady distance from him. The black SUV.

He was being tailed.

Chapter Nine

She'd tried to nap, but the cabin was entirely too quiet. At her place in Knoxville, there was a constant flow of background noise that never let her feel alone—traffic on the street outside her window, the hum of electrical appliances not only in her place but in those nearby, the whisper of heated air coming through the vents to warm the drafty old four-room apartment.

Here in the middle of nowhere, surrounded by nothing but trees and nervous little woodland creatures, the silence was nearly complete. The hiss of the space heater set into the hearth was the only noise, and though it was quiet, in the dearth of ambient noise, it seemed to ring through her head like whispered conversations just out of earshot. The effect was creepy and not at all conducive to sleep.

So when the phone rang just as she started to finally doze off, it set off dozens of little explosions along her nervous system, jerking her wide awake in a second.

The digital readout on the phone's display showed a number but no name. What was Darcy's number? She tried to calm her shattered nerves enough to remember.

Taking a chance, she picked up the phone but didn't speak.

"Rigsby?" Darcy's clipped accent rang over the line.

She slumped against the sofa cushions. "Yes."

"Listen carefully. I've picked up a tail. I'm trying to shake it, but you need to be prepared in case someone already suspects where we're staying. I'm fairly sure Bragg has extra firearms stashed somewhere in the cabin. You know he's worried about those hillbilly hotheads from over in Boneyard Ridge coming after Susannah."

McKenna knew well the potential threat to her cousin's life. She and her mother had taken Susie in when she was just sixteen, hiding her from a family of meth-dealing criminals determined to make her pay for killing one of their own when he tried to rape her. The Bradburys hadn't stopped looking for a chance to serve a little mountain justice to McKenna's cousin, finally catching up to her a few months ago.

If it weren't for Hunter Bragg and his colleagues at The Gates, Susie would probably be dead now. The agents from The Gates had issued a stern warning to the Bradburys that Susie was under their protection now. So far, the truce had held, but McKenna knew Hunter and Susie would always feel the need to keep their guard up.

"I'll look around," she said. "I'm armed, as well." Her Glock's magazine could hold thirteen rounds, but she'd used some rounds in getting away from the people who'd shot her. She had only nine rounds left. She needed to go ammo shopping soon.

"Listen closely. If you get surrounded, there's a way out of the cabin you need to know about." Darcy's voice was low and tight over the phone. "Downstairs in the basement, there's a big armoire near the back. Open the door and step inside. There's a pressure plate in the floor of the armoire that opens a trapdoor."

"How do you know about that?"

"Quinn told me."

"How does Quinn know?" As soon as she asked the question, she felt like an idiot. "Never mind. How does Quinn know anything? He's magic."

Darcy's soft chuckle bolstered her spirits. "If I can shake the tail, I'll be back. If I can't—if you don't hear something from me within an hour—I want you to take that basement escape tunnel. It comes out several yards into the woods. You'll need to start hiking due north. Within half a mile, you'll see a big mountain over the top of the trees. That's Laurel Rise. Keep hiking. You'll come upon a gravel road eventually. Follow that road up the mountain until you reach a big cabin at the top. That cabin belongs to Quinn. I've already called to tell him he might be getting a visitor."

Her gut tightened painfully. She wasn't sure what scared her more—the thought of hiking up a mountain in her weakened condition or coming face-to-face with Alexander Quinn again after all these years.

"Can you do that, Rigsby?" Darcy asked when she didn't respond.

She squared her shoulders. "Yes."

"I will do my best to get back to you." His voice held a hint of steel.

"I know."

He hung up without saying goodbye.

For a moment, she sat very still, still gripping the phone in one hand as her mind reeled beneath an onslaught of mental orders—find another weapon, find ammo, pack tools and necessities, pack water and food.

She shook off the paralysis and pushed to her feet, ignoring the punch of pain in her side. She didn't have time to indulge her weakness.

Her life was in danger, and once again, she had to figure out a way to save herself.

DARCY WAS RUNNING out of time, but he had to be sure he'd lost the tail—and any possible backup tail—before he risked going back to McKenna. She was depending on him to keep her safe, and the last thing he wanted to do was fail her the way—

He stopped himself short. He had to stop beating himself up over the past. The embassy siege had been eight years ago. He'd been concussed and outnumbered, along with those DSS and Marine Security Guard troops who'd survived the initial onslaught. Despite the wishful thinking of State Department bureaucrats sitting in their fancy offices in Washington, DC, there had been no way to get through that sort of relentless, vicious terrorist attack without sustaining casualties.

The real surprise had been just how many people had survived the siege, thanks to the efforts of people like Maddox Heller, McKenna Rigsby and, yes, even him.

He just didn't like losing. And so many dead embassy employees was a loss. No way around it.

He hadn't seen the black SUV in fifteen minutes. He'd backtracked, raced through yellow traffic lights, taken quick turns without signaling and broken about a dozen traffic laws trying to shake his followers, but there was still a vehicle behind him, about a hundred yards back. He couldn't make out much about it, except it was a lighter color. He couldn't even be sure if it was the same vehicle he'd spotted earlier, before he lost the black SUV.

Just in case, he whipped left down a side road that led toward Deception Lake and parked near a lakeside cabin. The place looked closed up for the season; April in the Smokies was still cool enough to dissuade tourists and part-time mountain dwellers from opening up their cabins until the advent of summer.

He got out of the Land Rover and hiked deeper into the woods, settling behind a large mountain laurel bush that offered both cover and a decent vantage point to watch the road.

After ten minutes with no sign of a following vehicle,

he returned to the Land Rover and settled behind the steering wheel, letting his racing pulse return to normal before he pulled his phone from his pocket and called Bragg's cabin again.

McKenna answered on the first ring, her voice tight. "Where are you?"

"On the road," he answered. "Listen to me. I still don't think it's safe for me to come straight back to the cabin, but if you haven't seen any sign of intruders, you're probably safe enough for now. Try not to worry. I'll be back there as soon as I can."

"Where are you going?"

He started the Land Rover, his muscles bunching with tension as the engine roared to life. "I think it's time I go talk to an old friend and find out just what the hell he's up to."

"I'M NOT HAVING you followed." Quinn kept his tone calm, though the man pacing the floor in front of his desk was anything but placid.

Nick Darcy halted suddenly, bending forward and slapping his hands on Quinn's desk. Though a lean man, he was tall and broad-shouldered, big enough to be imposing when he wanted to. If Quinn had been a different sort of man, he might have felt intimidated.

Instead, he mostly felt annoyed. And curious.

"You had a GPS tracker attached to my vehicle."

"I had them attached to every agent's vehicle."

"Without our consent?"

"Technically, I do have your consent," Quinn answered calmly. "Perhaps you should have read the fine print on your contract more closely."

Darcy's nostrils flared. "I'm on administrative leave."

"Doesn't negate your contract."

"Perhaps not. But I removed the tracker. And I'll be

checking my vehicle every time I leave here in order to be certain you haven't attached another. Is that clear?"

Quinn ignored the question. "Why do you think I'm having you followed?"

"Because it's the sort of thing you'd do," Darcy snapped.

Quinn quelled an unexpected flicker of dismay. He hadn't started The Gates to be anyone's friend. Everyone he'd hired had been brought into the company because he believed they could be valuable assets, not because he liked them personally or cared to be thought of as a friend.

He wasn't Darcy's friend. He wasn't anyone's friend.

But he valued Darcy's opinion, nevertheless. He supposed their long and often-colorful history together had made Darcy the closest thing Quinn had to a friend. He knew Darcy's thoughts on most subjects because the former DSS agent had been relentlessly honest with him, for good or for bad.

He didn't like hearing the disgust in Darcy's voice.

"I'm not having you followed," he said bluntly. "If I were, you would never have spotted the tail."

Darcy's lips flattened to a thin line.

"I am curious, however," Quinn continued, "why you spirited one of my agents out of here this afternoon for a private chat."

"Did she tell you?"

Quinn shook his head. "No."

"But you know about it."

"Of course."

Darcy sighed, dropping heavily into one of the chairs in front of Quinn's desk. "Do you know what we were talking about?"

"No. Would you like to tell me?"

Darcy was silent for a long moment, his dark eyes studying Quinn with disquieting intensity. Whatever he saw in Quinn's face seemed to answer some unspoken question, for his tense shoulders relaxed, and he nodded. "I wanted some information on an FBI agent named Cade Landry. Ava used to work with him at the FBI's Johnson City RA."

Quinn kept his expression carefully blank. "What did you want to know about him?"

"What kind of agent he was. Whether he could be turned."

"Did Trent have an opinion on the subject?"

"She shared her impressions of Agent Landry. We didn't come to a concrete conclusion."

"You know if you want my help, you need only ask."

"If I want your help, I will ask."

Quinn wasn't going to hold his breath. "If you care to know, the internal investigation into your activities over the past few months has nearly concluded. We should have something to share with you in a week or two."

"Kind of you." There was no warmth in Darcy's tone as he rose to his feet and started toward the door.

"I'm not your enemy," Quinn said, though he'd had no intention of speaking.

Darcy turned in the doorway to look at him. "But you're not my friend, either. Are you?"

Quinn had no answer to offer.

Darcy turned and left Quinn's office, letting the door click shut behind him.

Quinn sat in silence for a long moment, trying to clear his head. It wasn't like him to be thrown by the doubts of one of his agents. He knew most of them weren't certain they could trust his motives. They were probably right. He'd been working angles for so long, he wasn't sure he knew how to stop.

But he wasn't dealing Darcy an unfair hand, no matter what the agent thought. He was playing it straight as a board, giving Darcy all the leeway he could spare out of respect for their shared history.

Sooner or later, he hoped, Darcy would see what the

truth really was. And while he might never earn his cautious agent's friendship, he hoped he might earn back a measure of respect.

Three sharp raps on his door drew him out of his speculations. Before he could speak, the door opened and Olivia Sharp entered. "Was that Nick Darcy I just saw leaving?"

Quinn sighed. "You may enter."

Olivia made a face and dropped with easy grace into the chair Darcy had just vacated. "What did he want?"

Quinn was tempted to tell her to mind her own business, but he was becoming very curious about Olivia's connection to Cade Landry. "He spoke with Ava Trent about someone she used to work with."

Olivia's blue eyes went diamond hard, but that was the only change in her carefully schooled expression. "Why?"

"He wanted to know if Ava thought the man might be corrupt."

Olivia didn't blink. Her facial expression never changed. But most of the color leached from her cheeks, and her eyes went positively glacial. "It's Cade Landry. Isn't it?"

Well, Quinn thought, *isn't that interesting?*

TRY TO RELAX.

McKenna almost laughed aloud at the thought. Darcy hadn't shown up yet, though he'd called to reassure her she was probably safe. She'd been sitting there in the cabin's small front room, fondling her Glock and watching the minute hand on her watch go around the dial.

She wasn't sure she'd ever relax again.

The sound of footfalls on the porch steps sent a rattle through her nerves. She picked up the Glock from the coffee table and rose, willing herself to remain calm and focused.

The steps outside seemed to belong to only one pair of feet. She had nine rounds in the Glock. She liked her odds.

The door rattled and started to open. She settled in a shooter's stance and lifted the Glock.

The door stopped moving. Darcy's voice came cautiously through the narrow opening. "Rigsby? Are you aiming your weapon at the door?"

"I am."

"Please don't."

Unable to quell a nervous smile, she lowered the Glock, though she kept it gripped in one hand, ready to aim again if Darcy wasn't alone.

But he was. And he was bearing two large canvas bags that looked full of—

"Groceries," he announced, kicking the door shut behind him.

"You amazing man." She followed him to the kitchen and pulled up a chair while he started putting food away.

"I detect a hint of cupboard love in that declaration," he said with a smile, waggling a chocolate bar in front of her. "Your sweet tooth still in working condition?"

She grabbed the bar and set it on the table beside her. "It is, thank you. What else did you get?"

"I went for packaged frozen meals and canned foods. I know fresh would be better, but we may not have time to cook, and we might as well put the microwave to good use."

"Good point." She looked through the selection of meals he'd chosen, spotting several of her favorites. She and Darcy had shared lunch together dozens of times while working closely in Tablis; had he remembered her food preferences after all this time?

"However, since I was in town and the place was right there, I did stop and get this for our dinner." He pulled a large paper bag from one of the canvas totes and set it on the table between them. "There's a place in Purgatory called Tabbouleh Garden that serves the best falafel wraps I've had since I left the Middle East."

She opened the sack, breathing in the spicy aromas. In an instant, she was starving. "Definitely the most amazing man in the world. Though my hips may not thank you for the extra pounds they're about to pack on."

While she crossed to the sink to wash her hands, he put away the last of the groceries, finishing by the time she dried her hands and returned to the table. He turned to gaze at her, leaning back against the counter and crossing his arms as he gave her a look warm enough to make her spine tingle. "Rigsby, here's something you may not know. Most men—myself included—enjoy curves on women. And as delicious as yours clearly are, you're in no danger of 'packing on' too much flesh anytime soon. So indulge yourself." He smiled. "I used to enjoy watching you eat."

She didn't know whether to feel flattered or self-conscious. She settled on a little of both. "So *that's* what you were doing. I just thought you were grading my table manners on a scale from redneck to royalty."

He smiled at her lame joke as he turned to wash his hands at the sink. "Middle Eastern food is meant to be eaten with the hands. With gusto and appreciation for the flavors and textures." He dried his hands, pulled up a chair and reached into the bag, coming back with a container of hummus. He removed the top and set it on the table in front of them.

"You're right," she agreed. She looked in the bag and found something wrapped in aluminum foil. She set the packet on the table in front of them and peeled off the foil. "Mmm, pitas."

He took one of the pita rounds, tore it in half and handed another piece to her. He took his half, folded it into a scoop shape and dug right into the hummus. "So, how are my table manners now?"

"As much as I want to say closer to redneck than royalty, you somehow manage to look regal no matter what you're doing." She copied his actions, dipping hummus onto her half of the pita. A dollop of the spicy chickpea puree started to fall from the makeshift scoop. She caught it with her mouth, but not before some of it plopped onto her chin.

As she reached to wipe it away, he caught her hand, his dark eyes glittering with a dangerously sexy light. "Allow me," he murmured, releasing her hand and reaching up to slide his forefinger across her chin, catching the drop of hummus on the tip. He offered the tip of his finger to her. "Don't want to miss a drop."

Heat flooded her core and spread like wildfire along her nerve endings. Her heart pounding, she caught his hand in hers and drew his fingertip to her lips. Tentatively, she licked the creamy dip from his finger, then sucked lightly to catch every bit.

Darcy's eyes darkened as she finally released his hand.

"What are we doing?" Her voice came out hoarse and strangled.

Darcy rose slowly from his chair, sending it scraping back across the tile floor. McKenna found herself on her feet, as well, without quite remembering how she got there. As Darcy moved around the table toward her, she felt the tidal pull of him, drawing her relentlessly closer, steel to his magnet.

"I don't know," he answered her question as his head bent toward hers.

Then he kissed her, and she was lost.

Chapter Ten

Maybe it was the residual adrenaline coursing through his body. Or his growing sense of frustration at being relegated to what bloody well felt like house arrest. Or, if he was being perfectly honest, it might be his rather lengthy recent drought when it came to female company in his bed.

Whatever the cause, deep down he knew, even as he swept McKenna more tightly into his embrace, that kissing her was the absolute wrong thing to do.

Except it felt right. So right. She fit against him so perfectly, smelled so enticing, kissed him back with such a heady combination of honey and fire that he wanted to surround himself with her, breathe her into his lungs, taste the sweet heat of her mouth on his until she consumed him.

Was this how it would have been eight years ago if they'd given in to the temptation that had tormented them both? Or was the reward that much greater for having denied themselves so long?

Her tongue slid against his, tasting, testing, and he drank deeply from the well of her passion.

When she withdrew from him, tugging free of his embrace, the sudden loss of her soft heat felt like a jolting shock to his system.

"We can't do this, Darcy."

"Clearly, we can," he disagreed, reaching for her again.

She dodged his grasp, crossing the kitchen until her back was pressed against the refrigerator door. "Listen to me. We can't do this. Too much is at stake to be taking chances like this. This is why we stayed away from each other all those years ago. You know it is. It's just the business we're in."

Frustration burned in his gut. "People in this business have sex all the time. They take lovers. They take wives and husbands. They have flings, one-night stands, lifelong passions. They don't stop living. Why should we?"

"Which is it, Darcy?" She took a step toward him, her hands on her hips. Her unruly curls undulated around her head like Medusa's snakes, making him wonder if she was about to strike him dead with her crystalline gaze. "Is this going to be meaningless sex? Friends with benefits? Is it supposed to be a real relationship? What's it going to be?"

He stared back at her, at a loss for an answer. What *was* he expecting from her? Did he even know?

"That's what I thought." She pushed her hands through her hair and the auburn coils calmed beneath her touch, making him wonder what those magic hands could do to his body. Would he, too, grow gentle and compliant under her caress, or would she set him ablaze with every stroke?

He wanted it all. The tranquillity and the chaos. But he saw from the wary, rigid set of her posture that telling the truth would only drive her further away.

He couldn't risk it.

"So you're saying we can't touch each other?"

"I'm not sure we could avoid that, living in the same small cabin," she murmured, looking away as if the directness of his gaze was more than she could bear. "We just need to be professionals."

"Not friends?"

Her gaze snapped up to meet his. "We're friends. That's the one thing I'm sure about. You—" Her voice broke suddenly, and to his surprise, tears welled in her eyes. She cleared her throat and started again. "You got me through one of the scariest, most traumatic experiences of my life. And the fact that I didn't trust myself to stay in touch with you doesn't mean I didn't miss you in my life every single day."

Her words were so stark, so brave, so true to his own experience that he felt tears prick his own eyes. He blinked them away before they could fully form. "I didn't know."

"Of course you didn't." A smile curved her lips, and she knuckled away her own tears. "I worked damned hard not to let you know."

"I missed you, too," he admitted with a smile of his own. "Part of me wonders if I didn't take the job with The Gates so I could be surrounded by hillbilly accents like yours."

"Not a hillbilly." Still smiling, she rolled her eyes and returned to the table, opening the sack from the restaurant to dig inside. Her gaze rose to meet his as he took his own seat. "Oh, Darcy. You bought baklava, you wicked, wonderful man."

Pleasure flooded through him on a wave of warmth. "You loved that baklava you used to buy at that little sweetshop near the embassy. You even shared once in a while."

"Well, don't get your hopes up this time, hotshot. I'm starving." She tugged the sticky layered squares closer, flashing him a bright grin.

Too bright, he thought. She was trying to behave as if everything was fine. But she knew as well as he did that nothing was fine. She was in trouble. He had barely shaken a tail that afternoon. They had suspects but no proof that she'd been set up by people in her own bureau.

And they'd come damned close to going straight from tentative friends to reckless lovers in the span of a few minutes.

She was pure temptation. He had tried to pretend otherwise, tried to blame his lack of self-control around her on his recent romantic drought or the volatile emotions she'd unearthed by her mere presence, a part of his past with which he'd thought he'd finally made peace.

But the truth was, she'd always had this effect on him, long before al Adar had attacked the embassy. The day he met her, he'd felt as if something in his world had shifted, knocked his life off its steady, predictable axis.

Everything had changed for him in Kaziristan, long before the embassy siege.

"So, we got sort of distracted before," she said a few minutes later, about halfway through the falafel wrap she was eating with gusto. Her obvious pleasure in the food, and the improvement of both her spirits and her physical strength, came as a huge relief to Darcy.

"Yes, we did." And if he let himself focus on recalling the details of that distraction, he might end up throwing caution to the wind and going for another round.

"You didn't tell me how your talk with Ava went."

"Right." Nothing quite like the memory of his frustrating trip to The Gates to pour cold water on his reawakening libido. "It went fine, I guess. Her assessment of Cade Landry seemed to fit what you told me about him. She also had some interesting thoughts about the head of the Johnson City RA, Pete Chang." He told her what Ava had said about Chang's brownnosing habits.

She grimaced. "The sort who'll lick any boot on the ladder rungs above him?"

"Seems to be the case."

"Federal agencies are just chock-full of Pete Changs." She sat back in her chair, folding her hands over her stomach. "So if someone up the chain of command had asked him to sabotage my case—"

"He might have, especially if he's not the sort to question orders."

Her eyes narrowed. "But you don't think it's Chang."

"I don't think this feels like something that would come down the chain of command," he said. "It feels more—"

"Local," she finished for him.

He nodded. "I'd be looking at Knoxville or Johnson City if someone had put me in charge of this investigation."

"Someone *has* put you in charge," she said in a suddenly serious tone. "I have. I'm too close to the players to be objective."

"Are you?" he asked before he could stop himself.

Her brow furrowed. "Am I too close to be objective?"

"Are you close, period? To anyone. On the job or—?"

Her lips curved. "Isn't it a little late to be asking that question, Romeo?"

She had a point. They'd come bloody close to ripping off their clothes and having sex right there in the middle of the tiny kitchen. There was a part of him, fed by desire humming in his blood, that still wanted to give it a go.

"Are you involved with someone in Knoxville? Someone who might start looking for you?"

"No. I haven't had much time to date. I work a lot." She pushed her fingers through her unruly hair, once again managing to tame the wild curls, gentling them with her touch. A fresh surge of desire washed through him, and he struggled not to reach across the table for her.

"What about your family?"

"There's just my mom. Dad died a couple of years ago."

A stab of sympathy sliced his chest. "I'm sorry. I hadn't heard."

"Cancer. Hit fast and, mercifully, he didn't suffer long." She released a long, slow breath. "Could have been a lot worse. There are so many worse ways to die."

The last of his appetite fled. He and McKenna had seen a whole lot of death up close and very personal eight years earlier. And it wasn't the last time he'd seen the fleeting nature of life or how cruel death could be.

"Do you think you were followed back here?" she asked after a few long moments of uncomfortable silence.

He covered the remainder of his falafel wrap with the foil and put it back in the bag. "I don't think so. I think if I had been, someone would have already made a move on us."

She wrapped up her own leftovers and added them to the bag. "I think I'll save the baklava for later."

He reached across the table and caught her hand as she reached for the sticky dessert. "I'm going to protect you. Whatever it takes. You know that, don't you?"

"I'm an FBI agent. I don't need you to protect me." She lifted her chin. "But I know you'll have my back. And that means a lot."

"You'll have mine, too." He threaded his fingers through hers, giving them a light squeeze before letting go. "I need a shower. And we both could use some sleep."

"You go ahead. I'll clean up." She put the baklava back in the bag and headed toward the refrigerator.

In the bathroom, he stripped off his shirt and stopped short, his gaze snagged by his own reflection in the mirror. He looked rough. There was really no other word for it. His hair needed a trim, he hadn't shaved in a couple of days and he'd lost weight since joining The Gates, his natural bulk carved down to an almost feral leanness.

But he was stronger than he'd ever been. In better shape. And until that weak moment earlier in the kitchen, he'd been as clearheaded as he could remember being.

He was a different man from the Nicholas Darcy who'd worked in a suit and tie, playing by the State Department rules and living the same familiar life of embassies and receptions and protocol that he'd known since he was old enough to have a lucid memory.

But which man did he want to be?

The one who gets to kiss McKenna Rigsby whenever he wants.

Closing his eyes against the treacherous thought, he finished undressing and turned on the shower tap, adjusting the water to cool.

Bracing himself, he stepped under the cold spray.

WHILE DARCY SHOWERED, McKenna wandered around the small cabin, familiarizing herself with the place. It was just the big front room, a single bedroom, the kitchen and the bathroom, where Darcy was naked under a steamy shower, naked as the day he was born—

Focus, Rigsby.

What she needed was a computer and an internet connection. She'd ditched her phone once she realized she was up against someone in the FBI. Too easy to locate her by GPS, so she'd tossed the phone in a creek several miles back, hoping the water would render the damned thing useless. And even if it didn't, the FBI could track her only as far as the creek.

But she felt closed off from the world outside without her phone.

She smelled Darcy before she heard his footsteps, a clean, soapy scent mixed with something darker and more masculine. She turned and found him leaning against the bedroom door frame, his eyes narrowing slightly as her gaze met his.

"You're supposed to be resting." He softened his stern words with a faint smile.

"I'm not tired."

He'd shaved, she noticed. The lack of facial hair didn't temper the edginess she'd noticed right away when her fuzzy mind had cleared and she'd been able to take in the full impact of the man he'd become.

Age had made him leaner. Harder. But in a good way. He looked stronger. Fiercer.

He looked like a warrior.

"Then maybe we should sit down and go back over the details of your undercover assignment again. After I check your bandages." He backed out of the bedroom doorway, gesturing down the hall with his hand.

She followed him to the front room and settled on the sofa, grimacing as he sat on the footlocker and reached for the first-aid kit still sitting there from earlier that day. "It's not even really hurting."

"Good. Maybe we've got the infection on the run. But that's no reason to stop doing what's working, is it?"

She could hardly argue with such logic, so she lifted the edge of her T-shirt and turned her body toward him. "How does it look?" she asked as he eased the gauze and tape away from her wounds.

"Better, actually." He tore open a couple of antiseptic wipes and dabbed at the two holes in her side. "Sorry," he added quickly when she sucked in a sharp breath at the sting.

"It's okay. Doesn't hurt nearly as much as it did this morning."

"The inflammation appears to be receding." Finished with the cleaning, he applied more antiseptic, then soothed the renewed sting with the cool relief of aloe vera gel. A quick application of gauze and tape later, he sat back. "All done."

"Thanks." She felt shivery all over, and she knew it wasn't due to the pain of her injury. She needed to concentrate on figuring out what the BRI and their friend at the FBI were really up to and stop letting Darcy's proximity get to her.

They had a lead, didn't they? Cade Landry was as good a place to start as any.

"I want to look a little closer at Cade Landry," Darcy said before she could speak.

"I was just thinking the same thing."

"When I spoke to Ava, she said the man was on the fast track up the career ladder at the bureau for the early part of his career. But a year or so ago, something changed, and he was on a downward spiral, careerwise. She didn't know what that something was."

A memory twitched in the back of her mind. Something about an operation gone wrong. "Did Ava know where he was working before he was transferred to Johnson City?"

"I think she said Richmond."

The twitch got stronger. "There was a domestic terror investigation that went very wrong a little over a year ago. FBI agents had tracked a couple of bombing suspects to a warehouse. There were civilians inside and they were threatening to blow them all up."

Darcy nodded. "I remember that."

"According to FBI scuttlebutt, after SWAT arrived, the order came to hold position until the negotiation unit could get there."

He nodded. "Standard protocol."

"Right. But for some reason, one SWAT unit ignored the order and went in. Two members of the team and eight civilians were killed when one of the suspects detonated his bomb. Dozens of others were injured, including the rest of the SWAT unit that disobeyed orders."

Darcy was looking at her with a frown. "Hmm."

"What?"

He leaned closer. "When I was talking to Ava earlier, there was another agent in the office. And when I mentioned Cade Landry's name, that agent dropped a stack of files."

"And that's significant because…?"

"She was an FBI agent before taking the job at The Gates a few months ago. I remember Quinn saying she'd felt the FBI was a dead end for her and she was looking for new opportunities."

"I imagine for anyone who had been part of that unit that disobeyed orders, the FBI was probably a dead end," she said, finally following what he was saying. "You think Landry was part of the unit that blew the call, right? And your friend at The Gates might have been on the same team, too?"

"It's pure speculation at this point."

"But speculation worth investigating." She stood, driven by the need to do something besides hide in this cabin, living in fear of discovery.

Darcy rose with her, his brow furrowed. "You're supposed to be resting while I do the investigating."

"I'm fine. Most of my strength is back now."

"Really? Clasp your hands behind your back."

The mere thought made her wince.

"My point exactly."

The hint of triumph in Darcy's dark eyes annoyed her into action. "I don't need to put my hands behind my back to investigate." Dodging him, she grabbed her Glock from the coffee table and attached the holster to the front waistband of her jeans. The holster was meant to fit in the small of her back, but as Darcy had so annoyingly proved, reaching behind her back wasn't a good idea if she wanted to be fast on the draw.

She sat on the footlocker and picked up the tennis shoes she'd kicked off earlier, ignoring the hot pain lancing through her side at the exertion.

"Where exactly are you going to go?" Darcy asked, his tone dark with irritation. "You're in the middle of nowhere and you don't even know how to get out of here."

"You said hike north to get to Quinn's place, right?"

"You're going to Quinn?"

"You said he wants you to keep me safe. What's he going to do, turn me in to the FBI?" She grimaced as the pain in her side seemed to translate to fumble fingers. She couldn't seem to get the shoestrings to cooperate.

Darcy crouched at her feet, gently moving her hands aside and making quick work of the laces. He looked up at her, his expression a curious blend of annoyance and admiration. "It's at least two miles. Uphill most of the way. If you're determined to go see Quinn, I can take you in the Land Rover, but I think you need to seriously consider the consequences if you're wrong about what he'll do."

"What am I supposed to do? Sit here and wait for someone to finally track me down?" To her dismay, she felt tears burning her eyes. She blinked them away fiercely, determined not to show weakness. "Someone set me up, made me look like a traitor. Someone *shot* me, for God's sake. I don't think they were shooting to miss."

"I don't, either," he agreed, his voice rough. Remaining crouched before her, he took her hands in his. "But they haven't gone away. They're still out there looking for you, and you don't know which ones wish merely to bring you in for interrogation and which ones want you dead."

She looked down at their entwined hands. "I know."

"I really thought I'd never see you again." His voice dropped to a raspy whisper. "I'd run into people who'd seen you, and if I was brave, I'd even ask about you. But I never let myself go beyond the basics. I never asked if you'd met someone, if you'd married, if you were a mother now—" She heard an odd timbre to his voice, a hint of regret.

She couldn't stop herself from touching his face. "I didn't. I haven't. I'm not."

He curved his cheek into her touch, his eyes closing. "I shouldn't be glad about that."

Her heart pounding beneath her breastbone, she cradled his face between her hands, drawing him closer. "I shouldn't be, either. But I am."

Closing the distance between them, she kissed him.

Chapter Eleven

One hot summer night in Tablis, Darcy had gone for a swim in the embassy pool. Technically, anyone employed by the embassy could swim in the Olympic-size pool behind the embassy's fortified walls, but by custom, the daylight hours were left to the diplomats and their families, while the support staff, including the FBI's legat staff and the security personnel, waited until evening hours, if they were lucky enough to be off duty.

After ten in the evening was the best time if a person preferred to swim alone, Darcy had discovered. Most of the staff had gone to bed by then, leaving him alone to get in his laps and work off the day's stresses before bedtime.

But that hot summer night, he had not been alone. A young woman with a lithe, muscular shape had been cutting waves through the pool's clear water, powering her way from end to end as if racing a clock. He'd recognized her—barely—as the new legat agent.

She'd pulled up short as she reached the end where Darcy stood, water streaming from her chaos of curls and sliding with sensuous leisure over the curves of her breasts, so chastely but inadequately hidden beneath the modest one-piece bathing suit. Moonlight brought out deep auburn glimmers in her damp hair and cast her fair skin with a pearly glow that reminded Darcy of a Waterhouse painting he'd seen once at an art gallery in England, depicting young Hylas enchanted by naiads.

Brushing the water away from her eyes, his late-night intruder had offered a sweet smile worthy of those other-worldly water nymphs and apologized. "I thought I'd be alone at this hour."

It had been McKenna Rigsby's first day at the embassy, and Darcy had been utterly enchanted.

Getting involved with her romantically had been out of the question, of course. Tensions in Kaziristan kept all embassy personnel on alert, leaving them little time for anything but the most cursory of friendships. And they'd both worked high-stress, dangerous jobs that allowed no room for distractions.

Like kissing each other until they were utterly breathless.

She tugged him closer, her arms wrapping around his neck until she pulled his chest flush against hers. Her pulse raced in tandem with his as she parted her lips, inviting him to deepen the kiss.

Maybe she really was a naiad, he thought as her hair tangled around his hands, ensnaring him until he felt as though he was becoming part of her, helpless to resist her spell.

But he had to resist. This day, eight years later, was no less dangerous than that night at the US Embassy in Tablis. The enemy had changed, but terror was still afoot. People's lives were still in grave peril.

And as before, McKenna and Darcy stood in the breach, trying to keep death at bay.

He dragged his mouth away from hers, trying to catch his breath again. "We can't do this."

"I know," she murmured, reaching for him again.

Catching her hands, he held them together between his own to keep them still. "We can't do this, McKenna. Not now. For the same reasons as before. You know that."

She closed her eyes and leaned back. "Damn it."

"We need to keep our minds clear. We have to be able to function as a professional team. We've already lost precious time while you've been recuperating. It's not your fault," he added quickly at her stricken look, "but it's just the way things are. We're behind and we don't even know what the Blue Ridge Infantry might be planning. Do we?"

She shook her head. "I know it's big and it's going to be deadly. That's their goal. But I don't know what they have planned."

"Or who in the FBI is working with them."

"Right." She tugged her hands away from his, her composure back in place. She tamed her hair with steady hands and met his gaze with a look of raw determination. "I think we need to start with the second question first. Who is aiding the BRI in their plans? We have our suspicions about Cade Landry, right?"

He nodded. "But I don't want to get so focused on him that we drop the ball and fail to look at other suspects."

"I've known Glen Robertson for several years, even before I was transferred to the Knoxville Field Office." Her gaze followed him as he rose to his feet in front of her. "I can't imagine him doing anything that wasn't completely honorable."

"People can deceive you."

"I know that. I'm not naive."

"I know you're not." His voice softened. "Instead of going to talk to Quinn, why don't we go back to my cabin for now? Anyone who was looking for you in that area has probably moved on by now. And I have internet."

"We should probably wait until night."

He nodded. "Safer that way." He crossed to the doorway and grabbed his leather jacket from the garment hook nailed to the cabin's rough wood walls. "I'll be back."

She rose. "Where are you going?"

"To check the Land Rover. Make sure nobody has tampered with it. I'll knock four times fast and twice slow so you'll know I'm the one at the door and won't shoot me." Flashing her a smile, he lifted the collar of his jacket against the brisk April breeze as he stepped out onto the creaking porch, welcoming the dose of cold to help him get his simmering libido back under control.

The Land Rover was where he'd parked after returning from his roundabout tour of mountain roads in an attempt to shake the vehicles that had been following him. All four tires looked to be intact, and a careful check of the chassis and under the hood convinced him he hadn't picked up any trackers or other sort of electronic parasites.

He'd gassed up once he felt certain he'd lost the tail, so they should be good for the trip to his cabin on Killshadow Road.

When he got back to the cabin, he knocked using the code he'd told her to listen for. No gun pointed his way when he entered again. In fact, McKenna wasn't in the front room at all.

"Rigsby?" he called.

"Back here."

He followed the sound of her voice and found her in the bedroom, packing things back into his duffel bag. "I see you're ready to be gone."

She shot him a wry smile. "You had me at *internet*."

They cleaned up the cabin before they left, trying to put everything back the way it had been. Darcy stuffed their used linens and towels in a garbage bag he found under the kitchen cabinet. "I can launder them at my place and bring them back before Bragg and Susannah return," he told McKenna as she eyed the bag.

She fluffed the bed pillows and stood back to survey her

handiwork. "They'll know we were here when they find the extra food in the cabinets."

"Nobody ever complains about intruders who leave gifts."

She sighed, dropping onto the edge of the bed. "I don't know how I ended up here, in a situation like this. My career was my life."

Well aware he was playing with fire, he sat beside her on the bed. "I know the feeling."

"What happened to you, Darcy?" She twisted to look at him, a brief frown the only sign that the movement caused her any pain.

She *was* getting better, he thought.

"I stopped playing by the rules," he answered.

"That's cryptic."

"After Kaziristan, I saw how Barton Reid twisted everything I believed in to turn Maddox Heller into a scapegoat." He frowned at the memory of the sick, sinking feeling that had twisted his gut when he'd heard how Reid and his sycophants at Foggy Bottom had destroyed the good name of a brave, honorable Marine. "We were there, Rigsby. We saw how it happened."

"He saved our lives. He saved everyone but Teresa."

"We didn't know at the time how deeply indebted to the militants Reid had become."

"The bureau was only tangentially involved in the investigation of Reid," she said. "But I know enough to know he was corrupt to the bone."

"I helped bring him down."

She arched one ginger eyebrow at him. "That didn't make the papers."

"I guess, to be more accurate, I should say I helped the people who brought him down."

"Cooper Security, right?"

He nodded, remembering that night in Washington, DC,

when he'd gotten the call from Alexander Quinn asking for his help. He'd been inclined to ignore the call from Quinn—in his experience, cooperating with Quinn was rarely a good idea.

"Quinn called me. Told me a man named Jesse Cooper was on his way to Washington with a woman who was in grave danger from elements within the government who wanted to use her as leverage against her father."

"Her father?"

"Baxter Marsh." He saw the recognition dawn. "Yes, the same Baxter Marsh who headed the Marine Corps' part of the joint task force in Kaziristan."

"Reid was trying to get his hands on some coded journal, right?"

He nodded. "Jesse Cooper had the journal. They'd managed to decode the journal using the three keys General Marsh and his two fellow generals had created."

"Right. I remember that part of the story. Each man had entrusted the key to one other person, in case something happened to one of them, right?"

"Yes. And something did happen to one of them. General Ross died in a suspicious car crash. But he'd hidden his part of the key in a locket he gave his wife. So, eventually, his key was added to the other two keys to decode the journal and reveal the secrets that brought Barton Reid down."

"Along with several people in the previous administration," she said bluntly. "And you helped Cooper get his hands on that information?"

"I did. I also used my friendship with the British ambassador to the US to get Cooper and Evie Marsh into a big reception at the embassy."

"No wonder you hit a ceiling on the job."

He looked at her through narrowed eyes. "Do you think I did the wrong thing?"

She shook her head quickly. "Bad people got caught and put away. Wasn't that your job?"

He couldn't quell a smile. "Something like that."

"Then good for you, Nicholas Darcy. You didn't let the rules get in the way of doing the right thing." Her smile in return felt like the warm sun breaking through clouds on a cold day.

They made sandwiches for dinner and ate them on the winding drive back to Darcy's cabin. He watched carefully for any sign of a tail, but if there was anyone following them back to Killshadow Road, they were invisible in the darkness.

After an hour-long trip that took fifty minutes longer than the journey would normally take, he parked the Land Rover on the gravel drive in front of the cabin and cut the engine. "Wait here," he said. "And stay alert."

The cabin was dark and looked undisturbed, but that didn't mean anything when one was dealing with the FBI. He opened the Land Rover's back hatch and pulled out the toolbox he had stored there.

"What are you doing?" McKenna turned to watch him.

"Looking for this." He pulled out the small detection device that had come with the job at The Gates. Quinn had warned him that working for an agency that dealt with the sort of cases The Gates handled automatically made them all targets by enemies both domestic and foreign.

"You need to know if someone's listening," Quinn had warned him as he handed him the device.

Now he turned on the bug sniffer and headed up the porch steps, watching the little device do its work.

After covering the entire cabin without receiving any warning blips, he pocketed the sniffer and went back out to the Land Rover. "We're good."

McKenna climbed out of the Land Rover, moving a little more slowly than she had earlier in the day. She'd exerted herself more that day than she had since her injury, and the extra exercise was clearly starting to take a toll.

"Go straight to bed," he ordered. "I'll lock up."

She stared at him. "Are you crazy? It's not even nine o'clock. Just point me to your computer and I promise I'll sit still while I'm surfing the Net. We've already wasted more time than I like."

He decided not to argue for once. She was right. They were already behind, and time was running out.

"It's in my bedroom."

She started down the hall, then stopped, looking back at him. "What's the username and password?"

He froze in place. "Username is just my last name."

"And the password?"

Heat bloomed in his neck and cheeks as he realized he'd just stepped into a minefield.

"Darcy?" she said when he didn't answer right away.

He took a deep breath and got it over with. "It's Mc-Kenna, backward with no capital letters."

She stared at him a moment, her eyes luminous. "Oh, Darcy."

"*Tempus fugit*, Rigsby," he said gruffly, tapping his watch. "Time flies."

She flashed him a bright smile and disappeared down the hallway.

He glanced at his watch. Just after seven. There was a chance someone was still in the office, he knew. The normal hours at The Gates were eight to five, but none of the agents kept normal hours.

He'd worked deep into the evening several times himself. So it was possible Olivia Sharp was still in the office, wasn't it?

He pulled his cell phone from his pocket and dialed the direct number to the agents' bull pen. On the third ring, Cain Dennison's gravelly drawl answered, "The Gates."

"You're there late, Dennison. Sara out on the town with the girls?"

"If by 'out on the town with the girls' you mean on a stakeout over in Bitterwood, then yes. Yes, she is." The humorous tone of his voice didn't quite mask his wariness. "I heard you were in the office today."

"I was. Needed to pick Ava Trent's brain about something."

"Anything to do with why you're staying at Bragg's cabin?"

"No," Darcy lied. "Just following up on something. Is Olivia Sharp in the office by any chance?"

"Just missed her. She left around twenty minutes ago."

"Oh, okay. I'll talk to you later."

"Wait, Darcy."

The urgent edge to Dennison's voice made him do as the other man asked. "What is it?"

"Are you sure you're okay? You know if you need anything, all you have to do is call."

Darcy felt a niggle of guilt. "I know. I do. I'm fine."

"Okay." Dennison sounded unconvinced. "You know where to reach me if that changes."

The differences between Dennison and Darcy might outweigh the similarities, but Darcy believed him. If he ended up needing help, Dennison would come through for him.

It was gratifying to know he wasn't nearly as alone as he'd felt the past few years. "Thank you. I'll keep that in mind."

He hung up the phone and shoved it back in his pocket, wondering if he was going to have to take Dennison up on the offer before this case was over.

SHE WAS HIS PASSWORD.

As far as McKenna knew, she'd never been anyone's

password before. And Darcy's, of all the buttoned-up, unromantic souls in the universe...

"Grow up, Rigsby," she muttered as she powered up the laptop and waited for the log-in screen. But the corners of her lips still twitched at the thought of Darcy still thinking enough of her, all these years later, to use her name as a password.

She logged in, pulled up a browser window and typed in the name Cade Landry. Within seconds, she had pages full of Cade Landrys, so she narrowed the search by adding "FBI" to the parameters.

The entries narrowed down considerably. And most of them were about the explosion near Richmond.

As she clicked through the link to the first entry, she heard Darcy's footsteps coming down the hall. A moment later, his voice rumbled from the doorway. "Any luck?"

"Just got started." She patted the edge of the bed next to her and began scanning the online article. It was a pretty straightforward report of the incident and the injuries and deaths involved. Landry was one of the FBI agents mentioned. "If I was still able to access anything from the FBI database—but they cut me off."

"I'm cut off from most of the resources we have available at The Gates, too." He sat next to her. "Rather inconvenient, that."

She slanted a look at him. "You don't think that one has anything to do with the other, do you? You said you and your agency have been trying to dismantle the BRI and their affiliates—and the BRI is certainly part of what's happened to me..."

"I don't see how the two cases could be connected, though," he said thoughtfully. "I don't see how people would have linked you to me, or vice versa. We haven't spoken in years, and I doubt anyone in the BRI would have been at the American Embassy in Kaziristan nearly a decade ago."

She nodded, looking back at the computer screen. "It wouldn't have mattered if they were. We were always very careful not to let anything between us show. To anyone."

"Ourselves included."

He was so solid beside her. So strong and warm. The urge to curl up against his side felt like a physical craving.

She controlled the desire and clicked on another link. "We had our reasons."

The story in the second link looked to be longer and more substantial, she noted. It was dated a couple of days after the explosion, when both investigators and journalists would have had time to eliminate most of the misinformation and fill in the blanks of the story.

The tone of the story was much more critical of the FBI, of course. By that time, word of the botched standoff would have reached the ears of someone in the news business. Too many people in the bureau were happy to throw another agent or two under the bus in order to make themselves look good in comparison.

Cade Landry's name came up. Often. But it was a name near the middle of the page that caught her eye. "Well, would you look at that?"

Darcy leaned closer, the heat of him enveloping her with delicious warmth. "What?"

She pointed to the screen. "Look what group authorities believed the two bombers belonged to."

Darcy uttered a short profanity. "The Blue Ridge Infantry."

Chapter Twelve

Darcy had finally coaxed McKenna to bed around eleven the night before, but he'd stayed up a little longer, hunting down all the references he could find to the connection between the Blue Ridge Infantry and the two bombers involved in the Richmond incident that had cost Cade Landry his fast track up the FBI ladder.

Ava Solano had told him that Landry seemed to be apathetic about his job these days, but was apathy hiding something else? What if Landry had been involved with the Blue Ridge Infantry all along? What if the botched raid had been an attempt to help his comrades escape? The bomb detonation could have been accidental—all it would have taken was a nervous militia member with a twitchy trigger finger to set off a bomb belt.

Landry definitely deserved greater scrutiny, he decided the next morning when he headed to the kitchen to start a pot of coffee. And getting in contact with Olivia Sharp was the first place to start.

The aroma of freshly brewed coffee hit him halfway to the kitchen. He found McKenna at the table, sipping coffee and reading another article on his laptop computer.

"Grab some coffee," she invited with a cheeky grin. "Or maybe you could whip us up an omelet. I'm starving."

"You look a lot better."

"I feel a lot better." She stretched her arms over her head, not even wincing. "I slept like a log."

He could tell. She looked rested and beautiful. "Good. It seems to have done you a world of good."

"So, what's on our agenda this morning?" she asked as he crossed to the refrigerator for eggs.

"Breakfast," he said. "Then you can continue your internet research while I drive into town to track down Olivia Sharp."

McKenna turned from the laptop to look at him. "Right. She works at The Gates now, you said."

He put a skillet on the stove to heat while he stirred eggs, cheese, milk and spices together for the omelet. "I don't know her well. She came to work there shortly before I was put on administrative leave. But I'm hoping she'll be willing to answer a few questions for me about the incident in Richmond."

"And about Cade Landry?"

"Exactly."

"Well, do me a favor, will you? If you talk to her, ask her who the incident commander for her unit was. So far, all the news accounts keep referring to him by his job title. Not one has mentioned him by name."

He finished pouring the omelet mixture into the pan before he turned to look at her. "That's odd, I take it?"

"Very odd. I don't know why nobody supplied his name to the news outlets. They had no trouble naming any of the other agents on that team."

He dished up their omelets and set the plates on the table, taking his own seat opposite her. "Put away the laptop and eat."

With a sigh that reminded him of her workaholic days at the embassy, she slid the laptop to the side and picked up her fork. "Remember when we sneaked into the embassy kitchen in the middle of the night to make scrambled eggs for everybody getting off guard duty for the night?"

He smiled at the memory. "You always did know how to get people in trouble."

"How was I supposed to know the eggs were for some VIP brunch the next morning?" She took a bite of the omelet. "You still have the touch."

"I think it's just that you have the palate of a culinary philistine," he said, affecting his most plummy accent.

"Snob." She pointed her fork at him. "It is a truth universally acknowledged that a single man in possession of a good omelet must be in want of a wife."

"Nice. Paraphrasing Jane Austen. Which actually makes you a dilettante not a philistine."

"Don't make me look that word up." She shot him a saucy grin that made him want to sweep the plates of omelets aside and have his way with her right there on the kitchen table.

"Rigsby, you're better educated than I am. Now, finish your spectacular omelet and stop trying to distract me with your smart mouth."

He made quick work of his own omelet, moved his plate aside and slid the laptop computer in front of him. "Have you started looking into the backgrounds of any of the other agents on the suspect list?"

"Not since I found the articles on the Richmond bomb case." She stopped about two-thirds of the way through her omelet, pushing the plate aside. "Ugh, stuffed. You want the rest?"

He eyed the leftovers. "Since when do you leave food on the plate, Rigsby? Are you feeling okay?"

"I'm fine. I just—" Her reluctant tone made him look up. She was frowning, her earlier good mood gone.

"What's wrong?"

"I was just thinking about the past couple of weeks. Those men in the BRI aren't misunderstood. They're not mistaken or misled. They're cruel, chauvinistic bastards. They treat their women like property, to use or abuse as they see fit."

Something in her eyes made his chest ache. "What exactly was your role in this undercover operation, Mc-Kenna?"

"They have what I suppose you'd call 'groupies.' Women who like the mystique of their pseudo patriotism. You know, I've investigated other militia groups. Some of them aren't bad people. They just take individual freedom very seriously and worry about the encroachment of the federal government on matters that should be private or local. And I get that, Darcy. I do. I grew up in the mountains where federal programs have left whole generations of people on the draw. That's what we called it. The monthly welfare payments people draw. That's what happens when you let the government try to fix all your problems for you. But the BRI—they're just playing at that kind of 'don't tread on me' sensibility. They don't mean it. They want something else altogether."

The pain in her voice caught him by surprise. She'd talked about her North Carolina childhood quite a bit during their time together at the embassy, but most of the stories had been happy memories.

"What was your role?" he prodded, more gently this time.

She toyed with her fork. "I was supposed to befriend the groupies. Try to work my way into the perimeter of the group that way."

"You're not groupie material."

She smiled at that, and he felt some of the tightness in

his chest ease. "No, I'm not. But I was the only woman on the task force, so I got tapped anyway."

"How far inside did you get?" he asked, not certain he wanted to hear the answer.

"Not far," she said quickly, her gaze darting up to meet his. "Not far at all. They're very suspicious of outsiders. And I may have the right kind of accent, but this is a group of people who know everyone they're dealing with. The bureau tried to set me up with a backstory that would be convincing, but I think they sometimes forget that the BRI isn't just another backyard militia. They've been working hand in glove with some very bright computer geeks for a few years now."

"And someone saw through your cover story?"

"I don't think it was that, exactly," she admitted. "They weren't going to let me into the inner circle if they couldn't go deeper into my background, though. That much was pretty clear fairly soon."

"You told me before someone in the FBI found out you'd gotten close to putting something together on the BRI. How, if they wouldn't let you into the inner circle?"

"What I learned wasn't from the BRI. It was from one of the anarchists." A smile flirted with the corners of her mouth. "He was young. And hot for me. He wasn't particularly subtle about it, either. And I realized maybe there was more than one way to get the information I wanted. But—" Her smile faded, and she looked down at her hands.

Darcy leaned toward her, touching the back of her hand with his fingertips, his gut twisting with sudden alarm. "But?"

"He wanted sex. I wasn't going to give it to him. Definitely not in my job description." She turned her hand over, her fingers brushing lightly against his. Once, twice. Then she pulled her hands into her lap. "He got violent. I had to take him down, and after that, they looked a hell of a lot more closely at me, I guess."

"Is that when you overheard people talking about the Fibber?"

She nodded. "I had to sneak a lot at that point. People would clam up if they saw me coming. Honestly, I'm not sure why they didn't just kill me at that point. Maybe they thought I'd be useful in another way. Maybe by feeding me misinformation about what they were up to."

"How can you be sure they're up to something at all, then?" Darcy sat back, searching her face for any sign she was keeping something from him. It wasn't that he thought she'd intentionally mislead him about something important regarding the case they were investigating.

But maybe she'd keep to herself anything that happened to her when she was vulnerable and alone in a den of vipers like the BRI.

Was there something she wasn't telling him?

"You think I'm lying?" Her eyes narrowed in response. He should have known she'd see through his attempt to cover his doubts.

"I think maybe something happened with the BRI that you're not telling me. Did someone—?" His throat closed up before he finished asking the question.

She leaned forward suddenly, reaching across the table to close her hand over his. "No, Darcy. No. Nothing like that happened. I promise you."

He saw the truth in her eyes and felt his muscles relax, just a little.

She stroked the back of his hand with her thumb. "I know they're up to something because Ax let that much slip before I had to pull my best judo moves on him."

Darcy arched one eyebrow. "Ax?"

"It was his nickname, I'm sure. He never told me his real name. The BRI seem to go by their real names, but their anarchist buddies are all about the pseudonyms." She started to withdraw her hand, but he caught it, twining his fingers with hers. She looked up at him, her sharp green eyes softening. "I think he was trying to impress me."

"Are you sure it was the truth?"

"He tried to backtrack once I had him on the ground. Said he was just making things up."

"But you didn't believe him?'

"No. I'm pretty good at figuring out when someone's lying or telling the truth." She let go of his hand. "If you're going to catch up with Olivia Sharp, you should probably get a move on."

He couldn't tell if she was trying to deflect him from her experiences with the BRI or if she was simply eager for him to see what Olivia had to say about Cade Landry.

Either way, she was right. The earlier he showed up at The Gates, the more likely he'd catch Olivia Sharp on her way in or out of the office.

"Mr. Darcy has a concussion, but he's not showing any signs of a more dangerous injury." The military doctor looked tired and harried, his tone clipped but his eyes kind as he paused in the triage waiting area to update the ragtag handful of embassy security personnel who'd gathered to get information on their fallen comrades. "He's asking for someone named Rigsby?"

All eyes turned to McKenna. She felt heat rising in her cheeks.

"You can see him for a few minutes, but don't stay long. There's a lot going on in the triage area, as I'm sure you can imagine." The doctor nodded toward the door leading into the base's busy medical unit. "He's in bay number four."

Ignoring the curious looks of the other agents, McKenna entered the triage unit and followed the signs to exam bay *four, where she found Darcy resting on a gurney. His eyes were closed, and his face looked pale and haggard. But when she moved closer, he opened his eyes and managed a halfhearted smile. "Good. You're here. I need a lawyer."*

She moved closer, her fingers brushing the sheet beside his hand, allowing herself the ambient warmth but not the actual touch of skin to skin. She felt too vulnerable at the moment to trust herself. "You need a lawyer?"

"They're keeping me in this bloody hospital against my will," he grumbled, his dark eyes soft and persuasive as he gazed at her beneath the gauze bandage over his wounded head. "File a motion or something."

Relief fluttered through her. If he was well enough to complain, he was in better condition than she'd feared. "I have a better idea. Listen to what your doctors tell you to do. And do it."

He grimaced. "I was really counting on your rule-breaking tendencies, Rigsby. You've let me down."

Her knees felt wobbly, but there was nowhere to sit except the edge of the gurney. And she'd be damned if she'd do something so intimate with dozens of military doctors moving from patient to patient behind her. She found the steel in her spine and managed a smile, though she could feel the hot sting of tears at the backs of her eyes. "They'll let you out as soon as they think you're out of the woods. I should let you rest."

As she started to back away, Darcy's hand snaked out to circle her wrist. "Cameron?"

She shook her head, blinking back guilty tears.

"I'm sorry." He released her hand. "What about Jamil and the others in the kitchen?"

"Jamil is okay. He sustained some minor burns and a broken arm. Rafik is in surgery for a ruptured spleen. They haven't found Yusef. They're not sure if he was blown

clear of the kitchen by the rocket fire and managed to walk away or..."

"Or al Adar captured him." Darcy grimaced. *He knew as well as she did what the terrorists did to "collaborators."*

"Darcy, you need to rest."

"They're transferring me stateside as soon as they release me."

The twisting pain in her gut caught her by surprise. "So soon?"

He nodded, holding her gaze with his fathomless brown eyes. "I don't know where I'll be reassigned."

So this is goodbye, *she thought, seeing the truth in his troubled gaze.* "I'll be sticking around for a while. The bureau wants those of us who survived to help the incident investigation team."

He nodded, wincing a little at the movement. "That's why I wanted to talk to you. Because I don't think I'll see you again after this. We both know you won't try to look me up. Will you?"

The finality hit her like a body blow. Appearances be damned, she sat on the edge of the gurney before her legs gave out. "No. I won't," *she admitted, hating herself. Hating him. And wishing they were different people in a different place at a different time.*

"I don't think I would have survived the siege without you, Rigsby." *He brushed the back of her hand with his fingertips.* "Thank you."

She was not going to cry. She wasn't.

"Don't let the bureau break you. They'll try. They always do."

"I won't." *Tears burned the backs of her eyes but she didn't let them spill. She couldn't.*

Not while Darcy was watching.

McKenna woke with a start, her heart thudding heavily against her rib cage. Blinking away the sleep, she checked her watch. Only thirty minutes had passed since Darcy walked out the door. He'd told her as he left not to worry unless she didn't hear from him in a couple of hours.

Then she was supposed to call Alexander Quinn.

She rubbed her eyes, surprised to find tears dampening the skin beneath them. She'd been dreaming, she remembered. About that last day with Darcy at the base hospital outside Tablis.

Saying goodbye.

She knuckled away the tears and sat up from the sofa, eyeing the laptop she'd set on the coffee table before stretching out to rest her eyes. Her life was in danger. Her reputation as an FBI agent in tatters. It would be so easy to give up, to just hunker down and wait for everything to unfold. Sooner or later, the BRI would strike and everything she tried to warn people about would come to pass.

But she wasn't the kind of person who could sit back and let people die if she could stop it.

It was time to get back to work.

As she opened the laptop, she heard the thud of footsteps on the porch outside. She barely had time to grab her Glock when she heard the hard scrape of metal on metal and the door began to open.

She whipped the Glock up and brought it to bear on the broad-shouldered man who stepped through the door. The morning light poured in behind him, rendering him little more than a silhouette in the bright rectangle of the open doorway.

"Don't move," she commanded.

"Wouldn't dream of it," a familiar voice replied, his baritone tinged with amusement.

Son of a bitch.

"Nice to see you again, Agent Rigsby," Alexander Quinn said.

"Why do you want to know about Richmond?" Olivia Sharp crossed her legs, showing off an impressive golden tan and well-toned thigh muscles. She had an easy sensuality about her that reminded Darcy of a CIA agent he'd known back in Tablis. Tara Brady had worn her sexuality like armor, hiding the vulnerable woman underneath. Darcy had a feeling Olivia Sharp was not so different.

"I'm investigating the possibility that there's an FBI turncoat aiding the Blue Ridge Infantry." Darcy didn't see much point in lying.

"Investigating?" One honey-brown eyebrow arched delicately. "I thought you were on suspension."

"It's a personal project."

"What led you to me?"

"Cade Landry."

She flinched. It was only a slight twitch, but Darcy had been watching for any shift in her expression. She schooled her features immediately, her expression settling quickly back to neutral.

But she'd already given herself away.

"I worked with him," she said a second later.

"You both were involved in the botched raid."

Her jaw muscle twitched. "There was a miscommunication."

"Landry led your unit into the warehouse against orders."

"He said he received an order to go in."

"You didn't hear the order?"

Her eyes narrowed a notch. "I don't remember very much about the incident. I sustained a concussion from flying debris after the bomb detonation. I've never been able to remember the moments directly preceding or directly after the bombing."

He decided she was telling the truth, mostly because

he could see a hint of turmoil in those cool blue eyes. She didn't like not remembering what had really happened.

"How many people were in your unit?" he asked.

"Four, plus the unit commander, who wasn't directly on scene."

"Names?"

Her eyes iced over. "Why?"

"I told you. I think someone in the FBI might have been aiding the BRI members you had cornered in the warehouse."

"If so, he wasn't very good at it. One of the bombers blew himself up and the other was killed by sniper fire when he went for the detonator on his bomb belt."

That was new information, Darcy realized. "Sniper fire?"

"If he'd managed to set off the explosives belt, a lot more people would have died. The sniper made sure that didn't happen."

"Who were the members of the unit?"

"I was a member, of course. Cade Landry, as you know. We lost the other two members of the unit—Len Davis and Kevin Darnell. You must have seen their names in news reports if you've been looking into the incident."

He had, of course. Two FBI agents killed in the line of duty were big news. "And the unit commander?"

"I told you, he wasn't on the scene."

"No, I mean, who was he? What was his name?"

Her brow furrowed. "Are you testing me or something? If you've read the news reports, all of this information should have been in those articles."

"Most of it was," he admitted. "But not the name of the unit commander. He was even quoted. But not by name."

She looked genuinely puzzled. "Are you sure?"

"I'm certain. It's made me wonder how one manages to

head up an FBI operation that went entirely pear-shaped without his name being splashed across news accounts."

"I don't know," she admitted. "He has some decent connections in Congress. Enough that his career didn't go completely south." Her lips curved. "Though he himself went south."

"What does that mean?"

"I mean, he was transferred to a field office right here in Tennessee," Olivia answered. "He's a supervisory special agent in the Knoxville office. Darryl Boyle."

Chapter Thirteen

"You can put your weapon down, Rigsby. I'm unarmed."

McKenna didn't trust him, she realized. She'd talked big about going to Quinn earlier, but now she knew she'd have talked herself out of it. "I'll just hold on to this." She dropped the barrel away from him, however, waving him toward the armchair across from where she sat.

Quinn closed the door behind him and sat where she indicated. "You look well."

"I *am* well," she said firmly.

"You're favoring your left side," he said with a patient smile, crossing one leg over the other. "Subtle but there. You need to work on it if you want to convince anyone you're completely sound."

Alexander Quinn wasn't a tall man, nor particularly imposing. He had the sort of chameleon face that was perfect for spy work, she supposed. He could look very different from one day to the next with very little help from makeup or prosthetics.

Today, he looked like an ordinary, mild-mannered businessman in his midforties, his sandy hair touched with gray, his hazel eyes almost merry as he watched for her reaction.

"What do you want?"

"Darcy will protect you at all costs. Even from me. I assume you're aware of that fact or you'd never have come here looking for his help." Quinn's voice held a faint hint

of the Appalachian accent that tinted the language of most
people who lived here in the Smokies. McKenna's own
drawl was far more pronounced, but she hadn't spent most
of her life trying to hide her identity the way Quinn had.

"You're from mountain stock," she murmured. "From
right here in eastern Tennessee. Aren't you?"

"I was born in Purgatory. Spent my first eighteen years
here." His drawl broadened, as thick as her own. But with
his next words, the accent was completely gone. "You were
undercover for the FBI. Trying to infiltrate the Blue Ridge
Infantry. Or, I should say, their legion of female admirers."

She didn't respond.

"You were unsuccessful."

"Can you get to your point?" she asked bluntly.

"I want to destroy the Blue Ridge Infantry. Root and
branch."

"It sounds personal."

"It is" was his only response.

The sound of a vehicle approaching the cabin distracted
McKenna for a split second, but that was enough for Quinn
to reach behind his back and produce a big, black Ruger.
"Stay here."

He was at the window next to the door within a couple
of seconds, peering through the narrow space between the
curtain and the wall. His tense posture eased marginally.
"It's Darcy."

"He won't be happy to see you here," she warned.

Quinn flashed her a feral grin. "I know."

Darcy's footsteps sounded on the porch and stopped.
Waited.

"He knows you're here," McKenna murmured.

"He knows someone besides you is here," Quinn corrected.

"Quinn?" Darcy's voice came from the other side of
the door.

McKenna smiled. "He knows it's *you*. This is an Alexander Quinn stunt if ever there was one."

"Quinn, I'm coming in. Don't be armed." Though muffled by the door, there was no mistaking the commanding tone of Darcy's voice. McKenna saw that even Quinn arched an eyebrow at the sound.

"You gonna drop that Ruger or what?" she murmured, slanting him a sharp side-eye glance.

Quinn's lips pressed to a thin line, but he tucked the Ruger into the holster behind his back and stepped away from the door.

Darcy entered, his own weapon pulled. His gaze swept across McKenna, as if reassuring himself she was unharmed. Then he focused his intense gaze on Quinn.

"What the bloody hell are you doing here?"

"Checking on an old friend," Quinn answered, unperturbed.

"*Friend* is pushing it," she murmured.

Darcy looked at her. "Are you all right?"

"What exactly did you think I was going to do to her?" Quinn asked, more amused than offended.

Darcy finally put away his own SIG and closed the cabin door behind him. "What do you want?"

"I'm assuming the same thing you do. To find out who blew Rigsby's cover. Put them away and stop whatever they're planning."

"Why now?" McKenna asked.

Quinn waved toward the chair and sofa. "May I?"

Darcy shrugged and crossed to where McKenna stood, flattening his palm against the middle of her back. He led her to the sofa and sat closer, his thigh warm against her leg. "Talk."

Quinn sat in the armchair again, unhurriedly crossing his legs. "This morning, an FBI agent visited me at my apartment in town. Wanting to discuss my connection to Rigsby."

"What connection?" Darcy asked.

Quinn's sharp gaze met Darcy's. "Exactly."

"You mean, they're looking deep into my background," McKenna realized. "All the way to the beginning of my FBI career."

"That's my presumption."

McKenna felt Darcy's leg grow tense against hers.

"I assume if they connect you to me," Quinn continued, "they'll connect you to Darcy, as well."

"Are you suggesting we part company?" Darcy asked.

"Do you want to part company?"

"No," Darcy said firmly before McKenna could speak.

"Then no. But be aware that you may receive a visit from Agent Boyle."

Beside her, Darcy went utterly still. His thigh felt like a rock against hers. But otherwise, he showed no other sign of reaction.

Quinn looked at McKenna. "I assume you know Agent Boyle?"

"He's my supervisory special agent."

"Can he be trusted?"

Darcy's thigh pressed against hers for a moment, then relaxed.

"I don't really trust anyone at the FBI right now," she said. "But Boyle has always seemed to be a pretty straight arrow."

Quinn's scrutiny was almost uncomfortable. But his expression cleared, finally, and he rose. "I assume you'd like to be alone to discuss your options. You know how to reach me if you need my assistance."

"What makes you think you weren't followed here?" Darcy asked, rising to follow Quinn to the door.

Quinn gave him a pointed look as he opened the door and stepped out onto the porch.

"Call if you need anything." Quinn turned and left.

Darcy shut the door firmly behind Quinn and pressed his forehead against it. "We have to leave here again."

She sighed. "I know."

"I'm sorry."

"You're sorry?" She crossed to where he stood, impulsively sliding her arms around his waist from behind. She rested her cheek against his shoulder blade. "I honestly don't know what I'd have done if I hadn't come here, Darcy. You probably saved my life."

He turned, pulling her into the circle of his arms, his chin resting on her head for a moment. She felt utterly safe, she realized, despite the way danger seemed to be circling them, ever closer, seeking a chance to strike.

He let her go with a sigh. "We should pack. Quickly."

With a brief nod, she led the way to the bedroom to gather their things.

"So, THE ANONYMOUS unit commander was Darryl Boyle."

Darcy slanted a quick glance at McKenna. She sat straight and alert in the Land Rover's passenger seat, her gaze angled forward at the highway visible through the windshield. "You don't sound surprised."

"I got over the surprise back at the cabin when you telegraphed something was up with Boyle," she said drily. "You think there's any chance Quinn didn't notice your reaction?"

"No," he admitted. "Another set of eyes on Boyle won't hurt, will it?"

"Probably not," she admitted before falling silent.

They'd headed north when they left the cabin on Killshadow Road, bypassing the bigger tourist towns along the way in search of somewhere small and secluded to hide out for the next few days. Someone at the office had once told him about a motel in the Poe Creek area that took cash and didn't ask any questions.

Exactly the sort of place they needed.

They passed the highway sign announcing Poe Creek, Tennessee, was about fifteen miles ahead, before she spoke again. "Boyle has always struck me as a straight arrow. Law and order all the way. And—" She stopped short, pressing her lips to a thin line.

"And?"

"Well, I was about to say he's a fanatic about domestic terror investigations. Thinks we're ignoring the threat inside our own borders because we're too focused on foreign terror threats."

"He doesn't sound like a person likely to get in bed with the Blue Ridge Infantry."

"He doesn't," she agreed. "I find it hard to imagine he'd ever get involved with a group like the Blue Ridge Infantry. He's dedicated his life to bringing down groups just like them."

"But you're not certain about it, are you?"

She shook her head. "I've learned in this business, sometimes the perp is the last person you expect."

The Mountain Hideaway Motor Lodge in Poe Creek, Tennessee, was about what one would expect from a small, independent motor lodge on a main highway through the Appalachian Mountains. A rectangular two-story building constructed with now-fading red bricks and a flickering neon marquee in front of the office, the motel looked suitably shabby and anonymous for their purposes.

He parked the Land Rover in the side lot not easily visible from the street and turned to look at McKenna. "One room or two?"

Her gaze snapped up to meet his. "I'm really not sure how to answer that question."

He smiled at the wariness in her eyes. "For safety's sake. Do you feel safe in a room on your own or do you think we should band together so neither of us gets ambushed alone?"

Her lips quirked. "When you put it like that, one. I've been ambushed alone quite recently. It wasn't fun."

"Wait here. I'll pay for the room and get the key."

As promised, the clerk at the front desk of the motel office barely looked up from his paperback book to take Darcy's money and offer up a key. Darcy used his best American accent, in case the clerk was paying enough attention to remember later that his newest motel guest spoke with a British one, and signed in as Mr. and Mrs. Blake.

He found McKenna standing outside the Land Rover when he got back, stretching her legs. The afternoon breeze lifted her auburn curls and swirled them around her face. It was a good thing, he thought, that she'd stayed out here. Even the absentminded clerk couldn't have forgotten the sight of McKenna Rigsby and her glorious riot of hair.

"You should consider a ponytail," he told her as he unlocked the door to their first-floor room.

She gave him a side-eye glance as she preceded him into the room, reaching out to flick on the light switch as she passed. Dim light radiated weakly from the grimy overhead bulb. "Lovely."

"And a baseball cap."

She dropped the gym bag full of borrowed clothes they'd brought back with them from Hunter Bragg's cabin and looked at him, her head cocked to one side. "You don't like my hair?"

"I worship your hair," he answered with a smile. "But I'm not sure that it's good for the rest of the world to be quite so bedazzled by it if we're trying to keep a low profile."

Her smile felt like sunshine, warming the cool afternoon. "Duly noted."

The motel room was clean, at first glance. He'd stayed

in fleabag motels that hadn't put forth much effort at keeping up appearances, so he supposed it was to the Mountain Hideaway Motor Lodge's credit that he didn't automatically want to fumigate the entire room.

"I've stayed in worse," McKenna muttered as she set the gym bag on the bed nearest the bathroom and dropped to the edge of the mattress, her back to Darcy.

There was minimal furniture in the room—two full-size beds and a built-in dresser on the wall facing the beds. No chairs, no table, only two movable lamps by each bed, attached to the wall on a metal sconce. Darcy put down his duffel bag on the second bed and sat on the edge, as well, his gaze drawn to McKenna's slumped posture.

"Are you feeling well?" he asked finally when she didn't move.

She lifted her head and swiveled to look at him. "I have bullet holes in my side, I'm stuck in a cheap motel and I don't know who to trust. So, no. I'm not really feeling that well at the moment."

"Are you hungry? I could drive to one of those hamburger places we passed and get something for dinner."

"Maybe a salad."

He gave her a skeptical look, earning a hint of a smile from her.

"I know, veggies aren't my style, but I don't feel like eating anything heavy at the moment. Could go for a sweet tea, too."

He couldn't stop a grimace, but at least his show of distaste earned another smile from her. "I'll see if I can accommodate your culinary needs," he said in his most formal, clipped tone, determined to make that smile hang around a little longer.

"Knew I could count on you, Jeeves."

"Not a Brit," he murmured, getting up to leave.

Her grin followed him out the door.

He returned fifteen minutes later to the sight of Mc-Kenna sitting cross-legged on his bed, her fingers flying across the keyboard of his laptop. She looked up as he entered and set the bags of drive-through food on the dresser. "Hi."

"Hi." He was a little surprised she hadn't pulled her Glock on him. "I'm not sure you should drop your guard so easily."

"I saw you coming," she said with a cheeky smile. "Did you know you can tap into this fine establishment's security cameras by way of their free Wi-Fi?" She turned the computer around to show him the screen. Up in one corner was a small box showing a grainy black-and-white image of the breezeway in front of the external motel-room doors. "It's our own early-warning system."

"You know how to do that?"

The smile she flashed him sent tremors rolling through his chest to settle low in his belly. "Didn't the DSS teach you any computer tricks?"

"No, and why do I get the feeling you didn't learn that particular trick from the FBI, either?"

"Because I didn't," she admitted. "Remember that anarchist guy who had the hots for me?"

"Gecko?"

"Komodo," she corrected, slanting an amused look his way. "And it was Ax who had the hots for me. It was Komodo who thought he was dealing with a stupid hillbilly."

"Not a hillbilly?" he murmured.

"Not even close. I got Ax to show off all his tricks, pretending I didn't understand a thing about what he was doing. But, in fact, he was showing me how to do all kinds of things that are illegal as hell."

"Like tapping into a motel security camera?"

"Passive snooping. Barely illegal and nobody's likely

to find out in a place like this." She scooted over, making room for him on the bed.

He sat, trying not to touch her. But the soft mattress conspired against him, dipping with his weight and sending him arm to arm with her in the middle of the bed. "Any more tricks up your sleeve?"

When she slanted a look at him, her eyes were the deep green of the privet hedges that grew on the country estate where his mother preferred to spend most of the summers. "Lots."

His whole body seemed to flush hot, then cold, then hot again. This was worse than before, he thought. Back in Kaziristan, they'd kept a formal sort of distance from each other, physically, for the most part.

But now that he'd kissed her, doing so again—and doing so much more—seemed to be all he could think about.

He cleared his throat before he spoke. "Any more thoughts about Landry or Boyle? You've worked with both of them. You're in the best position between the two of us to know what we should do next."

"I honestly don't know. Right now, I'd say that Landry seems more likely, but that may be because I don't know him as well as Darryl Boyle. I've worked with Boyle almost a year now. Landry, I worked with for just a few weeks as part of a joint domestic terrorism investigation."

"But Ava Trent seems to concur with your assessment of Landry."

"What about Olivia Sharp? What did she say about Landry?"

"She seemed very cautious when speaking about Landry. There's something odd about her connection to him. I wish I'd had more time to delve deeper with her."

"How deep, exactly?"

The hint of jealousy he heard in McKenna's voice caught him by surprise. He let himself look at her again, bracing against the seismic effect she seemed to have on him recently.

Her wry smile told him she was mostly joking, but the curiosity in her eyes revealed he hadn't mistaken the slightly possessive tone of her voice.

"No more than skin deep."

"So she has nice skin?"

"Not nearly as nice as yours."

McKenna crinkled her nose. "I bet she's tall."

"Positively Amazonian."

"In ridiculously good shape," she ventured.

"Which indicates a rather unseemly obsession with one's appearance, wouldn't you say?"

"I would," she agreed, smiling so brightly he thought he could bask in her glow for the rest of his life. "I really would."

"She isn't you," he said softly. "No one else in the world is you."

"That's very cryptic."

He smiled. "Maybe you can get your friend Chainsaw to crack the code."

"Ax, Darcy. Ax." She set the laptop aside and shifted until she was on her knees beside him, gazing down at him with those fathomless green eyes. "I want this over with, Darcy. I want to be free again."

"I know. I want that for you."

"I've been thinking about how to do that. To get this over with faster."

He heard reluctance in her voice, as if she knew he wouldn't like what she was about to say. "What do you have in mind?" he asked.

"I think we should set a trap for both Landry and Boyle. I can contact each of them, tell them I want to come in from the cold and set a meeting time. Ask them to bring backup. Then we see which one of them brings backup and which one comes alone. The one who shows up alone isn't playing by the rules."

"What if they both bring backup? They'll take you in."

"At least we'll know neither of them is the mole in the FBI."

Darcy shook his head. "I don't want you putting yourself up as bait. Too much can go wrong."

"I'm tired of waiting around for us to stumble onto a break in this case. We need to make things happen or it's possible they never will."

As she made a move to get up off the bed, he caught her arm, stilling her movement. She gazed back at him, her eyes going dark. The air between them crackled with a sudden burst of heat, and even as he let go of her bare arm, he couldn't keep himself from letting his fingers trail down to the delicate skin of her slender wrist.

Her lips trembled apart. "Darcy—"

He tightened his grip on her wrist, tugging her to him until she stood between his legs, gazing down at him with a mixture of desire and consternation.

"Don't put yourself in danger, Rigsby." He wrapped his free arm around her waist, pulling her closer until her hips pressed against his belly.

"Are you going to try to seduce me out of it?" Her voice was warm velvet.

"Will it work?" he asked, pressing his mouth against the collarbone peeking out of her T-shirt collar.

"Worth a try," she said as she pushed him back onto the bed.

Chapter Fourteen

She felt reckless. Impulsive. Completely out of control. All the things she'd struggled with her whole life, that wild hare scampering inside her soul, yearning for wide-open spaces and spectacular adventures.

Her mother had warned her early about letting her feral side take control. Wild hares got eaten by predators. Run over by cars. They lived short, adrenaline-fueled lives. They never won the race.

But oh, the feel of flying along at breakneck speed, your heart galloping in your breast like a Thoroughbred going for the win—it was an intoxicating sensation. Darcy's arms around her were strong and solid, holding her so tightly as he kissed her that she thought she might break.

But she was stronger than his passion. Stronger than her own fierce response. She twined her fingers with his and kissed him deeply, with abandon, needing this freedom, this moment of surrender and demand.

But she couldn't let herself lose all control. She couldn't. Walking away from her friendship with Darcy had been one of the hardest things she'd ever done.

How much harder would it be to leave him behind if they gave in to this wicked fire burning between them?

Darcy dragged his mouth away from her jaw and looked up at her. "What's wrong?"

"This thing between us here—it can't go anywhere, can it?"

His chest rose and fell beneath her. "You are possibly the most confounding woman I've ever known."

He dropped his hands and she rolled away, lying on her back beside him. She stared up at the cheap light fixture overhead and wished her mother's voice had stayed silent a few minutes longer.

"I'm sorry," she murmured.

"I don't know if what's going on between us here can go anywhere. My life at the moment is nothing but a question mark. And you're wanted by the FBI." He reached across the narrow space between them and took her hand. "I just know that when I made it stateside after the siege, I felt utterly gutted because you weren't there. And I also know what we were about to do here was reckless and ill-advised."

"I'm sorry." She turned her head, taking in his handsome profile, the way his brow furrowed as he gazed up at the ceiling. "I know you think I'm a rule-breaking wild card compared to you, but I'm not the incautious type, really. I just—I missed you, Darcy. Every damn day."

He turned his head, his dark eyes meeting hers. "I missed you, too. You were an island of sanity in Kaziristan. Bloody levelheaded hillbilly. Nothing fazed you."

"Not a hillbilly."

"Yes, you are." He turned his body toward hers, reaching out to touch her face. "In the very best sense of the word. You're as solid as the mountains. As brave as the settlers who built a life on this rocky soil. As practical and unsentimental as any hardy mountaineer who's ever roamed these hills. I depended on every bit of that strength, McKenna, all those years ago in Kaziristan. I'm depending on it now."

His words brought tears to her eyes. She blinked them back. "So much for unsentimental."

He smiled and leaned forward to press his lips against her forehead. "I know you want this over with. But the thought of putting you out there like a piece of bear bait—"

"We can set it up so that it's safe." At his skeptical look, she added, "Or as safe as we can make it."

"If you insist on doing this, we need to bring Quinn in on the plan."

She shook her head, remembering Quinn's earlier visit to the cabin. "He's working his own agenda, Darcy. You know he is. It's what he does."

"Yes, but it so happens that his agenda coincides with ours."

"Until it doesn't." She sat up, letting go of his hand. "And there's the problem of the mole in your agency, too. I know it's not you. But there's someone leaking information from there, right?"

"Yes."

"Who else is under suspicion?"

"A man named Anson Daughtry. He, Quinn and I were the only three people who knew the real identity of an undercover operative working for The Gates. Someone got wind of that information, as well as what she was doing. She was lucky to survive. But she had to leave Tennessee."

"Is she in WitSec?" McKenna asked, her stomach aching. She'd dealt with a handful of people over the years who ended up in Witness Security, their names, their whole identities erased and replaced with new lives. Not all of them were innocent victims, of course, but there had been a few whose lives were shattered entirely through no fault of their own.

"No. And I don't know where she is now, because I could be the mole." His voice was tight with anger. "I need this to be over, but I don't know how to defend myself. All I have is my good name, my reputation, and that means nothing to Quinn."

"I think it means something," she disagreed, reaching for his hand and twining her fingers through his. "Quinn knows you're innocent. I could tell by the way he spoke to you. He respects you, and he doesn't respect traitors."

"Then why am I still on leave?"

"I think maybe because you're serving his purposes where you are. Such as your propensity for taking in wayward FBI agents in need."

He squeezed her fingers. "I'm a complete sucker for a wayward FBI agent in need."

"He trusts you." She looked down at their entwined hands. "The problem is, I don't trust him. Right now, I don't trust anyone but you."

He brought her hand to his lips and kissed her knuckles. "You know that question you asked me earlier? About whether I thought things between us could go anywhere?"

She nodded, not sure she wanted to hear the answer.

"I want it to. I do." He grasped her hand between his, holding it to his chest. "I have spent a very long time believing I would always be alone in life. And the thought never bothered me that much. I was an only child, raised by parents who loved me but never really enjoyed my company. They had their own lives to live, and they believed that coddling me too much would do me more harm than good."

Her heart contracted at the picture he was painting of his childhood. Her own had been nearly the opposite, she thought, a life spent under the watchful but loving eye of a mother who had made McKenna her whole world. "That must have been a lonely life."

He shook his head. "It didn't feel that lonely, really. The staff was kind. And my father's sister enjoyed my company a great deal when she visited. But she was so far away in America." He smiled. "It's one of the reasons I went to college in America instead of at Oxford as my father had hoped. Aunt Vivian was a graduate of the University of Virginia, and she talked me into going there."

"Sounds like you enjoyed it."

"Immensely." His smile faded. "But Aunt Viv died my senior year at UVA. Car accident. All very sudden."

"I'm sorry."

"So, I became accustomed to my own company." He slanted a look at her. "Until I went to Kaziristan to protect the ambassador and stumbled upon a wild-haired water nymph in the embassy pool."

She laughed. "Now you're just making things up. Water nymph?"

"Flitting through the water, all hair and fair skin and big green eyes. I was mesmerized."

"Darcy, you ordered me out of the pool."

"That's not the way I remember it."

"You told me I didn't have authorization to be there."

"I did no such thing."

"You were imperious and aggravating. You sounded like a snotty butler in a bad British movie."

He smiled more broadly. "Not a Brit."

"Yes, you are. The very best kind of Brit—smart, capable, steeped in traditions worth keeping and endowed with a dry wit that kept me sane in the middle of hell."

He cleared his throat. "Well, then. It seems we're both paragons."

She laughed. "We are. We really are."

His lips curled in a smile that didn't make it all the way to his eyes. "I know you want this to be over. I do, too. But if we just throw you out there to the wolves without a plan—"

"Who says we aren't going to have a plan?"

DARCY'S BURGER HAD gone cold by the time he pulled out their dinner from the take-out bags, but he ate it anyway, listening to McKenna work her way through their options between bites of her partially wilted salad.

"We're looking for somewhere that has public Wi-Fi and a decent video-surveillance system," she said after washing down a bite of salad with the sweet tea she'd ordered. "The more angles of approach we can cover the better. And we need to get our hands on another laptop computer so that we can cover both places we set up as the rendezvous points."

"I have a credit card, but if people are looking for me now—"

"You wanted to bring Quinn in on this plan, right?"

"But you said—"

"I don't trust him with the details. But if he can arrange for you to get your hands on a computer, I won't object."

Darcy set his burger on the bedside table and grabbed his duffel bag. He'd purchased a disposable phone shortly after going on administrative leave, aware that in his line of business, stealth might become a necessity before his ordeal was over.

Especially if someone in The Gates was setting both him and Anson Daughtry up for a fall.

He turned on the phone and checked the battery. Still had over 60 percent power. He'd need to charge it soon. But it would do what he needed for now.

He dialed a number only a handful of people knew. Even most of the agents at The Gates didn't have Quinn's personal number.

Quinn answered on the second ring. "Bradford Building Supply," he answered in a broad mountain drawl that made Darcy smile.

"It's your wayward son," Darcy replied.

"Is something wrong?" Quinn dropped the accent.

"I need a laptop computer. Performance oriented, with wireless and the means to monitor a video feed."

"Don't ask for a lot, do you?"

"Can you supply it?" Darcy asked, trying to keep his impatience from bleeding into his voice.

He could tell by the tone of Quinn's voice that he hadn't been entirely successful. "Would you like to tell me why I should?"

"Because you asked me to protect someone and I'm doing my best to accomplish that task. But I need a computer."

"What are you two up to?"

"Do you trust me to do this job or not?"

"Technically—"

"I'm on administrative leave. I know that. Believe me." Darcy glanced across the motel room at the other bed, where McKenna was conducting a web search for potential sites where they could set up rendezvous points with access to security-video feeds. "But you know as well as I do that you've given me a job to do. Do you trust me to do it or don't you?"

"I don't give jobs to people I don't trust."

Darcy felt the bunched muscles in his shoulders relax. "How quickly can you have the laptop ready for me?"

"Do you have twenty-four hours?"

"If need be."

"I'll try to make it faster. I don't have your phone number—"

"I know," Darcy said and hung up.

McKenna glanced up at him. "You're actually very sexy when you're being imperious and aggravating."

He smiled. "How's the search coming?"

"I have a list of six potential places. We'll have to check them out to make sure I can tap into the feeds. Some places may have heavier encryption than this motel. Some places won't. How long before Quinn can deliver a second laptop?"

"Twenty-four hours."

She nodded. "That will give us time. I think we should

try to get some sleep this afternoon and plan to go site hunting late in the evening. These sites I've picked out probably aren't going to shut down their Wi-Fi connections at night. If they do, they're probably heavily encrypted anyway and of little use to us."

He crossed to her side, looking over her shoulder at the list. There were two fast-food restaurants, a handful of motels, hotels or lodges, a campground and a coffee shop, all in or around the Poe Creek area. "The campground may be too remote. And I'm not sure what kind of security cameras they'd have available to tap into."

"We'll find out when we drive there tonight," she said with a shrug, handing over the laptop. "You figure out a plan of attack. I need a nap." She stretched out on her back, closing her eyes.

"We haven't treated your wounds since after your shower last night," he said. "I know you're feeling better, but we can't assume they're all healed up."

With a groan, she turned onto her side, lifting up the edge of her T-shirt. "Go for it, Marquis de Sade."

Forcing his gaze away from the curve of her slender waist, he grabbed the first-aid kit from his duffel bag and gathered his supplies. They were getting low on several, including gauze and other bandaging materials. "You didn't notice a drugstore near any of those places we need to go tonight, did you?"

"I think there's one not far from the burger place on Greenbrier Road." She looked at him over her shoulder. "How are we standing on money?"

"Good for now." He'd withdrawn five thousand dollars on his last trip to Purgatory, so with a little judicious budgeting, they wouldn't run out of cash anytime soon.

He eased the bandage away from her wounds, wincing a little as the tape pulled at her skin. She sucked in a quick breath but had no other reaction.

The wounds were healing. The redness of infection was all but gone, only the ragged edges of the wounds themselves still red with inflammation. And even they were starting to close up and scab over.

"How's it look?" she asked.

"Hideous," he said lightly. "But we've fought back the infection."

"Hideous, huh?" She shot him a wry grin. "You always know how to make me feel pretty."

Smiling back, he used a couple of his dwindling supply of antiseptic wipes to clean up the wounds. "Your wounds are dry and healing. You want to try going without a bandage awhile?"

She shot him an eager look. "I would love that. The tape pulls and itches like hell."

He tugged her T-shirt hem down to cover the wounds, his hands remarkably steady given how hard his heart was pounding. Even doing something as mundane and unsexy as cleaning her wounds was enough to get his pulse racing and his skin prickling.

He was so much more vulnerable to her now than he ever remembered being. Was it the proximity? The constant threat of discovery?

Or was it the fact that he'd finally allowed himself to touch her, to kiss her and hold her the way he'd wanted to that very first night at the embassy in Tablis? One taste and he was a helpless addict?

"Darcy?"

He made himself look at her. She was gazing back at him with a quizzical look on her face. "What?" he asked, his voice coming out low and hoarse.

"Is something wrong?" She touched his hand, the mere brush of her fingers sparking his nerves until they jangled.

He moved away from her, needing the distance. "Everything's fine."

He heard the mattress creak, then her footsteps as she walked up behind him. He looked up at the dresser mirror and saw her standing behind him, her gaze soft and worried.

"Darcy—"

He closed his eyes. "I should take the Land Rover down the road and fill up the gas tank if we're going to be driving around all evening."

Her hand closed over his shoulder, her grip gentle. "Are you running away, Darcy?"

He opened his eyes and met her knowing gaze. He couldn't quite stop a wry smile from quirking his lips. "Yes," he admitted.

She dropped her hand away and smiled back. "Go ahead. Just don't go far. I was serious about trying to get some sleep before we go back out tonight. I don't think we should try to get started before ten. We don't need a lot of people out and about, wondering what we're up to."

He left quickly, pausing beside the driver's door of the Land Rover for a moment, breathing in the chilled spring air. Clouds gathered in the west, promising rain.

It might turn out to be a miserable sort of night, he thought, wondering if they should postpone their hunting expedition for another night.

But what was the alternative—spending all night in bed across from McKenna, wanting her but not letting himself have her?

He pulled out his burner phone as he slid behind the wheel of the Land Rover and dialed Cain Dennison's number.

"HE'S UP TO SOMETHING," Olivia said from her perch on the edge of Quinn's desk. She didn't even bother with the niceties anymore, Quinn thought, watching her fiddle with the pencil holder in front of his desk blotter. "He was asking all sorts of questions about the Richmond incident."

"I suppose he suspects Cade Landry of blowing McKenna Rigsby's cover with the BRI," Quinn said, keeping an eye on Olivia's face.

Her expression didn't shift, but there was a flicker of something in her blue eyes. "Probably. He was also asking about another agent, Darryl Boyle. Last I heard, Boyle was an SSA in the Knoxville Field Office."

So, Quinn thought. They had two suspects. And Darcy wanted to get his hands on a second laptop computer, with wireless and reliable video-streaming capability.

Just what the hell was Darcy up to?

McKenna hadn't expected to fall asleep while Darcy was out, but apparently her stamina hadn't returned as much as she'd thought, for when she next opened her eyes, darkness had fallen outside the motel room, only the muddy light of the parking-lot lamps relieving the gloom.

She sat up, blinking away sleep, and reached for the bedside lamp to check her watch. Almost nine.

Then she realized Darcy's bed was empty.

"Darcy?" She got up and went into the bathroom.

Empty.

"Darcy?" She went back out to the main area and looked around thoroughly, though there was nowhere in the tiny room for anyone to hide, especially a man as big and solid as Darcy. She even ventured outside the motel room to check the back parking lot for any sign of the Land Rover.

It wasn't there.

She hurried to the room and closed herself inside, her heart hammering in her chest.

How long had he been gone? At least three hours, right? He had left around six, just as night was beginning to fall.

"Oh, Darcy," she whispered to the empty motel room as she sank onto the end of his bed. "Where the hell are you?"

Chapter Fifteen

Headlights appeared in the gloom, coming around a blind curve in the twisting mountain road where Darcy had parked the Land Rover. He was outside the vehicle, hidden, unwilling to make quite so easy a target in case Cain Dennison had double-crossed him.

The headlights dimmed and extinguished, and as Darcy's eyes adjusted to the gloom, he could make out the massive cab of Dennison's F-150 in the pale wash of moonlight. The driver's door opened, engaging the dome light inside the truck cab. Dennison hadn't come alone as asked, Darcy saw with a grimace. The girlfriend had tagged along.

The deputy-sheriff girlfriend.

Sara Lindsey's dark eyes scanned the scene, ever the cop, looking for signs of trouble in even the most mundane of situations. And Darcy supposed meeting a suspended agent up to his neck in skulduggery was hardly a mundane situation.

He stepped out of the shadows as they approached the Land Rover. "So much for coming alone."

Both Dennison and his girlfriend jerked their heads toward him in unison. "You try telling her no," Dennison drawled.

Darcy looked at Sara, who met his gaze steadily. "This is not a police matter."

Her lips curved, just a hint. "You're not a cop, so I'm not

sure you get to make that decision. But, for the record, I'm not here as a sheriff's deputy. And I know sometimes the letter of the law gets in the way of justice. I'm here to help."

"I've heard that before," Darcy murmured. He looked at Dennison. "Tell me why I should trust you after this."

"Because I'm all you've got," Dennison retorted. "I get that you don't do the friend thing. I've never been that great at it myself. But I know you're an honorable man. I know you're not the mole."

"You certainly should," Darcy said bluntly. "You've spent the last few weeks pretending to be my friend in order to investigate me."

"I wanted to clear you."

Darcy shook his head. "This was a bad idea. Forget I called." He started toward the Land Rover.

Sara caught his arm, her grip strong, stilling his movement. He looked down at her, irritated but also a little intrigued. Most of what he knew about Dennison's girlfriend had come from her part in a case Dennison had been investigating for The Gates, a twenty-year-old cold case involving Sara's deceased sister-in-law. Darcy's knowledge of that particular case was limited to what he'd heard around the office, but the subsequent news reports after the killer was captured had been enough to convince Darcy that Dennison's new girl was a hell of a lot tougher than she looked. And she looked plenty tough.

"Cain says you're in trouble. Let us help."

"I'm not in trouble," Darcy denied.

"But McKenna Rigsby is."

Darcy tried not to react to Dennison's soft reply. But when he looked up at his fellow agent, outlined in moon glow, understanding gleamed in Dennison's eyes.

"The FBI is trying to find you for questioning in her disappearance. They did a check of all the homes and businesses located on or around Killshadow Road, where the missing agent was last seen. Your name showed up, and a background check revealed your connection to her. You were both working at the US Embassy in Kaziristan eight years ago."

"So?"

"She's with you, isn't she?" Sara asked.

He looked at her, not answering.

"The FBI thinks she's gone rogue," Dennison said. "Ignored an order to come in from an undercover assignment. She fired shots at some hunters in the woods, unprovoked—"

Darcy arched an eyebrow at Dennison.

"I am aware that the hunters were probably militia members," Dennison added quietly. "And that she's the one being hunted."

Darcy looked away.

"Quinn knows something is up, but he's not talking. Not to me, anyway." Dennison shrugged. "I can't help if I don't know what's going on."

"I need someone to provide backup," Darcy said.

"Backup for what?"

"I'm trying to flush someone into the open."

"The real rogue in the FBI?" Sara asked.

Darcy didn't answer. He supposed Dennison and his girlfriend would find his silence answer enough.

"What do you need?" Dennison asked finally. "How much backup?"

"I need at least six people who can handle themselves in a fight."

"Do you plan to tell them more about what's going on than you've told us?" Sara's voice was tinged with doubt.

"I don't know," Darcy admitted. "I have to figure out all of the logistics."

"She doesn't know you're talking to us, does she?" Sara asked.

"No."

She closed her eyes and shook her head.

"I think I can rustle up six people who'll help you without asking a lot of questions." Dennison sighed. "That's the easy part."

"What's the hard part?" Darcy asked.

"You get to tell Agent Rigsby you arranged for backup without informing her." Sara turned and started walking toward the truck.

"Good luck." Dennison clapped Darcy on the back and followed Sara to the truck.

Darcy watched them leave before he climbed into the Land Rover and settled behind the steering wheel. Dennison and his girlfriend were right. He should have told McKenna what he was going to do.

Except he knew she wouldn't have agreed. Her current supply of trust was severely limited. There was no way she'd have agreed to bringing strangers into their plans. And now her trust in him was going to take one hell of a hit when he confessed what he'd done.

He still wouldn't change it. He'd done what he'd had to do.

But at what cost?

The hour hand of her watch clicked over. Ten o'clock. And still no Darcy. At first she'd been worried. Then angry.

Now she was worried again.

She'd tried to go back to sleep, reasoning that she could use the rest, and sleep would make time pass more quickly. But her nerves were too frayed for her to relax, and every time she closed her eyes in the dark motel room, a dozen different scenarios played out in her mind, dangers that she knew all too well were more than just her imagination at work.

There were people out there who wanted her dead. And if they'd connected Darcy to her the way Quinn said they had—

Car beams flashed through the motel-room curtains, painting arcs of light across the walls before the darkness swallowed the room again. She heard the growl of an engine die away in the night, followed a couple of minutes later by the sound of footsteps walking down the breezeway outside the room.

She sat up quickly, reaching for her Glock. It might be Darcy coming back. But considering how long he'd been gone, it could easily be someone else altogether.

There was a rattle of the doorknob. The swish of a card in the door lock. The door opened a few inches and Darcy's voice came through the narrow space. "Rigsby, it's me. I'm alone."

She didn't lower the pistol. But her heart leaped at the sound of his voice.

He entered slowly, sliding through the narrow doorway and shutting the door behind him. Only then did he flick the switch, turning on the overhead light.

McKenna checked him over quickly with her gaze, cataloging intact sets of limbs, the correct number of fingers, no signs of blood or injury. Relief set in, quickly eclipsed by anger, and she put the Glock down and crossed the room in four angry strides. "Where the hell have you been?"

"You know I went to get gas in the Land Rover."

"Hours ago."

"Large tank," he said, his tone infuriatingly dry.

"That's not funny." She thumped his chest with her hand.

He trapped her hand in place. "I didn't know the phone number for this room or I'd have called. I should have written it down."

"You could have called the front desk and had them patch you through." She wanted to stay furious at him, but his thumb was doing things to the back of her hand that made her want to curl up like a kitten and purr.

"We're trying to maintain a low profile," he reminded

her, his head dipping until she could feel his breath against her cheek. "I'm sorry."

"Where were you?" She tried to sound demanding, but her question came out on a plaintive sigh.

"Let's sit down." He led her to the bed and sat her down, crouching in front of her.

She didn't like the serious, troubled look in his dark eyes. "Has something happened?"

"Not yet," he answered, taking both of her hands in his. "But something's going to happen as soon as we figure out our plan of action."

"What's that?" She sounded breathless, even to her own ears.

"We're going to have backup."

A cold sensation swamped her with shocking suddenness. A soft buzzing sound rang in her ears. "We're going to have what?"

"I met with Cain Dennison. I told him we need backup for our plan."

She had to be dreaming still. It would explain the sudden, shivery feeling of unreality assaulting her with a vengeance, turning her limbs to liquid and making her heart thump with dread. "No. You wouldn't do that. You wouldn't go behind my back and set me up that way."

"I didn't set you up—"

She pulled her hands away from his, her fingers tingling. "Darcy, I told you no. I told you I wanted to handle this my way. Without bringing other people into it. My God, you told Dennison I was with you?"

Darcy pushed to his feet, sliding his hands through his crisp, dark hair. "He already knew. He's not stupid. The FBI has already connected you to me—you think Dennison didn't connect us, too? He saw me at Bragg's cabin. He knows I wasn't playing caretaker for Bragg—one phone call to your cousin's fiancé would have blown that story to pieces."

"That's not the same thing as you seeking him out behind my back and confirming it to him." She couldn't sit still, her legs suddenly jittering with nervous energy. "Darcy, your company has a mole working inside it. It's not you, but for all you know, it could be any other person who works there."

"At least you don't think it's me," he murmured, his gaze following her as she paced back and forth beside him. "Small favors."

She stopped in front of him. "Do you think that's funny?"

"I think we're outgunned, outnumbered and, if we don't improve our chances against the people gunning for you, we'll be outsmarted, as well."

"It's not your decision to make!"

"If I'm putting my life on the line for you, it damned well is!"

"Not without consulting me!"

"Would you have agreed to it?"

"No."

"Then what was the point of consulting you?"

She stared at him. He did not just say that. "I beg your pardon?"

"I don't think we can do this without backup. It would be foolhardy. Insane. Even if the plan works—even if you flush out the FBI's turncoat—what guarantee do we have that he's come alone? If he's in bed with the Blue Ridge Infantry, isn't it far more likely that he'd bring a crew with him to make sure his mess gets mopped up thoroughly?"

"We'll have advance notice."

"So we'll see our deaths coming."

"Damn it, Darcy!" She felt gutted, she realized. Upended, as if he'd jerked the floor from beneath her feet and sent her into free fall.

She sank to the edge of the bed, feeling sick.

"I know you're angry at me," he said quietly, reaching for her hand.

She jerked it away. "Don't try to handle me."

He dropped his hands to his sides.

"You had no right to do this without talking to me," she growled, trying hard not to let the tears beating at the backs of her eyes spill over. "Do you realize the danger you've put me in?"

"You were already in danger. I'm trying to get you free of it."

She made herself look at him, even though the sight of him right now made her want to punch him right in that beautiful mouth. "I came to you for help because I didn't have anywhere else to go. I should have remembered what you're like."

His eyes narrowed. "What I'm like?"

"Protocol says to procure backup, so that's what you do." Her voice was flint-hard. Good. She felt like stone inside. "You never even stopped to consider I might have my own ideas about how to protect myself, did you? Of course you didn't. You're the big bad security consultant. The man. Right?"

"This is not a man-woman issue."

"You're very right about that," she said coolly. "There's no man-woman anything about you and me. Not now."

His eyes closed for a moment. "McKenna."

"I think we function better when you remember that I'm Special Agent Rigsby with the FBI. Under suspicion or not, I do know what I'm doing. I don't need some civilian rent-a-cop telling me how to do my job."

His eyes snapped open, blazing back at her. "That was beneath you, Agent Rigsby."

"Do you think I haven't considered the idea that we could use backup? I have. The FBI may have painted me as a rogue agent, but I'm not one. I do know the protocols and the reasons they exist. I just can't depend on them under these circumstances. I don't know whom to trust." She leveled her gaze with his, making sure he was looking at her. "Maybe I would have been better off trusting no one at all."

"I don't deserve that." His voice was low and tight.

"Maybe you don't," she conceded. "But I can't take any chances."

He stepped backward, settling with his hips against the edge of the dresser, and fell silent.

She was tempted to walk out of the motel room and leave him behind for good. But she'd just made a big deal about not being stupid. It would hardly bolster her case to do something so monumentally dumb.

"I can call it off," he said a few minutes of silence later.

"It's too late."

"I trust Dennison," he added.

"But I don't even know him."

"You know me." Darcy pushed away from the dresser and crouched in front of her again, closing his hands over her elbows, holding her in place as he pinned her with his gaze. "You know me, Rigsby. You do. I'm the same man I've always been. And if there's anything in this world you should know about me, it's that I would never let anyone or anything hurt you if it's within my power. You have to know that about me."

She did know it. She might be angry now, might feel overturned and out of control, but she knew Darcy would put his life on the line for her, just as she would for him.

They'd always been bullet catchers, she and Darcy.

"I do know," she admitted.

"Then trust me. If I know anything at all about Cain Dennison, it's that he's a decent man. A good man. And he knows what's at stake. He will be as careful as you or I would be."

She couldn't be as certain as he was. She didn't know Cain Dennison. She didn't know how careful he would be or even if he knew what was at stake. And maybe if he was the only person she had to take a chance on trusting, she could do it for Darcy's sake.

"He's going to be approaching other people for you, isn't he?"

Darcy nodded.

"Do you know whom he'll be talking to?"

"No," Darcy admitted.

She rubbed her forehead, feeling the start of a headache between her eyes. "Every extra person who gets involved in this situation is another chance for betrayal."

Darcy released a long, slow breath. "Do you want me to contact Dennison and tell him to call it off?"

"Yes," she answered without thinking.

But as he reached into his pocket for his phone, she caught his arm, stilling his movement. He gave her a quizzical look.

"Just ask him to stand by. We need time before he contacts anyone else." She let go of him. "I need time."

With a nod, he pulled out his phone and made the call.

As he spoke in low tones with Cain Dennison, she pulled Darcy's notebook computer into her lap. She'd made a list of places to check out tonight, and it was past time for them to get started.

She'd worry about the question of backup later. Right now, they had to find out if there was any hope of their plan working at all.

BY TWO IN the morning, Darcy was beginning to wish he'd stuck around the motel room that afternoon and grabbed a nap. Between his lack of sleep and the monotonous hum of the Land Rover's tires on the road top, their circuitous tour of Ridge County's hinterlands was lulling him dangerously close to falling asleep at the wheel.

In the passenger seat, McKenna seemed to have found her second wind, though he could only infer her state of mind because she'd spoken very little since they climbed into the Land Rover almost three hours earlier.

"So we're agreed on the two venues?" he asked finally. His voice seemed loud in the silence inside the SUV.

"The Econo-Tel and the Blackberry Café," she answered briskly, as if she didn't want her words to linger long enough to permanently break the chilly silence between them.

The Econo-Tel was a small, low-budget motor lodge on Pike Road just south of Poe Creek. Set back from the road in an otherwise rural area, it was just isolated enough to pose a temptation to someone who wanted to catch McKenna out in the middle of nowhere, far enough from civilization to make running for help difficult at best.

The Blackberry Café in the tiny mountain town of Brightwater was a little less secluded, flanked on the left by a hardware store and on the right by a television-repair shop. But if they set up the rendezvous after five in the evening, both of those shops would be closed for the night, only the diner still open.

The bigger question was, would either Boyle or Landry show up if McKenna reached out to them? And what if both of them followed protocol and brought an FBI team with them to the meeting?

As he pulled to a stop at a crossroads, McKenna turned suddenly toward him, her eyes glittering darkly in the faint glow of his dashboard lights. "We need backup," she said flatly. "You were right."

He stared at her, not sure he'd understood her. "I'm sorry. Did you just say I was right?"

The corners of her lips twitched, but she didn't smile. "I'm still really angry at you for contacting your friend without consulting me. You had no right, and it shows a distinct arrogance I don't like at all. But if we're going to lure in a mole in the FBI, we need to be better prepared than two people can be all alone. So do it. Call Dennison and tell him it's a go."

Darcy pulled out his phone, pausing with his hand over the number pad. "And what if you're right and I'm wrong?"

She leaned her head against the headrest. "Then God help us all."

Chapter Sixteen

Smoky Joe's Tavern in Bitterwood, Tennessee, was doing a brisk business for a Thursday night. McKenna followed Darcy into the bar to a table in the back near the pool table, still feeling a little fuzzy-headed from a day spent trying to catch up with sleep before they put their plan into action that night.

Darcy held out her chair for her before taking a seat across from her, his gaze cutting toward a couple circling the felt-topped pool table. The man—tall, broad-shouldered, thirty-something—bent to speak in the woman's ear. The woman nodded and crossed to the bar to place an order, while the man set his cue stick against the wall and settled at a table next to Darcy and McKenna.

"You're late," the man murmured, his voice barely audible over the din of the bar.

"Didn't want to appear overeager," Darcy replied in the same conversational tone. "Rigsby, this is Sutton Calhoun. The woman who was trouncing him at billiards is his wife, Ivy. She's a detective on the Bitterwood police force."

McKenna let her gaze drift toward the woman standing at the bar, talking to a burly man with thinning brown hair and a bushy beard. Ivy Calhoun was small and slim, with dark hair pulled back in a ponytail under a faded blue baseball cap. She glanced back at the table where her husband sat, letting her gaze slide unhurriedly over Darcy and McKenna before she turned back to accept a couple of longneck beers from the bartender.

With the same nonchalance that had characterized her glance their way, she sat across from her husband, handing him one of the beer bottles.

Sutton took a sip of the beer before speaking. "Ivy, you know Darcy."

Ivy nodded, not looking at them. "I do. I suppose you're going to give me some code name for his lady friend, even though we all know exactly who she is, right?" She spoke with a drawl that was pure Appalachia, tinted by a mild exasperation that told McKenna just what she thought of the cloak-and-dagger aspect of the night's agenda.

"Call me Mac," McKenna murmured.

"Whatever." Ivy took a sip of beer. "Y'all ready?"

"We're going somewhere?" Darcy asked.

"Been a little change of plans," Sutton murmured, setting the bottle of beer on the table in front of him. He ran his finger over the lip of the bottle. "Dennison thinks we're too exposed here."

"I don't like sudden changes of plan," McKenna muttered to Darcy. "How do we know this isn't a setup?"

"Because my husband and I don't do setups," Ivy answered.

"Says the woman I've never met before in my life."

Ivy made a low snorting sound and took another sip of beer.

"I know them," Darcy said quietly. "And I know Dennison. If he thinks this place is too exposed, he has a reason."

God, she hated this. Hated being at the mercy of anyone, needing their help so much that she was actually sitting here considering the idea of following two complete strangers God knew where to meet more strangers she was supposed to trust, sight unseen, to help her stay out of the hands of people who wanted her dead.

Darcy reached across the table and covered her hand with his, his gaze intent. "Do you trust me?"

She closed her eyes and took a leap of faith. "Yes."

"You leave first," Sutton said. "There's a small clearing just across the bridge on the right. People use it to turn around all the time. Pull into that turnabout and wait for us. We'll head out of here in five minutes. We're in a blue Silverado. When we pass, follow."

As a buxom brunette waitress started to approach, Darcy waylaid her with a smile. "My wife has a headache. I think we're just going to pack it in for now." He pulled out his wallet and handed her a five-dollar bill. "For your trouble." He reached for McKenna's hand, his gaze locking with hers once more.

She took his hand and let him lead her back out to the parking lot. "I don't like this."

"Can't say I'm happy about it myself," he admitted as he unlocked the Land Rover's passenger door to let her in. "But if Dennison believes we could be compromised by staying here, I'm going to hear him out."

Darcy pulled off the road in the shallow turnoff Sutton Calhoun had mentioned, putting the car in Park and leaving the engine to idle. He turned to look at her, not speaking.

Waiting, she realized, for her to speak.

"I'm afraid." It wasn't what she'd planned to say, but it rang with the sound of truth.

"As am I," he admitted. "But you're right that we have to do something to draw your enemies into the open."

A moment later, a Chevrolet Silverado drove slowly past. Darcy put the Land Rover in gear and followed.

Old Purgatory Road wound south through Bitterwood, then changed names to Smoky Crest Road as it curved east into the mountains just outside the national park. "Where are we now?" McKenna asked as the Land Rover slowed into a sharp switchback.

"Smoky Ridge," Darcy answered, his brow furrowed.

"Is that good or bad?"

"It's neither at the moment," he said calmly. But the furrows in his brow deepened the higher they climbed up the mountain road.

Ahead, the Silverado turned off the main road onto a side road. It was paved, which was the best thing that could be said for the narrow, rutted avenue that cut a curvy path through deepening woods.

It ended near the top of the rise at a small, rustic-looking cabin set in the middle of a tiny clearing. A concrete patio about eight feet square led to two concrete steps up to a screen door. Lights were on inside the cabin, but the curtains were closed and there was no obvious sign of movement inside.

Anxiety crept up her back. "Where is this?"

"It's a cabin," Darcy said unhelpfully.

"Whose?"

"I'm not certain."

Sutton and his dark-haired wife exited the Silverado, not waiting for Darcy and McKenna to follow them inside.

Darcy looked at McKenna. "Your call."

"We're here already," she said after a brief hesitation. "Let's see what's going on."

On the walk to the cabin door, McKenna saw what the glare of the headlights had hidden—two more trucks parked off the road, hidden by the shadows of the sheltering trees. "Do you recognize the vehicles?" she asked Darcy as his gaze slanted toward the trucks.

"One is Dennison's. He probably has Sara with him."

"And the other?"

"I think it's Mark Fitzpatrick's truck. He just traded his

old one in for a newer model shortly before I went on suspension, but I'm pretty sure that's the new truck."

As they reached the patio, the door opened and a tall,
lean man stepped into the opening. "I'm Cain Dennison. I
hear we're supposed to call you Mac. Come on in. Everybody's waiting to hear what you want us to do."

With a glance at Darcy, McKenna climbed the shallow
steps and entered the cabin.

Inside, Cain Dennison went to stand next to a dark-haired
woman she assumed must be his cop girlfriend. Nearby, the
Calhouns were pouring themselves cups of coffee at the
counter. Two other men filled out the group gathered around
the small kitchen table—a tall, attractive man with short
brown hair and intelligent hazel-green eyes and a second
man whose dark, spiky hair and vulpine features reminded
her of a feral animal, all nerves and sinew. His mobile mouth
curved in a smile as she met his gaze, but she wasn't sure
she entirely trusted its sincerity.

"Mac," Ivy Calhoun said, with a slight arch of her dark
eyebrows indicating she was annoyed at having to pretend
she didn't know McKenna's real name, "you met Cain at
the door. That's his fiancée, Sara."

Darcy's gaze snapped up. "Fiancée?"

Cain's smile lit up his face. "She said yes."

"Congratulations."

"You're a cop," McKenna murmured to Sara as the
woman reached out to shake hands.

Sara's smile was tight. "And you're a rogue FBI agent.
Nice to meet you."

"I'm Seth Hammond, and for the sake of full disclosure,
I used to be a con man, but I'm no longer involved in that
deceptive art." The sharp-featured man grinned at her like
a used-car salesman.

Great. Just great.

"And I'm Mark Fitzpatrick," the other man said with a

mild smile that made him look like a choirboy, especially standing next to the former flimflam man with the friendly grin. "I was never a con man, for the record."

His dry delivery of the last statement almost made her smile. "I understand you're waiting for me to outline what we have in mind. But before I do so, I need to know something. If you don't like my plan, what do you intend to do about it?"

The Gates agents and the two women exchanged looks for a second. It was Cain Dennison who finally spoke, apparently for them all. "We'll tell you it's idiotic and suggest something that would actually work."

His blunt candor went a long way toward calming McKenna's rattled nerves. "Fair enough." She waved at the table, pulling up one of the kitchen chairs. "So, let's get started."

THE PLAN SEEMED to pass muster with the other agents, Darcy saw with some relief. He knew it wasn't a foolproof plan, but what plans ever were? McKenna's explanation of how she planned to tap into local video feeds to give them the equivalent of an early-warning system raised the eyebrows of both Sara Lindsey and Ivy Calhoun, the two cops in the room. But neither woman commented.

"We're trying to figure out which man brings backup and which one tries to meet me alone."

"Don't you think they'll suspect a setup?" Sara Lindsey asked.

"They may," McKenna conceded. "But if either of them is connected to the Blue Ridge Infantry, he'll try to lure me out of hiding rather than bring in the FBI. Because they don't know how much I know about what the BRI is up to. That's why I was targeted for death in the first place."

Her answer was met with tense silence at first. Then Sutton Calhoun stood to face them. "Make the calls."

McKenna turned to look at Darcy. "We've selected two rendezvous points," she told the others. "One is the Econo-Tel Motor Lodge just south of Poe Creek. Do you know it?"

Sara Lindsey nodded. "I worked a case near there recently."

"Then you can cover us there. Darcy's going to be with you," McKenna said.

Darcy stared at her. "You want us to split up?"

She caught his arm and took him aside, ignoring the curious looks from the others as they left the kitchen and entered the nearby hallway. "Look, I'm operating on a very thin layer of trust, as it is. We have two bases to cover, and I need someone I trust covering one of them while I take the other. I don't trust any of them. But I trust you."

He didn't know whether to kiss her or shake her. "But you trust them to cover your back?"

"I can cover my own back if need be. What I can't do is cover both feeds. I need you to make sure nobody screws this up. We have to know which man is the turncoat in the FBI. I need your eyes on the feed at the Econo-Tel."

He wanted to argue, but he knew she was right. For the plan to work, they had to have an advance look at both men and who, if anyone, they brought with them for backup.

"Okay. But I don't want you taking any chances. Understood?"

She nodded, and they returned to the kitchen.

"Everything settled?" Mark Fitzpatrick asked.

"Yes," McKenna answered. "As I was saying, Darcy will join Deputy Lindsey and Dennison at the Econo-Tel. One more of you will need to go with them."

"I'll go," Mark Fitzpatrick offered.

Darcy frowned.

"Or not," Fitz muttered.

"I think our friend Darcy is uncertain if I can truly be trusted," Hammond drawled, shooting Darcy an unoffended smile. At least, Darcy thought he looked unoffended. Seth Hammond had been a confidence man for years; even now, it was hard to know exactly what the man was thinking. "I'll go with him. The Boy Scout here can go with the lady."

Fitz rolled his eyes at Seth but gave a nod. "Calhoun, Ivy and I'll go with Mac."

"Our second rendezvous point is the Blackberry Café in Brightwater."

"I know where that is," Sutton Calhoun said with a nod.

"I don't want to confront either man," Darcy said, pressing his palm against the small of McKenna's back. "Understood? This is purely a reconnaissance mission. We're trying to figure out who has put Mac in danger. Then we can see about going to the authorities with what we know."

He felt McKenna's muscles tighten beneath his fingertips, but she didn't argue.

Dennison reached into his pocket and pulled out a cell phone. "I thought you might need another burner phone." He held it out to McKenna.

After a brief hesitation, she took it from him. "Thank you."

"There's a pay phone outside the Econo-Tel," Darcy said. "Mac's going to make the phone call to Cade Landry from there, then ride with Fitz to the café in Brightwater. Seth, you can ride shotgun with me."

As they split up to head for their cars, Darcy caught Sutton's arm on the way out, keeping an eye on McKenna as she followed Mark Fitzpatrick to his truck. "Whose cabin is this?"

"Belongs to Seth's mother. She's over in Nashville for the week visiting her cousin. Seth figured nobody from the FBI would think to connect this place to you."

Darcy nodded, hoping he was right.

Seth was waiting by the passenger door of the Land

Rover, smiling at Darcy across the top of the cab. "You don't trust me a bit, do you?"

"I barely trust anyone at the moment," Darcy answered.

"But especially not me."

Darcy didn't speak.

Seth shrugged. "I get it. I get it all the time, actually. But I reckon you'll just have to see for yourself whether or not I'm worthy of your trust."

"It would behoove you to be so."

Seth smiled as Darcy used the remote to unlock the doors. "Nice accent. You should hear my Irish one." He climbed into the passenger seat.

Darcy looked across the yard toward Fitz's truck. McKenna was standing next to the door, gazing at him across the dark yard. There was just enough moonlight to make out the glitter of her eyes.

Darcy smiled. He saw the slight curve of her lips, the faint glint of her teeth. Then she got into the truck, disappearing from his view.

For a moment, his stomach gave a sickening downward lurch.

He took a deep breath, gathering his wits. He hadn't seen her for eight years. They'd both survived the separation.

They would both survive a couple of hours apart, right?

At least, he hoped so.

CADE LANDRY ANSWERED on the second ring, his voice raspy and thick. "Yeah?"

Great, McKenna thought. Had he been drinking? "Landry, it's Rigsby."

There was a long pause on the other end of the line. For a second, she thought the call had been cut off and started digging in her pocket for quarters to feed the pay phone. Then Landry spoke again. "Where are you?"

"I need to meet you. I don't feel safe."

"Are you hurt?"

"Not badly," she answered, glancing over her shoulder at the Land Rover parked behind her. She couldn't see Darcy's face behind the glare from the motel sign bouncing off the windshield. But she felt his gaze on her. It warmed her, made her feel strong and weak at the same time.

"Tell me where to find you." Landry's voice was stronger now. Didn't sound nearly as slurred. "Are you alone?"

"I am," she lied. "Do you know where the Econo-Tel Motor Lodge is on Route 4 south of Poe Creek?"

"No, but I'll find it. Are you out of sight?"

"Not right now, but I will be as soon as I get off the phone."

"Good. Stay out of sight. You're in serious danger."

"I know. That's why I'm calling you. I need help coming in."

"I'll give it to you. You just get hidden and stay put. I'm in a black Malibu—remember what my car looks like?"

"I remember."

"I'll pull in the parking lot at the motel. Is there someplace you can hide where you can still see the parking lot?"

"Yes," she answered.

"Good. I'm on my way. Get out of sight and I'll see you soon."

She hung up the pay phone and walked over to the Land Rover. Darcy lowered the window and looked up at her. "Landry's coming?"

"Yes." She looked past him at Seth Hammond, whose used-car-salesman grin had disappeared now that the assignment was under way. "How's the video feed holding up?"

He met her gaze steadily. "Clear as a bell. This feed covers the parking lot perfectly. We should be able to spot the target as soon as he shows up."

"What's he driving?" Darcy asked.

"Black Malibu. Later model. It's not a bucar," she added, referring to an FBI fleet vehicle. "It's his personal car."

"Wouldn't he drive an FBI fleet car if he was playing this by the book?" Darcy asked.

"I don't know," she admitted. "Landry's an odd bird. And he loves that car. Just—keep an eye out for any sort of tricks."

"That's what we're here for," Seth said with a slight smile. He looked like an ordinary guy, she thought, when he wasn't trying so hard to play the role of the smarmy con man.

"I've got to hurry to the diner to make the second call," she said, patting the window frame as she started to turn to go.

Darcy caught her hand, holding her in place. "Be careful." His thumb slid over the back of her hand in a caress. "Don't take chances."

She turned her hand over until her palm pressed against his. "Everything in life's a chance. But I'll be careful."

"You do that." He let go of her hand, and she turned away, walking slowly back to join Mark Fitzpatrick in his truck.

Fitz, as he'd told her to call him, started the truck as she buckled herself in. "You ready for this?"

She nodded. "I appreciate this. That you're putting yourself on the line for me when you don't even know me."

"I know Darcy. He and the guys at The Gates helped me out not long ago when someone I know was in trouble. Darcy went to bat for her with Quinn. She needed a job and Darcy made sure Quinn gave her a chance. I don't think even Darcy knows how much he helped her."

"Your girl?" she asked, reading between the lines.

Fitz's lips curved, the boyish smile carving dimples in his cheeks. "Yeah. We're getting married soon." His smile faded. "So, let's get this done right tonight, okay? No surprises. No risks. I kind of promised her I'd come home alive. If I don't, she'll kill me."

"I'm all for coming home alive," she assured him, remembering Darcy's long, deep gaze at her as she walked away from the Land Rover.

They reached the Blackberry Café within ten minutes, parking near the edge of the lot where the glow from the street lamp on the corner didn't quite reach. The pay phone bolted to the wall of the hardware store was barely visible under the shadow of the store awning. It had been in working order when she and Darcy had checked it the night before, but a lot could have changed in a day.

She fed coins into the slot and sent up a silent prayer as she called SSA Darryl Boyle's cell-phone number.

It rang three times without Boyle answering. As she was about to hang up and start over, he picked up. "Boyle."

"Agent Boyle, it's Agent Rigsby. I'm in trouble and I need your help."

Chapter Seventeen

"They don't really think you're clueless about what they're up to, do they?" Olivia lowered the binoculars and turned to look at Quinn.

He shrugged. "I don't think they're actively trying to deceive me, no."

"The woman doesn't want you in on it."

"She doesn't trust me. Or anyone, I assume. She believes her own people were involved in trying to kill her." Quinn took the binoculars Olivia had set down and lifted them to his eyes. Through the lenses, he made out Darcy's Land Rover sitting at one end of the motel's parking lot. "What are they doing?"

"Hammond seems to be on a laptop computer," Olivia answered, drumming her fingers on the dashboard as if impatient for him to hand over the binoculars again.

Quinn ignored her jitters, trying to see if he could discern what was on the computer screen by focusing on the reflection in the Land Rover's passenger-side window. "They seem to be monitoring some kind of video feed."

"Did they set up hidden cameras somewhere?"

"I'm not sure. But I know how to find out." He handed her the binoculars and picked up his cell phone, dialing a number.

Seth Hammond answered on the second ring. "Yeah, boss?"

"Why are you parked in the Econo-Tel Motor Lodge parking lot, monitoring a video feed?"

Hammond muttered a profanity.

A moment later, Nick Darcy's voice was in Quinn's ear. "This isn't your business. Stay out of it."

"She didn't want you to come to me for help?"

"No."

"I'll keep my distance. But are you sure you're prepared for any contingency?"

Darcy's voice tightened, betraying his doubts. "There's no such thing as being prepared for any contingency."

"What are you hoping will happen?"

"We need to know who she can or can't trust at the FBI."

"And how is sitting in a vehicle looking at a video feed going to clarify that question for you?"

"You don't know what our plan involves, Quinn. And I'm not going to tell you." Darcy hung up the phone.

"You have such a way with your employees," Olivia murmured as he pocketed his phone.

"They've set up some sort of trap," Quinn said, reaching for the binoculars. "But Agent Rigsby is nowhere in sight."

"I spotted Dennison and his deputy girlfriend parked on the other side of the motel lot," Olivia commented. "Do we know who else is involved in this mysterious sting?"

"No. Ever since word got around of the GPS trackers in the agents' cars, they've been disabling them."

"Good for them," Olivia murmured, slanting a dark look his way. "We were wrong to try to track them like pets with microchips."

"Knowing where my agents are at the moment might come in very handy." Quinn considered what he knew about the agents he had in sight. Seth Hammond was with

Darcy. And Dennison had brought his girlfriend along for the operation, which meant they weren't necessarily sticking to agents from The Gates alone.

"Sutton Calhoun and his wife," he said aloud a moment later. "Calhoun and Hammond are close now. Rigsby must be with them."

"Just the three of them?"

"Probably one more agent to match the number here. There must be a second stakeout point."

"But where?"

Quinn picked up his phone and dialed Calhoun's cell-phone number. It rang three times before going to voice mail.

"Darcy warned them. They're screening calls from me."

"So what now?" Olivia asked.

Quinn picked up the binoculars and raised them to his eyes again. "They're staking out this parking lot for a reason. Right?"

"Right. You said you think they've set up some sort of trap. But who are they trying to trap?"

Quinn scanned the parking lot. "Rigsby claims there's someone inside the FBI gunning for her. Maybe they settled on a suspect."

"Or two," Olivia pointed out. "Since there's a second stakeout point?"

"One of them is Landry," Quinn said, slanting a look at Olivia.

"I know."

"Any thoughts on the other one?"

Her eyes narrowed as she peered through the windshield. "Darcy asked me some questions about what happened in Richmond. Specifically, he wanted to know who the incident commander for my SWAT unit was."

"Who was it?"

"Darryl Boyle."

"Rigsby's direct supervisor at the Knoxville office?"

"That's the one."

STAKEOUTS WERE GENERALLY boring affairs. Until they weren't.

Except for the call from Quinn twenty minutes earlier, Darcy's stakeout of the Econo-Tel Motor Lodge had been uneventful. If Landry was on his way to meet McKenna, he was taking his own sweet time.

Meanwhile, Darcy felt as if he was about to crawl right out of his skin. His nerves were jittering, his pulse pounding a heightened cadence in his ears, and every twitch of a leaf rustled by the night breeze outside set him on high alert.

He shouldn't have let McKenna convince him to split up. He should be with her instead of staying here watching a silent parking lot.

"Is that a phone?" Seth Hammond's drawl broke the silence in the Land Rover.

Darcy jerked at the noise. "What?"

"I'm hearing a phone ringing."

Darcy listened. Seth was right. A phone was ringing.

"The pay phone," Seth said.

It rang one more time, then went silent.

Darcy looked at Seth. "Coincidence?"

The other man shook his head. "Not damn likely."

The phone started to ring again.

As Darcy started to open the driver's door, Seth put a hand on his arm.

"What if someone's trying to draw you out in the open?"

"What if it's Landry trying to contact her again?" Darcy asked.

"You answering the phone isn't exactly going to make him feel real good about showing up for this shindig."

"It's a chance I have to take." Darcy opened the door

and hurried toward the ringing phone, catching it on the fifth trill. "Hello?"

There was silence on the other end of the line, but Darcy could feel someone listening.

"Hello?" he repeated.

"You're Nick Darcy, right?" The voice on the other end of the line was a deep drawl, broader and gentler than the hard-edged mountain twangs Darcy had grown used to hearing in this part of Tennessee. "This was a setup, wasn't it?"

Darcy didn't answer.

"Doesn't matter," Landry continued, sounding frustrated. "I need to talk to Rigsby. Now."

Cold crept up Darcy's spine and settled in his chest. "I can pass a message along to her."

Landry muttered a low curse. "She's not there, is she?"

"If you'll tell me your message—"

"He knows, Darcy. Darryl Boyle knows it's a setup. And wherever Rigsby's luring him, he's not going there alone."

The chill spread to Darcy's limbs. He clutched the phone more tightly. "You mean he's bringing FBI backup. Right?"

"I don't think so," Landry warned, his voice tight with tension. "Something's not right with him."

"Something's not right with you, either. I've talked to Ava Trent. I've even talked to your old SWAT team partner, Olivia Sharp."

"You talked to Olivia?" There was a shift in the tone of Landry's voice that caught Darcy by surprise.

"They both seem to think you're a dead-ender. On your way back down the ladder before you flame out for good."

Landry was silent for so long, Darcy feared he'd hung up. When he finally spoke again, his voice was flat and weary. "I guess I deserve that. But I'm tellin' you right now, you gotta get Rigsby out of there. I called Boyle. Told him about my call from Rigsby. He said he got one, too, and I should sit tight. He'd take care of it. But something about the way he was talking— I don't know. It didn't sound right. So I called the Knoxville Field Office, offered the Johnson City RA's assistance in the extraction. And nobody in Knoxville knew what the hell I was talking about."

"How do I know you're not setting us both up?" Darcy asked, trying to keep his head as his heart clamored at him to go get McKenna and take her somewhere so far away nobody could find her again.

"You don't," Landry said. Then the line went dead.

Darcy hung up the phone and ran back to the car. "Get Calhoun on the phone," he ordered, already dialing the number of the burner phone he'd given McKenna. The cell phone rang once and went straight to voice mail. "Damn it!"

"Calhoun's not answering," Seth said, looking at Darcy with a worried expression. "What the hell is happening?"

"I'm not sure," Darcy admitted, dialing another number. "But we need to pull up stakes and get to Brightwater as fast as we can."

On the second ring, Alexander Quinn answered. "Ready to talk to me now?"

"Yes," Darcy snapped. "So listen very carefully, because we may already be out of time."

McKENNA LOOKED AT her watch. Only four minutes had passed since the last time she'd checked. It felt more like an hour. "Maybe we should check in with Calhoun and his wife," she suggested, glancing at Fitz in the driver's seat. "See if they've seen anything suspicious."

"I'm sure they'd have called us if they had," Fitz said reasonably.

"I'm climbing out of my skin here. Can't we just call someone? Anyone? Maybe we could call Darcy and see if his crew has seen anything from Landry."

Fitz looked her way, amusement crinkling the corners of his eyes. "You try Darcy. I'll call Calhoun."

She tugged the burner phone from her jacket pocket and dialed the number he'd stored for her.

Nothing happened. She looked at the display and saw there were no bars. The phone wasn't receiving any signal from the cell tower.

"Hmm," Fitz murmured.

"What?"

"No reception."

Alarms blared in her head. "We were able to check in with Calhoun just fifteen minutes ago. The signal was great."

"I know." Fitz frowned.

McKenna looked down at her laptop, checking the video feed. There was nothing new there. She could see Calhoun's truck parked at the other end of the small shopping strip in one of the diner's security cameras. Fitz's truck was still visible in the feed from the second camera. Nothing had changed.

She narrowed her eyes and reached for the power-window switch on the passenger door.

"What are you doing?"

She reached out the passenger window and waved toward the camera, keeping her eye on the feed.

Nothing in the image on her computer screen changed. No hand, no wave.

"Oh, hell." She raised the window again and pulled her Glock from the holster behind her back.

"What?"

"Someone's hacked our feed. They're out there." She peered out the window at the quiet street in front of the diner, looking for any sign of movement. "And I don't think it's the FBI."

Fitz muttered a curse and started the truck's engine. As he

put the vehicle in Reverse, a hard thud shook the chassis, and the truck began to shimmy as Fitz tried to steer it backward.

"Son of a bitch," he growled. "Someone shot out a tire."

"Drive anyway!" McKenna twisted in her seat, trying to see behind them. The road appeared deserted, but out of the corner of her eye, she saw a rush of movement toward her.

The truck came to a hard stop, flinging her against the seat belt and sending the baseball cap covering her curls flying onto the dashboard. Her hair tumbled into her face, blinding her for crucial seconds.

When she shoved her hair out of her eyes again, she was staring down the barrel of a shotgun. Her heart sank as she recognized the shaggy-haired man with cold blue eyes gazing back at her from behind the weapon.

Calvin Hopkins. Current head of the eastern Tennessee branch of the Blue Ridge Infantry. As cold and nasty a son of a bitch as she'd come across in a long, long time.

The man she'd hoped to bring down by going undercover.

"Hey there, Maggie." He bared his teeth at her in a parody of a smile. "Or should I call you McKenna?"

THE DINER WAS DESERTED. No sign of Fitz, Calhoun or the women. No sign, in fact, that anyone had been here recently at all. Until the headlights of Darcy's Land Rover swept over a shard of tire tread near the far end of the shopping-strip parking lot.

He put the Land Rover in Park and got out, bending to examine the tread. It had been pitted by buckshot, he realized. Several bits of shot remained in the rubber tread.

Fear rose like bile in his throat. He swallowed with difficulty, trying to maintain control over his emotions. Panic wouldn't help anyone.

Panic got people killed.

"Is that buckshot?" Seth Hammond's tone was uncharacteristically serious. "Son of a—"

Darcy pulled out his cell phone and dialed Sutton Calhoun's number. He heard a trilling sound coming from somewhere nearby.

Seth crossed to the front of the diner and crouched by one of the bushes that flanked the walkway into the diner. He rose again, now holding the ringing phone, his expression grim. "Sutton's."

"Damn it." Darcy raked his hand through his hair, furious and terrified at the same time. He should have made her reconsider her crazy plan. He should have insisted on being with her.

"Don't waste time second-guessing yourself, man." Seth put his hand briefly on Darcy's shoulder. "We've got to figure out where they've taken them and get them back."

If they're even still alive, Darcy thought, his heart pounding with dread.

Chapter Eighteen

McKenna had no idea where the others were. Whether they were even alive. Frankly, she was surprised Calvin Hopkins hadn't blown her away on sight. But apparently he wasn't the one calling the shots.

Darryl Boyle was.

"Whom have you involved besides Darcy?" Boyle leaned against the wall of the cellar where she was being held, his arms folded and his expression placid. He spoke in a slow, measured tone, his Baltimore accent mostly neutralized, coming out only now and then in his vowels. They could have been sitting across from each other at the Knoxville Field Office, calmly discussing the latest case.

Except she was tied to a water pipe, her feet duct-taped together and two loaded shotguns aimed at her, wielded by bushy-bearded, cold-eyed Blue Ridge Infantry members flanking Boyle.

Jutting her chin toward him, she forced herself to smile. "Do your boys here know what you're really up to?"

"My boys, as you call them, are sovereign citizens and answer only to themselves. Don't you, boys?"

They both nodded.

"He's using you," McKenna said. "He's goading you into doing what he wants, and then he's going to make an example of you. Crack down on sovereign citizens like

yourselves because he thinks you pose a dangerous threat
to the government you hate so much. The government he
works for."

"The boys know you're the government plant, Rigsby."
Boyle's smile was placid. Almost friendly.

He was so sure of himself, she realized. So certain he
had everything under control.

Except he didn't. If he really had everything under control, she'd already be dead. There was something he wanted
from her, and she had a sick feeling it had everything to
do with Nick Darcy.

"Who else is involved besides Darcy?" Boyle repeated.
"The Gates, I presume. Considering who you were with
when we found you."

"What did you do to them?" she asked, her heart in her
throat. If Fitz, Calhoun and Ivy were dead because of her—

"They're enjoying the hospitality of our friends in the
BRI," he said with a feral smile that made her skin crawl.

"You can't kill us all," she growled. "Too many people
know what's really going on."

"Just a few, really. Your friend Darcy and the people he
has with him at the Econo-Tel Motor Lodge."

Terror poured through her body like ice water. He knew
where Darcy was staked out?

Was Darcy even still alive?

Boyle walked closer, bending to look her in the eye. He
had warm brown eyes, the same color as Darcy's. But behind the manufactured friendliness lurked a cold hatred
she'd never noticed before. He spoke in a soft, even kind
tone, but it sent a shudder up her spine. "I need you to tell
me if you've contacted anyone else."

"I'm not telling you anything."

"Yes. You will." He motioned over the man on the right.
The bearded man came over quickly, the shotgun still point-

ing at her chest. "Keller, show our guest what buckshot can do to a knee—"

A banging sound on the door to the cellar caught the attention of all three men. McKenna felt her whole body go hot, cold, then hot again with sheer relief as the man named Keller swung the barrel of his shotgun away from her.

"Trouble's comin'," the voice on the other side of the door called. "All hands needed."

Boyle nodded toward the two men. "Go. I'll watch her."

They climbed the stairs and disappeared through the cellar door, leaving McKenna alone with Boyle.

"I guess your friends tracked us down." He grabbed a metal folding chair leaning against the wall, unfolded it and set it in front of her. He sat down, crossing one leg over the other. "Wonder how they did that."

"Darcy knows the BRI is behind what happened to me. And he works for The Gates, who seem to have made taking the BRI down a personal project."

"I have nothing against The Gates or their agents," Boyle said calmly, "but they're a small group with limited influence. They may eventually take down the BRI, but other groups will continue rising up in their place. It's like trying to take down a jumbo jet with a peashooter. Something big needs to catch the attention of the public. Then the public will press Congress—"

"You're willing to sacrifice thousands of people just to change public sentiment about domestic terrorism? You're sanctioning the very thing you're trying to stop!"

"Wars have casualties."

"It's a war you've started!"

"Not true. Look at Oklahoma City. The Olympics bombing."

"Isolated acts. It's not a pattern."

"You don't see the pattern because you've blinded yourself to the reality." He leaned forward, his eyes alight with

passion. "It's not just the big bold acts, Rigsby. Do you
know how many police officers die at the hands of so-called
sovereign citizens like our friends Keller and Shelton out
there? Scores every year."

"In a nation of over three hundred million," McKenna
protested.

"Whom have you involved besides Darcy, Agent Rigsby?"
She pressed her lips together, not answering.

"THERE ARE TEN men in the compound, but if they get on
the horn, they can probably bring in thirty or forty more,"
Alexander Quinn warned Darcy as they surveyed the BRI
enclave in the heart of Bridal Veil Woods near the tiny town
of Thurlow's Gap. Four families linked to the Blue Ridge
Infantry lived in small, well-fortified cabins in the woods
nestled between two mountains in the southernmost part
of Ridge County. Those cabins were now barely visible in
the faint light of dawn rising over the mountains in the east.

"They probably have already," Seth warned, nodding toward sudden movement outside the small compound. Several men armed with shotguns and rifles had gathered in
front of the houses like a phalanx of palace guards.

"This kind of situation never ends well for anybody,"
Seth warned. He was crouched beside Darcy, viewing the
scene through a pair of high-powered binoculars. "Waco,
Ruby Ridge—"

"There has to be a way to get her out of there," Darcy
said gruffly. "We just have to figure it out."

"Boyle isn't their friend." Cain Dennison spoke for the
first time since they'd set up in their surveillance position
atop Thurlow Rise, east of the conclave. Next to him, his
dark-eyed fiancée was checking the magazine of a com-
pact Kel-Tec PF-9.

Darcy wondered what had become of McKenna's Glock.
What had become of her…

He made himself focus. She was still alive. He could feel it, like a second heartbeat in his own chest. She was alive and she was looking for a chance to get free.

He had to figure out a way to give her that chance.

"I'm going down there alone," he said aloud.

The other agents in earshot all turned to look at him as if he'd lost his mind.

"No, you're not," Quinn said, his tone dismissive.

"Hear me out. They have Calhoun and his wife. Mark Fitzpatrick. And McKenna. They don't know who else might be helping her. Except me. They know about me because Darryl Boyle knows about me. The FBI has been looking into her connection with me. I can go down there. We can use that buttonhole camera you brought—"

"They might shoot on sight."

"They want to know what we know. Boyle needs to have plausible deniability with the FBI. Right now, it's our word against his. Nobody's seen him with any BRI members. It's all speculation. But he knows we brought in some of the Gates agents."

"What if Rigsby's already spilled everything she knows?" Sara Lindsey asked.

Darcy shot her a pointed look. "She'd die before she'd give up anything."

"I hope she doesn't have to," Sara responded, a grim look on her pretty face. But the look in her eyes was more sympathetic than Darcy had expected.

"Do it."

The quiet response from Alexander Quinn drew their attention his way. He was looking toward the enclave below, his eyes narrowed. A moment later, he turned and pinned Darcy with his sharp gaze. "You know the stakes. You're invested. Do it."

"Any idea how we're supposed to get him in there without them shooting him on sight?" Sara asked.

"Wave the white flag?" Seth suggested.

Darcy grimaced. "Surrender?"

"Those men down there are a bunch of thickheaded cowards, but they think of themselves as honorable, patriotic men," Seth said with quiet urgency. "They'll hesitate to shoot an unarmed man turning himself in to them."

"Hesitate," Sara reiterated. "But that doesn't mean they won't shoot, sooner or later."

"It's a risk I'm willing to take," Darcy said, unclipping the holster from his jeans. He handed the pistol and holster to Quinn. "Can we contact them? Get me in there?"

"I know at least one of them. Randall Farmer. I ran some cons with him over in Barrowville," Seth said. "I can contact him, see if I can get through to Calvin Hopkins. He's taken the reins of this cell since Billy Dawson went to jail for that mass-poisoning attempt."

"Make it happen," Darcy said.

DARRYL BOYLE GOT up from the metal folding chair and started pacing slowly in front of McKenna, a faint smile on his face. "I suppose we must assume your friends have found Calvin and his boys."

"And you," she said.

"They think I'm one of them." He smiled more broadly. "That's what undercover is really about, Rigsby. Selling yourself as one of them. You never could pull off that part."

Because I'm not a raving lunatic like you, she thought, her stomach twisting. She'd worked with Darryl Boyle for over a year. Took his advice, spent long hours in research and discussions with him, even socialized with him now and then with other field-office agents and personnel.

She hadn't had a clue that he'd lost his bloody mind.

She had to get out of here. As soon as possible.

Another knock on the cellar door set her nerves rattling again.

"What do you want?" Boyle snapped.

It was Calvin Hopkins himself who walked through the cellar door and down the rough-hewn wooden steps. He slanted a hard look at McKenna before turning to Boyle. "Darcy wants to talk."

DARCY FELT EYES on him before he made it ten feet onto Calvin Hopkins's property, but he tried not to let his twitching nerves show. He had one chance to get this right. One chance to stay alive and get McKenna safely out of here.

He just had to get on the inside somehow. Get to her and make sure she was still alive, then work the angle he and Quinn had discussed while Seth was on the phone with Randall Farmer.

Dew clung to the legs of his jeans as he climbed the grassy hill. A hundred yards up the rise, the line of armed militia members came into view. And though Darcy had known they were there, had prepared himself for the sight of them, his blood still froze when he saw a dozen gun barrels pointed straight at his heart.

"Hands up," ordered one of the men.

Darcy stopped and raised his hands. "I'm unarmed."

The man who'd spoken nodded toward Darcy. "Check him out."

Another man, younger and clean-shaven, handed his rifle to the man next to him and crossed to Darcy. He patted him down, his touch less rough than Darcy had expected. Darcy gave him a considering look as the man backed away, his curiosity piqued. But he didn't have time to figure out why. The older man, the one clearly in charge, motioned him forward.

He walked slowly toward the gun line, half expecting with each step to walk right into a volley of rifle fire. But the BRI members held their fire.

"I'm Cal," the older man said, flashing a disarming smile. "You're Nick, right?"

"Darcy," he said.

One dark bushy eyebrow rose, but Cal just nodded. "Darcy. I understand you want to talk?"

"I know something you need to know about Darryl Boyle."

"Boyle?" Cal tried to sound puzzled, but he didn't pull it off. "Don't know any Boyle."

"Yes, you do. You think he's your secret weapon. But he's not. He's not your friend. And he's not on your side."

WHAT THE HELL was Darcy thinking, coming here? And alone, if the snippets of overheard conversation between Boyle and Calvin Hopkins could be believed.

Boyle came back down the stairs slowly, a smile on his face. But McKenna was beginning to read the SSA a little better, now that she had the key to understanding him.

He was obsessive and narcissistic. But he was also in a very vulnerable position where the BRI was concerned. And like any vulnerable man faced with an unexpected wrinkle in his plan, he was showing signs of stress. Sweat beading on his brow. A nervous twitch to his gaze, as if he was afraid to let it settle too long on any given point.

"What are they going to do to Darcy?" she asked.

"Talk. For now."

And that was what Boyle was afraid of, she realized. That Darcy would say the wrong thing, reveal the wrong fact about Boyle's real reason for rubbing elbows with the Blue Ridge Infantry.

"He doesn't know about you," she lied.

"You didn't tell him?" Boyle looked skeptical.

"I told him about Landry. I didn't mention you. I was hoping I was wrong about you, and nobody else would have to know. I respected you. Your record, your work."

His eyes narrowed. "I don't believe you."

She shrugged. "I can't do anything to change your mind."

"You can tell me how many other people are out there right now."

"I have no clue. Darcy was my only contact until last night. He's the one who brought the others into this mess. I didn't want anyone else involved."

Her words had the ring of truth, and she could tell Boyle knew it. "So they think Landry's the one behind all of this."

"They did. And if you stay out of sight, they'll continue to think so. But if anything happens to Darcy, his friends won't stop looking for answers." She tried not to let her fear show. "You need to tell Calvin to send Darcy packing back where he came from."

"That's touching, really. Trying to protect your friend." Boyle's eyes glinted with curiosity. "Or maybe he's more than a friend?"

So much more, she thought with despair, and she hadn't ever had the guts to say it out loud. "Make him think I've been taken somewhere else. He'll go looking for me, and then you'll be rid of him."

"You'd give up your own life to save him?"

She shook her head, suddenly terrified by the gleam of understanding in the SSA's eyes. "I didn't say that. I'm trying to get out of here alive, too, believe me. Darcy's got a lot of people who'll look for him. I don't. Thanks to you, everybody thinks I'm a crooked fed. Nobody's going to care what happens to me. So I can help you with your plans. And then, I hope, you'll let me go free. What am I going to do, tell the FBI I helped you commit an act of terror? They already think I've gone native with the BRI, right?"

He nodded slowly.

"Get Darcy out of here, and then I'll help you with whatever you're up to. Just give me my life in return, and I'll disappear. Nobody will ever see me again."

"I don't believe you," he said again. But this time, she heard a hint of uncertainty.

"Fine. Let Darcy get taken prisoner or worse. Then you'll wish you'd never heard his name. Because there are people out there, very powerful people, who haven't forgotten he's the son of an influential former US ambassador. He has friends in very high places. And they won't stop trying to find out what happened to him until they have all the answers."

Boyle held her gaze for a moment before he looked away. Slowly, he crossed the small room and started climbing the steps.

But before he got there, the door opened and Calvin Hopkins filled the doorway. "Just the man I was looking for," he said, a feral grin splitting his bearded face.

Boyle took a step back, almost losing his balance. But Hopkins grabbed him by the front of his shirt, jerked him through the door and shut it behind them with a loud slam.

The ensuing silence seemed thick and oppressive. Left alone for the first time since they'd brought her to the cellar, McKenna started twisting the rope holding her tied to the water pipe, trying to loosen the knots enough to give her a chance of breaking free.

For several minutes, the only thing she heard was her own accelerated breathing and the rasp of the hemp rope against the metal pipes as she struggled to loosen her restraints. But as she felt the bindings finally begin to loosen around her raw wrists, she heard a furtive *snick* sound, followed by the quiet thud of footsteps on the wooden stairs.

She looked up, blinking away the sweat dripping into her eyes. Blinked again to be sure she was really seeing what she thought she was.

"Darcy?"

He came the rest of the way down the steps quickly, hurrying to her side. "Are you all right?"

"How did you get in here?"

"I did someone named Cal a favor. Calvin Hopkins, I presume." He tugged at the knots around her wrists until they finally loosened enough to pull her hands free. He then ripped the duct tape away from her ankles and pulled her to her feet. "We have five minutes to get out of here before they come back from dealing with him. Don't ask questions. Don't look back."

He took her hand and pulled her with him up the steps, pausing only when her knees started to wobble as she reached the top landing. He bent to look at her. "Do you trust me?"

She stared back at him, her heart pounding. "Yes."

He kissed her forehead, his lips lingering for a breathless moment. Then he tugged her hand again. "Let's get you out of here."

Epilogue

Night had fallen over Knoxville, Tennessee, after a long day of debriefing. SAC Robertson had brought in a doctor to check on her gunshot wounds, but she'd talked them both out of admitting her for treatment. "They're practically healed by now," she'd protested, and they'd been able to tell by her stern tone that she wasn't going to agree to any attempts to trundle her off to the hospital for further tests. Besides, the doctor had been forced to concede that Darcy had done a good job of keeping the wounds clean and treated.

"You should follow up with your own doctor in a day or two," the bureau doctor had told her with a firm look before he gathered his supplies and left her alone with Glen Robertson.

The next few hours had been a series of in-depth interviews, not just with Robertson but video interviews with high-ranking officials at FBI headquarters in Washington. She'd told them everything she knew about Darryl Boyle's involvement with the Blue Ridge Infantry, including the fact that she'd been forced to leave him behind when making her escape.

"I suppose that doesn't exactly cover me with glory," she said.

"I'm not sure any of us is in a position to judge your

choices, under the circumstances," Robertson murmured. "And you have no idea where they could have taken Boyle?"

She shook her head. "I don't. There are places in the hills where secrets have stayed hidden for centuries."

Finally, close to 10:00 p.m., apparently everyone interested in what she had to say ran out of questions. The video links shut down and Robertson finally turned to her in the silence of his office.

"I don't think you have a chance in hell of going anywhere in the FBI, Agent Rigsby."

She nodded, unsurprised. "I know."

"It's a damned shame. You're a good agent."

"I'm not. I can't play by the rules enough to be a good FBI agent."

Robertson put his hand lightly on her shoulder. "Maybe not. But I think you did more to stop a terror attack these past few days than you realize."

She hoped so. She just wasn't sure the Blue Ridge Infantry would let one little setback stop them.

"Am I free to go?" she asked.

"You need to stay in the area until the case is officially closed. But yes, you're free to go. Do you need a ride?"

She wasn't sure what had happened to her car. She'd have to see if it was still where she'd left it before everything went crazy, or if it had been towed already. "Yeah, I guess I do."

A little while later, SAC Robertson pulled up in front of her apartment building and let her off at the curb. "You want me to park and walk in with you?"

She couldn't help but laugh. "I think I can probably handle it." She headed up the sidewalk to the awning-covered double doors.

Inside, the apartment lobby was quiet and mostly empty, except for a man sitting on one of the white lobby chairs.

He looked up as she entered, and for a moment, she thought she was seeing what she wanted.

Then he stood, tall and lean and so familiar, her heart started to ache.

"Thought you'd never get here," Darcy said with a smile.

SHE LOOKED TIRED, he thought. No doubt the FBI had put her through the wringer before letting her leave. He'd undergone similar questioning from the Ridge County Sheriff's Department, especially since one of their deputies had been tangentially involved in what had happened the night before.

"I heard you found Fitz, Calhoun and his wife safe and alive."

"They managed to free themselves from the shed where they'd been stashed," Darcy told her, waving off her offer of something to drink. She looked strangely out of place in this clean, utilitarian apartment she apparently called home. Wild-haired, makeup-free and still wearing the grimy clothes she'd been wearing when she was abducted by Hopkins and his crew, she seemed like an alien presence in this city flat.

"Everybody's okay?"

He nodded. "And Quinn took me off paid administrative leave. I've been cleared to resume duties."

She smiled. "Good. About damn time."

"That's what I told him." He fell silent, wondering how to approach the next topic.

Them.

Before he could speak, McKenna grimaced. "I need a shower."

"I could use one, too." He crossed to where she stood by the kitchen counter and took a deep breath before speaking. "We could share."

She looked up at him, smiling as if she thought he was kidding.

He wasn't.

Her smile faded. "You're serious, aren't you?"

"I thought I'd lost you." He touched her face, let his fingers tangle in her hair. "I thought you were dead. And I realized that I've been in love with you for over eight years."

Tears filled her eyes. She let them fall. "Oh, Darcy. I love you, too. I always have. I just didn't think—" She knuckled the tears away.

He tugged her closer. "Didn't think you could put up with such a priggish rule-keeper?"

She laughed. "You are anything but priggish. And I'm pretty sure you broke more rules than I did over the past few days."

"I try."

She touched his face. "I thought you'd never be happy with someone with one foot still in the hills. I am what I am. These hills made me who I am, and I don't know how to be anything else."

"I wouldn't want you to be anything or anyone but exactly who you are." He cradled her face between his hands. "I depend on you being you. I need you, just the way you are. So, tell me. If I said I wanted you to come to Purgatory and be with me for good—could you do it? Would you?"

She tugged him to her, kissing him deeply. He pulled her closer, his heart starting to race as she pushed him back against the kitchen counter.

He dragged his mouth free. "I'll take that as a yes."

She laughed again, the sound beautifully free and light. "That's definitely a yes. And while we're at it—think you can talk Quinn into giving me a job?"

"What about the FBI?"

She arched her eyebrows. "I'd be a dead-ender like Landry."

"Oh," he said. "Did you hear about Landry?"

She shook her head. "SAC Robertson didn't mention him. Did something happen to him?"

"Nobody knows. He didn't show up for work this morning, and when his supervisor sent an agent to check on him, his apartment had been cleared of any personal items. His landlord said he'd paid up the remainder of his lease, told the manager to dispose of the furniture as he saw fit and left."

"Wow. I thought you said he tried to help us."

"I think he did," Darcy admitted. "He seemed honestly worried about you and what Darryl Boyle was up to."

"Robertson said there's no sign of Boyle." Her expression darkened. "I don't know that I feel very good about leaving him to the tender mercies of the BRI."

"I didn't, either," Darcy admitted. "But it was the only way to get you out of there without a standoff. And a standoff with that many armed, reckless men never ends well."

She pressed her cheek against his shoulder. "I was so afraid for you."

"I was so afraid for you, too." He kissed the top of her head. "But we're both safe now."

"Till the next time we butt heads with the BRI." She kissed his shoulder and looked up at him. "Quinn's not through with them, is he?"

"No."

She shot him an impish smile. "Well, we'll worry about that later, okay? We have a shower to take."

"Yes," he agreed, tugging at the hem of her T-shirt, "we do."

She dodged free, laughing. "Race you, Jeeves!"

"Not a Brit!" he protested as she darted toward the hallway.

She stopped in the doorway and turned, gazing at him

with so much happiness it made his chest ache. "You are. You're *my* Brit."

He closed the distance between them, pulling her tightly into his arms. "I guess that makes you my hillbilly, then."

"It does." She wrapped her arms around his neck and pulled him down for a kiss.

* * * * *

Award-winning author Paula Graves's miniseries
THE GATES *continues next month with*
TWO SOULS HOLLOW.

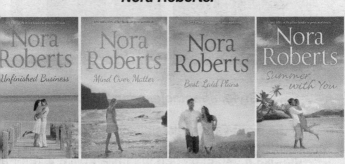
15_ST_11

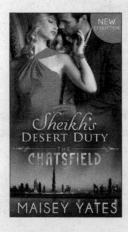

Join our *EXCLUSIVE* eBook club

FROM JUST £1.99 A MONTH!

Never miss a book again with our hassle-free eBook subscription.

★ Pick how many titles you want from each series with our flexible subscription

★ Your titles are delivered to your device on the first of every month

★ Zero risk, zero obligation!

There really is nothing standing in the way of you and your favourite books!

Start your eBook subscription today at www.millsandboon.co.uk/subscribe